RAIDERS OF SPANISH PEAKS

Zane Grey

Laramie had saved the young man called Lonesome from hanging and had helped get Williams out of jail. Now they were as close as brothers and their fame as The Three Range Riders spread all over the prairie. Their goal was to be cattlemen, rich and honest ones, but the path ahead was full of gamblers, desperadoes and gunmen. They were all out to stop the three. And then there were the young boy and the girl to complicate matters. It came down to a question of just how fast Laramie's guns could be!

ZANE GREY'S WESTERNS IN
LARGE PRINT

ZANE GREY

Raiders of Spanish Peaks

John Curley & Associates, Inc.
South Yarmouth, Ma.

Library of Congress Cataloging in Publication Data

Grey, Zane, 1872–1939.
    Raiders of Spanish Peaks.

    1. Large type books.   I. Title.
[PS3513.R6545R3 1985]   813′.52   85–9850
ISBN 0–89340–934–0 (lg. print)

Published in Large Print by arrangement with Harper & Row, Publishers, Inc. in the U.S.A. and Loren Grey for the U.K. and Commonwealth.

Distributed in the U.K. and Commonwealth by Magna Print Books.

Printed in Great Britain

Raiders of Spanish Peaks

Chapter 1

Laramie's horse went lame, and as Wingfoot was the only living creature he had to care for, he halted at midday, without thought of his own needs.

That long journey of yesterday, calculated to put a hundred miles between Laramie and a certain Kansas ranch where his old habit of gun-play on little provocation had rendered him unpopular, had aggravated a sprained tendon Wingfoot favored. Laramie slid out of the saddle.

"Heah, let me see, yu uncomplainin' deceivin' hawse," said the rider, "How was I to know about it?"

Wingfoot might have traveled miles farther without serious result, but Laramie chose not to take the risk. He liked the pleasant prospect at hand – a widening valley bright with the spring green of cottonwoods and willows and a gleam of water. He would camp there until the following day. It was nothing for Laramie to go hungry.

"Wal, Wingfoot, heah we stop," he drawled as he removed the saddle. "Plenty grass an' water for yu. If I see a cottontail I'll shore make up for thet pore shootin'.... I've a pinch of salt left.... Now yu be around heah in the mawnin'."

Wingfoot was not so lame that he could not roll. After thus indulging himself, he made for the running stream and the patch of green on the bank. Laramie packed the burdened saddle beyond the edge of the grove to a willow thicket. Another of his range habits was that of caution. He needed sleep about as much as Wingfoot needed rest, but he decided to exhaust the meat possibilities of this valley before lying down. To that end he spread his saddle blankets to dry in the sun, and cut an armload of willows for a bed, after which he went hunting.

This particular section of southern central Kansas was unknown to him. It was a cattle country, a vast sweeping prairie-land, rolling and grassy, where a steer appeared to be as hard to find as a needle in a haystack. Few indeed had been the hoof tracks he had crossed that day. A long tramp down this winding lonesome swale earned Laramie no more than an appreciation of the ranch possibilities of the place. How many beautiful, fertile, lonely bits of range-land had inspired the same desire for a farm, a few horses and cattle, a home! That hope never

2

died, though Laramie was well on, as years counted at that time. Still, as many riders of twenty-five died with boots on as lived to herd cattle.

Somewhere to the northwest lay the railroad and Dodge, for which Laramie was headed. Cattlemen and riders were as thick there as flies on a freshly skinned cowhide. He would get another job and try again, knowing that sooner or later he would straddle Wingfoot again for a grub-line ride. Thinking of meat made him more than usually keen-eyed, with the result that soon he espied a rabbit. It ran off a few rods, and then made the mistake to stop and squat down, after the manner of cottontails. Laramie shot the top of its head off.

"Wal, dog-gone!" he ejaculated, very pleased. "I reckon I couldn't hit nothin' no more. Now if thet had happened to be Luke Arlidge..."

Laramie did not end his speculation. He skinned and dressed the cottontail, and returning to camp, built a little fire over which he broiled the rabbit to a nice brown. The addition of some salt made it so toothsome that Laramie wanted to devour it all. But he saved half for the morrow.

The heat of the day was passing. Wingfoot grazed contentedly down the valley. Laramie left his fire to look around. There was not even a bird to see. He had come from the north and had a curiosity to see what it looked like to the west, up over the low slope. But with the thought that there was no sense looking for trouble he went back to the willows and was soon asleep.

Upon being rudely awakened by some noise, Laramie thought he had scarcely closed his eyes. He heard a thud of hoofbeats on soft ground and then a harsh voice:

"We're goin' to string yu up to this heah cottonwood, thet's what."

"Fer no more'n yu've done yourself, Price," came the reply in a young, bitter voice.

"If I done so, nobody ever ketched me. Haw! Haw!"

Laramie considered himself a judge of men through their voices. He sat up silently, a cold little thrill stiffening his spine, and peered out between the willow leaves.

Four horsemen had ridden under the great spreading cottonwood, three of whom were in the act of halting. The foremost, a boy of about twenty, was short and sturdy, his figure bearing the hallmarks of a rider. His homely face might have been red ordinarily, but now it was tense and pale. He had singularly fine eyes, neither dark nor light,

4

and on the moment an expression of scorn appeared stronger than a somber horror. He was too young to face hanging with a spirit which no doubt would have been his in later years. Price was a typical cattleman of the period, no longer young, and characterized by a lean hard face of bluish cast under his short beard, and slits of fire for eyes. He looked more at home in the saddle than on the ground, and packed a blue Colt gun in the hip pocket of his jeans. The position of that gun told Laramie much. The other two riders were mere boys, even more youthful than the one they were about to hang. They did not look formidable, wherefore Laramie wasted no second glance on them.

"Price, yu ain't goin' through with it?" asked the doomed rider, hoarsely.

"Didn't I ketch yu dead to rights?"

"Yes, an' it wasn't the first time I done the same. But yu hadn't paid me a dollar fer six months....An' the boss was away....An' I had to have some money."

"Say, Mulhall, air yu tryin' to make excuses for rustlin'?" queried Price, loosening out a small deadly-looking noose in his lasso.

"Show me a rider who never stole a head of stock – if yu split hairs on it!" ejaculated Mulhall, passionately.

5

"I ain't splittin' hairs. Yu're a rustler."

"Yu're a liar. If yu wasn't every damn rider on this range would be a rustler. *Yu* would an' yu know it."

Price gave the noose a little careless toss and it fell perfectly over Mulhall's head. He flinched in his saddle. And Laramie, watching with intent eyes, felt that shock communicated to him. Such brutal justice had become the law of the range. In this case it might have been deserved and on the other hand it might not. Laramie thought it no business of his. But could he sit there and see them go through with it?

"Thet's my answer, Mulhall," replied Price, curtly. "I'll tell somebody yu took yore medicine yellow."

"——!" burst out the bound rider, furiously. "I knowed it. Yu're hanging' me 'cause *she* has no use fer yu. . . . Go ahead an' string me up, you ——! . . . She'll be onto yu. Hank or Bill will give yu away some day. An' she'll hate you –"

"Shet up," snapped Price, jerking the lasso so tight round Mulhall's neck as to cut short his speech and sway him in the saddle.

"Aw – Price!" interposed the older of the other two riders. He was pale and it was plain he wanted to intercede. "Let Mulhall off – this time."

6

Whereupon Price cursed him roundly, and then flinging his end of the rope over the branch just above Mulhall's head he leisurely dismounted to pick it up.

"I've seen more'n one of yore brand dangle from this cottonwood," he said, with a coarse grim humor that failed to hide passion.

This inflection of tone decided Laramie, who had been wavering. Silently he arose, and strode out from behind his covert. Price appeared about to haul the lasso taut and tie it to a sapling. The ashen-faced Mulhall saw Laramie first and gave expression to a more violent start.

"Bill, get set to kick his hoss out from under him," ordered Price.

When Bill failed to move and, moreover, betrayed his alarm, Price wheeled. Laramie had advanced half of the distance from the willows. He halted, standing slightly sidewise. His posture, as well as his appearance, would have given any Westerner pause. Laramie had counted on this many a time, though in this instance it was more habit than design.

"Hullo!" cut out Price, suddenly springing erect. He was genuinely astounded.

"Howdy yoreself," returned Laramie, in

7

slow, cool speech. "See yu're aimin' at a necktie party."

"Yu ain't blind, stranger," replied Price, sharply, as his gaze roved over Laramie, to grasp the significance of his stand. "Where'd yu come from?"

"Down the draw heah with my outfit. Been huntin' rabbits an' happened to see hawses."

"Rabbits, huh?" rejoined Price, slowly. "Wal, go on with yore huntin'."

"Shore, when it suits me."

"This ain't no bizness of yourn."

"I'm makin' it mine."

"Hell yu say!...Who might yu be, stranger?"

"No matter. I'm just ridin' through."

"Wal, go back to yore outfit an' ride on. Mixin' in heah might not be healthy."

"Wal, somehow I've thrived on unhealthy soil."

Price threw down the end of the lasso and reddened in angry amaze: "What yu up to?"

"I cain't fool about heah an' see yu hang thet boy," drawled Laramie.

"He's a rustler. We ketched him brandin' calves fer an outfit who's been payin' him."

"Shore. I heahed yu talkin'."

"Hell then, man! Don't yu know this country?" fumed the cattleman.

8

"Wal, yes, if yu reckon Texas, Abilene, Dodge, an' the Pan Handle."

"Ahuh. Texas rider. One of them Chisholm Trail drivers?"

"Shore. If thet means anythin' to yu, Mister Price."

It meant considerable, as was plain by the man's visible vacillation in the face of a doubtful issue. Laramie had gauged him shrewdly.

"But what fur, damn yu? Mulhall ain't nothin' to yu. He's admitted his guilt."

"Yes, an' the way he did it is why I'm callin' yore bluff."

"Bluff! . . . There ain't no bluff in a rope."

"Yu'd swung him shore if I hadn't come along. But I did – an' now yu won't."

That was the gauntlet flung in this matured rider's face. It flamed. He was the kind in whom rage gave rein to impulses, but obviously there was something about Laramie's front that restrained him.

"Yu'd fight fer this calf-stealin' boy?" burst out Price, incredulously.

"Shore. Reckon I've fought fer less. But if yu want to know, Price, I just don't like yore face an' yore talk."

"No? I ain't takin' a hell of a fancy to yourn," retorted Price, sarcastically.

"Wal, I'm a better judge of men than yu

9

are," retorted Laramie, with even more sarcasm.

"Like hell yu air! Willin' to take chances an' fight fer a cowpuncher who admits he stole! Yu must be hard up fer a fight, stranger. As fer me – I pass. Mulhall ain't even wuth gettin' scratched fer."

Price's spurs jangled a discord as he stamped to his horse and flung himself in the saddle.

"Hold up a minute," replied Laramie, dryly, as he walked around Price to see if he had a rifle on his saddle. The saddles of the other two riders were likewise minus a long-range gun. "Price, I size yu up to be some punkin on talkin', an' thet's aboot all. Mozy along."

The chagrined rider complied, while his two companions reined their horses in beside his.

"Take him an' be damned!" shouted Price, over his shoulder. "He'll thank yu by stealin' yore shirt."

"Hey, Price, all I ever stole from yu was yore gurl," Mulhall shouted after him, in fiendish glee.

The rider called Bill looked back and his young face gleamed.

"Goodbye, Mull. I'm glad we –"

Price swung a vicious hand on Bill's lips,
10

nearly unseating him. Then the riders rode on, breaking from trot to canter, and disappeared under the cottonwoods.

Laramie drew a knife with which he carefully cut the cord around Mulhall's wrists. The boy swiftly lifted his hands to tear the noose off his neck so violently as to dislodge his sombrero. It went flying with the rope.

"My God, stranger!" he burst out, in terrible relief. "Price'd hung me – but fer yu!"

"I reckon. There's many a slip, though," responded Laramie as he bent to recover both lasso and sombrero. The latter he handed up to Mulhall, then began to coil the lasso, "It'd be bad luck, boy, not to keep this.... Any chance of Price fetchin' back an outfit?"

"Aw, hell! He wouldn't have the nerve if he had any more outfit," replied the rider, contemptuously, as he rubbed his red wrists.

"Wal, in thet case we needn't be in such a hurry," replied Laramie. "I'm alone. Was ridin' through, an' my hawse went lame. An' while restin' him I was takin' a nap heah in the willows. Yu waked me up."

"It was sure a good wakin' fer me, stranger," rejoined Mulhall, fervently, and swinging a leg over the pommel he began to

11

roll a cigarette. His fingers trembled slightly. Then he met Laramie's upward glance. Their eyes locked – the one shamed, grateful, curious, the other grave, searching, kindly. Naturally such an exchange of looks could not have been ordinary, but this developed into something unusually strong and potent.

"What's yore name?" queried Mulhall.

"Yu can call me Laramie."

"Mine's Mulhall. Yu can call me Lonesome."

"Funny handle for yu. Bet yu're not the lone-prairie kind...Mulhall....Any kin to thet big stockman, Silas Mulhall?"

"No kin to nobody," replied Lonesome, hurriedly, with evident distaste or a habit of evasiveness. "I'm alone in the wurr-ld."

"Wal, yu came dog-gone near takin' a trip alone," concluded Laramie, dryly. "Let's move out of this heah neck of the woods."

Laramie dragged his saddle and things out of the willows, and dividing these with the rider made his way down the valley, keeping to the thick plots of grass.

"Reckon it'd take a good tracker some time workin' our trail out," remarked Laramie, thoughtfully, as he picked his way.

"Sure. But say, Laramie, I had a pard once thet could track a bird," returned Mulhall, enthusiastically. "Honest to Gawd, he was

12

the grandest boy on a trail! His name was Ted Williams, an' I called him Tracks. Stuck to him, too. . . . Heigho! – dear old Ted! Wonder where'n hell he is now. . . . We was pards two years."

"What became of him? Stop some lead?"

"No! He made the other fellow do thet. Ted was slick with a gun – leanin' toward bein' a gunman, they said."

"I see. But yu're not tellin' me about him."

"It happened over in Nebraskie. We was ridin' for a cattleman – what was his name? . . . Spencer or somethin'. Anyway, he ran an X-Bar outfit, an' he had a daughter. I was only sixteen an' she was twenty. Red-headed girl! – Gosh, she was peaches an' cream. About to marry a stock-buyer, a mean cuss, with lots of money. I didn't want to get sweet on her – dog-gone it! She was to blame. Stockman's name was Cheesbrough. Never will forget that, because it was my callin' him a big cheese that led to the fight. He beat me somethin' awful. Ted rode in, found me all bunged up. An' he called Cheesbrough out an' shot him . . . I've never seen Ted since then. Thet's what made me a raomin', lonesome, grub-line rider."

"Wal, yu must be hell on girls," drawled

13

Laramie, as he walked on, looking under the trees for his horse.

"I can't help it if they like me," declared Lonesome, stoutly. "An' I couldn't help lovin' any girl to save my life.... This deal of Price's yu mussed up – thet was all on account of a girl. Annie Lakin. She couldn't read or write, but she sure was there on looks. Rancher up the draw three or four miles. Bruce Allson, a fine man to ride for when he was flush. But he's been broke ever since thet big raid some rustlers worked awhile back. Annie is the daughter of Allson's sister, who'd come to be housekeeper for him. Natural she upset the triangle outfit. Price is foreman, an' was loony over Annie. He had a chance, the boys said, till I rode along a few weeks ago. Thet fellow sure hated me. He'd done for me, too! Hung me!..."

"But how aboot Annie?" interposed Laramie.

"Thet girl!... I was sure sweet on her. Cross-eyed little skunk! Laramie, I don't know if yu've had experience with girls, but I'm tellin' yu they're no good, as a rule. But I had one onct thet... This Annie was crookeder than any rail fence yu ever seen in yore life, an' just as sweet. She had all the boys on Allson's ranch an' everywhere daft

14

about her. When I come – well, *I* was new an' somethin' to egg the other fellows along with. An' all the time she was lettin' Price make up to her! On the sly, thet was. But I queered his game if I didn't do nothin' else.... My Gawd! how thet kid could hug an' kiss. An' dance – say, I've seen her dance the whole outfit so done they couldn't get their boots off."

"Wal, then it's not breakin' yore heart much to leave heah?" went on Laramie.

"Not so terrible much, now I think of it. But I'd liked to have had a little money from Allson. I'm clean busted."

"Yu're welcome to some of mine.... Heah's my hawse. I'd begun to worry thet he'd strayed up the draw."

Laramie secured Wingfoot, and throwing blankets and saddle loosely over him, and the bridle round his neck, led off down the widening valley, with Mulhall beside him. Cottonwoods grew thickly here, and the stream was lined with green willows.

"Yore hoss is a little lame, Laramie," observed Mulhall.

"Yes, thet's what kept yu from havin' a new hemp necktie. But he's not so lame as he was. A night's rest will make him fit again."

15

"Travelin' light, I see," went on Lonesome.

"Light an' hungry."

"No grub atall?"

"Half a rabbit an' some salt."

Mulhall appeared frankly curious, and not without misgivings concerning this new-found friend; nevertheless he restrained his feelings.

"Let's camp here," he said, halting. "We'd have to come back up this draw, an' it's travel for nothin'. We can kill a couple of rabbits anywheres. Where yu headin' for?"

"Just haidin' away, Lonesome," drawled Laramie.

"Ahuh! – I sure had a curl up my spine when I seen yu step out of them willows. . . . It's a funny world. . . . By ridin' forty miles tomorrow we can strike a cattle-camp. Next day Dodge."

"Suits me. Haven't hit Dodge for a couple of years," rejoined Laramie, reminiscently.

"She's a hummer these days."

"If Dodge is any livelier than Abilene or Hays City, excuse me. . . . Pile off, Lonesome. We'll camp heah an' have some hot biscuits, applesauce, a lamb chop, an' some coffee with cream."

"Say, I'd kinda like you even if you hadn't saved my neck," observed Lonesome,

16

thoughtfully. "An' for me to like a *man* is sure a compliment."

They found a thicket with a little grass plot inside where they made beds.

"Reckon we better hunt some more meat," said Laramie, when their tasks were done.

"I'll go with you, Laramie. There ain't a damn bit of use in my huntin' alone. I can't hit a flock of barns. An' if I happened on to one of Price's calves I'd run it down."

So they went out together, stepping quietly and watching sharply. Lonesome sighted the first rabbit and as he drew Laramie closer to where it was squatting it hopped away. Laramie killed it on the move. Lonesome gasped his amazement, and thudding across the open space he picked up the kicking quarry.

"Top of his head gone!"

"Wal, shore thet was a lucky shot," drawled Laramie, looking to his gun.

"I'm reservin' opinions till I see you shoot again. But I've the same hunch Price must have had."

"An' what's thet, Lonesome?"

"It ain't wise to try to throw a gun on some men," returned Mulhall, his eyes bright and keen.

"Thet's so," admitted Laramie. "I've met a few I'd hate to have tried it on."

17

"Humph. Who, for instance?" asked Lonesome, as he took out a knife to skin the rabbit.

"Buck Duane, Wess Harkin', King Fisher – to mention three."

"All Texans. Ain't there any other Westerners quick on the draw?"

"Heaps of them, if yu can believe range talk. Wild Bill Hickok shore is one. I seen him kill five men all in a row. Thet was at Hays City."

"He's sheriff over at Hays. We won't go... Look! Another rabbit. He's stoppin' under thet bushy cottonwood. By the little bush.... Laramie, if you hit him from here I'll –"

Laramie espied the rabbit and interrupted Mulhall with a quick shot. This one flopped over without a kick.

"Dog-gone! I'm shootin' lucky today. Reckon it's because I'm so hungry," said Laramie, in a matter-of-fact tone.

"Ahuh. So I see," rejoined Lonesome, sagely.

They went back to camp, where Lonesome busied himself in the task of dressing the rabbits for broiling. He declared frankly that he was a first rate camp cook. He built a hot fire and let it burn down to a bed of red coals. Then, having spitted the rabbits on clean whittled willow sticks, he broiled them close to the coals, by turning them over and over.

Laramie watched him covertly. How many boys like Lonesome had he seen enter and exit on the hard stage of the range! Lonesome had the qualities to make him liked around a cow-camp, but scarcely those that might insure his survival. He was easy, careless, amiable, probably a drifter and perhaps not above the evils of the outdoor life. Still, he did not show any signs of being addicted to liquor – that bane of riders. Laramie felt a strange pleasure in having saved his neck and in his presence now. Long years had Laramie been a lone wolf. By this experience he was brought face to face with the fact of his loneliness.

"Come an' get it, Laramie," called Lonesome. "An' dig up your bag of salt. We could fare worse."

"Done to a brown," declared Laramie as he took the spitted rabbit tendered him. It had a most persuasive scent.

Whereupon the two sat cross-legged on the grass and enjoyed their meal. Lonesome, however, showed his improvident character by eating all of his rabbit while Laramie again saved half of his.

Meanwhile sunset had come and the grove of cottonwoods was a place of color and beauty. A tiny brook tinkled by under a grassy bank; mockingbirds were singing off somewhere in the distance; a raven croaked overhead. The grass shone like black-barred gold and there was a redness in the west. Tranquil, lonely, and sad, the end of day roused feelings in Laramie that had rendered his breast heavy many a time before.

"Nice place for a little ranch," he said, presently.

"Ain't it, though? I was just thinkin' thet. A bunch of cattle, some good horses, plenty of wood, water, an' grass – a home.... Heigho!... It's a hell of a life if you don't weaken."

Laramie had touched on a sensitive chord in his companion's heart. Somehow this simple fact seemed to draw them closer together, in a community of longing, if no more.

"Wal, when yu said home yu said a heap, boy.... Home! Thet means a woman – a wife."

"Sure. But I never got so far in reckonin' as thet," replied Lonesome, thoughtfully.

"Lonesome, why don't yu marry one of these girls yu swear bob up heah an' there?"

"My Gawd! What an idear!... Thet's one thing thet never struck me before," ejaculated Mulhall, profoundly stirred, and

20

his homely young face was good to see on the moment.

"Wal, since it has struck yu now, how about it?" went on Laramie.

Lonesome threw his rabbit bones away in a violence of contention, with alluring but impossible ideas.

"Marry some girl? On this range – this lone prairee where the wind howls down the wolves? Where there ain't any girls or any cabins for the takin'. When a poor rider can't hold a steady job.... When – Aw, hell, Laramie, what's the use talkin'."

"Wal, I wasn't puttin' the difficulties before yu, but just the idee."

"Ahuh, I wisht you hadn't. I've got a weak place in me. Never knowed what it was. But thet's it."

"Like to have a corner to work on – a homestead where every turn of a spade was for yoreself – where every calf an' colt added to yore ranch? Thet how it strikes yu?"

"Sure. I've got pioneer blood. Most of us riders have. But only a few of us beat red liquor, gamblin'-hells, loose wimmin, ropes an' guns."

"Yu said somethin' to think about," mused Laramie.

"Laramie, have you beat them things?"

"I reckon, except mebbe guns – an' I've done tolerable well about them."

"I take it you're ridin' a grub-line, same as I have to now?"

"Shore. But more, Lonesome. I'm ridin' out of this country. Colorado for me, or New Mexico – mebbe even Arizona."

"Laramie, if I ain't too personal – air you on the dodge?"

"Nope. I've a clean slate," retorted Laramie, with the curtness of the Southerner.

"I'm thunderin' glad to hear thet," burst out Lonesome, as if relieved. "I wish to Gawd I had the nerve to ask you – Aw! Never mind. My feelin's run away with me at times."

"Ask me what, Lonesome?" queried Laramie. "I'll lend yu some money, if yu want it."

"Money, hell! You're good to offer, knowin' it'd never be paid back.... I meant to let me ride with you out of this flat Kansas prairie – away off some place where you can get on a hill."

"Wal, why not? If yu'll take a chance on me I will on yu."

Lonesome strangled a wild eagerness. The light in his eyes then decided Laramie upon the real deeper possibility of this lad.

22

"But I'm no good, Laramie, no good atall," he burst out. "I can ride, I like cattle, I ain't lazy, an' I'm a good camp cook. But thet lets me out."

"How about whisky?"

"Haven't had a drink for six months an' don't care a damn if I never have another. I'm a pore gambler, too, an' a wuss shot. Reckon I'm some punkins with the girls. But where'd that ever get a fellow?"

"Lonesome, all yu say, 'pears a pretty good reference, if I needed any."

"But you heard Price accuse me of rustlin'.... It's true.... An' thet wasn't the first time by a darn sight." Lonesome evidently found this confession a shameful thing to make. No doubt Laramie had roused a respect which drove him to be loyal to the best in himself.

"Boy, it's only the last couple of years that cattlemen have counted haids. An' it's no crime to kill a beef to eat," rejoined Laramie.

"But, Laramie, it ain't only cattle," rushed on Lonesome hoarsely. "I – I got an itch to – to approperate any damn thing thet ain't tied down."

Laramie laughed at the boy's distress, not at the content of his confession.

"Wal, then, all the more reason for somebody to look after yu," he replied.

23

"By thunder! I told you, an' thet's more'n I ever did before," declared Mulhall, in the righteousness of sacrifice. "But I ain't guaranteein' no more.... I'm afraid I'm just no good atall."

"Yu make me sick," replied Laramie, with severity. "Hidin' facts about yore people – talkin' about wantin' a girl, a ranch, a home, an' all thet. Then in yore next breath tryin' to make yourself out a low-down thief! I cain't believe both, an' I choose to believe the first."

"Gawd only knows what a pard like you might do for me!... But I've told you, Laramie, I've told you."

"Shore. An' as likeable a boy as yu must turn out a straight shooter. Yu'll have to if yu trail with me. Let's go to bed, Lonesome."

Long after dark, and after his companion had fallen asleep Laramie lay awake, vaguely pleased with himself and more than usually given to hopeful speculations as to the future.

Chapter 2

Late in the afternoon of the second day Laramie and Lonesome rode into Dodge, the wide-open cattle town of the frontier.

They had gotten only far enough down the wide main street to see through the clouds of dust the vehicles, horses, and throng of men that showed Dodge was having one of its big days – the arrival of trail drivers with their herds from Texas.

A voice called: *"Lonesome! Lonesome Mulhall!"*

The owner of that name stiffened in his saddle while he reined his horse. "Laramie, did you hear some one call my name?" queried Lonesome, incredulously.

"I shore did," replied Laramie, halting beside Lonesome to gaze up and down and across the street.

"Gosh! I reckoned I had the willies... Somebody knows me, Laramie, sure as I'm the onluckiest –"

"Lonesome! For Gawd's sake – is it you?" called the voice, husky of accent.

Laramie located whence it came. "Come,

Lonesome, an' don't make a yell. . . . Looks like a jail to me. Shore wasn't heah on my last visit to Dodge. The town's growin'."

On the nearer side of the street a solid-looking squat structure had a small window with iron bars across it. Between those bars peered out a pale face from which piercing black eyes fastened upon Lonesome. It required no more than that to acquaint Laramie with the likelihood of their having found the much-talked-of Tracks Williams, Lonesome's one-time partner.

They rode up to the window, which was about on a level with their heads as they sat mounted. Lonesome had not let out the yelp Laramie had anticipated, a fact that attested to deeper emotion than Laramie had given him credit for. But his face had paled, and his chin wabbled.

"Don't you know me, pard?" came from the window.

"*You,   Tracks!* . . . Alive? . . . Aw,   I'm thankin' the good Lord! I reckoned you was dead."

"I'm damn near dead and I will be soon if you don't get me out of here," replied the other bitterly. Laramie saw a handsome thin white face, lighted by eyes black as night and sharp as daggers. Black locks hung dis-

26

hevelled over a fine brow and a thin downy beard bespoke youthful years.

"You locked in?" queried Lonesome, swiftly.

"Yes, with a lot of lousy greasers and drunken cow punchers."

"It's a jail, huh?"

"Do you think it's a ballroom? ... Who's your riding pardner?"

"He hails from the Handle, Tracks," answered Lonesome, as he turned to his friend. "Laramie, stick your hand in there an' shake with my old pard, Tracks Williams."

Laramie did as bidden. "Hod do. I cain't say I'm glad to meet yu in heah, but I would be if yu was out."

"Are you Mulhall's friend?" came the eager query.

Laramie was about to admit this when Lonesome burst out, vehemently: "Tracks, he saved my neck. I was about to be swung up. We're ridin' away from Kansas."

"Don't ride away without me," implored Williams.

"Huh! Did you have any idee we would?" grunted Lonesome, fiercely. "Not if we have to wipe this here Dodge off the map."

"Lonesome, don't waste time. Let me talk," replied Laramie, who could see

27

through the window that other inmates were listening. "What're yu in for?"

"Not a damn thing," declared Williams, with passion. "Wasn't in any shooting fray, nor drunk, nor anything. It's an outrage. Sheriff and his deputies made a raid to lock up a lot of newcomers. And I happened to be one."

"Wal, we'll get yu out one way or another," declared Laramie.

"Come back after dark with a pick or crowbar. You can dig a hole through this wall in ten minutes."

"What'd be the best time?"

"Any time after night. The guard leaves us here and goes into the saloon. We'd broke out long ago if we had anything."

"Look for us about middle of supper time," whispered Laramie, his sharp ears and eyes vigilant. A moment later a heavily armed man appeared around the corner.

"What you doin' at thet winder?" he demanded.

"Howdy, officer. We was ridin' by an' some one begged for a cigarette. I was about to pass some makin's in," replied Laramie, his hand on his breast pocket, where the little bag of tobacco lay.

"So long's you let me see you do it," returned the guard.

Whereupon Laramie passed his tobacco-pouch in with the words: "There yu are, cowpuncher. Hope yu get out soon. Good luck an' so long."

He and Lonesome rode on up the street, and when they had reached a safe distance Lonesome breathed low: "Say, Laramie, but you are a quick-witted cus. I was about to throw a gun on thet guard."

"Think twice before yu do anythin', now yu're with me," replied Laramie, sharply. "Let's get our haids together. We'll need another hawse, saddle, bridle, an' such. Some grub an' water, for we'll have to rustle out of heah pronto. Also somethin' to break a hole in thet wall."

Before they reached the busy section of Dodge, inquiry led them up a side street to a stable and corral maintained for incoming riders. Bargaining for an extra horse with equipment took but a few moments. While Laramie paid for this and feed for the horses, Lonesome went sauntering around. Upon his return Laramie gathered from his bright wink that he had hit upon something interesting or useful.

"Leave the hawses heah in the corral. We'll be rustlin' out before sunup," said Laramie.

"Ain't youse a-goin' to paint the town?" queried the stableman, with a grin.

"Shore. But thet takes us only one night. . . . Come on, pard, let's rustle some fodder for ourselves."

They made for the main street, boots scraping and spurs jangling, after the manner of riders unused to walking.

"Wal, do we hunt up a hardware store?" drawled Laramie.

"Nix. I spotted tools under thet open shed. We'll approperate a couple of them," replied Lonesome, grinning.

"Lonesome, this heah approperatin' habit of yorn worries me," declared Laramie, humorously.

"It ain't no habit. It's a disease."

"Wal, whatever it is yu must curb it. That cowman at the camp last night – he was shore decent. An' right under his nose yu stole his tobacco-pouch."

"Aw, not stole."

"Dog-gone-yu. Thet's what he'd say. If we ever fall into respectable company yu'll disgrace us."

"No fear then. . . . Gosh! you can't see the town for the dust. Regular roarin' place, this Dodge. No wonder Tracks got run in."

"Let's buy a canvas bag to pack grub in,

an' a couple of water bottles," suggested Laramie.

They sallied into a merchandise store, where they made more purchases than Laramie had bargained for. Manifestly being in town went to Lonesome's head. It was dusk when they arrived back at the corral with their supplies. The stableman evidently had locked up his stable for the night. While Laramie filled the canvas water-bottles at the watering-trough, Lonesome went to secure some tools. He came jingling back almost immediately.

"Got a pick an' a crowbar," he announced, highly elated. "We can bust thet jail wide open in a jiffy."

Hide 'em along the corral fence," replied Laramie. "I shore hope this heah job doesn't land us in jail."

"Now I've found Tracks, I'd rather be with him, in jail or not."

"Wal, I can appreciate that," rejoined Laramie, dryly. "But if it's all the same to yu we'll stay out."

They returned to the main street and approached the center of the great stock town. Lights shone yellow through the dust. Wagons and riders were on the move. Lonesome wanted to walk on forever, but Laramie dragged him into a restaurant. Only

31

a few customers were there, which was fortunate for the two riders, as by the time their meal was served to them the place had filled up with a noisy throng of teamsters, cowpunchers, trail drivers and ranch hands, with a sprinkling of hard-looking individuals whose calling Laramie had his doubts about. Their conversation was loud, punctuated by guffaws, and the content was movement and sale of cattle, and the excitement of Dodge.

Laramie had to drag Lonesome out of the eating-hall. By now the dust had settled and the main street was no longer obscured. Not so many pedestrians passed to and fro. But the saloons, restaurants, and dance-halls were already roaring.

"Wal, Dodge is a sight tamer than she used to be," was Laramie's comment.

"She's wild enough for me," declared Lonesome, halting in front of a wide-open palace of iniquity. "Gosh! it's sure good we can't linger in this burg.... Look at them pale-faced black-coated gamblin' gents. They wouldn't fleece us, not atall. An' look –"

"Come on, yu tenderfoot," interrupted Laramie, dragging him on.

"Tenderfoot! Me? Say, thet's a good one."

Lonesome chuckled over that, very sincere in his own opinion that it went wide of the mark. They came abreast of an open lighted door whence issued strains of music. A young woman, bare-necked and bare-armed, with a pretty painted face and eyes of a hawk, about to enter the hall, gaily hailed Lonesome:

"Hello, sweetheart!"

A yoke of oxen could not have checked Lonesome more effectively. There was a dash of gallantry in the manner with which he doffed his sombrero.

"Howdy. Where'd I ever meet you?" he replied.

"It was on the boat from Kansas City to New Orleans. Come in and dance."

Laramie felt the urge in the lad and held on to him.

"Sorry. I – I got an important job on hand," floundered Lonesome.

"Who's your gun-packing pard?" queried the girl as she backed into the doorway, with her hawk eyes on Laramie. "I've seen him somewhere."

"I'm his dad an' he's a bad boy," drawled Laramie.

She trilled a mirthless laugh. "I thought his mother didn't know he was out."

Lonesome flounced out of Laramie's grip and lunged on down the street.

"Smart Alec of a girl! I never rode on no boat to New Orleans."

"Reckon yu don't know her kind, Lonesome. Boy, yu'd be a lamb among wolves in this heah town. Let's rustle to dig Williams out an' then hit the road."

As they strode off the lighted street into the dark one Laramie decided the best plan would be to saddle the three horses and lead them out to a clump of cottonwoods at the edge of town, then return with their implements to free Williams. All was dark and quiet in the vicinity of the corral. They lost no time saddling up. Then they set out, with Laramie leading the horses and Lonesome following with the tools. They proceeded cautiously and kept to the back road which soon led out into the open country.

Laramie halted. "Lonesome, this heah is haidin' east. We want to strike west."

"Sure we do. An' we'll ride straight back through this here Dodge town," asserted Lonesome.

"Suits me, unless we get surprised breakin' open the jail. Now let's work down to the main road an' find thet bunch of cottonwoods."

Soon these were located and the horses haltered. Whereupon the rescuers hurried into town again. Lonesome was excited, hard to hold back and keep still. Fortunately there

34

was not a light in one of the several houses they passed before reaching the jail. It too was dark. Laramie had forgotten that the small window was high off the ground. After peering through the darkness up and down the road, listening the while, Laramie lifted Lonesome up to a level of the window. The inmates were not by any means silent, but Lonesome's sibilant whisper brought instant results.

"All right, pard. Coast's clear. Got any tools?"

"Sure. Crowbar an' pick," replied Lonesome, in his shrill whisper.

"Pass the bar in. Then you keep watch outside. Tap on the wall if any one comes."

Laramie had to let Lonesome down to get the crowbar, then hoist him aloft again. The implement was easy to hand in, but not so with the pick. Dull thuds sounded on the inside of the wall. Crumbling sounds were soon deadened by rough jolly songs of the cow-camps. Williams had coached his accomplices in this jail-breaking. Laramie could not have heard any approaching footsteps. It was all a matter of luck. Suddenly the crowbar split through the outside planking. Lonesome then attacked the place with his pick, and in less than two

35

minutes there was a hole as large as the mouth of a barrel.

"Pile out, yu jailbirds," called Laramie, low-voiced and grim. If they were discovered it meant gun-play.

A dark form crawled out to leap erect. In the starlight Laramie recognized the pale face and black head of Williams. The next instant Lonesome was hugging him.

"Pard! – My Gawd – I'm glad!"

"Dear old Lonesome! To think it had to be you!"

Other forms crawled out of the hole, like rats out of a broken trap. Laramie lingered as Lonesome hurried Williams down the road. Nine men emerged, all of whom except the last, scuttled away in the darkness. This fellow was burly of shoulder, bushy of head and beard. He loomed over Laramie, peering with big gleaming eyes.

"I don't forgit a good turn. Who air you, stranger?" he said gruffly.

"Laramie, for short."

"Steve Elkins is mine. Put her thar."

They shook hands.

"Anyone left inside?"

"Hell yes. Some drunk an' some asleep. Don't risk wakin' them. Thet new Dodge Sheriff shore goes off half-cocked."

Laramie stole away in the gloom and

presently broke into a light trot. Soon he espied two dark forms in the middle of the road.

"Thet you, Laramie?" called Lonesome, eagerly.

"Shore. All safe," panted Laramie.

"Meet my pard, Ted Williams.... Tracks, this is my new pard. Calls himself Laramie. Salt of the earth! An' by Gawd! I'm a lucky an' a reformed man."

That ceremony over, the three hurried down the road to the clump of cottonwoods, to find all well with their horses.

"Lonesome, I've changed my mind about ridin' through town," said Laramie. "We'll circle an' hit the road somewhere west."

"Dog-gone! I'd like to have had a peep at thet girl who called me sweetheart," complained Lonesome.

They mounted and rode out into the starlight, where each instinctively halted. It was a fresh start – new and different life for each. Laramie heard Lonesome choke up. But it was Williams who broke the pregnant silence.

"Two's company. Three's a crowd. Hadn't I better go my own way?"

Laramie sensed loyalty to others in Williams' terse query. He belonged to the best of that fire-spirited breed who rode the ranges of the West, though perhaps, like so many others, had a name or a deed to hide.

"Not on my account," replied Laramie.

"Ted, it'd kill me to lose you now – an' Laramie – how could I ever split from you?" cried Lonesome, poignantly.

"Wal, I reckon three's as good a combination as two," rejoined Laramie.

"Thanks for putting it up to me," said Williams, his voice ringing. "We'll stick together.... Three for one and one for three!"

Months afterward a rancher over on the Platte wanting to keep Laramie and Tracks but to discharge Lonesome, called them The Three Range Riders. And that name, augmented by gossip from cow-camp to cow-camp, traveled over the prairie ranges. Laramie's fame with a gun, Williams' as a tracker, Lonesome's irresistible attraction and weakness for women, preceded them in many instances, and in all soon discovered them. Cattle thronged the immense area of western Kansas and jobs were easy to be had. Keeping them, however, was a different matter. Trouble gravitated to the three range-riders. If it was not one thing it was another. If a cattleman wanted one of them he had to hire all: if he wished to get rid of one he lost the three. They rode a grub-line from camp to camp, from range to range; and they got on at this ranch and then at that. At Tellson's Diamond Bar an irate and jealous cowpuncher made an illuminating remark: "Them three flash range-riders never spend a dollar!"

This was almost true and Laramie was the genius. He bound his two comrades to an oath agreement that they turn over their earnings to him to save. Lonesome and Tracks kept their word, but not without wailings and implorings. Laramie was inexorable. The three wore clothes so ragged that they resembled the scarecrows of eastern Kansas fields, and they made a pouch of tobacco go a very long way. No drinks! No candy! No new gloves or other accounterments! Laramie had become obsessed with a great idea and was relentless in its fulfillment. When the three had earned enough money they would find a good lonely range over in Colorado or New Mexico and buy cattle enough to start ranching on their own account. All three were heart and soul in the hope, but it was Laramie's will that might make it possible.

In the little town of Pecord, upon which they happened one hot summer day, they halted long enough to eat a much-needed meal. Tracks begged for ice cream and

Lonesome begged for apple pie. But Laramie was obdurate.

"Yu galoots can starve for dainties," declared their chief, scornfully. "Do yu heah me shoutin' for blackberry jam when I love it better than my life?"

Tracks restrained his longings, but when, once more riding along the road, Lonesome produced a sadly mashed piece of apple pie from inside his open shirt, then Tracks exploded, "Where in hell did you get that pie?"

"Um-yum-yum," was all the satisfaction he got from the ravenous rider.

"Wal, yu ugly little bowlegged toad!" exploded Laramie, when he saw the pie. "Yu approperated thet!"

"Give me a bite, you hawg!" importuned Tracks.

All to no avail were his importunities. Lonesome gobbled all the pie and even went to lengths of picking bits of crust off his chaps to devour them also.

"Tracks, he *stole* thet pie," declared Laramie, in an awful voice. "Shore as the Lord made little apples, Lonesome will ruin us yet."

"Beat hell out of him first!" quoth the fiery Williams.

So they rode on to the next cow-camp,

40

where they worked for three weeks and were elated, feeling that their luck had changed. Yet not so! Vast as the Great Plains were, they constituted only a small world. Who should ride in with a herd of steers but Herb Price, two hundred miles and more from the range where he had aimed to hang Lonesome! Laramie was for calling Price out, saying he would be sure to bob up again. But Lonesome would not hear of that. "Fork yore hosses, pards. We're on our way," he said, and without word to the kindly rancher and with wages due, they rode away into the melancholy autumn night.

They drifted west and at the approach of winter were glad to accept poor pay from a trail-driver boss on the way back to Texas to fetch up another herd. Down the Pecos to the Braseda they rode, and on to the gulf part where the big cattle herds formed. They lost that job to find a better, and drove stock with vaqueros during the winter months, to start north in the spring over the old Chisholm Trail. That was a tough trip, and when they ended up at Abilene they were a tough trio, though still motivated by their cherished dream. And their savings had mounted to almost incredible proportions.

Out of Abilene one night the three rangers made camp on the river, where they were joined by several self-styled cowmen riding home. They were jovial fellows. That night, despite the fact that Laramie slept on his precious wallet, it was stolen from him. In the morning the home-riding strangers were gone. But they could not shake a tracker like Tracks Williams. A hound on a trail, he tracked them to Hays City. Laramie conered them in a gambling-hall, killed the leader, crippled the second, and held up the third, who confessed and swore that the money had been gambled away.

It proved a terrible blow to the three range-riders. They let down. Lonesome got drunk and Tracks picked a fight. Laramie, almost too discouraged to begin all over again, looked upon red liquor himself. Yet when destruction threatened he pulled out, got his partners away, and faced the long trail once more.

Vicissitudes common to range-riders of the period dogged their tracks for a year, at the end of which they were as badly off as ever. What they did not experience in life on the ranges was certainly inconsequential. All the mean and hard jobs around cow-camps fell to their lot. Beggers could not be choosers. Laramie recaptured his spirit and clung to it unquenchably because he realized Lonesome and Tracks were slipping down the broad and easy trail. They had come to be more than brothers to him. He fought them with subtle cunning, with brawn and actual threat. But the frontier was changing from the bloody Indian wars and buffalo massacres a few years back to the cattle regime and the development of the rustler. For young men the life grew harder, for not only did the peril to existence increase, but also the peril of moral ruin. The gambler, the prostitute, the rustler, the desperado, the notoriety-seeking, as well as the real gunman, followed hard on the advent of the stock-raising.

Laramie had his work cut out for him to save his young fire-brands from going the way of the many. And the worst of it was he realized that another backset or two would break his shattered hopes. Something extraordinary had to happen soon or he would funk the job and that would be the end of Lonesome and Tracks. Laramie prayed for a miracle.

One weary day in the spring the inseparable three rode into a growing prosperous town. Laramie did not know it or that it was on the railroad. Both Lonesome and Tracks balked when they discovered it.

"I'm gun-shy," said the aloof Williams, growing harder and harder to reach.

"An' I'm girl-shy," added Lonesome, doggedly.

"Wal, I've done my best for yu both," replied Laramie, with bitter finality. "If yu don't brace an' come on I'll be drunk in half an hour."

That dire threat fetched them. The idea of Laramie getting drunk was insupportable.

"Tracks, we *got* to stick to Laramie," swore Lonesome.

"We're a couple of measly quitters," replied Tracks, with remorse. "But, Laramie, old man, it's not that we don't love you and swear by you. It's that we're hopeless, hungry, ragged, and sick. We're for holding up a stagecoach."

"Wal, let's try once more," entreated Laramie, for the hundredth time in less than that many days. They rode into the town and dismounted at the livery stable.

"Boy, what place is this heah?" asked Laramie, of the lad who came to take their horses.

"Garden City."

Laramie turned to his comrades. "Shore it's a new town for us. Heah our luck will change."

"Ahuh. What's the idee?" queried the glum Lonesome.

"We're three ragamuffins," declared

44

Tracks, hopelessly. "We'll be taken for rustlers on the run."

"Let's go eat. I've got some money left. Then we'll feel better to tackle this heah place.

"You son-of-a-gun!" ejaculated Lonesome, admiringly.

"He's a magician," declared Tracks. "How many times has he had a little money left!"

With a square meal in sight the downhearted trio brightened, and they forgot their tattered garments, their worn-out boots. Laramie would not enter the first eating-shop, nor the second, though his friends dragged at him.

"Not good enough for us," he asserted.

"Hell, we'll get throwed out," replied Lonesome, giving up.

It was about the noon hour and the broad street did not present numerous pedestrians, though sidewalks on each side were lined with vehicles and horses. Laramie strode on until he came to a pretentious hotel, and was entering the lobby, followed by his reluctant and grumbling partners, when suddenly he was halted by a man.

"Look out, Lonesome! Duck!" called Tracks, who was ahead.

But the Westerner with the broad-brimmed sombrero let out a whoop.

"*Laramie!* ... By the Lord Harry, where'd you come from?"

Quick as a flash Laramie recognized the lean, lined, tanned face with its gray eyes of piercing quality.

"Buffalo Jones or I'm a daid sinner! I shore am glad to meet yu heah."

Their hands met in a grip that bespoke a period in the past which had tried men's souls.

"You're older, Laramie, a little peeked an' drawn, but I wouldn't have known Old Nigger Horse any better, if he'd come along," said Jones, heartily.

"Wal, Buff, yu haven't changed a whit," declared Laramie.

"I'm fit as a fiddle. ... You look like we did after that Comanche campaign. ... Say, man, come to take you in you're a sight ... An' your pards here – they're about as tough. What you been fightin'? Wild cats in a thorn thicket?"

"Nope. Greaser hawse-thieves down in the river bottom," replied Laramie, lying glibly. "Boys, meet Colonel Buffalo Jones. Yu've often heahed me speak of him. ... Buff, meet my pards, Mulhall an' Williams."

The plainsman's greeting defined Laramie's status and the regard in which any friend of his must be held. Then Jones turned to a pale, rather handsome man, with whom he had been talking before the interruption and who had stepped back.

"Lindsay, you must meet these boys," said Jones, drawing the man toward Laramie. "This is Laramie Nelson. He was with me when I had the campaign against Old Nigger Horse, the Comanche chief. You heard me tell the story to your daughters only last night. Laramie was a boy then."

Laramie quickly responded to the Easterner's genuine interest and pleasure. Then he introduced Lonesome and Tracks. To do them credit, they acquitted themselves with modest restraint. Laramie was not now afraid of their appearance. That was a recommendation. This meeting augured well.

"Laramie, it'll interest you to learn Mr. Lindsay is from Ohio," went on Jones, "and has come West for his health. With his wife, three daughters, and a son! Isn't that just fine? The West needs Eastern stock, good blood with the pioneer spirit."

"We're shore glad to welcome yu," said Laramie, warmly, and Tracks and Lonesome seconded him.

"Laramie, you know this country like a book. Lindsay has bought a ranch and a big herd of cattle over in Colorado. Pretty high up on the plains. Lester Allen sold out to him. I'm curious about the deal. Maybe you know Allen?"

By the merest chance Laramie was able to connect the name of Lester Allen with Spanish Peaks Ranch, and he said so casually.

"Lindsay, you're in luck," declared Jones, with a flash of his wonderful eyes. "You're an Easterner, a tenderfoot if you'll excuse me. You've bought a strange ranch from a stranger, without seeing either. It's an irregular transaction. You must have a man you can trust. Here he is, Laramie Nelson. I vouch for him, stand back of him. He knows the West from Texas up. He knows cattle, and what's more to the point – the ways of cattlemen, honest and dishonest. Last he had few equals with a gun – and that was years ago."

"Mr. Nelson, you're spoken so highly of that I'd want you even if I didn't need you, and indeed I do," said Lindsay earnestly. "My family and I are up a tree, so to speak. Can I persuade you to come along and help us run Spanish Peaks Ranch?"

"Thanks. I'll be glad to talk about it,"

48

replied Laramie, biting his tongue to restrain it within bounds, and he had all he could do to keep from kicking Lonesome and Tracks, who kept edging in, eyes wide, mouths agape. "We're pretty tuckered out an' need a rest. But I might take yu up, provided, of course, I could bring my riders, Mulhall an' Williams. I don't want to brag about them, but i never saw a rider as good with a hawse an' rope as Mulhall, or a tracker in Williams' class."

"To be sure I'd want them. By all means," replied Lindsay, hastily. Then he turned to Jones. "The wife is waiting for me. Suppose you excuse me now and meet me here in an hour, say?"

"We'll be here, Lindsay. Meanwhile I'll try to talk Laramie into going with you," said Jones.

Whereupon Lindsay bowed and left them, to join two ladies who were waiting at the corner. It discomfited Laramie to become aware that the younger of this couple bent grave, fascinated eyes upon him. As he wheeled he was in time to see Lonesome come out of a trance, apparently, and turn a radiant face to him. Sometimes that homely, dirty, bearded face could shine with beauty. It did so now.

"My Gawd, Tracks, did you see what I seen?" he whispered.

"No. What was it?"

"A girl — a slip of a girl — inside the lobby here. She had the wonderfulest eyes.... But she's gone!" he ended, tragically.

"So are you gone," retorted Tracks.

Laramie heard all this while Jones was questioning him further.

"Boys, go in the lunchroom an' order some grub. I'll be along pronto." And after they had rushed in Laramie turned to Jones.

"No, I'm not acquainted with Lester Allen, but if Luke Arlidge is his foreman there's shore a nigger in the woodpile."

Buffalo Jones cracked a huge fist in a horny palm, and his eagle eyes flashed as Laramie had seen them years before.

"Laramie, that deal had a queer look," he declared, forcibly. "It had been settled — money paid — papers signed — before I met this merchant from Ohio. And Allen had gone. Allen is not well known here. No one would say good or bad of him. And that's bad. If you know Luke Arlidge is off color —"

"Shore I know that," interposed Laramie, as the plainsman hesitated.

"Then another trusting Easterner has been bilked. It's a damn shame. Fine man. And the nicest family. The boy, though, he'll

50

blow up out here.... Do you want my advice?"

"Shoot, old timer, an' yu bet yore life I'll take it."

"Chance of your life to help a worthy family and get –"

"Thet's enough for me. Never mind what I'll get. But, Jones, I was throwin' a bluff. We're daid broke. We haven't had work for weeks. We hadn't any in sight. An' we just cain't go alone with this Lindsay outfit half naked."

"I'll fix that, Laramie," replied the plainsman. "Lindsay has plenty of money. I'll get you an advance.... No. It might be better to lend you some. I'll do it. But don't you be in a hurry sprucing up. Let this Eastern outfit see you in real Wild West rags. Savvy? Go and eat now. Meet me here in an hour."

Chapter 3

The Lindsay family, late from Ohio, were assembled in the upstairs parlor of the Elk Hotel, Garden City, Kansas. They had arrived that morning, and now, intensely interested though bewildered, they gazed out upon this new country with many and varied feelings.

It was a raw day in early spring, with puffs of dust rising down the wide street and the windmills in the distance whirling industriously. Evidently Saturday morning was an important one to that community. Old wagons with hoops covered with canvas, and laden with all kinds of farm produce lumbered by the windows; light high-seated four-wheeled vehicles, drawn by fast trotting horses, rolled down the street toward the center of town, some few blocks westward; a string of cattle passed, driven by queer-garbed big-hatted riders; knots of men stood on every visible corner; women were conspicuous for their absence.

John Lindsay, head of the family, an iron-gray-haired man of fifty years, and of fine appearance except for an extreme pallor which indicated a tubercular condition, stood with his back to a window, surveying his children, and especially his wife, with rueful and almost disapproving eyes.

"It's too late. I'm committed to the deal with this cattleman, Allen. And I couldn't get out of it if I wanted to," he said.

His wife's red eyes were significant, without her expression of misery.

"Upper Sandusky was good enough for me," interposed Neale, the eighteen-year-old son of the Lindsays, a rather foppish youth, whom the three sisters eyed in some disgust. Harriet, the oldest, was thinking of the embarrassing incidents they had had to suffer already through this spoiled only son.

"Neale, you were hardly good enough for Upper Sandusky," retorted the father, curtly. "This raw West may improve you."

"Improve Neale! It couldn't be done," declared Lenta, the youngest, who was sixteen. She was little, auburn-haired, with innocent baby-blue eyes that could conceal anything.

"Aw, shut up! You could stand a lot of improvement yourself," replied Neale as he snatched his hat and arose.

"Dear, don't go," implored the mother,

with words and looks that betrayed her weakness. "We were to hold a conference."

"What I think or say doesn't go far with this Lindsay bunch," he growled, and strode out.

"The Lord be thanked!" cried Lenta, after him.

"Mother, you must give up coddling Neale," said her husband, earnestly. "We're out West now. Start in right. He must take his medicine."

"But such rough-looking men!"

"Yes, the men we meet will be plain and rough, and the West will be hard," went on Lindsay. "Once and for all, let me have my say. I begged you all to stay home at Upper Sandusky. But none of you, except Neale, would consider that. The doctors held out hope for my health, if I came to live in a high dry country. I wanted to come alone. That was not easy to face. You had plenty of time to decide. And come West you would. So I sold out – and here we are. Let's make the best of it. Let's not expect too much and fortify ourselves against jars. Naturally we feel lost. But other families have become pioneers before us. Honestly, I lean to it. I always had a secret longing to do this very thing. It certainly will be the saving of me if you all pitch in, take what

54

comes, and work out our destinies and happiness here."

"Father, it will all come out right," rejoined Harriet. "Mother is tired out and blue. You go down and look around. Meet people. Inquire about this Lester Allen, to whom you have committed yourself. We'll cheer mother up and tackle our problem."

"Thanks, Hallie, you're a comfort," replied Lindsay, with feeling, and went out like a man burdened.

As soon as he had gone Mrs. Lindsay began to weep again.

"Mother –"

"Hal, let her cry," interrupted Lenta. "You know ma."

Florence, the second daughter, sat looking out of the window, at once dreamy and thoughtful. She was nineteen and the beauty of the family, a dazzlingly pretty blond with dark eyes. Harriet had her fears about Florence. Vain, coquettish, now amiable and again perverse, her possibilities in this new country were uncertain. Lenta crossed to the window. "Flo, I'll bet you see a man," she said.

"Lots of outlandish gawks going by, all hats and boots," observed Florence.

"Girls, wouldn't it be more sensible of you to help me with mother and our immediate problem?" asked Harriet. "Just think! In a few days we will be traveling in canvas-covered wagons across the plains to this new home. We have endless things to buy, to plan for, as well as screwing up our courage. And here you are curious about men!"

"Who's curious?" queried Lenta.

"Both of you. Weren't you all eyes at the station? You never looked out across the prairie. But that prairie is important for us to get used to. It's no matter what kind of men there are here, at least not yet."

"But – there *is,*" burst out Mrs. Lindsay, in a fresh outburst. "That terrible little greasy, hairy man who called me sweetheart. *Me!* . . . He had the most devilish eyes. He carried my bags to the bus and when I offered to pay he grinned and said, 'Lady, your money's counterfeit.' I protested it was not and insisted he accept pay. Then he called me sweetheart. I believe if you hadn't come he would have chucked me under the chin. . . . Oh! Outrageous!"

"Mother, I'd take that as a compliment," said Harriet. "He took you for our sister instead of mother."

"Ma, you should be tickled to death," added Lenta, teasingly. "That proves you still have some of the beauty grandma raves about."

"Oh, be serious!" cried the mother, distracted. "What in heaven's name – will my daughters do – for husbands!"

Lenta shrieked with delight. "Flo, can you beat that?"

Harriet was for once taken aback that she had no ready reply. Florence took their mother's wail in a grave, superior, smiling sort of way which intimated a confidence in the future. Harriet got her mother's point of view. Their father's health and the making of a new home were matters of importance, but in the long run nothing could equal the need of husbands.

"Mother, there seem to be plenty of men to pick from," finally replied Harriet, her sense of humor dominant.

"Such men!"

"But, mother, you are unreasonable. They may be fine, big-hearted, honest, splendid fellows."

"Listen to our man-hater!" exclaimed Lenta, impishly.

By that Harriet realized that in her earnestness she had broken her usual reserve. Lenta was an adorable girl, but she could say things that stung. Years before, it seemed long ago, Harriet had formed an attachment for a handsome clerk in her father's store. It had been Harriet's only romance, and an unhappy one. Her father's estimate of Tom Emery was justified and Harriet, heartbroken, withdrew in secret sorrow and felt that she was done with men.

"Hallie, do you really believe so?" queried Mrs. Lindsay, hopefully.

"Certainly I do. Appearances are nothing. Out here men must work hard. They have no time to think of clothes and looks. Then what have we seen? Only a few dozen horsemen, farmers, and whatever they were. Let's give the Western men a chance."

"Flo, what's got into Hal?" inquired Lenta.

"Lord only knows, Lent, unless we may expect a rival in her," replied Florence, complacently.

These younger sisters had infinite capacity for rousing Harriet's tried spirit and the present was no exception. Only Harriet reacted differently this time.

"My darling sisters, you put it rather vulgarly, but you may expect just that," replied Harriet, with a cool audacity somewhat discounted by a furious blush.

"Hal Lindsay!" ejaculated Florence, confronted by an incredible and disturbing idea.

"Look at her! Handsome, shameless thing! She ought to blush," cried Lenta, trillingly.

"What's that your sister may expect?" interposed the mother, quite mystified.

"Mother dear, for some years past Flo appropriated every young man who happened around. And lately Lent has more than followed in Flo's footsteps. I was just warning them that now we have arrived out in this wild West I shall contest the field with them."

Harriet had spoken on the spur of the moment, out of need to hide her hurt, and she had gone farther than she had intended.

"Thank God you've come to your senses," declared Mrs. Lindsay bluntly.

"Hal, you know darn well we wouldn't look at one of these louts," asserted Florence, spiritedly.

"Humph! I'd like to see the masculine gender you wouldn't look at – twice, and then some," returned Harriet, dryly.

"This is great. Gosh! but we love each other! I'm going to have the time of my life," said Lenta, with immense satisfaction. "I hated school, and the idea of spending all my life in that Upper Sandusky was sickening. Out here something will happen. We can *do* things."

"Yes, you can work," rejoined the mother, with equal satisfaction. "I declare. Harriet has bucked me up. If *she* can talk that way, coming West is the best move we ever made in our lives.... I can think again. Here we are. And some miles out on that gray flat is our new home. There's a ranch-house, an old Spanish affair, almost a fort. So this Mr. Allen wrote father. I supose it's a barn. I hope it's empty. What we need to know most is what's *in* it. Thank goodness we're not poor. We can buy things for our comfort."

"There! All mother needs to buck her up is a chance to spend money on a house," said Harriet, pleased with her diplomacy.

"We'll have to buy a thousand things we know are not in that ranch-house. Suppose we go out to look in the stores?" suggested Mrs. Lindsay.

"I'll go," declared Florence, with vivacity.

"Ma, I must write to Bill and Jack and –" said Lenta, tragically.

"We'll come later, mother, or go with you after lunch," interrupted Harriet.

"Good. It would never do to leave Lenta alone," replied the mother, practically, and followed Florence out.

Lenta's baby-blue eyes held an expression no precocious infant's ever held.

"Hal, I'll bust out some day," she said, as if over-burdened.

"What for?"

"Just because mother expects me to."

"Nonsense! You know mother is the best ever. She has been distressed over father and us. If we can only get her started right!"

Lenta left the window and came to sit on the arm of Harriet's chair. Long and earnestly she gazed at this elder sister. When Lenta was sweet and serious like this no one could resist her, not even Harriet.

"You did start her right. Hal, you're the kindest, most thoughtful, helpful person. I *do* love you. I do appreciate you; and I want you to start *me* right," said Lenta, with emotion.

"Why, child!" returned Harriet, deeply touched. Praise and affection from this younger sister had never been too abundant. But back in Ohio Lenta had been absorbed in her school, friends, affairs. Here in the West it would be different, and Lenta recognized it. Harriet hugged and kissed her warmly, as she had not for long. "And I adore you, Lenta. Nothing could have made me any happier. I will help you. I'll be more of a sister to you. Something tells me we have a tremendous experience ahead of us. It thrills while it frightens me."

"I'm thrilled to death. . . . Hal, I hope you weren't deceiving us – just to help buck mother up."

"Oh, that – about contesting the masculine

61

field with you and Flo?" queried Harriet, embarrassed. But she did not need to fear the light in Lenta's eyes now.

"Yes. It'd be great, if you meant what you said."

"Well, honey, it was sort of forced out of me. Self-preservation. I didn't know I had it."

"Hallie dear, you are all *over* that – that old love-affair?" asked Lenta, softly.

"No, not quite all.... But I shall get entirely over it out here."

"Oh, I'm glad!... I remember Tom Emery, though I was only ten. You couldn't help but like him.... Bosh! We've got to say good-by to old friends and find new ones. No wonder Ma went under!"

"The idea grows on me, Lent. I feel sort of giddy – like I used to feel. Young again!"

"Why, you dear old goose!" ejaculated Lenta, fondly. "You're not old. Only twenty-five and you don't look that. And you're darned handsome, Hallie. Your brown hair and white skin and gray eyes are just the most fetching combination. And what a figure you have, Hallie! I'm a slip of a thing and Flo is a slim willow stem. But you'd take the eyes of real men. If you weren't so aloof – so reserved!"

"You flatter me, dear," murmured

Harriet. "But, oh, how good it sounds! I think you have helped me to face this thing."

"Well, I'll need a lot of help by and by," said the girl, returning to her roguishness. "Sufficient unto the day!... I'll write my letters, Hal. Then we'll paint the town."

"And I'll unpack a bag or two."

"Do. That gray one of mine. We'll dress up and knock their eyes out."

To Harriet's amazement they found stores far more pretentious and better equipped with important supplies and necessities of life than they had left in their home town. And as far as wearing apparel was concerned, Harriet thought they had brought enough to last forever, judging from the backwardness in styles of this Western metropolis of Kansas.

They found the clerks polite but cold, the other customers too busy with their own purchases to concern themselves with strangers. Lenta put the situation precisely when she giggled and said: "Hal, when we raved how we'd turn this burg inside out with curiosity we were barking up the wrong tree. Nobody but a few *bold* red-faced freebooters, or whatever they were, ever saw us at all. And I heard one of them say, 'Tenderfeet!'"

"You're right, Lent. I feel taken down a

peg or two. Wonder what Flo will report. But then she's so pretty she'd stop a parade."

They were to learn presently that Florence's beauty had not set the town into a furor.

"Had some peace once in my life," declared that little lady, calmly. "Funny lot, these Western men. The women, though – you should have seen them stare at me – particularly my shoes and bonnet."

It was Mrs. Lindsay, however, who had been most susceptible to the peculiar aloofness of Western folk. "Never saw such a town. Most uncivil people. You can't spend your money in these stores unless you raise a fuss with the proprietor. I declare we might be a family of hicks."

"You hit it, Ma! That's just what we are. Ohio hicks!" shouted Lenta, in glee. "I've had the darndest good time ever. This West is going to win me. Who cares who we are? I'll bet it's what you *do* that goes out here."

They changed dresses for dinner, and it was Harriet's opinion that Florence overdid the privilege, which was not usually one of her faults. Still she looked too stunning for the other Lindsays to be anything but proud.

Mr. Lindsay had not been seen by a member of the family since early morning, nor had Neale put in an appearance. This latter circumstance caused Mrs. Lindsay much concern, and she was finally silenced by a caustic remark from Lenta to the effect that Neale did not have nerve enough to get into real trouble. Finally, Mr. Lindsay returned, tired out and pale, but quite excited. He bade them go into dinner and he would follow promptly.

This they did, and to Harriet's satisfaction they did not go unnoticed, especially Florence. Then the father joined them to announce that "he had been and gone and done it."

A contrast to Harriet's consternation was Mrs. Lindsay's inquiry about Neale.

"Last I saw of that nincompoop he was playing pool," replied Lindsay, shortly.

"John, you should have looked after him," said the mother, reprovingly.

"Neale will look after himself and I hope he gets his eye-teeth cut." He was impatient with his wife and turned to Harriet and her sisters. "Eat your dinners. I'm too excited to eat. Besides, I had three or four stiff drinks. I'll talk."

And he did, with the effect of shocking his wife and taking Harriet's breath. He had met Allen and his foreman, as agreed, and had gone over maps and papers and figures, to consummate and settle the Spanish Peaks

Ranch deal then and there. Before giving them time to ask questions he explained that he had really committed himself to the deal by correspondence, and as long as he was satisfied with representation, had decided to close the thing at once.

"John, you should have seen what you bargained for before paying," reproved Mrs. Lindsay, severely.

"Well, after I heard the ranch described I knew you womenfolk wouldn't let me buy it if we saw it, so I took the bull by the horns. Allen is a bluff Westerner. Selling ranches and cattle is common with him. He introduced me to Garden City business men who evidently regarded the deal one of mutual advantage. The location is extremely healthful and beautiful, which I made clear was the main issue. Allen sold approximately ten thousand head of stock, including horses, mules, steers, cows. His foreman Arlidge – Luke Arlidge, who by the way, will catch the eye of you girls – could not give an exact estimate of the number, but it was around ten thousand. Finally I told Allen the price was a little high. He said he did not care to sell to anyone who was not perfectly satisfied, and asked me what I'd pay. I told him. He accepted. We went to a bank where the transfer was made.... We now have a ranch,

66

a home to build up. So don't look so sober. It's done, and I won't squeal if I do get a little the worst of it in a business way. I can afford it. The big thing is I feel a new man already. Instead of being cooped up over a desk all day I'll be out in the open – in the sun."

"Father, you have trusted men before to your sorrow," was all Harriet ventured to say. What more could be said? He had been set on the Western ranch idea from the very beginning, and now he had had his way. No doubt his feeling of gain and hope should be taken into consideration.

"Both Allen and Arlidge will drop in at the hotel later," went on Lindsay. "I asked them to dinner, but they begged off on that, having come in their ranch togs. They are driving out tomorrow, so it is just as well you meet them when the chance offers. I couldn't remember the things you wanted to know about."

Mrs. Lindsay joined in the discussion then, relative to the property and its prospective needs. The dinner ended without Neale having joined them, but the girls encountered him on the stairs. He was in no mood to be questioned and rushed on to his room.

"He had a black eye," asserted Florence,

certainly more speculative than sympathetic. "Did you see that, Lent?"

"I should smile," retorted Lenta, highly diverted. "Some Westerner has punched our darling."

"Oh dear! Oh dear!" cried Mrs. Lindsay, who had seen and heard. At the head of the stairs she left them, presumably to console her afflicted favorite. The girls went into the parlor while Mr. Lindsay waited downstairs for his callers.

"Flo, old girl, we're stuck. Pa's done it," remarked Lenta. Florence's silent acceptance was not conducive to hopefulness. Nevertheless, Harriet did her best to bring up pictures of prospective work, fun and home-making, and of the undoubted fact that they were committed to the wild and lonely West for good.

Presently their father entered the parlor accompanied by two tall men, of striking enough appearance to have interested any Easterner. They were introduced to Harriet and her sisters. The rancher, Lester Allen, was no longer young and had a face like a hawk. He wore a dark suit, the trousers of which were tucked in high top boots. He carried a huge tan sombrero and a whip. It did not take a moment to prove him shy and awkward in the presence of women.

The other man, Luke Arlidge, did not suffer from his marked contrast. He manifested a bold and admiring ease. He made a superb figure of a man, still young, scarcely thirty, though his bronzed hard, lean face, his eagle eyes, indicated long years of experience. His garb was what Harriet took for that of the plains rider. He was spurred, booted, belted over rough dusty apparel, and most conspicuous was the ivory-handled gun that swung from his hip, and the absence of any coat.

Mrs. Lindsay came in, and presently all were seated in a half-circle.

"Now, Allen, you must allow yourself to be questioned," said Lindsay, happily. "This is my family, except my only boy, and they want to know things."

"Fire away," replied Allen.

Lenta was not in the least embarrassed in the presence of these impressive Westerners.

"Is it lonesome?" she asked.

"Wal, I'd say shore, if you mean the ranch-house. The coyotes and wolves howl at night an' the wind moans. Only three ranches inside of fifty miles. Two days by hossback to La Junta an' six by buckboard to Denver."

"Heavens!" was Lenta's reply, but undaunted she ventured one more query.

"Any young people?"

"Wal, if you call my cow-punchers people, there's shore a heap of them. Ten all told, isn't it, Luke?"

"No. Only nine. I let Happy go," replied the foreman.

"*Only* nine!" murmured Lenta.

"Thet's all now. But your father will need three or four more."

"No girls?" queried Florence, thoughtfully.

"Let's see. There's one – two – at the nearest ranches. No more closer than La Junta."

That seemed to exhaust the interest of the two younger members of the Lindsay family, whereupon their mother had her opportunity. The upshot of her swift and numerous queries brought out that Spanish Peaks Ranch consisted of weather, landscape, a stone-and-clay house with two wings, porches, doors, and patio on the inside, facing east.

"It used to be an old fort. Built by trappers who traded with the Utes an' Kiowas. There's a fine spring comes right up inside the patio an' some big cottonwoods. It's shore pleasant summer or winter."

"And the house itself is practically empty?" concluded Mrs. Lindsay.

"Wal, it will be. I'm movin' some wagons of furniture beddin' an' sich, which you wouldn't want. My other ranch is about two days' ride north. I've a cabin there an' some stock. How many haid of cattle there now, Luke?"

"I don't know, boss. Mebbe two thousand, mebbe four," replied Arlidge.

"We must figure on hauling in everything to make a home?" asked Lindsay, rubbing his hands as if the prospect was alluring.

"Wal, I reckon so, if you want comfort," drawled the rancher.

"How far to drive loaded wagons?"

"Four days, with good luck."

"And La Junta is only two?"

"No. It'd be more fer wagons. We figured Garden City was your best startin'-point, because of the good stores where you can buy, an' then mostly level road out to the ranch."

"How about wagons and horses? Did you fetch some in for me?"

"No. We've been bad off for wagons an' teams. I'm leavin' you the chuck-wagon. You'll have to buy wagons an' teams here. Luke has made a deal for you. Man named Hazelit will call on you here. Wagons, though, you'll get at the Harvester Company store. There's saddle hosses aplenty."

71

So the practical questioning went on, with Harriet listening silently and her two younger sisters losing interest. Harriet's deductions during that half-hour were not reassuring. Allen did not inspire her with great confidence, though he seemed frank enough. She had dealt with thousands of men while bookkeeper in her father's ship-chandler and general merchandise business, and her intuition never went wrong if her perspicuity sometimes was amiss. As for Arlidge, he was quickly gauged as a strong, subtle personality, bold and crafty under a pleasing exterior. It was only a blush that mantled Harriet's neck, which her gown had left modestly bare: she felt burned by a lightning glance from Arlidge's piercing eyes. But it had been so swift that she could not be sure some of her reaction was not due to her habitual reserve. Later, however, this glance leaped upon Florence, as she sat there in her young fair beauty. Only then did Harriet yield to distrust of her father's venture. Toward the end of that interview Harriet chose to break silence.

"Mr. Arlidge, I understand a foreman's duty is to manage the ranch. Am I correct?" queried Harriet, looking him in the eyes.

"Yes. An' managin' a ranch is most

handlin' the riders an' stock," replied Arlidge, pleased to be questioned by her.

"What's the number of horses and cattle my father has purchased?"

"She'll pin you down, Arlidge," laughed Lindsay. "She was my foreman for years."

This manifestly was not so pleasant. Arlidge kept his smile, but he shifted a little uneasily.

"I don't know, Miss Lindsay. We sold in a lump. Somewhere around ten thousand haid."

"Don't you count the heads when you sell?"

"Sometimes, in small bunches."

"Oh, I see. You mean then in this case a number a little more or less than ten thousand?"

"Not more. An' mebbe a good deal less. Your father was satisfied with a rough estimate. But I'll have a count when you come out, if thet will please you."

"Yes, do. But it's a matter of business. I shall continue to keep my father's books, and will take immediate steps to learn the ropes – or lassoes, I suppose I should say," returned Harriet with a laugh.

"A bookkeeper on a big ranch is somethin' new, especially when it's a handsome young

73

woman," said Arlidge, sincere in his dubiousness.

"Thank you. I dare say it's a much-needed innovation in your slipshod method of cattle-selling," returned Harriet, lightly. "Mr. Arlidge, are you going to remain at Spanish Peaks Ranch as my father's foreman?"

"He shore is, Miss. I sold him along with the stock. Nobody but Luke could ever handle thet fire-eatin' outfit of riders," interposed Allen as he rose, sombrero in hand.

Arlidge likewise got up, lithe and graceful, a forceful, doubtful character. He fastened eyes of admiration upon Harriet.

"No, Miss Lindsay, I wasn't shore I'd stay on at Spanish Peaks until I met you – an' all," he replied, gallantly.

Then the Westerners bade the company good-night and left, with Lindsay accompanying them to the door, where he was heard planning to see them early next day, before they left. He hurried back to confront his family. It thrilled Harriet to see him so keen and enthusiastic.

"Tell me, one by one, what do you think," he beamed.

"Well, John, there is one good thing about this deal. It'll take plenty of work and money to make your old fort livable," replied his wife, complacently, and that from her was assuredly favorable.

"Well, Lent?"

"Pa, I'll shore upset thet outfit of cow-punchers," returned the youngest of the Lindsays. Already she was imitating the drawl and words of the Westerners.

"You, Flo?"

"Like it fine. Why didn't you tell us the place was Spanish? That porch all around the patio – the big cottonwoods and the spring! I must have a Spanish hammock, embroidered shawl, lace mantilla, castanets – and the rest of the duds. If they can't be bought here, I surely will find them in that La Junta town."

This was a long speech for the beauty of the family and it had telling effect.

Lindsay turned to Harriet: "My bookkeeper lass, what is your say?"

She smiled tenderly upon him, and suddenly kissed his cheek. When had she seen a little color in them?

"Father darling, you have been tricked – robbed so far as the cattle deal is concerned. But if you are happy and are sure you'll get well and strong – I am heart and soul for our Spanish Peaks Ranch."

Chapter 4

On Sunday Garden City appeared to become a deserted village, as far as the main street was concerned. The short walk that Harriet took with her mother discovered but few people and these were on the side streets. Outside of this interval the whole of that day was devoted to planning of purchases for their newly acquired home. Fortunately they were not limited as to means; otherwise they would have faced a sorry prospect.

Naturally there were several squabbles in the family, precipitated by the younger Lindsays. Mrs. Lindsay gave Harriet the duty of censorship over each individual list. To Florence she said: "Substitute these articles I checked with things that will make your room livable." To Lenta: "Child, you've done pretty well, but if you ate all the candy listed here we'd need a doctor." And to Neale: "I'll talk to father about the saddles, chaps, guns, on yours. I should think one of each would be sufficient to start on, *if* you are to be permitted freedom with such."

What this trio said to Harriet was vastly more forceful than elegant. Neale left in high dudgeon to take his case to his court of appeal – his mother.

After dinner Mr. Lindsay summoned them to meet a remarkable Westerner. This was the famous plainsman, Buffalo Jones. Upon first sight Jones struck Harriet singularly and not favorably. He was a rugged man in the prime of life, tall, erect, broad-shouldered, with a physiognomy that baffled her. Like so many of these Westerners he had a hard cast of face, and eyes narrowed by years of exposure to the open. They were light-blue eyes and looked right through Harriet. His smile however, seemed to change the ruthless, craggy set of mouth and chin. After all the Lindsays had been introduced Jones won Harriet over in a single speech.

"Wal, I shore am glad to meet you-all. It's a lucky day for the West. Lindsay, you're still a young man an' in a few months you'll be strong as an ox, ridin' all day. Mrs. Lindsay, you will soon accustom yourself to the plains an' be a pioneer's wife. It's a hard but wonderful life.... An' what shall I say to these handsome, healthy girls? Wal, I wish I were a young man again. Three strappin' riders somewhere out there don't know the great good luck in store for them. ... Young man, you've got good eyes – at least one of them is – an' a good chin. But you're kind of pale round the gills an' your hands are soft. Look out for the cow-punchers, keep quiet an' work – that's Buffalo Jones' hunch."

Jones appeared to strike them all, except possibly Neale, to be the Westerner they needed to meet. Lenta did not show the least awe and her first wide-eyed query, accompanied by her irresistible smile, evidently pleased him: "Why do they call you Buffalo Jones? Are you another Buffalo Bill?"

"Yes, in a way. Bill an' I are friends and we both were buffalo-hunters, but now I'm putting my energies to savin' buffalo. I lassoed an' captured most of the live buffalo left today, of course when they were calves."

"How thrilling! Oh, tell us about it," burst out Lenta.

"Hold on, Lent," spoke up her father, gaily. "I lassoed and captured Buffalo Jones. I'd like to hear wild stories as well as you. But let's not wear him out. What we need to get straight is the thing we're up against. This West – our lately acquired ranch – what we must expect – and do – in fact all a family of blessed tenderfeet need to know."

Jones presented a contrast to most of the aloof Westerners they had seen and met.

78

Harriet was quick to grasp that it was because he loved the country, had been and no doubt still was a factor in its development, and that he delighted in the acquisition of new pioneer blood.

They led him upstairs to the parlor, which was empty, and all of them seemed inspired by his presence. It was Jones, however, who took the initiative by plying Mr. Lindsay with questions. In a few moments he was in possession of all the facts about Lindsay's deal with Allen.

"Wal, wal, you are a fast stepper. I hope it's all right. I'll look into it. . . . Spanish Peaks Ranch? It's over in Colorado. Beautiful country, fine range, ideal for cattle. A high dry climate."

Then he asked further questions as to distances from towns, railroad, market, water, and lastly the ranch-house.

"Big place, stone and mortar, built round some cottonwood trees and a spring –"

"O Lord! Is that your ranch-house? Wal! – I've been there. You needn't fear that it'll blow down or that you can't keep the wolves and cold out in winter."

"Dear me!" sighed Mrs. Lindsay. Harriet hid what the two younger girls expressed. But Neale was eager to know more about the wolves, the hunting, the wildness. Jones rather endeavoured to retrieve the dismaying impression he had conveyed, despite the fact that if he was not dismayed for them he certainly was concerned.

"May I ask if you are prepared to spend considerable more money to make this place possible for your women folk?"

"Oh yes. I expected that. I can afford it."

"Wal now, that puts a different light on the matter," said Jones, with satisfaction. "You can make that old fort one of the show places of the West. Like Maxwell's Ranch over in New Mexico. . . . Will you arrange for me to meet this Lester Allen and his foreman?"

"I'm sorry. They left town at daybreak. I had planned to meet them here at the hotel. But they had breakfast before I was up."

"Wal, you don't say!" ejaculated Jones, plainly surprised. "An' the deal was only settled yesterday?"

"We kept the bank open after regular hours to settle it."

"What was their hurry?"

"They didn't say. I confess I was a little put out."

"Humph! . . . Of course Allen will send his foreman back to help you buy your outfit an' pack it to the ranch."

"No. Nothing was said about that. Arlidge

did not seem keen to take charge for me. But he finally agreed. I think my daughters decided him."

"Arlidge. Who's he?"

"Allen's foreman."

"Not Luke Arlidge?" queried the old plainsman, quickly.

"Luke Arlidge. That's the name."

"Wal, Lindsay," went on Jones, constrainedly, "we'll talk that all over later. It'd bore the ladies."

"Now tell us why you're called Buffalo Jones?" begged Lenta.

"Wal, for a number of reasons, all to do with buffalo. But I like to feel that I deserve it most because I did preserve the American bison," replied the plainsman. "The fact is, though, that the name never stuck till after the massacre of the last great herd of buffalo an' the bloody Indian fight it raised.

"In the late 'seventies the buffalo hide-hunters chased the buffalo to their last stand. This was in Texas, south of the Panhandle. Thousands of hide-hunters were scattered all along the range an' millions of buffalo were butchered for their hides alone. The Indian tribes saw their meat going, their buffalo robes, and that if they did not stop the white hunters they would starve. The Comanches were the fiercest tribe, though

81

the Kiowas, Arapahoes an' Cheyennes were bad enough. If they had joined forces the West never would have been settled. As it was the buffalo-hunters banded together an' broke the power of the redmen forever.

"It was in 1877 that the big fight came off – also the end of the buffalo. But the hunters had to quit killin' buffalo to kill Indians. I was in the thick of that campaign. Comanches under a fierce chief named Nigger Horse made repeated raids on hunters' camps, murderin' an' scalpin'. I organized a band of hunters an' we tracked Nigger Horse to his hidin'-place up on the Staked Plains. I had Indian and Mexican scouts who tracked the wily old devil over rock an' sand. I surrounded Nigger Horse's force in a deep rocky gulch an' planted part of my men to block the escape of the Comanches. That was about the bloodiest fight I was ever in. We surprised them at dawn an' all day the battle waged. Then when Nigger Horse saw he was beaten an' was in danger of bein' wiped out completely, he sent his son at the head of the hardest-ridin' bucks straight for the mouth of the gully. That was a magnificent sight. The Comanches were the grandest horsemen the West ever developed. An' the war-cry of the Comanches was the most blood-curdling of all Indian yells. We all saw what was comin'. The Indian riders collected at a point below out of rifle-shot. Comanches were vain, proud, fierce warriors, an' this was a race their hearts reveled in. Our men yelled along the line. The son of Nigger Horse – I forget that buck's name – pranced his horse at the head of the band. It was somethin' that made even us hardened old buffalo-hunters thrill. Then with him in the lead an' with such a yell as never was heard before they charged. What ridin'. But Nigger Horse's son, swift an' darin' as he was, never got halfway. He fell at a long shot from one of my sharp-shooters. That broke the back of the charge an' Nigger Horse's last defense. Only a few of those riders got away. An' the rest of the great Comanche band that escaped climbed out on foot. I reckon no other single fight had so much to do with breakin' the redmen as that one. Certainly not with the Comanches."

"Oh – terrible!" cried Lenta, breathlessly, her eyes shining. "But I don't see how – why they called you Buffalo Jones, just for that."

"Wal, I don't see, either," laughed the plainsman. "It's true, though. That night in camp it turned out the sharpshooter who killed Nigger Horse's son was a young North Carolinian named Nelson. Laramie Nelson.

He got the front handle here on the plains. I never knew his right name. Wal, he stood up among us as we sat round the camp fire, a crippled dead-beat outfit, an' liftin' his cup high he yelled, 'Heah's to Buffalo Jones!' The men roared an' they drank. An' from that night they called me Buffalo Jones."

"So that was it? Oh, how I'd like to be there!" cried Lenta.

"Was it coffee they drank your health in?" asked Lindsay, quizzically.

"Wal, no."

Harriet felt an unfamiliar impulse, that seemed to come from a thrilling heat along her veins.

"And what became of the young man?" she asked.

"Nelson, you mean? Wal, he made other great shots after that," replied the plainsman, reminiscently. "He belonged to that Southern breed of wild youngsters who spread over Texas an' the West. Laramie was one of the finest boys I ever knew. But those were hard days, an' if a man survived, it was through his quickness with a gun. He shore earned a name for himself. For years now I haven't heard of him. Gone, I reckon. An unmarked grave somewhere, out there on the 'lone prairie,' as his kind called the plains."

An unaccountable pang assailed Harriet's

breast. Poor brave wild boy! The West took its first strange hold upon her. There were things she had never dreamed of. History, story, legend, were somehow unreal. But here she was listening to a man who had seen and lived great events of the frontier, whose face was a record of those unparalleled adventures about which Easterners could not help but be skeptical and cold.

Soon after that narrative Jones left with her father, and Harriet went back to her room and the growing puzzle of plans and lists, of what to discard and what to retain. Bedtime came with Lenta's yawning entrance. The young lady, while undressing, delivered herself of a last humorous remark:

"Dog-gone-it, Hallie, I'm goin' to like this West!"

Bright and early next morning, all the Lindsays, except Neale, assembled for breakfast and with visible and voluble anticipation of an exciting day.

"Oh, yes, I nearly forgot," said Lindsay, in the midst of the meal. "Jones bade me be sure that you womenfolk bought heavy coats and woolen shirts, rubber buskins, slickers, and warm gloves. He said it wasn't summer yet by a long chalk and we might hit into a storm."

This interested all except Florence, who

leaned more to decorative than useful purchases. Harriet saw that she added these new articles to her list. After breakfast they sallied forth, with Harriet, for one, realizing that they were furnishing covert amusement to employees of the hotel

That was a day. Harriet found herself so tired when evening came that she scarcely had appetite for dinner. Her father appealed to her for help in making out a list of food supplies to purchase on the morrow.

"I don't believe I'm equal to that – at least not tonight," replied Harriet, dubiously.

"Jones was right about the foreman. Arlidge. He should have stayed to advise me. What do I know about supplies in this country?"

"Or I? But we know what we have been accustomed to and can easily buy that, so far as it is supplied here. I discovered one fine big grocery, I dare say they keep everything."

Another day saw their personal wants wonderfully and fearfully attended to. Mrs. Lindsay had bought furniture, kitchen ware, bedding, linen, and in fact, Harriet's father said, enough truck to fill several of the six big wagons he had obtained.

"What we can't take we'll send back for," he concluded, ending that mooted question.

Buffalo Jones had dinner with them that evening and his keen interest and sympathy were nothing if not thrilling. He laughed over some of their purchases.

"Wal, you're a lucky outfit!" he drawled. "Just suppose you hadn't any money. That you had to tackle the plains with your bare hands, so to say!... I wish my family was here. I've got two girls. I'd like you-all to meet them."

Harriet was drawn away to her father's room, where he and Jones desired a little privacy. To Lindsay's explanation that Harriet was his right-hand man and would handle the financial end of the new enterprise, Jones gave hearty approbation.

"She looks level-headed," he went on, "an' I reckon will stand up under the knocks you'll get.... Now, Lindsay, for the first one. You've gone into an irregular deal, an' some way or other are bound to be cheated."

Lindsay never batted an eye.

"Father, I told you," said Harriet.

"You've to learn that Westerners are close-mouthed. They almost *never* talk to strangers about other Westerners. It's not conducive to long life. But no matter – I'm goin' to waive that.... Your man Allen had not the best of reputations. An' Arlidge has been in several shady deals, over the last of which he killed a man. In fact, he has several killin's to his credit, an' at that he has not been many years in western Kansas. You've bought a ranch, all right, an' if my memory is good it's one that will *make* a wonderful place. But you'll find probably less than half ten thousand head of stock, maybe only a third. There's where the trick came in. It always does in deals where tenderfeet buy Western stock. Couldn't be otherwise. Can you swallow that?"

"I have, already. I'm no fool. The gleam in Allen's eye and Arlidge's glib tongue were not lost on me. I've swallowed this and can stand more."

"Good. Now brace yourself for a harder jolt. The worst is yet to come. It's a safe bet that Allen, with another so-called ranch thirty miles from Spanish Peaks Ranch, an' his foreman Arlidge workin' for you, will clean out most if not all the stock they sold to you."

"Clean out! Steal it?" ejaculated Lindsay, his jaw dropping.

"They'll rustle it off. Let me explain. We are now in the midst of what I might call the third great movement of early frontier history – the cattle movement. First came the freighters, wagon-trains, gold-seekers, fur-trappers, an' the Indian fights. Next the era of the buffalo an' the settler. This is the cattle movement. For years now vast herds of cattle have been driven up out of Texas to Abilene an' Dodge, the cattle terminus. From these points cattle have been driven north an' west, an' shipped East on cattle-trains. The cattle business is well on an' fortunes are bein' made. With endless range, fine grass an' water, nothin' else could be expected. I sold out my own ranch a year back. Reason was I saw the handwritin' on the wall. Cattle-stealin'! There had always been some stock stole. Every rancher will tell you that. But rustlin' now is a business. The rustler has come into his own. He steals herds of cattle in a raid. Or he will be your neighbor rancher, brandin' all your calves. The demand for cattle is big. Ready money always. An' this rustlin' is goin' to grow an' have its way for I don't know how long. Years, anyway. You'll be in the thick of it an' I want to start you right."

"You're most kind, Jones," replied Harriet's father, feelingly. "I appreciate your – your breaking a Western rule for me. However I'm not dismayed. I'll see it through. Only tell me what to *do.*"

"That's the stumper," rejoined the plainsman, with a dry laugh. "You've got to live it. But the very first thing you must do is to get a man – a Westerner – who will be smart enough for Allen an' Arlidge. They sold nine range-riders with the range. It's a foregone conclusion that most of these riders, if not all, will remain on Allen's side of the fence. You won't be able to tell who they are until they prove themselves. I must find you a hard-shootin' range-rider who knows the game."

"Hard-shooting?" echoed Lindsay in consternation.

"That's what I said, my friend. The harder an' quicker he is the better. I reckon there'll be some powder burned at Spanish Peaks Ranch this summer."

"O Lord! What will the wife say? Hallie, look what I've got you all into."

"Father, it makes my stomach feel sickish," declared Harriet. "But we can't back out now."

"Back out! I should say not. Damn those two slick cattlemen! . . . Jones, where'll I get the range-rider I'm going to need?"

"Stumps me some. I can't put my hand on anyone just now. But I'll look around. An' if no one can be found I'll go myself back to Dodge an' fetch one. I like your spirit, Lindsay. I like your family. An' I'm goin' to do what I can to help you."

The plainsman's gray-blue eyes gave forth

a narrow piercing gleam, hard to meet, but wonderful to feel.

"I reckon you'd better keep all this to yourselves," he advised. "An' don't be in a hurry to leave."

With that he departed, leaving Harriet deeply perturbed and her father downcast. As in the past, Harriet endeavored to cheer and inspirit him. And they managed to hide their feelings and fears from the rest of the family. Neale, however, threw a bombshell into the midst of their breakfast the next morning by blurting out: "They're talking about us in this hayseed town. Say we're a family of rich tenderfeet and that we got properly fleeced."

"Where'd you hear such gossip?" queried Lindsay, red in the face.

"In the saloon. But it's common talk all over."

"Well, if it's true, that'll give you a fine opportunity to help support this tenderfoot family."

"Neale couldn't support a baby if he had a cradle and a flock of cows," retorted Lenta, sententiously. "Never mind, Dad. We came out here for you to get well. And we can stand anything."

The girls were in and out of the hotel all morning, so that Harriet lost track of them.

91

About noon they came in, giggling, and left packages strewn from one room to another.

"Hal, you missed something," said Lenta, mysteriously.

"Did I? Thank goodness. I've sure missed a good deal of money I had figured up."

"Ha! Ha! You will. But honest, sis, this was rich. Flo came staggering into the hall downstairs, and as she could hardly see from behind her pile of bundles, she ran plump into the handsomest strangest-looking Westerner we've seen. I nearly burst myself laughing, but I kept out of it. Flo knocked him galley-west and of course the packages went flying. She was flabbergasted – and you know to flabbergast Flo isn't easy. This handsome ragamuffin laughed, doffed his old sombrero, and apologized with the grace of a courtier. His manners and speech were hardly what you'd expect from such a tramp. His dusty clothes hung in rags. He had a big gun in a belt and that belt had a shiny row of brass shells. He was young, thin, tanned almost gold, and his eyes – oh! they were wonderful! Black and sharp as daggers. His hair was black, too, and all long and mussed. I saw all this, of course, while he went to picking up Flo's packages. Then, will you believe it? he said: 'Permit me to carry these for you, miss.' Flo blushed like a rose. Fancy

92

that. And she stammered something. They went upstairs. I hope she was not so rattled she forgot to thank him."

"Well, that was an adventure," replied Harriet, with interest.

"It wasn't a marker to what happened to *me*, retorted Lenta, her eyes shining. "I had stepped aside into the doorway of that storeroom. I didn't want to meet that black-eyed cavalier on the stairway. I heard his spurs clicking on the steps. He passed without seeing me and he said to another fellow who had come in, and whom I hadn't seen yet, 'My Gawd! Lonesome, did you see her? She was a dream.'

"This other fellow let out a yelp. 'Did I? Lordy! Lock the gate!'

"Well, they went out and I ventured forth," continued Lenta. "But I tripped on the rug. Honest I did, Hallie! One of my bundles dropped. Then, lo and behold! this second fellow appeared as if by magic. He was young, rosy, ugly, bow-legged. He wore the awfulest hairy pants. His shirt was in tatters. He smelled like – like the outdoors. He picked up my bundle and laid it on top of the others in my arms. And he said:

" 'Sweetheart, look out for Western range-riders. Even my pard is a devil with the women.'

"His eyes fairly danced, they were so full of fun. If his pard was a devil, I'd like to know what *he* is. . . . I know I got as red as a beet and I rushed away without giving him a piece of my mind."

"God help us from now on! It has begun," exclaimed Harriet, solemnly.

"What has begun?" asked Lenta, innocently.

"I don't know what to call it. Slaughter of the Westerners might do."

"All right, old girl," retorted Lenta, half offended, for in her excitement evidently she had been sincere. "But you look out for yourself. Everything will happen to you!"

That occasioned Harriet some uneasiness. It seemed to be in the nature of a prophecy. But she passed it by and went on with her work until called to lunch. Her father was waiting at the head of the stairs. All the shadow of worry and uncertainty had disappeared from his face. He was bright, smiling, more than his old self again. Somehow he had gained.

"Now, father!" queried Harriet, in wondering gladness.

"What do you think, Hallie? I've had a stroke of fortune. At least Buffalo Jones swore it was. He ran across one of his scouts of buffalo days – in fact the very young fellow who killed Nigger Horse's son in the Indian fight, you remember. Nelson – Laramie Nelson. He it was who was responsible for Jones being called Buffalo Jones. Well, Nelson just happened to ride into Garden City with two other range-riders. Jones said he whooped when he saw them. No wonder! Talk about Westerners! Wait until you see these."

"Three – range – riders," returned Harriet, almost faltering. Could two of them be the young men Florence and Lenta had encountered? Could they! There was absolutely no doubt of it, and Harriet could not account for her feelings. Suppose the third one happened to be this Laramie Nelson, already picturesquely limned against the difficult background of Harriet's fancy!

"Well, after introducing me," went on Lindsay, "Jones went off with Nelson. I met them later in the saloon where Nelson's partners were playing pool. It seems the three had just returned from some hard expedition after horse-thieves, or something, and that accounted for their bedraggled appearance. Jones had made a proposition to Nelson about joining up with me. Evidently it wasn't so promising to him. But Jones and I importuned him until he said he reckoned he'd go if I hired his friends. I agreed. So the two young men were called from their game and introduced to me. Their names were Lonesome Mulhall and Tracks Williams. Had been with Nelson for years. In fact, they were inseparable. Strange to me both these young Westerners demurred. They did not want to come. Mulhall said: 'Laramie, I don't mind work, as you well know, but I kick against a lot of tenderfoot girls in the outfit.' And Williams backed him up. Whereupon Nelson swore at them. 'Yu're a couple of contrary jackasses. Heah's your chance to help a family that'll shore need it. Lonesome, only awhile back yu were lamentin' yore lack of feminine inspiration – I reckon yu called it. An' Tracks, heah, he was sore at me 'cause ridin' with me left him nothin' to be chivalrous about.'

" 'Pard, mebbe we'd better reconsider,' said Mulhall to Williams. ' 'Cause it's a shore bet Laramie is goin' to line up with this Peak Dot outfit.'

" 'Ump-umm,' replied Williams.

" 'Wal, if yu haven't got stuff in yu to want to help a fine family, maybe yu'll go for my sake,' snorted Nelson, with fire in his eye.

" 'How come, pard?' asked Lonesome, curiously.

" 'Wal, the foreman Allen turned over to

Mr. Lindsay happens to be Luke Arlidge. Now will you stick to me?"

" 'Hell yes!' yelled Mulhall.

" 'How about yu, Tracks?' asked Nelson of his other partner.

" 'Laramie, I hate to give in, but I wouldn't miss seeing you kill Arlidge for a million dollars!' "

Mr. Lindsay had recited all this in a thrilling whisper. He waited to see if it had made any impression on Harriet. Manifestly he was more than satisfied. Then he concluded:

"That ended the argument. And I engaged Nelson and his friends on the spot. I feel pretty good about it, as much for you girls' sake as my own. Jones declared Colorado wasn't big enough for both Nelson and Arlidge. And sooner or later Nelson would take charge of our ranch. The best of it is that the expectations Jones had roused in me, regarding this Laramie Nelson, were more than fulfilled. What a quaint soft-voiced fellow! You'd never believe he had killed men."

"Mercy, father!" burst out Harriet, with a revulsion of feeling. "Don't say he's a – a murderer!"

"Hallie, these Western folk have got me up a tree," declared Lindsay. "They talk of shooting and killing as we do of – of plowing corn. Jones said Nelson had killed men – he didn't know how many that he was a marked character in the West. I gathered in spite of a gun record, Jones regarded Nelson as the salt of the earth."

"Oh, these bloody frontiersmen!" exclaimed Harriet, aghast. "How can we have a man like that around?"

"Well, I'm getting – what do they call it? – a hunch that before long we may be damned good and glad to have him," declared Lindsay, bluntly. And when her father swore he was most genuinely in earnest. They went to lunch, at which time Lindsay casually announced that it was possible they might start for their ranch in a very few days. This upset his hearers in one way or another. Lenta was in raptures; Florence had some secret reason for wanting to linger in Garden City.

"Say, dad, are you going to give me a job?" demanded Neale.

"Yes. You drive one of the wagons," returned his father, concisely. To which the remainder of the family took instant exception.

After lunch the Lindsays scattered on their various errands. Harriet, coming in alone, encountered her father in the lobby in company with the most striking man she had ever seen.

"Harriet, come here," called Lindsay, dragging his tall companion forward. "This is my new man, Laramie Nelson.... Meet my eldest girl, Nelson. You must get acquainted. She will be my mainstay out on the ranch."

Harriet bowed and greeted Mr. Nelson with all outward pleasantry. Inwardly she was shrinking, and wondering why that was so.

"Wal, Lady, I shore am glad to meet yu," drawled Nelson, removing his old sombrero. His low voice and quaint manner were markedly Southern.

Before more could be said Lenta and Florence bounced and floated in, to be presented to Nelson. This gave Harriet opportunity to look at him. He was tall, slim, sandy-haired, slightly freckled, and his eyes, gray and intent, shone with something which reminded her of those of Buffalo Jones and Luke Arlidge. His lean face wore a sad cast. He did not smile, even at the irrepressible Lenta, who was nothing if not fascinated with him. His garb was travel-stained and rent. His shiny leather overalls, full of holes, flounced down over muddy boots. Great long spurs bright as silver dragged their rowels on the floor. His right side stood toward Harriet, and low down, hanging from a worn belt and sheath, shone the dark deadly handle of a gun. All about him suggested long use, hard service. So this was the killer Laramie Nelson – this strange soft-spoken, singularly fascinating Westerner? Harriet was as amazed as she was repelled. He did not look it.

Suddenly attention was directed upon Harriet again and she almost betrayed herself in confusion. The girls made demands for money.

"She's our treasurer, Mr. Nelson," declared Lenta, gaily. "Dad never handles money.... Look out for your wages!"

"Oh, Lenta, that's unkind!" exclaimed Harriet, flushing. "Indeed, Mr. Nelson, I am not that bad."

And it was an indication of Harriet's unusual preoccupation that she handed her purse to Lenta, who whooped and ran out, to be pursued by Florence.

"There, do you wonder I need to be careful of father's money?" queried Harriet, with a laugh.

"Wal, miss, I'm wonderin' a lot," replied Nelson, with his first smile, a slow dawning change that made him younger. "Most of all

I'm wonderin' how yore paw will ever run cattle an' range-riders with three such lovely daughters around. It cain't be done."

Chapter 5

Laramie surveyed his two arch conspirators in mingled disgust and apprehension. Wonderful to realize the three of them occupied a real room in a real hotel. Not only did they have a roof over their heads, but also each possessed a complete new outfit of wearing-apparel. Their fortunes had changed. Laramie felt a sick emptiness at the thought that the perverseness of these beloved comrades might prevent him from grasping straws.

"You borrowed money to buy all this?" Lonesome was saying, with a sweep of his hand to indicate the beds littered with shirts, scarfs, suits, sombreros, chaps, boots.

"Do yu reckon I robbed a store?" countered Laramie, testily.

"From Lindsay?"

"No. From Buffalo Jones. An' I can pay it back any time. These Eastern folks won't know. But at thet I shore ought to tell ... or – at least – Miss Lindsay."

"*Which* one?" asked Lonesome, sarcastically.

Tracks turned from the mirror, where he had been shaving a week's growth of beard from his dark face.

"Lonesome, you've coppered the trick," he said. "You didn't need to ask which one. Laramie has gone down before the oldest – Hallie, I think they called her. I don't blame him. A sweet, serious, level-headed girl!"

"Ugh-huh. The volluptuss one," agreed Lonesome. "I can't say I blame him, either. Didn't I go bloomin' loony over thet sassy baby-faced, red-lipped kid? It ain't that. What I want to know is this? Why the hell didn't Laramie tell us these girls belonged to the Lindsay rancher we was goin' to rid for?"

"*Are* goin' to ride for," corrected Laramie.

"How in hell did Laramie know?" queried Tracks, in defense of their leader. "I should think you'd be loonier than ever. I am. Go! Well, I guess I'll go. Range-riding for the Peak Dot outfit looks like heaven for me. Even if it didn't I'd never desert Laramie when he's bound to buck into that Arlidge galoot. Lonesome, I want to be around when they meet."

"Me too. I'm not so thick-skinned as that," rejoined Lonesome, gloomily. "But you've gotta bid me good-by, pards. I ain't goin'."

"Cheese and skippers!" ejaculated Tracks, ironically. "If you want to cut off your nose to spite your face, that's not our outlook. God knows you're ugly enough now."

"Every fellar can't be handsome like you an' fascinatin' like Laramie," replied Lonesome, sadly. Then his spirit roused. "Just the same, I never noticed you two corrallin' all the girls."

"Lonesome, yu're forgettin' how I broke up thet little necktie party some years back," said Laramie, reproachfully. "*Why* won't you go?"

Lonesome appeared driven into a corner. He sat down weakly upon the bed and his homely face took on a woebegone expression.

"'Cause I called that kid 'Sweetheart,' an' snitched this from her when I handed back the pack she dropped," admitted Lonesome, producing a small leather case, quite suggestively plump.

Laramie was dumbfounded. Lonesome at his old bad habit again – his besetting sin – his one weakness!

"What's in it?" demanded Tracks, curiously.

"Darn if I know. Didn't dare open it. Reckon I just wanted *somethin'* of hers, a keepsake to remind me of her when I got out on the lone prairee again."

Tracks snatched it out of Lonesome's caressing hands.

"It's a pocket-book . . . full of greenbacks!" exclaimed Tracks as he opened the case. "Tens and twenties. . . . There's a fifty. . . . Oh, a century plant! First one of them I've seen since I hit the range."

"My Gawd!" groaned Lonesome. "I didn't know there was money in it. S'pose she felt me take it! – Pards, I gotta vamoose out of this Garden City, an' pronto!"

Laramie strode across the room, and taking the pocket-book from Tracks he shook it in Lonesome's face.

"Yu — — bow-legged little —!" he drawled. "Yu're shore goin' to ruin us yet. Yu set there till I get back."

"Where you goin'?" asked the rider, in impotent alarm.

"I'll return this money. Let on it was accident –"

"Laramie, it *was* an accident. I swear to Gawd! . . . An' good-by, old pard –"

"Go on, Laramie, I'll keep him here," interposed Tracks, "if I have to bust him a couple on his red snoot."

"I can lick you any day," Lonesome was retorting, belligerently, as Laramie went out into the hall.

He felt that this lapse of Lonesome's had

105

roused an inspiration. By frightening him it had made distinct the clear soft voice of conscience. He would make haste to profit by the opportunity, and meet the situation coolly, no matter how he might be affected inwardly. When Laramie approached Miss Lindsay's door some way down the hall he heard the delightful laughter of her younger sister.

Laramie knocked. A contralto voice called, "Come in."

He hesitated long enough for the door to be opened by the oldest sister, the one called Hallie.

"Oh – it's Mister Laramie!" she cried, and surprised deep-gray eyes met his. Laramie had looked over his gun at many pairs of challenging eyes, but never at two which so made chaos of his faculties. But as he had prepared himself, it was possible to overcome all that was outwardly betrayed, and to inquire with his usual slow drawl:

"Anybody about heah lose a pocket-book?"

Before Miss Lindsay had time to reply there came a shriek of joy and a rush of steps. The youngest sister confronted him.

"I should smile somebody did," she cried, joyously, expectantly, her pretty face distracting in its youth and freshness.

106

Laramie kept the pocket-book behind his back.

"Wal, what was the one somebody lost like?" he asked, smiling down on her.

"It was yellow leather, with a gold clasp.... Please let me see."

"An' what was inside?"

"Money. Stacks of bills! Mostly mother's, and she has been wild since I lost it."

"I'm shore glad. Yu must have dropped it in the hall," replied Laramie. "Heah yu air."

The girl received it gratefully. "Oh, I thank you, Mr. Nelson. Mother will be so – so relieved. She hadn't told dad. Now he needn't know .... I could just hug you.... Maybe I *will* some day!"

With a gay and mischievous laugh she ran down the corridor, evidently to acquaint her mother with the good news.

"How lucky you found it, Mr. Laramie!" said Miss Lindsay. "Buffalo Jones insisted that your association with us would be fortunate. And here you live up to his extravagant praise at once!"

"So Jones spoke high of me, Miss Lindsay?" asked Laramie.

"Indeed he did."

"Wal, I reckon it's more'n I'm wuth. An' I'd shore like to straighten it out in yore mind. An' I'm askin' yu to tell yore father."

"Certainly. Any message you care to give. He pleases to call me his right-hand man."

"Wal, he'll shore need yu," went on Laramie, bluntly. "Miss Lindsay, what I cain't stand about this deal is Jones givin' yu'all false idees about me an' my two pards. Don't misunderstand. I'm downright shore yore father couldn't get nowhere three better men for this queer range deal. But all thet talk about us – thet was pure taffy. The fact is we are only three tramp grub-line range-riders. We cain't hold a job nowheres. I'm the wust, I reckon. I cain't keep out of trouble. My gunman record follows me. I swear it's not my fault. The way of the West is hard on my breed. Now, for my pards, Williams is a strange rider, a true pard, but I know next to nothin' about him. He shore comes of a good family, as I do myself. But what's thet in this wild country? Tracks is just another fine boy gone to the devil – run off from home, I expect, a rollin' stone. An' Lonesome, thet little son-of-a-gun, is wuss. He has a heart of gold, but thet's about all, 'cept he cain't be beat at ridin' an ropin'. But he drinks, fights, gambles, swears, an' long ago would shore have been daid – but – for me."

108

Laramie gulped over the last. What relief to his breast! He could look straight into the clear, earnest, grave eyes without a qualm.

"Well – Mr. Laramie – you – you surprise me!" she ejaculated, in embarrassment. A rich color mantled her cheeks. "Are you deliberately repudiating Buffalo Jones' tribute?"

"I reckon, 'cept about us bein' as good range-riders as yu could get for this heah tough job."

"You want me to tell father all that you said?"

"I shore do. I'd feel a heap better. I do already, tellin' yu. It shore went against the grain to pretend I wasn't out of a job – thet I had to be bargained with an' coaxed. But Jones is to blame. He lent me money, so we could look decent again. I never rode under false colors. He swore yore father needed us plumb bad, an' thet it'd be better to make up a little story about us. Eastern tenderfoot family – some romancin' girls, yu know, an' we oughtn't disappoint yu. But I got to thinkin' better about it an' so I've told yu."

"I see, Mr. Laramie. I must say I – I respect you for this admission. But you – you almost distress me. I am afraid I had already begun to rely on you – somehow."

"Wal, what I've told you is shore no reason why yu cain't," drawled Laramie.

"This West flabbergasts me!" She flushed, averted her darkening eyes, and then, turning quite pale, she looked at him searchingly.

"Is there any reason why you could not come to us honestly?"

"Not now. There was. I told yu. Easterners air bound to see the West strange an' hard an' wild. It is. An' we men air thet way. But I can face my mother an' sister just as I am facin' yu now."

"Thank you. I think that – relieves me. And can you vouch for Williams?"

"Yes, so far as I know him."

"And Mulhall?"

"All I can promise, Lady, is thet I'll answer for Lonesome, I'll be responsible for him."

"What will father say?" she mused, soberly.

"Wal, I hope he doesn't take it to heart. Thet foreman Arlidge is a man who wants a Westerner to figure him."

"Buffalo Jones said Westerners never speak ill of other Westerners."

"They don't if they air afraid of their health. What I'm hintin' about Arlidge yu'll heah me say to his face – thet is, if yore father

110

takes me. Yu must put it up to him, Miss Lindsay."

"I – I could almost answer for him," she returned, nervously. "But we'll see .... Thanks for your – your frankness .... Oh, I almost forgot. Father commissioned me to ask you three to have dinner with us tonight – at six. He said not to accept a refusal."

"Wal, I reckon I cain't refuse," responded Laramie. "It's shore been long since I set at table with nice folks. Mebbe I'll never get a chance again. Good-day, Lady."

As Laramie bowed himself away from the door she stood gazing in perplexity, as if she had more to say. But she did not speak and he passed on down the hall, conscious of an inward commotion. He could not withhold a slight swagger as he burst in upon the boys.

"Say, you was gone a hell of a long time," accused Lonesome, with awful eyes.

"I shore fixed it, pard," replied Laramie, loftily. "Give the pocket-book into the kid's hands. Said I found it in the hall. She was plumb glad. Swore she'd like to hug me an' would some day."

"Aw!" breathed Lonesome.

"Laramie, did it take you all that time to return a lost article?" queried Tracks, suspiciously.

"No. Fact is I was talkin' to Miss Hallie," drawled Laramie, casually.

"What about?"

"Myself, most of all. Did yu reckon I'd rave about yu an' Lonesome? ... An' I shore got us all invited to dinner tonight."

"*No!*" exclaimed Tracks, incredulously radiant.

"Shore did."

"Laramie, forgive me. I was afraid you might have told her that we're a rummy outfit, instead of The Three Musketeers, as Buff Jones made us out."

Lonesome rose off the bed in such profound consternation, and awe that he appeared tall.

"Din – ner!" he blurted out, weakly.

"Shore. An' I reckon I'm slick enough to set yu close to thet pretty kid or leastways across from her."

"Aw, my Gawd! – Tracks, where's my gun? I'm gonna blow out my brains! ... Aw, aw! What a chance I missed! If I only hadn't spoke out that vulgar! ... Called her *sweetheart!* Took her for a common Western street girl!"

In his abject misery Lonesome crawled under the bed and his bare callused heels showed through his worn boots. There he moaned to himself.

"Yu ought to be thankin' Gawd an' me for keepin' yu out of jail," declared Laramie, resentfully.

"What do I care about snitchin' that pocket-book? I'm thinkin' about *her!*" replied Lonesome, furiously.

"Come out from under, Lonesome," chirped in Tracks, cheerfully. "Don't show yellow. Take a bath and shave, get your hair cut. Then spruce up to beat the band and make that pretty kid think you're the greatest range-rider the West ever knew."

This sally fetched Lonesome out. "Dog-gone-it, I'll do that or die!"

Laramie did not slight preparations for the occasion, but long before the boys returned from a visit to the barber's he had made himself look a vastly different man and took some slight melancholy pride in the fact. Not that it made a difference one way or another, but he happened to think of his sister Marigold and would have liked her to see him thus. "Long time now since I wrote Marigold," soliloquized Laramie. "I'll shore make up for thet before we leave this heah hotel."

Lonesome and Tracks came rushing in, their faces shining pinkly, their hair trimmed, and in Lonesome's case at least, pasted down flat.

113

"Boys, yu look almost human," remarked Laramie. "But I don't know about yu. This heah dinner may be too much."

Tracks was whistling. Laramie went back to his newspaper, an old one from Kansas City, and let the parade go on. He read every line in the paper, including the advertisements, and when again he looked up Tracks and Lonesome were still primping.

"Wal, if fine feathers don't make fine birds I'm shore a barnyard owl," declared Laramie.

"Laramie, it ain't easy to stack up against such an Apollo as Tracks or such a wonderful Southern-lookin' planter's son gent as you," complained Lonesome. "Gawd A'mighty didn't do a fair job on me. I'm short an' dumpy, like a duck. No girl could look at me standin' without seein' how you can ride a cayuse between my laigs. An' my face would stop a clock. Dog-gone-it, I ain't bootiful. No use deceivin' myself! I've gotta work my wiles on women. Tell 'em how lovely they are. Tell 'em wild yarns of battle an' blood. An' when you make love lay it on thick."

"Lonesome, may the good Lord warn me in time – before yu cut any of yore shines with this Lindsay family!" ejaculated Laramie, fervently.

"Right you are, pard," agreed Tracks.

114

"But when you're aiming to win a girl of class, like this Lenta Lindsay, don't eat with your knife."

"Aw, you joy-killer!" cried Lonesome, aghast at the truth. "How'n hell will I know how to eat?"

"Watch me and do and say exactly the same as I do," declared Tracks, earnestly.

"Ugh-huh. It's a bitter pill to swaller, but I'll take your hunch."

"An' Lonesome, don't eat like a hawg," put in Laramie, "a grub-line rider starvin' to death."

"But I *am* starvin' to death," protested Lonesome.

"You can eat heartily without giving yourself away," said Tracks.

"Can I ask for another helpin' if somethin's particular good?"

"Shore yu can. But not for three," replied Laramie.

Between them they coached Lonesome until Tracks appeared satisfied. But Laramie felt dubious about the irrepressible boy, and had some qualms about himself. At last they were ready, and with only a half hour to wait for dinner they went down to the lobby, where Laramie made the gratifying observation that not even the clerk recognized them. Lindsay himself, entering with the

115

expectation of meeting them, had to look twice. And Laramie, studying his pale mobile face, expressive of good will and kindness, breathed a great sigh of relief. No doubt Lindsay had been told by his daughter the truth about these three range-riders, and he was big and fine enough to waive the delinquencies. Right here Laramie added gratitude and loyalty to his former interest.

The other Lindsays were waiting just inside the dining-room, which had not yet begun to fill up with guests. Before they drew close Laramie had a long look at Hallie Lindsay. An unfamiliar commotion within his breast must have had to do with her appearance in white. She greeted him and introduced him to her mother, a bright and vigorous woman whose face held traces of former beauty. Then Lindsay attended briefly to the rest of the introductions. On the moment two incidents struck Laramie forcibly. Lenta bowed to Lonesome and said: "How do you do, Mr. Mulhall. . . . Dad, I've had – the pleasure of meeting the gentleman before."

"That so. You didn't say."

"It was in the hall, I think," replied Lenta, her wide baby-blue eyes apparently so innocent and guileless.

116

Lonesome arose to the occasion like a cavalier.

"Yes, Mr. Lindsay, it was in the hall," he said, blandly. "Miss Lenta came in so packed with bundles that I couldn't see she was a grown-up young lady. An' when she dropped one I picked it up for her, an' made a pleasant remark, I forget what, such as any lonesome rider in from the plains might make to a pretty child. That was the meetin' she meant."

The Lindsays laughed their agreeable acceptance of this explanation, even Lenta showing a mirthful surprise. Laramie marveled at Lonesome. He also noticed the interchange of glances between Florence Lindsay and Tracks Williams. Not only was she amazed to recognize in Tracks the gallant though uncouth person who had carried her load of parcels upstairs, but also to see the transformation of a ragged tramp rider to a strikingly handsome young man. She murmured her acknowledgement of the introduction.

Then they were escorted to a table arranged for eight, where Mrs. Lindsay seated herself at the foot and her husband took the head. Laramie was given the seat at Lindsay's right, Hallie the next, and Tracks the third on that side. Lenta sat across the

117

table from Laramie, Lonesome next between her and Florence. Thus the astounding thing had come off without any hitch or awkwardness. Laramie felt easier to be off his feet, and glad to have Miss Lindsay beside him instead of where he might have to meet her glance. Yet her nearness had a perturbing effect.

"Well, boys, I've dispensed with the formalities and had my wife order the dinner," said Lindsay. "How'll turkey, cranberry sauce, bread, gravy, ice cream and so forth strike you?"

Lonesome uttered a boyish laugh of sheer content.

"If my pards will let me eat all I want, that dinner will strike me terrible good."

This pleased and rather flattered Mrs. Lindsay, who took interest in Lonesome at once.

"Wal, I tired of wild turkey an' buffalo rump once, but thet was years ago," added Laramie.

Tracks looked across the table at Florence and said, feelingly, "Turkey! It will make me think of home."

"And where's that?" asked Florence, languidly.

"Boston, I'm a down-easter."

Her gaze came up to study him. Laramie thought he had never seen so fair a girl, and in truth her white skin and golden hair, in striking contrast to her proud dark eyes, gave her a dazzling beauty. Alas for Spanish Peaks Ranch! There could never be any riders faithful to their range duties so long as that girl remained unwon.

"Indeed," interposed Lindsay, "I'm a Yankee myself. How long have you been West?"

"Seems a lifetime. Only eight years. I'm twenty-four now. I was sixteen when I ran away from school."

Laramie flashed a glance across at Lonesome and that young man intercepted it swiftly. Nevertheless, he did not so much as wink. Laramie knew that he and Lonesome were of one mind in regard to their mysterious and aloof partner. Silent all these years, yet when a dark-eyed girl watched him, with all of romance in her gaze, he would give up his secret!

"So you ran off to seek your fortune out West?" asked Florence, tremendously impressed.

"Yes, but I never have found it – yet."

"And your folk at home?"

"I'm ashamed to confess, I've never written them, in all these years," went on Tracks, sadly. "But it was a bad mix-up. I hated school. Dad intended me for law. I was preparing to enter Yale. We quarreled. I told him I never could be a lawyer. He vowed he would disinherit me if I did not go on. So I ran away. Some day he'll find me. I'm sorry now, because I've wasted my life, perhaps broken mother's heart. I'd like to see her."

Florence was intrigued. For that matter, Tracks held the stage. Although no doubt he had meant only to excite Florence's interest, he had gained that of the others. What if that story were untrue? But Laramie had no reason to doubt Tracks. Never had he spoken of himself until now. There had been a ring of truth in his voice, a sadness and a self-reproach probably not lost upon any of the Lindsays. It was, however, decidedly lost upon Lonesome. Was he to see himself outdone by this scion of a rich Boston family? Not much! The instant Laramie laid eyes upon him after Tracks had concluded he fortified himself against what was coming.

"My pard stirs my memory," began Lonesome, addressing the wide-eyed Mrs. Lindsay – a most strategic approach. "Sure the range-riders had to come from somewhere, 'cause there ain't been years enough of cattle-raising yet for him to be born out here. They come from all over, though I reckon the South furnished the most – an' sure the best riders." Here

120

Lonesome bowed flatteringly to Laramie. "Texas an' the Carolinas made the West. That's an old sayin' out here. I've ridden for an outfit that had a nigger, a greaser, an Indian, a Rebel, a Yankee, an Englishman an' Dutchman all together. For all I knew the Englisher might have been a dook an' the nigger a runaway slave an' the Rebel a rich planter's son. This range-riding is a pictooresque profession."

Lonesome paused for effect, casually including everybody in his slow glance, and winding up on Lenta, whose face wore an expression that would have inspired a cigar-sign post.

"I'm from Mizzourie, myself. My dad was one of Quantrell's Guerillas, a Rebel, an' my mother came from blue-blooded Yankee stock. She had an uncle or somethin' who came over in the *Mayflower* an' kicked redskins off the ship in that Tea Party you read about in school books. Reckon I never thought it much of a party.... We was turrible poor an' I had to do odd jobs while I was gettin' my education an' when my ma was takin' in washin'. When I was ten I had a chance to come West on a cattle-train. Naturally I took to horses like a duck to water, an' I was singin' 'Lone Prairee' before I was fifteen. Gosh! but that's a long time

121

ago – an' I'm younger'n Tracks here, in years. I've rode from Montana to the Gulf, an' been in everythin'. There was a rope around my neck when Laramie met me first, an' but for him I'd kicked the air. All 'cause a measly foreman named Price was jealous of my way – er, of me – where a lady was concerned. Since then Wild Bill hasn't anythin' on me –"

Lonesome was getting in deep. Talking liberated something in him, which mounted while being set free. But suddenly his remarkable fabrication suffered a break. Laramie knew from Lenta's eyes that she knew Lonesome was lying. If she did not repress a giggle, Laramie missed his guess. Mrs. Lindsay, however, was deceived and enthralled, and perhaps that was Lonesome's main objective. His abrupt pause manifestly had to do with the arrival of two waiters carrying huge trays, conspicuously on one of which lay a huge turkey, nicely browned. It was not clear to Laramie whether the sight of the wonderful bird or a rush of saliva had checked Lonesome's outburst. Anyway he could not go on.

"Oh, what wonderful lives you boys have lived!" exclaimed Mrs. Lindsay. "It scares me for my son Neale. . . . John, please carve the turkey. . . . Mr. Nelson, I suppose you too have had a great career?"

"Me? . . . Wal, no. I reckon I was born on a hawse an' growed up with a bridle in one hand an' a gun in the other," drawled Laramie.

This speech established in Laramie's mind a fact that he had once before favored his imagination or over-sensitiveness in one particular. And it had come from an almost imperceptible shrinking or revulsion in Miss Lindsay. The table was small, necessitating the chairs being close, and a propinquity to her charming person that had played havoc with Laramie. He had not realized that until after he had felt her slight shudder. What else could he have expected? A young Eastern woman of education and refinement, suddenly thrown into the company of a range-rider who had killed men, must have felt horror at such contact. Others soon would add to Buffalo Jones' characterization of him, and then he would stand out clearly as the notorious Laramie Nelson. Somehow it hurt Laramie deeply. It was unjust. He could not change the West or help what had gravitated to him. He did not imagine he had been such a fool as to grow sentimental over the eldest Lindsay girl, yet he had dreamily felt something vague and sweet, unutterably new to him, that would have to die a violent death. Romance surely would be Tracks' portion and even the almost hopeless Lonesome's – if he could be reformed. But for Laramie Nelson it must be a secret thing and never bear fruition.

From the moment the turkey and other savory victuals were served to the three range-riders the conversation became limited to the Lindsays, of whom Lenta was the liveliest. Laramie, in his supreme obtuseness, did not wake up to her demure and subtle wit, exercised at Lonesome's expense, until the little minx winked at him. Laramie had a shock. What that tenderfoot girl of sixteen would do to Lonesome seemed appalling. Yet Laramie reveled in the thought. The Lone Prairie gallant had at last found more than his match.

To do Lonesome full credit, he did not disgrace himself as to the consumption of food, and the dinner ended a huge success for the riders and their hosts.

Several times Miss Lindsay had addressed a casual or polite remark to Laramie. He divined she had felt something different and aloof arise in him. But that did not matter. He replied as he would have to his employer.

"Nelson, how soon can we get away?" asked Lindsay.

"That's the very question I had on my lips," said Miss Lindsay, eagerly.

"Oh, when do we start?" burst out Lenta. Florence looked dreamy, silent words across the table at Tracks.

"Wal, we're ready for sunup in the mawnin'," drawled Laramie.

"What! It'll take a week yet," declared Lindsay.

"Tomorrow? How bewildering! It's not possible," added Miss Lindsay, but plainly she was excited.

"What's the sense of hangin' around heah any longer, spendin' more money for hotel bills?" queried Laramie, shortly.

"Nelson, you hit me plumb center, as you Westerners say. What *is* the sense of it?" replied Lindsay.

"Air yu ladies through yore buyin'?" asked Laramie.

"We can't think of another single thing," rejoined Harriet.

"How about packin'?"

"A good deal of that is done, too."

"Wal, how about day after tomorrow, early mawnin'?"

"Mr. Nelson, you take our breath," ejaculated Mrs. Lindsay, and Lenta gasped in rapture.

"By Jove!" burst out Lindsay, slapping

the table with an emphatic hand. "Nelson, you take charge."

"Very wal, sir. Let me have yore lists to go over."

"Mother, you and the girls excuse us," said Lindsay, rising.

"Better pack tonight, so tomorrow will be free to pick up odds and ends."

Excitement and delight prevailed among the feminine contingent. Laramie added to these by advising Mrs. Lindsay and the girls to leave unpacked warm clothes, heavy coats, slickers, buskins or riding-boots, gloves, which they should don on the morning of the journey.

"An' excoose me, Mrs. Lindsay," interposed Lonesome. "Laramie never stops at midday for nothin'. Better pack a big basket of grub for lunches. An' the other half of this turkey we couldn't eat – it'd be a shame to waste that."

"You're a bright and thoughtful boy," declared Mrs. Lindsay. "Come, girls. We've had a pleasant hour. Let's get to our packing."

"Hallie, fetch down all your lists so we can go over them," said Lindsay, as they went out. "We'll be in the lobby. Come, boys, and have a cigar."

Smoking was not one of Laramie's habits.

There were reasons why his nerves should never be unsteadied by tobacco or liquor. It amused him deeply to see Lonesome tilted back in a lobby chair, puffing a huge and expensive cigar. Tracks, however, betrayed signs of having smoked one before.

"Nelson, it's certainly good to have you on the job," declared Lindsay. "I was up a stump."

"Wal, I reckon I'm glad yu decided to take us on, after all," returned Laramie.

"Eh? – Oh, I see – why, of course," said Lindsay, somewhat disconcerted. Then Harriet arrived with a batch of papers.

"Shall I stay to go over these with you?" she asked.

"Heavens, yes!" answered her father. "Begin this ranch business right now."

"Wal, it's not a bad idee, if Miss Lindsay is yore bookkeeper an' is goin' to handle money," rejoined Laramie.

Tracks brought a chair for her, and they formed a little circle of five around a small table.

"You may smoke, gentlemen.... Here are my lists. Which will you see first?"

"Wal, all of them, if yu don't mind," replied Laramie.

"But our – our personal lists – they're of

127

no – no interest to you?" inquired Harriet, blushing.

"Powerful interestin' to me, lady, but not really necessary," drawled Laramie. "Give me your supply list first."

Harriet gave him four pages full of a neat and legible handwriting.

"Is this heah yore writin', miss?" inquired Laramie.

"Yes. Why?"

"Wal, it's so nice I'd shore like to get a letter from yu. . . . Enough grub heah to feed an army for years. Too rich for range-riders! They'd get lazy an' fat. An' Lonesome would die of his indigestion."

"What's eatin' you? I ain't got any such ailin'," retorted Lonesome.

"Tracks, write down on yore paper there two wagons to pack food supplies. . . . How many wagons did you buy, Mr. Lindsay?"

"Six. There were no more new ones in town. But I can obtain two second-hand, in good condition."

"Put thet down, Tracks. . . . Now, Miss Lindsay, let me have the furniture, beddin', hardware, household goods list?"

Laramie scanned two more pages. "Tracks, this stuff will take four wagons. We'll have to cut down an' take only what's needed first off. Then send back for the rest.

Say two wagons first trip. . . . Thet leaves us four wagons. . . . There are no tents on this list."

"We never thought of tents," rejoined Miss Lindsay.

"Yu'll need four. Put thet down, Tracks. Also canvas an' hoops for the wagons."

"Oh, we'll be traveling in prairie-schooners. A regular caravan!" exclaimed Miss Lindsay, evidently thrilled.

Laramie held out his hand for another list.

"Here's one made out for us by Buffalo Jones."

"It ought to do. But Jones is stingy. . . . Let's see. Harness, tools, farm implements, saddles, blankets, bridles, salt, grain, camp utensils, seeds, oil. . . . Ah-huh. Pretty good for an the plainsman. . . . It'll take four wagons to pack this. Tracks, put down two wagons for first trip out. . . . Thet makes six wagons, with two left. An' we come down to the personal lists of the ladies."

"We have trunks and bags galore, besides all the endless things we bought here," Miss Lindsay informed him.

"How many trunks?"

"Sixteen. And twenty-eight bags and boxes."

Laramie threw up his hands. "We'll pack what we can an' leave the rest for the second trip out. Got thet, Tracks? ... Now, Mr. Lindsay, I'll make out a list of things yu couldn't be expected to know of. An' Jones is a buffalo-hunter, not a cattleman.... How about teamsters an' hawses?"

"Brown, the storekeeper, has engaged six drivers with teams for me."

"We'll need two more an' a cook."

Lindsay scratched his head dubiously. "My wife and the girls are good housekeepers. I – we thought they might take care of the cooking on the ride out."

"Why, man, yu're plumb loco," drawled Laramie.

"I don't know what that is, but I agree. I am."

Harriet laughed, the first time in Laramie's hearing. "I know. It means you're crazy."

"No offense, sir. Thet's just a range word. But we can't have the ladies cookin'."

"We are not afraid of work," retorted Harriet, spirited almost to resentment.

"I reckon not, an' I'll bet my sombrero yu-all can cook up a delicious meal. But this will be tough sleddin', Miss Lindsay. Not a picnic. We'll have rain, wind, maybe snow on the way out. An' cookin' for ten, eleven, twelve hands like Lonesome heah, an'

130

yoreselves – why it'll be one hell of a job. I object."

"Your objection is sustained," replied Harriet, won over in spite of herself. She gave Laramie a penetrating look that he found strange and sweet to meet.

"Anything you say, Nelson," added Lindsay, spreading wide his hands.

"Wal, I'll rustle up a cook. Hope he won't be like the last one I hired. Had to shoot him."

Miss Lindsay was wordlessly shocked.

"Only his laig off. I caught him stealin' an' he drew on me.... Wal, everythin' looks easy. We could get away tomorrow if we were rushed," returned Laramie, amused at the girl's struggle to recover. "I'll keep these lists to consult again. That's all, Mr. Lindsay. We'll leave day after tomorrow, early mawnin', shore."

"Mr. Laramie, you are either what you called father or else a magician," said Miss Lindsay, with what seemed forced admiration.

"Wal, I'm loco, all right."

"But what is loco?"

"It's a weed the hawses eat an' go right off their haids."

Miss Lindsay arose suddenly: "Father, here's Neale," she said, and if there was not

131

a warning note in her voice Laramie guessed wrong.

A young man, rather flashily dressed, good-looking, but with his pale face marred by a darkly swollen eye, came hurriedly up to Lindsay, and clutching his shoulder with one hand he extended the other with shaking finger at Lonesome.

"There – there he is," he burst out, accusingly. "That's the little rooster of a bow-legged, pool-room loafer who punched me in the eye?"

132

Chapter 6

Lonesome reluctantly removed the cigar from his mouth and retorted: "Yes, an' I'll black your other popeye if you'll come outdoors. I'm too much the gennelman to hit even a rummy tenderfoot like you in front of a lady."

Consternation was written large in the faces of Mr. Lindsay and his daughter. Laramie shared it. Could a day pass without Lonesome falling from grace? This newcomer was undoubtedly the Lindsay youth and therefore Harriet's brother. He appeared upon the verge of apoplexy.

"I'll – have – you horsewhipped!" he flamed.

"Nope. Not me. I ain't packin' my hardware, but nix on that hosswhippin' game. It's been tried on me. An' there was a funeral."

"Oh, this is dreadful," cried Miss Lindsay, in mortification. "Neale, you should not air your grievances here. We are in an important discussion."

"I – don't care," panted Neale.

133

"Something's got to be done with this fellow."

"Neale, what's ailing you now?" inquired Lindsay, and his patient and resigned expression conveyed much.

"He punched me in the eye."

"The result is evident, if he's the culprit. But what for? How do I know you didn't deserve it?"

Here Lonesome got to his feet and his small stature expanded. To be sure, Laramie had been fooled before but as a rule Lonesome betrayed it when he was guilty. In this instance he appeared righteously incensed.

"Mr. Lindsay, excoose me, but this here young fellow cain't be with your folks?"

"I regret to say he is, Mulhall."

"Dog-gone! . . . Laramie, can you beat my luck? Why'd he have to pick on *me?*" After which plaintive speech Lonesome went on: "But, Mr. Lindsay, he just cain't be no relation to you?"

"Unfortunately, I cannot deny the existing blood-tie," replied Lindsay, with a dry humor that tickled Laramie. "He's my only son."

"Aw, my Gawd, no!" wailed Lonesome. "Not this cocky cub tenderfoot in a boiled shirt?"

134

Neale moved as if to assault Lonesome, but was prevented by his father. "I'll whip you myself!" he fumed.

But Lonesome was beyond reach of such challenge. He sensed dire disaster. Turning to Harriet, he appealed in desperation: "They're foolin' me. You an' him couldn't be related?"

"He's my brother, Mr. Mulhall," replied Harriet, and it was not patent to Laramie that she had any pride in the fact.

"Aw, no! Such a lovely lady as you – to have that – that –"

Miss Lindsay nodded with a smile that rather hinted that she was fearful of being victim to mirth.

"See here, Mulhall, let's hear your side of it?" demanded Lindsay.

"No help for me, Laramie. I'm a doomed man an' you better let me slide," said Lonesome, pathetically. Then with a dignity, that might have been assumed, but which was vastly convincing, he addressed the father. "It happened the day we rode in. Not an hour after! Me an' Tracks was playin' pool as peaceful as a couple of kittens. We was playin' for the drinks an' could afford only one game. I seen this – your son stalkin' around the table. An' he says, 'Lemme in the game.' I thanked him an' declined the honor.

He comes back, 'I could spot you ten balls.' That riled me, but I kept my mouth shut. Tracks was beatin' me, but I made some nifty shots an' was catchin' up. I come to a decidin' shot, an' if I made it that beat Tracks. It was a particular easy one for me, too, but I wanted to make sure, so I was slow. Up speaks your young Mr. Lindsay. 'That's the wrong way. Lemme show you.' An' I swear I never batted an eye. But as I was about to shoot he directed my cue from behind, an' I missed. Tracks offered to let me do it over, but I was too mad. An' I says to your boy, 'I'll spot you one on the eye,' which I did pronto.... An' that's the honest Gawd's truth."

"Serves him right," declared Lindsay, with finality. "Neale, I know your weakness of meddling in other people's business. But for your own sake – and your skin – mend your ways. You're out West now."

"But, dad, that's the blamedest lie I ever heard," declared Neale, astounded, outraged, defeated. "I wasn't in any pool-room. It happened on the street. I – I met a girl. We were talking. Along came this little runt in his woolly pants. He winked at the girl. I – I resented it...."

Suddenly Laramie had an inspiration and

he judged it was high time, if he were to save Lonesome.

"Listen to me, young man," he drawled. "We're about to undertake pioneer work on the range. We cain't afford to fight over little things or with each other. There'll shore be guns an' blood out at Spanish Peaks Ranch."

Neale's flushed face lost its heat. He had been impressed.

"Can yu ride a hawse?" went on Laramie.

"Yes – of course."

"Can yu drive a team?"

"I've driven a pair of fast trotters many a time," replied Neale, eagerly.

"Wal, yu're on. I'm shy a couple of teamsters. Yu'll drive one of the wagons. So dig up yore warm togs an' heavy boots an' gloves. We're leavin' early day after tomorrow mawnin'."

"Dad, is it true?" cried Neale, wild despite uncertainty. "Am I to get a man's job?"

"Nelson has charge. You've my permission. Get your mother's."

"Yours is enough, dad. I've been tied to mother's apron-strings long enough. Thanks, Nelson. You seem to understand me. Dad, you must let me have money to buy a teamster's outfit."

"Ask Hallie. She has the purse-strings," replied Lindsay, evidently much relieved at

137

the turn of the situation. Neale took Harriet's arm and dragged her away.

"Dog-gone, Laramie, you struck fire from him," said Lonesome. "Mebbe he's got stuff in him, after all."

"Shore. Thet young chap will have tough sleddin' out heah. It'll make him or break him."

"Let us hope it will make a man of him," responded Lindsay, fervently. "You've started him well, Nelson. I'm indebted to you. I look to you for much. See you tomorrow. Good-night."

Lonesome talked a blue streak on the way upstairs, disturbing Laramie's reflections. They shared the same room. It would never have done for Laramie to leave Lonesome alone. Tracks came along with them. Once the door closed upon them, they gazed at each other with rapt eyes.

"Wal, pards, I've landed yu good," drawled Laramie.

"Too good to be true!" mused Tracks, dreamily.

"Laramie, I just love you," declared Lonesome, which remark had all the sincerity of truth.

Laramie was about to suggest that they sit down and plan tomorrow's labors when he espied Lonesome smoothing out something on the bureau.

"What's thet? What yu doin'?"

"Aw nothin'."

Tracks, however, snatched it away from Lonesome and held it up – a small white handkerchief with a lace border. Laramie caught a faint scent of perfume.

"Gimme that back," said Lonesome, snatching it in turn. "Belongs to Miss Lenta. She dropped it, an' I forgot to give it to her."

"Like the old lady who kept tavern out West," scoffed Tracks.

Laramie gave his erring and irrepressible friend one reproachful look. "God help me!" he sighed.

Lindsay's caravan, as Buffalo Jones christened it when he bade the party good-by, got away a little after sunrise on the morning scheduled. They had, however, to take the sunrise for granted, because the sky was dull and overcast.

Jones' last word, meant only for Laramie, matched the gleam in the old plainsman's eye: "Hangin' rustlers has come in strong on the range these last few years!"

"Shore has. I hope none of my outfit takes to rustlin'. Good-by, Buff, an' look for me in town some day."

There were eight wagons and they were

loaded. Laramie prayed that the impending storm would hold off. But he would not delay an hour for anything. Let the Lindsays take what came. They were Westerners now, and rain, wind, snow, hail, heat, drought, grasshoppers, work, loneliness, horse and cattle thieves, and all the other gifts of the Great Plains were to be their portion. Laramie had his doubts about Lindsay's strength holding out and of Neale's backbone being sufficiently stiff, but for the rest of them he had sincere hopes.

After all, not only did Neale have to drive a team, but also Lonesome and Tracks. And as Mrs. Lindsay and Lenta rode on Lonesome's wagon, and Harriet and Florence on Tracks', these two proud and unrestrained range-riders were suddenly as mild as lambs. Laramie chuckled to himself over this. "If this heah trip don't beat trailin' Injuns for excitement I'll shore swaller my sombrero."

It had chanced that he had been fortunate to engage a cook who had worked for some of the greatest outfits of the cattle country. Jud Lawrence was a marvel of industry, good humor, and culinary skill, but as so often happened in the case of such treasures he had a weakness for the flowing bowl. He had passed his sobering-up period in the Garden City jail, a fact he begged Laramie to conceal from the Lindsays: "An' I swear to Gawd, Nelson, I'll keep sober so long my friends'll figger I've got religion."

"Yu're on, Jud, with this provision. Thet if yu break yore word to me, I'll beat the everlastin' stuffin's out of yu."

Lawrence would have agreed to more than that to get out of town, and Laramie calculated on the fact that he had seen some fellows keep sober a long time. He gritted his teeth over a resolve that Lonesome and Tracks would stay in a like condition indefinitely.

Laramie felt good to bestride Wingfoot once more on a real journey with real work at the end. And the horse seemed to respond to its rider's feeling. Laramie was the only horseman in the party. Lonesome's and Tracks' horses, together with several new mounts the boys had picked up cheap, trotted behind the last wagon, where Laramie brought up the rear. Young Neale Lindsay drove this last wagon and Laramie wanted to keep an eye on him when they came to bad places. This unfledged young man had taken a sudden liking to Laramie that might be put to good use. "He'll shore be a damn nuisance if no wuss, but his sister is wuth standin' it for – an' mebbe makin' somethin' of him," soliloquized Laramie, quite unconscious that he had omitted the fact that the lad had two other sisters, to say nothing of a mother and father.

The cavalcade passed the last ranch, out over a rolling hill, upon the open gray prairie sloping by leagues up to the vague and dark horizon. The wind cut down raw from the north, and bore ill tidings. Tomorrow it would rain or snow, and Laramie decided he would be sure to tie on some firewood at the first camp, which would be Cottonwood Creek, thirty miles to the northwest.

Spring was backward. The ridges still held to their gray bleached hue, but down in the swales green showed. Willows and cotton-woods had begun to leaf. It was just as well that the Lindsays saw the prairie in its gray monotony, because they would have that to contrast with summer's rich and purple bloom. Then when the bleak north winds brought the snow they might be better prepared. The only good word Buffalo Jones had had for the Spanish Peaks Ranch was: "Wal, anyway, they won't freeze to death in winter. Thet stone house will shore be warm."

Like a scout on duty, Laramie kept his eye on all the wagons, particularly the last. And he settled back into the pleasant idle, dreamy state of the range-rider once more out in the open, with the winding road ahead and the wild country somewhere lost in the haze. He liked the Lindsays and refused to answer his accusing questioning conscience as to which one he liked best. If Lindsay survived this long cold ride in the raw spring, he would probably be cured of his lung weakness. The Colorado slope down from the Rockies was high, clear, dry, with wonderful curative properties in the sun and air. Solitude and simple living would be good for a sick man, however hard it might be upon his family. Eastern Colorado, however, had growing towns, to which an occasional visit might save the girls from too great loneliness. If they took hold of the work! That eldest girl, Hallie, she would win over all the hardships. Laramie wondered about her. What had given her the sad far-away look of eyes, the firm grave sweet lips? No doubt she had left a lover back there in Ohio. Laramie soliloquized that if he had been that luckiest of fellows he would have pulled up stakes and taken the ride with her. For he had been given to understand that the Lindsays had burned bridges behind them; they had threshed it all out together; they would stick to their ailing father and to this chosen new home, come what might.

They made fast time all morning,

considering the loads, and by noon were twenty miles out. And Laramie's practiced eye began to note the lessening number of black dots on the prairie. Cattle were thinning out. But it was a vast country, with enough swales and draws and river bottoms to hide a million cattle. A pale sun shone after a while, making the ride less raw and giving the landscape something of brightness. Coyotes and deer and antelope fell under Laramie's keen eye for distance, and once he espied a group of dark riders, far off, topping a ride against the sky. Such sights always led to speculation. He had made inquiries about the road, the water, the grass, the wood, and the settlers. But of the last he had not observed much sign, and none during the last two hours.

About mid-afternoon, from the top of a hill which had taken an hour to climb, Laramie espied a wooded stream-bed some few miles on the downgrade. He rode ahead.

"How yu makin' it, Neale?" He asked, as he rode by.

"Fine. But my arms are most pulled out," shouted the lad, gaily.

"Hang on. We're most in camp."

Passing Lonesome's wagon, he was accosted by Lenta: "Hey, cow-puncher, where you been all day?"

"Taggin' along, lass. How you ridin'?"

"I've been driving the team."

"Wal! ... An' yu, Miss Hallie – how about yu?"

"Me? Oh, I'm scared, happy, weary, hungry – altogether enchanted," replied Harriet.

Lindsay could not be seen. No doubt he was lying down under the canvas of his wagon. Tracks looked as if he had driven a chariot all day. Florence had a flushed face and bright eyes. Mrs. Lindsay was asleep on the seat.

"Step out, Wing, old boy," called Laramie, and loped down the winding road to the river bottom. It was a wide valley, grassy and thicketed, with groves of trees here and there, and running water. He required far more time than usual to select a camp site, and at length, up toward the head of the stream, where the valley notched, he found a most desirable spot, yet still close to the road. He sat his horse a while, meditatively, until he remembered where he was, and then dismounting, he soon had Wingfoot free to roll and drink and graze. Then he went over to the road to wait for the caravan. They soon reached him, all in a bunch, horses as glad as the travelers for the prospective halt.

"Turn off heah under the trees," he shouted, waving a hand, and when the drivers reached the desired spot and halted, Laramie gave his further orders.

"Unhitch, water the hawses an' hobble them. Jud, get busy an' send two men to cut firewood. Lonesome, yu an' Tracks haul out the tents an' beddin'. Neale, lend a hand if yu ain't daid. Rest of yu get off an' come in."

Laramie swung an ax with avidity that afternoon, pausing now and then to attend amusedly to the several Lindsays limping around. Presently Lenta ran to him.

"Oh, Laramie," she called, before she got to him. "Come. I'm afraid Lonesome an' Tracks will kill each other."

"What about?" asked Laramie, mildly.

"About how to put up our tent."

"Wal, I'll come along. Lug thet chunk of firewood, lass. Yu may as wal begin now."

"You bet," declared the girl, and little as she was she lifted the heavy block with ease. "I'm having the time of my life."

When Laramie gazed down upon his two partners he realized that their heated faces were not proof of his suspicions that they were showing off before the girls, but really because they disagreed about how the tent should be put up. It was a new-fangled complicated affair.

146

"Wal, I shore don't see how yu boys have gall enough to figger on ranches, wives, children, an' all such when yu cain't put up a simple tent," drawled Laramie.

This effectually squelched them, with the result that they soon got the tangled canvas straightened out. Laramie built a sparkling fire against a cottonwood stump near at hand, and went to fetch a bucket of water and basins. Also he appropriated a stewpot from Jud's kit to heat water in. Then he helped the boys put up two more tents.

"Dig up the beddin', Lonesome, while I fetch a bundle of grass and ferns. Thet ground is damp an' hard."

"There's a dozen or more tarps," interposed Tracks.

"Thet's so. Ted, yu do have an idee once in a while," drawled Laramie, and in lower voice. "Shore surprises me, seein' yu so bad in love."

"You stone-hearted gun-thrower!" flashed Williams. "I hope and bet you get it so bad you'll nearly die."

"What Me? ... Wal, if I got it atall I'd die shore enough."

When these three tents were ready and the particular bags the girls needed were unpacked, Laramie went on down the line of wagons. Neale, to do him credit, had elected to sleep under a cottonwood and had unrolled his tarpaulin there. Mr. Lindsay and his wife were to occupy one of the covered wagons. Jud Lawrence, with his helpers, were busy about two fires. And about dusk the cook yelled out in lusty voice, "Come an' get it before I throw it out!"

"What on earth does he mean by that?" asked Mrs. Lindsay, in amaze. The younger girls made laughing conjectures, while Harriet asked Laramie if it had not something to do with supper.

"Wal, yu can take thet literal, Miss Hallie," replied Laramie.

Whereupon the girls ran merrily to the chuck-wagon, near where Jud had spread a tarpaulin, with packs, boxes and bags for seats. They made a merry and a hearty meal, and were loud in the praises of the cook. No doubt Jud had planned to establish a reputation with this first meal.

Laramie, with his riders, and the other men, were served next, and ate standing or squatting after the manner of range-riders. And as usual they were too hungry to be very talkative.

"Wal, fellows, we're in for weather by mawnin', I reckon," said Laramie.

"Feels like snow. But mebbe it'll hold off.

148

Hope so. Wood powerful scarce tomorrow an' next day."

"Tie up some bundles heah while we can get it dry."

Lonesome and Tracks evinced a desire to linger about the camp fire of the Lindsays, leaving Laramie to have a look at their horses. This first night, at least, Laramie was glad to see, was a comfortable and absorbing one for the Easterners.

"Hey, yu-all," he called, when he had returned from his tasks. "Better roll in. Yu won't feel so powerful awake about five in the mawnin'."

But he did not impress either the Lindsays or his two bewitched partners. Laramie unrolled his bed under a wagon and crawled into it, conscious of both familiar and disturbing sensations. He was glad to be out on the range again, and particularly with a prospect of a permanent job. Sleep did not come as readily as usual. Soon his old wild comrades of many a lonely night encompassed the camp – the coyotes – and began their hue and cry. He heard Lenta Lindsay call out: "Listen to those awful yelping dogs. I didn't see any dogs with us. Where'd they come from?"

"Wild dogs on the plains, miss," replied Lonesome.

149

"Wild! . . . Are they dangerous?"

"Not so very much. But in winter they eat you alive."

Mrs. Lindsay screamed at that, and the girls uttered dismayed exclamations.

"Coyotes is what they're called," said Ted Williams. "Perfectly harmless except in case one happens to have hydrophobia."

"Oh, what have we come to!" exclaimed Mrs. Lindsay, in distress. "Uggh! They curdle my blood. How can we sleep?"

"Upper Sandusky wouldn't be so bad just now," admitted Lenta. "Might not those beasts crawl in our tents?"

"They might. But we'll make our beds in front, so they'll have to go over our dead bodies –"

At this point Laramie fell asleep. He did not awaken until he heard the ring of Jud's ax on hard wood. Dawn was pale gray in the east. Thick gloom hung over the camp. Laramie pulled on his boots. His first move was to stalk over to where Lonesome and Tracks lay wrapped in slumber. Tracks was always easy to awaken, but Lonesome slept hard and he hated to be roused, and if that was done rudely he roared like a mad bull. Laramie pretended to stumble over him and did fall upon him. Lonesome, of course, awoke bewildered and forgot where he was.

He yelled murder, stampede, redskins, and then launched upon a volley of range profanity. Tracks, careful to keep out of reach, leaned down to whisper hoarsely: "Cheese it. The girls will hear you."

"Huh!"

Laramie beat a retreat. The girls had heard something, for as he passed their tent he heard whispers and titters. Laramie could not resist the temptation to stoop behind the nearest tent and scratch upon it.

"Mercy! Hallie, listen! – What's that?"

"Sounds like a beast of some kind. I suspect it's a two-legged one. . . . Let's get up."

"In this pitch dark? Not much."

Laramie stole away silently and from a safe distance called out: "Breakfast in half an hour. Pile out. It's mawnin'."

Daylight came pale and cold, with a raw wind. Laramie did not need to hurry the men, as everybody wanted to be on the move before the rain began. But the storm held off and the journey began under a dark lowering sky. Driving or riding was no fun that day. Young Neale lagged behind most of the time thus keeping Laramie in the rear. When they came to a hill Laramie got off.

"Yu walk a bit an' lead my hawse," he

151

suggested to Neale. "Thet'll warm yu up. But don't get gay an' try to ride him."

That slope was long. From the next summit Laramie saw the country was getting more rugged, and during a brighter interval, when the clouds broke, he noticed dim mountains to the west. Grass was good only in spots. Laramie decided that the cavalcade would not make the camp he had wanted to reach, and that he would do well to find any place possible. Late in the afternoon the leading teamster waited for the others to come up, anticipating Laramie's judgment. A rather deep swale furnished shelter from wind, fairly good water, but scant grass and no wood. So camp was made. The wood hauled on the wagons had to be conserved for Jud's cook fire, around which the Lindsays huddled, rather silent and subdued. Lenta kept up her spirits. It was significant that they all went to bed before darkness really set in.

Sometime in the night Laramie was awakened by cold rain on his face. "Wal, too bad! We're shore in for it. Why couldn't we have had fine sparklin' weather?"

Morning came cold and wet under a gray-blanketed sky. The teamsters and riders tramped around with pancakes of gray mud on their feet. It was funny to see the

Lindsays troop to breakfast, bundled up in heavy coats and slickers. Mr. Lindsay, however, did not leave the shelter of his canvas wagon. "He caught cold yesterday," explained his wife, "and I think he'd better not come out. I'll take him some breakfast."

"Keep him warm, ma'am," advised Jud, solicitously. "An' if yu need anythin' hotter'n coffee come right heah."

The rest of the Lindsays ate standing in the drizzling rain, trying to keep warm by the bed of sizzling coals.

"Rustle, everybody," ordered Laramie. "We want to get along. If we cain't pass these bottom-lands before it starts rainin' hard we'll lose two days an' more. Ten miles ahaid we climb out on good road."

Laramie had his tasks cut out for that morning. After the first wagon bogged down in a creek-bed, Laramie took Neale's team and the lead. They had four hours of wet, slippery, muddy, tedious travel before getting up on hard ground again. After that he had no concern, except for the welfare of the Lindsays, about whom he felt some misgivings. Mr. Lindsay was ill, Neale had given out, and the girls, according to Lonesome, were a lot of bedraggled mud-hens. Getting on and off the wagon at intervals during the morning, wading

153

through creeks and across bottom-lands, impeded by boots and long slickers, they had but a sorry time of it. In the afternoon as the horses made fair progress on an almost imperceptible slope, wind and rain grew colder. Laramie drove on long after dark, making Laclade Grove, completing thirty miles of travel for the day. This was, according to his information, a fine camp site, from which the road to Spanish Peaks Ranch forked to the left. Three wagons rolled in close upon Laramie, the last of which was Jud's chuckwagon. So far as Jud was concerned, an abundance of firewood and water supplied his most urgent needs. The other wagons straggled in one by one, the occupants of which were loud in acclaim of the blazing fires. Lenta expressed the significance of the case for tenderfeet when she naïvely said. "I never knew how good a fire could feel."

The rain had turned partly to snow. Laramie remarked to Jud, "Wal, if it changes into a real storm we'll hang right heah."

"Too late fer a blizzard, Nelson."

"Shore, but a right perty May storm would be tough enough for these Eastern folks."

The girls were game, but in the way of becoming pretty miserable. Laramie had a word with Lindsay. He was sick, but

154

cheerful! That night all the Lindsays slept in the wagons, and Laramie doubted not that they had a cold and dreary time of it.

Next day Laramie's salutation was: "Cheer up, yu-all. We're in Colorado an' tonight we'll make the Peak Dot."

"And what's that?" asked Lenta.

"Wal, didn't yu know? That's the brand on yore cattle."

"If it gets any colder I'll be branded myself."

"The wust is yet to come. Hang around the fire till yu're dry an' warm. It'll be a tough day."

So it proved. Laramie did not care for sleet and snow and bitter winds although he was used to them. Lonesome hated anything approaching winter. Ted did not suffer from cold. But by this time apparently he had been rendered impervious to everything save a pair of dark proud eyes.

Laramie got the outfit started early and he kept everlastingly at it. After a few hours the snow changed to rain again, and that held, with lulls at intervals. Cattle huddled in the lea of ridges. Laramie calculated that the last fifty miles of this country had taken them up out of the plains. The road wound around the heads of deep wooded draws. For the most part, however, even at midday

Laramie could not see a mile out on the range. He passed several landmarks he had been told to look out for, the last of which, gray roofless walls of an old fort, gave him the satisfaction of knowing the distance to Spanish Peaks Ranch was now a matter of only a few more miles.

But they were long ones, and piercingly cold in the driving rain. Laramie felt the lighter quality of a higher altitude and he seemed to smell the mountains. Poor Lindsay! He hoped this Allen range-outfit would be expecting them and have fires going at least, but a second thought dismissed that hope. As darkness came on he looked for lights. But there were none. And he had almost begun to fear that he had gotten off on a wrong road when a big square rough-ramparted structure loomed up before him.

Laramie halted the team. "Wal, Neale, we're heah, I reckon," he said, to the youth lying back of the seat.

"Here! Where?... That's a wall of rock," replied the weary Neale.

The restiveness of the horses excited Laramie's attention. Wingfoot, tied behind the wagon, snorted in a way to acquaint Laramie with the presence of water. Then above the gusty wind he heard the flow of

156

water somewhere close in the darkness. Laramie clambered off the seat, stiff from the long cold drive. Jud, who had been next to him, must be coming close. The grating sound of wheels attested to this surmise.

"Hi thar, Laramie," called the cook. "Yu turned off the road."

"Mebbe I did, but anyway we're heah," shouted Laramie, and he moved forward toward the gloomy structure. Its close proximity had been an illusion: he had to walk some paces to get to it. Rough stone met his groping hand. He felt his way along the wall toward the sound of running water, and at length reached the end of the wall. Between where he stood and the dim continuation of the wall opposite ran a brook, which soon leaped off in the darkness downhill. Laramie knew he had arrived at Spanish Peaks Ranch. But this stone fortress-like house appeared deserted. He went back.

Meanwhile Jud had driven down and the grind of more wheels and pound of hoofs sounded.

"Laramie, didn't you know you turned off the road?" asked Jud, as he fumbled under the seat of his wagon.

"I shore didn't. Case of luck. Wal, it's about time we had some.

"Aw, this is fine. We might had to lay out another night. Heah, I'll have a light in a jiffy."

When the lantern was lighted Jud swung it to signal the coming drivers. "Laramie, this heah is all right. Fine windbreak. Line the wagons close to the wall. I'll take a look inside. Where'n hell is the outfit that was supposed to be heah?"

Laramie wondered about that, too. He walked out to meet the incoming wagons and directed the drivers where to go. Indeed, he had turned off the main road. Six wagons had passed him, leaving one more, the driver of which was Tracks Williams. As he could not yet be heard Laramie hurried back to the wagons. The drivers were unhitching the horses.

"Howdy, pard," called out Lonesome, cheerily. "It was a rummy drive, huh? Gosh! you gotta hand it to these girls! But they're about all in, countin' spunk. I seen a light off to our right. It looked downhill. There's a jump-off here, where that water tumbles down."

"So there is. I forgot. A big draw opens heah. Barns, corrals, pastures down below, accordin' to Buff Jones."

"Reckon that Allen outfit must be bunked

158

in the draw. It's a safe bet they ain't up here in this wind."

Jud came back with his lantern. The yellow light showed dripping horses and wagons, the wet drivers, and the falling rain, mixed with snow.

"Snug an' dry inside, Laramie. Stack of cut firewood big as a hill. I'll lead the chuckwagon in. Send after the lantern soon as I start a fire."

"Give me yore light, an' yu drive in," replied Laramie, encouraged by Jud's satisfaction.

When Laramie turned the corner of the wall he was surprised at the size of the gloomy enclosure. The brook ran under stone slabs through the gateway; a group of huge old cottonwoods stood up spectrally in the center. Wild animals of some species scurried out into the open. He halted for Jud to catch up. And as he lifted the lantern high above his head he discerned a huge courtyard, stone-flagged, with a mound of mossy boulders in the center, around which the gnarled old cottonwoods spread mighty branches. The spring evidently flowed from under these boulders. On this left side ran a long porch-like succession of rooms, resembling stalls, opening to the outside. Laramie surmised that this tier ran all

159

around the inside of the walls. His instant impression was most favorable. Gloom and wet, dank odors and gaunt beasts, empty leaking rooms and rotting porch timbers, the feel of having walked into a huge old barn, long vacant – these could not keep Laramie from recognizing a haven with wonderful possibilities. He knew what high stone walls meant. He knew the rigors of summer and winter, and he had vision. He experienced an intense relief.

Jud drove his chuck-wagon clear to the far corner, where Laramie saw an enormous pile of firewood stacked under the roof.

"Darn place was full of varmints," declared Jud. "But I ain't smelled any skunks yet. Have you?"

"Not yet."

"Nifty dug-out this," went on Jud. "There's a stone fireplace in heah thet was built by a mason who was a cook." He leaped off the seat. "Come in heah with the lantern, Laramie.... Dry as punk. I call this nifty.... Cedar an' piñon wood – oak too, Laramie, dry as a bone. You can bet there are foothills somewhere near.... There. I got her started. You can show the other fellars in, Laramie. Room for a regiment."

Laramie went out. "Heah, men. Follow me in an' unhitch. Better grain the hawses, then turn 'em loose." As he showed the way for the wagons and turned into the gateway, Jud's fire, already blazing brightly, brought more than one word of satisfaction from the teamsters. Then Laramie started out to look for the eighth and remaining wagon. Lonesome followed him.

"Gosh, pard, the kid's cryin'," he whispered. "An' Miss Hallie is plumb saggin'. I ain't got the heart to stay there an' see them wake up to thet hawg-pen.... Tell you what I'll do, pard. I'll yell up the Allen outfit. What say?"

"Good idee. I'll look for Tracks. How fur was he behind?"

"Aw, he lagged along. Tracks can drive four hosses without battin' an eye. It's the gurl."

"Ahuh. I savvied that. Wal, if he keeps her cheered up it's somethin'."

"Hope he has more luck than me. I talked myself black in the face about the bootiful country an' this old Spanish ranch. What'd I get?"

While Laramie strode out to the main road Lonesome found a position below the ranch, from which he yelled in stentorian voice: "HEY, DOWN THERE!... HEY, YOU ALLEN OUT-FIT.... WHERE'N HELL ARE YOU"

Lonesome waited a couple of moments

161

and then repeated his calls, with variations. This time there came a reply from far down in the black void.

"Go to hell an' find out!"

There followed a moment's silence. "Laramie, you hear that?"

"I shore did."

"What you make of it?"

"No more'n I expected."

"The low-down lousy –! . . . Pard, shall I call again?"

"Shore. An' say something this time," replied Laramie, and strode on.

"HEY, COWPUNCHER!" bawled Lonesome.

"Hey yourself!" came the reply.

"YOU'RE TOO WINDY."

"Aw, shut up, you grub-line rider!"

"I'M THE RIGHT-HAND MAN OF YOUR BOSS, YOU COYOTE!"

"Haw! Haw! Haw!"

"YOU'LL GET THE WIND PUNCHED OUT OF YOU FOR THAT!"

"Who'll do it?"

"I WILL. COME UP, YOU —— —— ——!"

"Heah's rarin' to meet ya!"

By this time Laramie heard grating wheels round a dark thicket. He stepped off the road to wait, as well as to listen. Lonesome was making the welkin ring. Laramie sensed a fight before his outfit even got unhitched,

162

and he sighed. What was the use? Lonesome could no more avoid trouble than could he keep his mouth shut.

The last wagon came rolling round the bend. Laramie picked up his lantern, which he had set down in the grass, and as he lifted it the light flashed full on the wagon-seat. Laramie gasped. Either he was dreaming or else he saw Florence Lindsay's beautiful face, white and rapt, pressed close to the dark one of Tracks. Swiftly he moved the lantern, throwing the wagon into shadow again.

"Thet yu, Ted," he called.

"Whoa!...What's this, a hold-up?" shouted Tracks, sharply.

"Nope. It's only me. I was some worried. We've got heah. Follow the light down."

So there was a reason why Tracks, usually the most prompt of riders, had been delayed along the road. What did he care for rain, cold, dark road, or worried partner? Laramie would not soon forget that girl's white rapt face, her dark eyes staring out into the night. Not until he had reached the house did he halt to wait. Tracks was not long in arriving. A broad belt of light flared out of the gateway. Laramie went on. A big fire, halfway down the courtyard, lit up the interior of the stone structure, giving it giant proportions and a most weird and dismal aspect. Snow and rain were swirling down. Smoke floated aloft, to be blown away beyond the ramparts. The teamsters were bustling at their tasks; the horses were munching grain; Jud whistled over his cook-fire under the shed, and rattled his pans. Laramie surveyed the scene with satisfaction. He had brought the outfit through in four days without an accident, which was little short of marvelous. He saw Ted leap down off his seat to help Florence, and heard her call, "How perfectly wonderful!"

"Not so bad," replied Tracks, with a queer little ring in his voice. "Go up by the fire. I'll fetch your bags."

Laramie wended a thoughtful way around on the right side of the courtyard, realizing that enthusiasm and happiness depended on the point of view. This right side presented a more dilapidated and forlorn aspect than the left. In places the wooden roof had caved in. Some of the rooms had been used for stalls. But all this in no wise detracted from Laramie's picture of what might be made of the old fort. The spring itself was worth the money Lindsay had paid for the property, and the gnarled old cottonwoods were beyond price.

Laramie continued on around the square. The western wall was not so wide as the northern and southern. A black aperture opened through it and had evidently been a door. A blank space flanked it, from which on the north side led stone steps to the ramparts. No doubt all around these ramparts on the inside, ran a walk from which soldiers had once stood on guard.

Presently Laramie became aware of a pathetic and disturbing spectacle. He halted in the shadow.

"Oh – my – God! What – a hideous place!" sobbed Mrs. Lindsay. She sat upon the stone step in the flare of the courtyard fire. Her appearance was pitiful. Wet, cold, miserable, she sat there, bareheaded, her iron-gray hair straggling down, glistening with raindrops, her bonnet fallen to the ground, every line of her face and person indicative of abject disillusion, hopelessness, and panic.

Laramie looked from the mother to the son, Neale, who sprawled upon the porch, a lax, spent figure significant of despair. Florence sat somewhat apart, leaning elbows on her knees, also bareheaded, her fair locks shiny, wet, and disheveled, her white face expressive of extreme fatigue, her wonderful dark proud eyes fixed upon the fire with piercing intensity. But she did not see the blaze, nor the opalescent heart of the burning cedar sticks. She was not conscious of the weariness and havoc her looks and posture suggested. She gave no indication of having heard her mother's disheartening speech. Lenta stood out in the rain, a ludicrous little figure. She had been too tired to lift the yellow slicker off the ground, and she had dragged and trampled it into the mud. She held her red little hands and wet gloves out to the heat. Her hat was on awry and from under it strands of hair hung down. Her pale pretty face was woebegone, and she, too, was weeping unrestrainedly.

"I'm so tired – and cold – and sick. I – I want to die," she faltered. "I just – don't care."

Harriet had thrown aside the burdening slicker, and she too was trying to warm benumbed hands. Raindrops dripped from the narrow brim of her hat. Her face was ghastly in its pallor and there were big dark circles under her eyes. She was biting her lips. It was not only raindrops that rolled down her cheeks. Her breast heaved as if laboring under an oppressive burden.

"Mother – don't cry," she said. "Don't give up.... To be sure it's a – a horrid place.... After all we – we dreamed! ... And father is flat on his back. But the ride's over.

166

We're here. For mercy's sakes don't let him see how – how terrible we feel!"

"But he – he'll die out in this desolate frigid place," moaned Mrs. Lindsay.

"Oh no, he won't, mother.... Let's not give up. It *might* not be so – so bad."

The strain under which Harriet labored betrayed her struggle, as her face and speech made clear that she was the sanity and strength of this family. Suddenly Laramie saw the situation from their point of view, and he suffered a poignant pang. He had forgotten that they were Easterners unused to privation and loneliness. Harriet no doubt was appalled at what they had come to. But she fought to conceal her dismay, her fears. She probably saw the worst of it more clearly than any of them.

Whatever Laramie's state of mind had been before, he felt staggered under a rushing tide of feeling for this girl. That was the moment when he fell in love with her. It affected him with a strange, fierce spirit to protect and help her, and through her these other unfortunate Lindsays.

"Wal, folks," he drawled, genially, as he stepped out of the shadow, "I see yu're all heah an' enjoyin' the fire. Shore's nothin' like a hot blazin' bunch of cedar."

Then stepping over to the wagon that

167

contained Mr. Lindsay, he called out: "Hey, boss, we're heah, an' darned lucky. How'd yu ride it?"

"He's very ill," cried Mrs. Lindsay. "Please don't excite him."

"Not so good, Nelson," replied Lindsay, in a weak voice.

"Wal, I'm shore glad yu're not daid," drawled Laramie. "Shows yu're pretty husky yet, Lindsay. Thet was a hell of a cold, mean, rough ride. I'll fix yu up a drink of hot whiskey. Pile out an' walk about a bit. This heah house shore hits me plumb center."

"Oh no! No! John, you mustn't get up," cried Mrs. Lindsay, in affright, as she ran over. "This hor –"

Laramie put a gentle yet firm hand over her lips, effectually stifling her speech.

"Shore he'll get up, Lady," said Laramie, with a different note in his voice. Harriet came running in alarm, but if she meant to expostulate, Laramie silenced her with a look.

"Yu're out West now, Lindsay," went on Laramie, as if that mere fact itself was a marvelous difference. "Colorado weather never hurt nobody. Shore it's hard. But, man, in a week yu'll be jumpin' up an' kickin' yore heels together."

"By gum!" muttered Lindsay. "Mom, where'd you hide my boots?"

Mrs. Lindsay clambered up into the wagon. "John, darling, you mustn't think of going out in the wet. That terrible Nelson is crazy. You would catch your death."

"Stop mollycoddling me!" declared Lindsay, testily. "Nelson may be terrible, but he's not crazy. Strikes me.... Where's my boots and heavy coat?"

Laramie turned to face Harriet. She seemed frightened and uncertain. Lenta came slushing her slicker over the wet stones to join them. Thereupon Laramie took their arms and drew them back to the fire.

"Girls, listen," he said, without his usual drawl, and he still held to Lenta's arm while he looked down into Harriet's pale face. "I could almost laugh at yu. This heah ain't nothin' atall what yu reckon it is. Yu air seein' it with an Easterner's eyes. Yore feelin's air those of a tenderfoot. But yu want to see this heah old house an' this night with my eyes."

"But – Mr. Nelson," faltered Harriet, as Florence, finally aroused from her reverie, joined them. "Aren't you asking the impossible?"

"Shore. But yu're plumb extraordinary girls. The way yu stuck out that hard ride shows me. Why I'm so proud of yu-all thet I could bust. An' Lonesome an' Ted – they feel the same.... This place ain't what it 'pears to yu. It'll make the wonderfulest ranch-house in all the West. An' the country round about is grand. Yu couldn't ever get lonesome or tired, lookin' up at the Rockies, all snow-capped an' beautiful, or down across the Great Plains, thet Lone Prairie Lonesome sings about, all so purple an' lovely. This heah Colorado will change yore hearts. Yu'll never want to leave it. So much for yore surroundin's. An' as for makin' this a home – why it'll be the most satisfactory work of all yore lives. In a week or so we'll have the wagons back with more lumber an' whatever we'll need. Just s'pose yu didn't have any money atall or any of these wagon-loads. *Then* yu might feel blue. But yu're the luckiest girls who ever rode out to make the West a better country. Cain't yu see it? Close yore eyes."

It was significant that Laramie's suggestion acted so powerfully upon them that they did as bidden. Laramie stretched his imagination and invoked all the gods of fortune to sustain his claims.

"Cain't yu see this ranch-house as I see it? Work makes a home, after yu find the place. There's one of the wonderfulest springs this side the mountains. To drink that water is to become Western. An' I'll get a dipper from Jud an' prove what I say. In the mawnin' this storm will break. The sun will shine. Yu'll fall in love with these old cottonwoods under which Spanish padres have told their beads an' trappers have traded with the Indians an' soldiers have tramped on guard. Cattlemen before Allen have hanged rustlers from these wide-spreadin' branches. This court will grow green an' beautiful in yore hands. We'll clear out this old corral of stone walls. Then we'll repair an' build an' whitewash. We'll cut windows.... It'll be like as if the fairies of yore kid story-books has visited heah with their magic wands. An' all yore own work! Yu'll look back at that terrible ride an' at this miserable night an' be glad yu had them. Yu'll be glad for all thet's hard out heah.... Wal, then, cain't you see ahaid a little?"

Harriet gazed up at Laramie fascinated, unconscious of her surrender to something so splendid, so unexpected. But Lenta burst out impulsively: "Mr. Laramie, I'll be dog-goned if I don't see somethin'.... Oh, Hallie, he has made it endurable."

At this juncture a trampling of many boots on the stone flags and a jingling of many spurs gave Laramie a start. Dark forms of men showed down the court.

"Whar'n hell is that loud-mouthed puncher?" called out a ringing, raucous voice.

Laramie spread wide his arms and forced the three startled girls back under the shadow of the porch. "Stay heah," he said.

"Nels, who's that yelpin'?" queried Jud, sharply.

"Don't know, Jud," replied Laramie, as he strode out and set the lantern down. "Throw on some more wood an' keep folks back up heah."

"Show yourself, puncher, if yore gall's as strong as yore yellin'," bawled the leader of the approaching squad.

Chapter 7

Nelson's iron arm across Harriet's breast gave her a vague and unaccountable sensation dominant despite the sudden alarm occasioned by this leather-lunged intruder. Nelson, looking backward over his shoulder down the court, was not aware of any physical contact.

"What is it?" whispered Harriet. There seemed to be a menace about him, a transformation. His face in the fire-glow looked somber, the brows knit, the eyes like sparks. Lenta grasped her convulsively as Nelson left them, and gasped: "Hallie, something's – up!" Florence sat down on a box as if her legs had buckled under her. Neale struggled up to a sitting posture, muttering in concerned accents. And Mr. Lindsay put his head out between the canvas covers of his wagon to ejaculate: "What's this? ... Girls, who's yelling?"

Meanwhile the group of visitors trooped up into the firelit circle, headed by a lanky red-faced youth of motley garb and most sinister aspect. He might have come farther but for Nelson's significant move, which placed him just out of the bright light, away from the porch. Harriet did not miss the fact that Nelson stood erect, sidewise, like a statue.

"Heah, applejack, better be less noisy an' more civil," advised one of the teamsters, roughly.

"Whar's thet brayin' jackass?" demanded the red-faced individual, glaring all round. None of the Lindsays, except possibly Neale, could have been visible to him. Tawny hair stood up like a mane; his gimlet eyes roamed back to Nelson. Harriet felt her heart pound up out of normal position to hamper her breast.

"Air you alludin' to me?" queried a cool voice. And Lonesome emerged from behind a wagon to confront the irate visitor.

"Shore am, if you're the galoot who was hollerin'."

"I'm that same gennelman."

"Haw! Haw! You sure look it – you banty-legged little rooster," declared the other, derisively, and he took a couple of long strides, which fetched him close to Lonesome. "What you mean bellarin' like a bull, to wake riders up? You got outfit enough to take care of yourselves."

"Say, if your outfit is all as hospitable as you we got it figgered," retorted Lonesome.

Muttered ejaculations sounded back in the group of dark restless figures. An authoritative voice and ringing boot-thuds came from the entrance to the courtyard. Two more men were approaching. Meanwhile the teamsters had lined along infront of their wagons and Jud stepped down off the porch.

"Puncher, you're talkin' to Slim Red," announced the instigator of this disturbance, and he was more than arrogant.

"Which don't mean nothin' atall to me," sneered Lonesome. At this juncture Tracks Williams stalked out: "Lonesome, what –" he panted, as if from hurried effort.

"Stay back, pard," replied Lonesome, waving his friend aside without even turning. "Look 'em over from –"

"You bellyachin' little geezer," snorted the self-introduced Slim Red. "I'm gonna bounce on you an' jam your square head down into your gizzard so you'll look like a smashed toad. I'm the rarinest wrastlinest wildcat on this range –"

"Save your wind. An' look out what you say," warned Lonesome. "Mebbe you don't savvy this outfit. We've got ladies in camp."

"Aw, to hell with your emigrants! What'd

175

you bust in on us for with your lousy petticoats –"

"Shut up, Slim!" called the ringing voice from behind. "This is Lindsay's wagon-train."

Bam! A sound like a bass-drum appeared to come simultaneously with Lonesome's sudden lurch and swing. Slim Red uttered a hoarse gasp. He doubled up like a jackknife, and opening back again he began to sink down to the ground, his hands on his abdomen, his face distorted hideously, his mouth agape, from which issued a whistling expulsion of breath. He sank to his knees, sagged and flopped down.

"Mebbe that'll shut off your wind," declared Lonesome.

Then a bareheaded man leaped by the group. He held a coat over his shoulders, as if he had hastily thrown it there to keep off the rain. This lithe, bronzed, eagle-eyed newcomer was Luke Arlidge. With a start Harriet recognized him. And what had been amazed perturbation for her suddenly augmented to fright. A chill shot over her, and she trembled. She clutched Lenta who had appeared to freeze against her. Nelson had not moved. What was the meaning of his strange immobility? Hints about Arlidge flashed confusedly through Harriet's

176

mind. Something dire impended. Was this the –"

"Did you hit him?" demanded Arlidge, harshly, of Lonesome.

"Me? Naw, I didn't *hit* him. I just caressed his windbag."

"Luke, that's nobody but Lonesome Mulhall," declared a short, thick-set individual who had followed Arlidge.

"Hullo, Price!... Well, I wouldn't be surprised now at anythin'," said Lonesome, in a low tone.

"Luke, I had a rope round the neck of thet bow-legged little rustle –"

"Cut any talk about rustlers heah!" broke in Nelson, his voice remarkably piercing and arresting.

Arlidge whirled with a violent start. He espied Nelson. He peered, he crouched as if to see under a shadow. Then with slow rigidity he straightened up, his face full in the fire-flare. The bronze had changed to ashen hue.

"What'd you – say?" Arlidge queried, with a husky break in his voice.

"Yu heahed me."

"Luke, so help me Gawd it's that Texas rider who beat me out of hangin' Mulhall!" rasped Price. "I told you. It happened three – four years ago."

177

Lonesome shook a burly fist in Price's agitated face. "You bet your sweet life it's that Texas rider who saved my neck. An' what was you hangin' me for? I'm a-roarin' it at you, Price. I want my outfit to heah. I cut you out with a girl an' to get rid of me you tried to hang me as a rustler."

"Didn't I ketch you brandin' a steer?" shouted Price, furiously.

"Mebbe you did. I forget that. But I wasn't no rustler."

"Yes, you are. A two-bit cow-punchin' rustler!"

Price, take that back or go for yore gun," interposed Nelson, coldly and slowly.

The stocky pallid-faced man gulped. "All right, if you're so testy about it. I crawl."

"Riders who live in glass houses shore oughtn't throw stones about," returned Nelson, with a hint of his habitual drawl.

"Who the hell are you?" demanded Arlidge, in fierce uncertainty.

"Wal, yu ought to remember an old Nebraskie rider who shore remembers yu."

"*Laramie Nelson!*" exclaimed Arlidge in a hoarse whisper. His fingers snapped audibly and his hand moved as if to flash in sudden violent gesture. But it froze to the sleeve of his coat, which had begun to slip from his shoulders.

178

Suddenly the seven or eight spectators behind Arlidge split and leaped frantically to each side. Price too made a flying leap to get out from line with Arlidge. A teamster sang out: "Fellars, hell'll be poppin' heah pronto!" And he dove under a wagon.

Harriet, though a thorough tenderfoot, did not fail to grasp the significance of the moment. She had been half prepared. There would be shooting – blood spilled – men murdered. Perhaps Nelson! And she sickened with revulsion while some other unknown and violent sensation attacked her.

"What you – doing – out here?" asked Arlidge, haltingly.

"Wal, I might ask yu the same."

"I was foreman for Allen. He sold out to Lindsay. . . . I went with the deal."

"Shore. I heahed thet. But my idee is – if yu do any more ridin' it won't be with Lindsay's outfit."

"Hell – you say," panted Arlidge. Sweat stood out on his face. He gave an impression of intense preoccupation, of an uncertainty which he needed to have time to meet.

"And why won't I?"

"Wal, I'm ridin' for Lindsay an' this ranch won't be big enough for both of us, seein' yu won't live up to yore brag."

Arlidge tossed his coat to Price, who stood

aside. He appeared violent, furious, yet singularly relieved.

"I'm not toting my gun, which I reckon you seen," he retorted.

"Ahuh. I see thet now. Wal, I reckon it's good luck for yu an' bad for the range."

Arlidge made a passionate gesture. He seemed torn within. His roving gaze sighted Lindsay's white face peering out of the wagon-tent.

"Lindsay, is it true? Have you hired this Laramie Nelson?"

"I have. And he was highly recommended by no less than Buffalo Jones," replied Lindsay, emphatically.

"Then I quit. I wouldn't have Nelson in my outfit," snapped Arlidge. "You'll be left flat. My riders will stick to me –"

"Don't speak for all of us," interrupted one of the bystanders. "You've kept me an' Dakota an' Clay slavin' for months without pay, all on the chance of this Lindsay deal goin' through. An' since it 'pears to have done so we'll have a talk with him."

"Split my outfit, will you?" shouted Arlidge, further enraged. "Look to yourself, Mayhew."

"Aw, you can't bluff me," returned the rider called Mayhew. "I just heerd you called to your face. An' I ain't denyin' I'm damned

180

curious. . . . Come on, pards. Let's mosey."
Then as he and his two comrades turned
away Mayhew wheeled to say: "Mr. Lindsay,
we three ain't tied to Arlidge an' we'd like to
talk to you."

"Certainly. Glad you'll stand by me,"
replied Lindsay, spiritedly. "And as for you,
Arlidge – I'm pretty curious myself, and bet
I'll be better off without you."

"Tenderfeet have stopped lead for less
than that," rejoined Arlidge, contemptuously. "You'll have a fine time
ranchin' it here, with less than half an outfit.
Rustlers made off with four thousand head
of your cattle just three days ago. Let's see
your gun-slingin' Nelson drive them back.
Ha! Ha!"

"You insolent fellow!" ejaculated Lindsay.

"Out of this, Price, an' you gapin' fools.
Get up, Slim, before you show yellow like
Mayhew an' his cronies."

Whereupon Arlidge stalked away down
the courtyard with the remainder of his men.
Lonesome was the first of those watching to
break silence.

"Dog-gone, Laramie, it couldn't have
come off no better," he declared. "An' all
without upsettin' our lady folk."

"Oh, no, we're not upset atall!" cried
Lenta, hysterically.

181

"No one woulda guessed it," said Jud, approvingly, as he moved away. "Thunder an' blazes! Smell my burnin' biscuits!"

"Well, I'm glad that's over," declared Lindsay, feelingly. "Our first experience with the enemy, girls.... Nelson, come help me down."

"It might have been bad, Lindsay," replied Nelson, as he complied. "But even if it had it'd only been an incident of range life. I'm shore pleased at the way yu-all took it.... There yu air on yure feet. Walk about a bit, sir."

Harriet felt further repulsion toward this strange, soft-voiced man, yet could not resist the desire to confront him.

"Only an incident of range life?" she asked, endeavouring to be flippant.

"Thet's all, Miss Hallie."

"I may be a tenderfoot, but I'm not without sense. Have not you and Arlidge clashed before?"

"Wal, I reckon."

"Bad blood between you?"

"There is some, now yu tax me about it."

"He appeared stunned upon recognizing you. He went white in the face. He was a man possessed of devils."

'I reckon Luke did feel riled. Wal, don't

182

worry, Miss Hallie. His bark is wuss than his bite."

Jud sang out: "Somebody spread a tarp to eat on an' pile on some wood so we can see."

Lonesome appeared to help Lenta out of the burdensome slicker.

"I sure was sorry I had to be so rude before you girls," he said gallantly. "But that Slim Red fellar was too windy."

"Lonesome, I could have shrieked when you slugged him," cried Lenta, ecstatically.

"Dog-gone!" murmured Lonesome, astounded at this amazing speech. Even Harriet could not reprove her young and impulsive sister. Things were happening, multiplying. The rain has ceased. A few white stars shown through a rift in swiftly moving clouds. The air had grown lighter and colder.

Fragrance of fried ham, hot coffee, and bread acquainted Harriet with the meaning of one of her queer sensations. She had never felt half starved before. It also acquainted her with the fact that the rest of the Lindsays were in the same condition. Lame and stiff, still wet and bedraggled, they flopped down round the tarpaulin with a heartiness that was a crowning surprise of the day. They had been crushed by disappointment, overcome

183

with fatigue and cold, frightened by the rude visitors. Yet they could eat.

Laramie Nelson loomed out of the shades to gaze down on them with his penetrating eyes.

"Wal, yu see how good a fire is when yu're froze an' grub when yu're hungry," he drawled. "I reckon none of yu ever knowed before."

"Nelson, there's something in what you say," replied Lindsay.

"Ahuh. Yu're shore a turrible sick man – the way yu're pitchin' into Jud's grub," returned Nelson, humorously. "But the best after this killin' ride will be when yu stretch out in warm soft blankets with a hot stone at yore feet. The boys air spreadin' yore beds now. Miss Hallie, I'm advisin' yu girls to sleep three in a bed. Leastways we're makin' only one bed for yu. I reckon Miss Lenta, bein' the kid of the family, should have the middle. But we'll fix bags an' things all about so the bugs, rats, mice, bats, snakes, centipedes, tarantulas an' such cain't find yu. Ha! Ha!"

"Oh mercy!" cried Lenta. "Once in my life I accept being the kid of this family. I'll sleep between Flo and Hallie."

"Mr. Nelson, why not tell us the very

worst, so we can die promptly?" said Mrs. Lindsay, resignedly.

"You can't – faze me – Nelson," retorted Lindsay, his mouth full of victuals.

"Boss, I knowed yu was a real pioneer at heart. What I come particular to tell yu is this. I've found three dry store-rooms at the gate end of the house. Two of 'em full of wood. Wal, we'll move that wood an' clean 'em out an' pack the supplies from the wagons in there temporary. Then I'll send five or six of the wagons back for the rest of our loads, an' more lumber. We want glass, putty, paint, an' a lot of things we forgot. It'd be better to pay cash, for when yu run up accounts these storekeepers charge more. Besides, after this we'll do our buyin' at La Junta, which's only half as far. I reckon thet's about all. I'll call around later."

When Nelson had gone, the head of the family remarked: "Buffalo Jones vowed I'd find this Nelson fellow a veritable mountain of strength. I've begun to believe it."

"Dad *I* knew that the instant I clapped eyes on him," observed Neale, with a superior air.

"He's the most wonderful man I ever met in my whole life," declared Lenta.

Harriet felt it would be justice to add her little to the encomiums being distributed, but somehow she could not. Nelson inhibited her, alienated her. To be sure, besides being a fighting-man – which antagonized her – he was a jack-of-all-trades. For that matter all these Westerners appeared to be singularly efficient when it came to necessary physical things. Harriet had observing eyes, and she gave due credit. She would not have admitted just then that the trait she approved of most in Nelson was his thoughtful economy on behalf of her father.

The girls ate prodigiously, but did not remain long away from the fire. "Hallie, let's toast ourselves brown and then run to our triple bed," suggested Lenta.

"Where is it?" queried Hallie.

"Must be on the other side."

Just then Lonesome came ambling along from across the court.

"Clearin' off fine an' cold, gurls," he said, cheerily.

"Where's our boudoir?" asked Lenta.

"Say, was that somethin' we packed at Garden City?" he asked, scratching his head.

"I mean our bed," replied Lenta, with a giggle.

"Right across there. We built a fire in front. An' we wrapped hot rocks in clean burlap sacks, so your dainty tootsies won't get soiled. You'll be as snug as three little

186

bugs in a sheepskin rug. It'll be rippin' cold in the mornin', though. Better sleep late, till the sun gets goin'."

"I won't get up atall," sallied Lenta, as the rider went on.

"Let's walk up and down," suggested Florence, her eager dark eyes roaming everywhere, to linger on dark forms round Jud's fire. Harriet calculated that Florence had a severe case. She had cases periodically, but never had her eyes shone with such an intent, hungry, uncertain light.

"All right, let's walk," agreed Harriet. So arm in arm the three limped and dragged themselves across the court, found their bed most carefully made and protected, and went on to the dark gateway, beyond which they were afraid to venture. But Hallie said: "We're three tenderfeet, all right. Suppose we were thrown upon our own resources?"

"Ridiculous, Hallie!" ejaculated Flo.

"It'd be great fun – if we could survive," responded Lenta, dreamily.

"For shame. Are you both going to be dependent upon men? Well *I'm* not," declared Harriet, and to prove it she ventured boldly out into the darkness. Her sisters, not to be shamed or else too scared to stay alone, joined her and they walked out beyond the protection of the walls.

A few stars were showing, by the light of which black clouds could be seen scudding across the sky. The air stung Harriet's cheeks and ears; the wind swept by strong and pure, redolent of great spaces; somewhere off in the darkness there was a roar like the sound of trees in a storm. But for that bleak, black, stone house the place seemed empty, a vast windy hall of the night.

"Let's go back. We might bump into that Slim Red. Wasn't he a devil?" said Lenta.

"Listen," replied Flo, nervously.

Off at a distance short wild barks sounded. "Coyotes," affirmed Hallie. "We've heard them every night. I almost like them."

"No. This was different. You know how a hound bays in the dead of night when death has come to some one?" whispered Florence. "It was a little like that – only infinitely more.... Oh! there!"

Hallie's ears were smote by a clear, cold, low-withdrawing mournful wail, like nothing she had ever heard. It curdled her blood.

"That can't be a dog. It's a wild animal," she whispered.

"Sounded far away, thank goodness. Let's sneak in like the tenderfeet we are.... But oh, it's strange and wonderful!"

"What is? That mournful beast? Ughh!"

188

"Just everything. But how glad I am my sisters are with me."

Lenta at rare intervals expressed a note of the child that still survived in her. They groped their way back to where the light shone from the gateway and went in. Mr. Lindsay was still up, talking and coughing, to his wife's despair. He scarcely had time to answer the girls' good-night. He seemed tremendously excited, which rather augmented the impression of frailty which clung to him.

"If he goes into pneumonia!" whispered Lenta, her big eyes dark with fear. "What Doctor Hurd always fought against!"

"Don't say such things, Lent," responded Florence, shuddering. "It would be dreadful! ... Way out here in this wilderness. After all we've given up!"

"Girls, I really don't understand how we ever got here," said Harriet, solemnly. "But we *are* here – in the hands of God and these Westerners."

They crawled over the ramparts of bags which surrounded their bed, and with whispers and laughs and starts they removed their heavy buskins and stiff clothes. Harriet's stockings were still wet, her feet still cold. Heroically she crawled under the blankets on her side and wearily stretched out, with the feeling that she would never move again. Suddenly her cold wet feet came in contact with something hot. Then she remembered.

"Oh – heavenly!" she murmured.

"Isn't it just?" returned Lenta, snuggling close and lovingly. "Do you know, Hallie, I'm just finding you out. You're a deep old darling. Isn't she, Flo?"

"Who's darling?" asked Florence, dreamily.

"Well, I don't mean that black-haired, gimlet-eyed Adonis," burst out Lenta, and she gave Hallie a significant hug.

"Shut up and go to sleep, Lent Lindsay," rejoined Flo, languorously.

"Sleep! Not for hours.... Oh, Hallie, hasn't it been an adventure? I'm just daffy.... I like these Western fellows, Hallie. They can *do* things. They're so easy, slow, cool, and somehow... I don't trust that Lonesome. He's just what that Slim Red called him. I was sorry for Slim. Didn't he get an awful wallop in the tummy? It actually hurt me. Mr. Mulhall may be little, but he's mighty. I'll bet he's a lot of things.... But Laramie – he's the wonderful man! I could certainly love him."

"Child, don't talk such nonsense," remonstrated Harriet.

"I'm talking sense, Hallie. But if you want me to be sentimental and weave a fairy story, here goes.... Dad will get well and strong, like I remember when I was a kid. He'll wax rich and powerful on this range and Spanish Peaks Ranch will grow famous far and wide. For the hospitality of its hostess – dear old mom, who always had a weakness to entertain, to show off, to play the grand lady. And famous for the beauty and charm of its three fair daughters, ahem!... Flo will elope with Ted Williams and they'll come back like turtle-doves. Then his wealthy family will find him out and will be reconciled to him, and adore his lovely Flo, and beseech them to go East to live on Ted's inheritance. Ted will take the inheritance for Flo's sake, but will only go back home on visits.... And I – I will play the merry devil with these gawky range-riders, until retribution overtakes me and I am scared stiff or stung by remorse for my heart-breaking ways, or worse – I fall really in love with some homely bow-legged vociferous little giant.... And as for you, Hallie – oh, you're the cream of this outfit. They will find you out, these long-legged, still-eyed nice cattlemen and will come a-riding and a-wooing. But you will not be easily won. You will break more hearts than your wicked little sister. And you will inflame
191

such men as Arlidge and rustlers, bandits –
until your own Laramie, our desperado,
wades through blood to – to –"

Lenta's voice trailed off and she dropped
into the land of her dreams.

Harriet lay awake, gratefully aware of
Lenta's warm cheek and trustful hand in
hers, and of the fitful firelight on the walls,
the cold stars blinking, and moving clouds,
the moaning wind, and the wild voices of the
beasts of the night.

She wanted to think over the last day of
their never-to-be forgotten ride, and
especially of their arrival at the monstrous
place that had to be made home, and of what
had already transpired. But physical
sensations dominated her. No longer were
her feet dead weights of ice, but living,
glowing, tingling members of her anatomy!
She felt a drowsy fullness of the well-fed
animal. The cold wind that whipped in
rather invigorated than otherwise. The fire
crackled, blazed up, died down, and always
there was that steady musical murmuring of
flowing water in her ears. Voices, too, came
dully, and an occasional rasp or bump, and
the grate of wheels. After a while all these
sensations went blank.

When Harriet opened her eyes she saw
azure-blue sky behind a great rounded thin

mass of cottonwood foliage, still tiny leafed and delicately green. Wonderingly she asked herself where she was. And instantly she knew, though all appeared different.

Lenta lay wrapped in deep slumber, purring like a kitten, her cheeks rosy, her hair tousled. Florence likewise was asleep, and more beautiful even than in wakeful hours. Her opal-hued face was turned toward Lenta, and she had a hand under her cheek. Her long black lashes hid her dreams and contrasted wonderfully with her golden hair. Never had Hallie been so stirred by Lenta's dependency or Florence's beauty. Soon these beloved sisters would awaken to this new life in the West and they were going to need their elder sister. Hallie prayed that she would not fail them.

The sun was high in the heavens and dazzlingly bright. There appeared to be a bustling activity around the courtyard, punctuated by a sing-song rollicking voice and the sound of hammers. Hallie felt ashamed that she had not been up to help initiate the home-building. But as she essayed to move she got a twing like a stab of a blade. That roused her combativeness and she manfully struggled out of bed, careful not to awaken her sisters. With boots and coat in hand she crawled over the bags to get outside. There she espied a nice little fire of red coals, boiling water in a queer black iron pot, shiny tin basins on a slab of rock, and a bucket of water.

"Thoughtful of somebody," soliloquized Hallie, and she gazed around the strange courtyard, at the upheaved mound of boulders in the center, at the magnificent old cottonwoods, and the gray walls of stone above the slanting remains of wooden roofs. She heard Jud whistling over in his cook-shack, and she smelled things that instantly made her hungry. She had forgotten the bag that contained her toilet articles, so she crawled back to get it, this time disturbing Lenta, who murmured, "Don't leave me, Hallie."

In a few moments Hallie had put on her skirt, stockings, boots, had washed her face and brushed her hair, after which she made haste to warm her hands over the fire. She had neglected to use the hot water. At this juncture Lonesome came along. Without his woolly chaps he appeared smaller and his bow-legs were less prominent. His smile positively eliminated his homeliness.

"Mornin', Miss Hallie. I sure am glad to see you up. Near on to ten o'clock! You should see the work we've done, Wagons on the way back to town, wood all stacked outside, stores packed, an' now we're stowin' away furniture an' such. That Laramie Nelson is a wonder, once he gets goin'. An' I never seen him goin' so good."

"Good-morning, Lonesome. I think you all must be wonders. Thanks awfully for the fire and water. You are very thoughtful."

Lonesome scratched his head dubiously, so that his sombrero tilted.

"Dog-gone-it, I wisht I'd been that thoughtful. But no use lyin'. You got Laramie to thank.... How're your sisters ridin' this mornin' – I mean, feelin'? Sure they're awake? It's powerful late, an' I want to give you a hunch. Jud is the best ever, but he hates to keep meals hot."

"I'll look," replied Hallie, and took a peep over the rampart of bags. Flo was indeed wrapped in slumber, but Hallie had a suspicion that Lenta was only pretending. Her flushed face bore too innocent a cast.

"They're asleep, lazy girls," replied Hallie. "Take a peek, Lonesome. Aren't they the babes in the woods?"

Lonesome rested his hands on the bars and slowly, as if impelled beyond his bashful fears, peered over. It certainly was a picture that greeted his eyes – Florence in her exquisite beauty and Lenta so young, so fresh, so rosy and innocent. Lonesome drew back as if his gaze were sacrilege.

"My Gawd! To think the West is goin' to have two such girls!... An' you, too, Miss Hallie.... It just ought to make honest men out of a lot of no-good range-riders!" And wagging his head he slouched back across the court, a queer, funny, sturdy, somehow impressive little figure. Hallie found herself liking him, hoping for him, with a birth of what must have been maternal interest.

"Lent. Wake up," she called.

"Ah-huh.... Wh-e-re – am I? – Ooooo?"

"The world has changed over-night.... Florence. Wake up."

"Oh-h! – Is that you, Hallie?" replied Flo, in her lazy contralto.

"Yes. Get up. Your night of dreams is over."

"Lord! Did I talk in my sleep?"

"Did you? – Well, you had better be good.... Nice little fire out here, and hot water."

Hallie found her mother stirring, vastly a different being from the preceding night. "Morning, daughter," she said, brightly. "Isn't the sun gorgeous. How thankful I am! What do you think? Father is still sleeping like a baby. And he did not cough one single time!"

"Oh, I'm glad," cried Harriet, and stepped up on to the porch to take a peep at him. How pale and drawn he looked – how quiet!

"Last night after you went to bed that Nelson man came over and said: 'Boss, heah's a drink me an' Jud fixed up for yu. We'll have yu understand we don't do this for everybody. Drink this firewater, go to bed, an' in the mawnin' yu'll have hair on yore chest!' "

All Harriet could ejaculate was, "Well!"

"They didn't happen to see me, as I was in the wagon. Father grinned, and taking the thing – it was a good-sized dipper – he said, 'Here's to my foreman and cook!' And he drank it down, quick, as if he had an idea it would be unpleasant. It must have been some kind of explosive; you never heard such splutterings. Father gasped: 'My God! what was that?' And Mr. Nelson replied: 'Just a little dose Jud an' I brewed. No man never needs but one.' "

"Mother, do you suppose it could have been a trick?" queried Harriet, in shocked voice. "These Westerners are not to be trusted."

"I don't care what it was," declared Mrs. Lindsay. "The blessed truth is John never coughed a single time last night. Think of that!...Hallie, come out of your old shell. These Westerners may be sudden and rough. But they've won me."

"Mother, I – I'm glad of that, too," faltered Harriet, in her surprise.

"Look at your brother. Neale Lindsay! Up with the sun! Breakfast long ago! Working for hours, crippled as he is!"

"Indeed! Miracles are happening. What, forsooth, induced all this astounding transformation?"

"I don't know, unless it was that Nelson man, who gave Neale a dig, waking him. 'Pile out, son. The day's busted. I'm countin' on yu a lot. Yu see there's only yu, me, Ted an' Lonesome, beside Jud, an' we got a man's job on hand, mebbe includin' a fight with this Arlidge outfit. So buckle on yore gun an' line up with us.'"

"Mercy!" gasped Harriet.

"Hallie, that was my first thought," replied Mrs. Lindsay. "I had to choke back a scream. I've always babied Neale. And I vowed, after that lecture John gave me in Garden City, I'd never baby him again. It almost kills me to think of – Neale sweating, swearing, fighting maybe, drinking and smoking, with these Wild Westerners. But I've had an illumination of mind. This Nelson is not what he looks. You can't fool me on men. He's a godsend. He'll cure your father and make a man of your brother."

"God bless him, then," murmured Harriet, with emotion, not all of which was surprise and gratitude.

Her sense of fairness, as well as an eagerness to pass on anything hopeful, prompted her to go back to the girls and tell them, word for word, what her mother had said.

"How perfectly splendid!" exclaimed Florence, her eyes flashing magnificently.

"*What* did I tell you, Hal Lindsay?" burst out Lenta.

But Harriet fled down the court, laughingly calling back that she would meet them at breakfast presently. She crossed to the mound of boulders. Old flagstones, worn hollow in the center by years of footsteps, led winding up to an open space, at the back of which from under great mossy rocks flowed the most marvelous spring Hallie had ever seen. It was a fountain. What a tremendous volume of sparkling water! Where it flowed from the well to a deep pool, before it took its first leap, there was a faint bluish, cloudy cast to the water. She wondered what caused that. An aged green drinking-cup, iron, she thought, hung on a chain. Hallie dipped it in the spring and lifted it to drink. Cold as ice! Tasteless, pure as the rain from heaven! She gazed around. Flagstones and moss, boulders and the spreading cottonwoods all betokened age. Straightaway she fell in love with that place, and Laramie's extravagant hyperbole came back to her. But was it hyperbole? She followed the little brook by the stepping-stones that kept pace with the miniature waterfalls, down to the courtyard, and out of the gateway. There she became aware of the labor going on at that end of the court. But she did not pause to look. The open called her. What would greet her outside that wide portal?

She expected to see a bleak barren gray waste of land. She forgot that a fog of rain and snow had obscured the landscape for the whole of the two days' journey into Colorado. Wherefore she was not prepared for grass and green growths which escorted the brook in its evident leap down a hill. Harriet paused. How brilliant the sunlight! How cold, sweet, intoxicating the air! Frost glistened like diamonds on rocks near by, on the long grass. Just to the right of the gateway a road led out toward a brushy ridge, beyond which she could not see. Directly in front of her there appeared to be a gulf that ran on into the blue of sky. She gazed mystified. Was she standing upon a mountain top? Below the blue the dim gray shapes and streaks took form, until it dawned upon her that the streaked gray must be land – distant range on range.

Whereupon Harriet strode out along the brook to the verge where it leaped down with murmur and splash. There was unconscious defiance in her action. By some strange circumstances she had not yet seen any extensive or formidable section of the West. Only monotonous Kansas prairie lands from the window of a railroad coach!

Suddenly the ground fell away from her feet. A V-shaped gully, all grass-benched and thicket-sloped, opened before her, to widen and descend to a colorful valley that spread out to merge into purple range. Pastures full of cattle, and log-fenced bare spots of land, and cabins nestling among the cottonwoods, and a silver stream winding parallel with a yellow road, arrested her gaze while seeming to lead it onward to an immensity of space out there. But Harriet attended to what lay close at hand and intimate enough to grasp. This valley constituted part of the ranch. Harriet had to concede its astounding fertility, beauty, and tranquility. Cows were mooing, calves were bawling, horses were neighing, and above all sounded a raucous bray. A rollicking masculine voice, young and strong, floated up from the green. She saw a mounted rider cross an open patch. Beyond the valley spread the range, rolling and purple, ridged and swaled, dotted with cattle in the foreground and gradually merging into boundless expanse. League upon league stretched down to what she realized was the descent to the Great Plains. She was confounded. No landscape had ever approached this. It drawfed Lake Erie from the highest hill. She began dimly to grasp its meaning.

To south and north stretched infinitude, the same purple sea of rolling verdure, on and on to uneven horizon. Her view of the west was obstructed by the wide stone structure. So she walked back to the gateway, crossed the brook, and went on to the opposite corner.

Gray-sloped, twin-peaked, snow-capped mountains apparently loomed right over her. These must be the Spanish Peaks from which the ranch derived its name. They were her first sight of high mountains and the effect seemed stunning. But they were only a beginning. Beyond rose a wall of black and white which she had imagined was cloud. Suddenly she realized that she was gazing at the magnificent eastern front of the Rocky Mountains. Pure and white, remote and insurmountable, rose the glistening peaks high into the blue sky, and then extended, like the teeth of a saw, beyond her range of vision.

Harriet stared. Greater than amaze and ecstasy something had birth in her. The thing she had waited for all her life seemed to be coming – the awakening of a deeper elementary self. A vague, sweet, intangible feeling of familiarity smote her. But where and when could she ever have seen such a glorious spectacle? Perhaps pictures haunted her. This scene, however, was vivid, real, marvelous, elevating. Lonely and wild and grand – this Colorado!

She put a hand to her breast. And on the moment, startling to her, she remembered Emery and the blighted romance of her early twenties. Strange that she thought of it then, and stranger that she was not loth to do so! How long ago and far away! The millions of wheel-turnings that had fetched her here seemed to have lengthened the past, as well as the distance back to the old home. In that moment Harriet realized poignantly how the old home and all which pertained to it belonged to the past. Here began a new life. Deep in her heart a sore and hidden knot swelled and seemed to burst with a pang. This pain was release. It had come to her from these far-off glooming mountains, so vast, so apparently eternal. The strength she had prayed for flowed to her mysteriously. Her ailing father, her mother, the dreamy Florence and the coquettish Lenta, and Neale, callow, vain, overindulged but still with good in him – how they all would need her, and how desperately she would need strength! It was there. She sensed it in the purple beckoning range and in this up-flung white-capped world. Her heart went out to meet them. Something before unknown welled up in her.

Tears dimmed Harriet's eyes and shrouded the scene, and she walked out into the open lest some one pass to notice her. Stunted little trees that looked as if they had endured hardships to survive grew there, and grass, and a fragrant gray bush pleasant to the eye, and tiny pink-blossomed flowers, and everywhere gray stones large and small. Harriet sat down. When her sight cleared she was further surprised to see that the whole panorama had subtly changed and was, if anything, more arresting and beautiful. The magnitude of the West thus unfolded to her gaze, the tremendous sense of solitude, distance, wildness, and loneliness all grew with every moment of watching. And all of a sudden she felt glad that they had come, for their own sakes now, as well as her father's.

From where she sat the house appeared a rough-walled portholed fort, as indeed it must have been during the Indian days. It could never be made a thing of beauty on the outside, but within there were limitless possibilities. She returned to the courtyard, with courage now to look about the inside and to speculate upon what could be made of it. Before she got far, however, Lonesome Mulhall hailed her.

"Lady, everybody's been callin' you. Jud's roarin' how he'll throw the ham an' eggs out if you don't come."

Harriet replied gaily that she would run, and she did, not, however, without becoming aware of muscle-bound and stiff legs. The girls did not greet her, for the reason that they were too gastronomically busy. Her father sat up, attended by her mother, and he asked: "Hallie, where have you been?"

"Good-morning, father," she replied. "I have been seeing Colorado for the first time. And once was enough!"

"What for? I'd hoped against hope you –"

"Enough to fall in love with it," she interrupted. The girls laughed incredulously, to the peril of choking over their food. Her

205

father brightened perceptibly. He looked worn to exhaustion.

"Hallie, Jud left your breakfast on the fire. He's a funny little fellow. Fussed and fumed because you girls didn't get up early. Says Nelson was a slave-driver and that it was tough to be blacksmith, carpenter, mason, wagon-builder, and I don't remember what else, besides being cook. I'm bound to admit he can cook. And clean as any housekeeper!"

While Harriet was verifying her mother's praise, and agreeing with it, Nelson came up to them with some kind of a tool in hand. He was in his shirt sleeves and he still wore the ugly gun bumping his thigh. What a lithe, virile man he looked, young too, in the morning light, and Hallie had to acknowledge, singularly attractive! She hardly recognized in this genial, smiling man the sinister one of last night.

"Mawnin" girls. It shore is good to see yu up again. I was afraid maybe yu was daid," he drawled. "An' how yu ridin', boss?" he inquired of Lindsay.

"Not so good, Nelson. Sit down and talk a little," replied the other. "I slept like a log, though. Never coughed once. But this morning my breast hurts and my ears ring. And my legs feel dead."

"Nothin' but the altitude. Yu see it's plumb high heah. Thet'll pass, boss."

Mrs. Lindsay intercepted her husband as he was about to reply: "Nelson, I'll tell you if he won't. It's worry as much as ill health that's pulled him down."

"I reckon," replied the rider, solicitously. "Wal, there's nothin' to worry about now, Lindsay. Yu're heah an' in pretty good shape, considerin'."

"I believe I am, by jingo!" rejoined Lindsay, who manifestly could not resist Nelson's persuasive speeches. "I ought to have croaked, if all Doc Hurd and our friends prophesied had come true. Honest, Mon, I'd feel free – if I wasn't scared, or worried. It's just wonderful to be here."

Mr. Laramie, why isn't there anything for father – or me – to worry about?" asked Harriet, seriously.

"Wal, I'm not so shore about you, Miss Harriet," he drawled. " 'Cause yu're a young an' handsome tenderfoot of the opposite sex from all the punchers, riders, an' rustlers who infest this country. They're shore not goin' to let grass grow under their hawses' feet, makin' up to yu. An' I just cain't guess how yu'll stand under thet."

The merry laugh rang out at Harriet's expense, and her absurd blush made it worse.

"Don't let me worry *you*, Mr. Laramie," retorted Harriet. "I can look after myself. I was thinking of father, his health and the business end of ranching."

"If yu please I cain't abide bein' called Mister," rejoined Nelson. "Wal, heah's what Lonesome just said to me. An' I shore can recommend it. 'Dog-gone, Laramie,' says Lonesome, 'if our Lindsay outfit can only see this deal yore way, why, it'll come out fine.'"

"Very well, Laramie, I am almost convinced myself," replied Lindsay. "Explain what this way is that Lonesome places such store upon."

Instantly the rider sobered a little and his eyes took on their usual piercing light. Harriet divined that his spirit leaped at an opportunity, for them as well as for himself and comrades.

"About yu first, sir. Yu air not so sick a man as yu think. I've seen many a man twice as bad off as yu come out cured an' strong. Thet was in Nebraskie, which is shore not so wonderful as Colorado to put men back on their feet. . . . Now listen, boss. Forget trouble, loss, health, but take an interest. Rest a lot, but keep goin'. Sleep outdoors. Breathin' this sage an' mountain air all the time, livin' out in the sun – why, it'll cure yu.

There's a Mexican down in the valley. He raises all kinds of fruit an' vegetables. He raises chickens, geese, turkeys, pigs. An' cows, say, there's a hundred milk cows. Shore he's in yore employ an' yu will live on the fat of the land."

"Laramie, I feel a well man already. I'll follow your advice absolutely," declared Lindsay, earnestly.

"Wal, thet's fine. Now about the business of ranchin'. Take an interest, shore, but don't worry. If Miss Hallie has been yore manager an' bookkeeper back in Ohio, she shore can fill the job heah. Anyone can see that she's smarter'n a man. It'd take more than Allen an' Arlidge to cheat her. An' they shore cheated yu, Mr. Lindsay, how bad I cain't reckon yet. But pretty bad. Let me handle the men an' the stock. Miss Hallie can handle the money. I'll guarantee we could make this ranch pay if we started *now* without a dollar, an' with only half the cattle I see out there on pasture. I know cattle. I know riders an' rustlers. I can handle both. This ain't no blowin' my horn. Once for all I want yu to know thet. All my life I've wanted a chance like this. It's the finest range I ever saw. We can run a hundred thousand haid of cattle heah despite the rustlers. Course I'm allowin' for the usual run an' work of thet breed. This mawnin' I went below, after the wagons left, an' I looked about. Allen's outfit of nine riders were there, but Arlidge had gone. I reckon he did some tall thinkin' last night. Anyway, I figgered he'd do just thet. Shore he could have taken these riders away, most of them, at least, but he thought better of thet, an' for reasons I've got a hunch about. Some of these nine riders air no good, we can gamble on thet. An' some others, maybe four or five of them, air or can be made faithful cowmen. It won't take long for me to do thet. Then we'll be ridin' pretty."

"Laramie, I feel tremendously encouraged – after being way down," replied Lindsay, heartily. "Hallie, don't you feel the same?"

"I think Nelson has a gift to inspire," responded Harriet, gravely. It was impossible not to trust this Westerner, to feel his fire and force.

"If my daughter agrees, it is settled," concluded Lindsay.

Laramie's lean bronze face took on a dusky red. Probably it was a tremendous issue for him to have his chance hang upon a woman's judgment. Harriet felt keenly for him, but all that she had of intuition and judgment were exercised in behalf of her father. As she met Laramie's eyes they lost something of their piercing intensity, that eagle-look of

210

pride, in a softening appeal which she trusted. He might be a blood-spiller, this cool, easy, drawling Southerner, but he was honest and he had her father's interest at heart. Harriet felt a reluctance to association, even in the most impersonal business way, with a man notorious for his skill with a gun, for his killings. She struggled for the common sense she prided herself upon. She could not foster Eastern ideals upon this crude wild West. It might well be that only such a man as Laramie Nelson could bring success out of disaster. She had a glimmering that, out of gratefulness to him already, would rise something even stranger, perhaps respect. She endeavoured to face the West with open mind.

"I agree, father," she said, with finality. "I will work with Nelson."

"Thanks, miss," returned Nelson, somewhat huskily. "I hope I can live up to yore trust."

"I hope and pray *I* do not make a mess of ranching," said Harriet, fervently. "Now – where do we begin?"

"With the house heah," answered Nelson. "There's shore a lot of work. My idee is to have Fork Mayhew, who was the rider thet spoke up for himself an' pards last night – I'll have them herd the cattle pretty close in, while I put the rest of the outfit to work heah with us. Then I'll take a ride out occasionally or send Lonesome an' Tracks. An' thet reminds me, boss. Do you happen to have a spyglass?"

"I brought both a telescope and field glass. Both presents to me. Didn't know what to do with the darned things, so I packed them."

"Good!" The rider rubbed his strong brown hands together. "We can sweep the whole range from the wall, an' also see a lot of what's goin' on below, without anyone seein' us. Shore I'm suspicious. Don't overlook thet.... The place I've picked out for yore office, Miss Hallie, couldn't be beat. It's next to the gate on the left side. All stone walls, with heavy log door thet'd have to be chopped or burned. It's got a large porthole front an' back, which cut out some will do fine for windows. We've cleaned this all up spick an' span. Nice stone floor. We'll whitewash the walls, build in shelves, a desk, table, an' whatever else yu want. In another day or two yu can move all yore papers, valuables, money, an' such in there an' lock the door with a feelin' yu cain't be robbed."

"How you anticipate my wants!" exclaimed Harriet, warmly. The man was perplexing her with his practical suggestions.

"Shore, an' thet ain't nothin'," returned Nelson, visibly pleased. "Lonesome has got some wonderful idees, but he won't tell me. Says he wants the credit himself.... Wal, it's work now. Yu folks camp out right heah till we get the rooms done, one by one. Girls, any bags or trunks yu need just point out to us an' we'll lug them over to yore camp."

"But we'd better not unpack much until we have rooms all fixed up, new and clean," replied Harriet, dubiously.

"Shore not. An' yu-all better go the rounds with me to pick out just which of these stalls yu want for rooms. There air four big stone fireplaces with chimneys goin' up through the walls, an' thet is shore one grand thing for this ranch-house. It'll get cold as blue blazes, but with plenty of wood yu'll never know it's winter.... Now, folks, I'd like to make a suggestion."

"Nelson, you can't make too many suggestions to suit us," declared Lindsay.

"Wal, unfortunately, these heah stone fireplaces are not close together. I didn't count this one Jud is usin'. Come to look about, this would make a first-rate kitchen. Wal, suppose we fix up the next stall with fireplace as a sittin'-room for yu, Lindsay an' Mrs. Lindsay, with a door leadin' into the next stall, which can be made into a bedroom. If yu want we can haul in a wood stove for thet, an' for all bedrooms. Yore son Neale has already picked his on this side. Those stalls – or rooms, I reckon I should call them, for they shore were rooms before cattlemen ran horses in heah – across on the other wing are bigger than these. Fifteen by thirty feet. Thet's a big room. It'll take a lot of lumber, paint, an' such to make them comfortable for all yore furniture, rugs, an' nice things. It's good I bought chisels an' mauls. Else we'd had he – hail Columbia cuttin' the portholes into windows."

"Come on, Laramie," cried Lenta, breaking her long rapt silence. "Help me pick a big room for Hallie and me, with a sitting-room next, where we'll have a fireplace."

"Shore. An' where will yore other sister be?" rejoined Nelson, smiling.

"I'd like to be next to them. But I'm not afraid to be alone," replied Florence.

"Strikes me funny," laughed Mrs. Lindsay. "Here we are cooped in an old fort and planning offices, bedrooms, sitting-rooms. It's just rich. I'll have you all know that I want a parlor, a reception-room, a library."

"Ha! Ha! Where you can entertain our numerous neighbors," exclaimed Harriet

214

gaily. "Wait, mother dear, till you have a long look at our neighborhood."

"Wal, thet's about all, I reckon. No, I forgot somethin'," went on Nelson, turning to Lindsay once more. "Where would yu want me an' Lonesome an' Tracks to bunk, sir?"

"Not far away, that's certain," declared Lindsay, bluntly.

"Wal, so we figgered, leastways til yu-all get broke in to the West."

"Laramie, *I* would like you boys to camp right in that gate, at nighttime, anyhow," asserted Lenta, vigorously.

"Wal, it'd never do to tell Lonesome thet," drawled Nelson, with a grin. "He'd be unrollin' his tarp under yore front door. Come on, girls. Pick out yore rooms an' then I'll go back to work."

Chapter 8

Harriet pondered over her ledger and her diary, and she could have wept at the entries there. But the fact that kept back her tears, that made her rejoice in spite of all, was the truth about her father. After spending a week flat upon his back, during which he appeared to sink toward the verge, he had gotten up and stayed up, to the despair of his family. Then had come what Harriet believed one of his short improved spells that, like the others, would soon end, leaving him worse than ever. But this last time there was no relapse. And now six weeks had gone by! She could doubt no longer. He was on the mend. The high cool dry air of Colorado, with its wonderful quality to restore, had saved him. And that was enough. That was what they had all come West for, worked and endured and prayed for. Harriet wondered why she could not be unutterably happy and humbly grateful. But she was. She might not be able to show it like her mother, who cared for nothing except her husband's recovery; or Florence, whose dreams had magnified in this

216

benign environment; or Lenta, who adored everything and everybody, particularly the riders, around their new home; or Neale, who rode bucking broncos, or tried to ride them, and otherwise gravitated toward the life of the range. Nevertheless, Harriet knew that in her heart she was as deeply thankful as any of them. Only somebody had to run the ranch, and that devolving upon her, was a nightmare.

It was mid-June. She could look through the open iron-barred window of her cool stone-walled office down upon the green ranch and out upon the purple range. The air was full of dry sweet fragrance; flowers waved in the prairie grass; flocks of blackbirds swirled in clouds over the tilled fields and verdant pastures; the brook that had its source in the cottonwoods of the courtyard sang by her open door and crashed musically over the rocks down into the valley. If she chose she could step out and climb the stone steps to the ramparts of the old fort, and from there see a panorama of ever-changing mountains, ever-growing in magnificence, ever strengthening in her trails.

A month of such labor as Harriet had never seen equaled had transformed the interior of the old fort to a unique, spacious, comfortable and even luxurious home, and the courtyard, with its great cottonwoods, its mossy boulders and welling spring, into a shady, beautiful bower, which inspired rest and happiness.

Laramie Nelson had been the genius of this work. Early and late he had slaved at it, driving his faithful partners to their limit, and somehow extracting service out of Arlidge's uncertain outfit. The debt of the Lindsays to Laramie Nelson could never be paid, yet it kept growing in what seemed to Harriet leaps and bounds.

Wherefore, then, had she any cause to be unhappy? Was this longing, half-bitter, frustrating burden a real or an imagined unhappiness? No shadow of the old heart-sickness had returned. That was past. But some new ill, secret and persistent, pervaded Harriet's soul.

For one thing, the affairs of the ranch, so far as cattle were concerned, were disheartening. According to Nelson's account, which he would not absolutely vouch for, Allen had left seven or eight thousand head of cattle, out of the ten thousand he received payment for, on the Peak Dot range. Of these more than four thousand head had been driven off by rustlers a few days before the Lindsays had arrived, and since then straggling bands, of a few head each, had disappeared. So that not many more than two thousand cattle remained, mostly cows and calves. All pertaining to this ranching business was amazing to Harriet; however, the fact that Nelson claimed he could find out where the stolen cattle had gone, but he could not recover them, surely had a good deal to do with Harriet's seeing her ledger all red. She concealed her gathering wrath. It had grown upon Harriet that Nelson, though un-questionably honest, concealed the worst from her. She could not tell, however, whether this had to do with the impossibility of raising cattle in that country without fighting rustlers, or of some complexity in the situation Allen had left behind, the smoothing out of which she herself un-consciously combated. She had given Nelson to understand once for all, if he was to stay on at Spanish Peaks Ranch, that he must not resort to bloodshed. Had she tied his hands? Something Lonesome had been overheard to say had disquieted Harriet. And it had begun to dawn upon her that she must be poorly equipped for the task imposed upon her.

Harriet's sense of duty and responsibility, as much as her pride, fired her to an ambition to succeed at ranching. She had been no small factor in her father's success as a ship-chandler back on Lake Erie. He had still considerable means, but Harriet looked forward to the time when they could live on their ranching income. At the present day, however, that desirable contingency seemed far remote. According to Nelson the herd needed to be added to, built up, and guarded before it could command an income, but there was no sense in that until the rustlers moved away from Colorado or died of old age.

"They shore never will die with their boots on," Nelson had concluded, with a hint of sarcasm.

That was the grave situation in regard to the main issue – cattle-raising. For the rest there were a number of perturbing developments for Harriet to cope with.

Nelson had been able to hold the Allen outfit of riders together until one and all of them had caught a glimpse of Lenta on a horse – then, according to the disgruntled Lonesome, "the dinged sons-of-guns couldn't be druv off."

Lenta's reaction to the wild West was not wholly unexpected, although not even Harriet had seen the abandon with which the girl threw herself into everything around the ranch, from work to play. No one could accuse Lenta of shirking her share of the manifold tasks of homemaking. Florence had confined herself to the things that concerned her own comfort, pleasure, and appeal. It was Lenta's play, however, that lay open to criticism, and which vastly concerned Harriet. Her mother could not see it and her father only laughed. Neale took exception to Lenta's carrying-on, as he termed it, which only added fuel to the flame. When Harriet was not worrying herself frantic for fear Lenta would be killed by a horse – the girl had already been thrown four times – or kidnapped, or worse, Harriet was rendered almost as desperate by her sister's flirtations.

Neale, too, presented a problem. He had amazed them all by his hitherto undeveloped ability to stick to hard work, as he had outraged them all, especially his mother, by his drinking and fighting. To be sure, Harriet guessed that Neale was not soley to blame for this. All these riders, even Nelson, had an itch to play tricks on tenderfeet, and Lonesome was the worst of the lot. That boy was as incorrigible as he was likable; moreover, it appeared that Neale and Lonesome did not hit it off well together.

Like wildfire the fame of Florence's beauty and Lenta's charm had spread over the range. For three Sundays now riders from all over had called at the ranch. Lindsay made them welcome and his wife indulged her passion to entertain. What a picturesque group these range-riders made! They had come to see and to be seen. Lean, youthful, intent faces, some of them clean and fine, many of them hard, a few of them sinister – how Harriet reveled in a study of them! So far as the beauty of the Lindsay family was concerned, however, these riders might better have stayed away, for Florence could not see anyone except Ted Williams. That fact had become patent, accepted by all about the ranch.

"Where do they all come from?" asked Harriet, in amaze. "This lonely wilderness! So many young men!"

"Wal, I reckon they come from all over," Nelson had replied. "An' some of them air rustlers an' hawse-thieves, Miss Hallie."

"Oh no! . . . Nelson, how can you say such things?" exclaimed Harriet, almost indignant. "They seem not at all different from own own riders."

"Wal, yu hit it plumb center. They shore ain't any different atall from ours," drawled Nelson, his light eyes, with their un-fathomable clearness, making Harriet uneasy. "An' I suppose yu even have a good word for Luke Arlidge?"

Nelson's dry tone had added to Harriet's embarrassment. She blushed, and that always annoyed her. No one else at the ranch had the power to bring the blood to her cheeks. It infuriated Harriet, and like a woman she sought to wound in return.

"Oh, Mr. Arlidge? Yes, I can say a good word for him. It seems he has parted with that disagreeableness he showed when we arrived. He's entertaining. Father likes him. And you know he doesn't want either Arlidge or Allen to be our enemies. And – we girls think Mr. Arlidge quite handsome – in a sort of bold and flashy way."

"Shore. Luke has a bold, flashy look all right. He'd look fine danglin' from a rope." And after that cool, inscrutable, almost insolent reply Nelson had turned on his heel, leaving Harriet repulsed and angry.

No one had to tell Harriet – as her sisters persisted in doing – that Arlidge visited Spanish Peaks Ranch to see her. He made that plain enough. And it annoyed rather than pleased Harriet. How silly that she should give Nelson a contrary impression! Women were complex and unfair. It troubled her a little that she might hurt Nelson's feelings – he to whom they owed so much. But she could not help it. On the two occasions of Arlidge's visits, however,

Harriet saw to it that he never got a moment alone with her.

Then there were many other lesser grievances or annoyances that helped to swell the total. One was a real dismay over Lonesome Mulhall's abject worship of Lenta. Harriet liked the boy. He was far from good, she supposed, but he was so many other contrasting things that it was impossible not to love him, almost. Lenta did not love him, that was certain, though she led him a dance no poor range-rider had ever endured before. Lonesome had constituted himself a champion of the Lindsays, even of Neale, who rubbed him the wrong way. His loyalty was beautiful, and in that way he resembled Nelson. But he was an unhappy wretch and persisted in confiding his woes to Harriet.

Another matter, inconsiderable yet perplexing, was the disappearance of innumerable articles of no particular value to anyone except the girls, that had been noted increasingly during the last few weeks. Some of these had been lost, of course, in transit, and some, no doubt, had been mislaid, but Harriet began to suspect others had been pilfered. She did not know whom to suspect, however, unless one of the several Mexican lads who lived below and were always hanging about the ranch.

A slow step and a tinkle of spurs interrupted Harriet's pondering. She recognized them with a little start and stir of lethargic nerves. Following a tap on the open door, she called, vaguely ashamed of her deceit: "Who is it? Come in."

Nelson entered. She had not seen him for three days, the lack of which now occurred blankly to her. Dust trailed off his riding-garb. He brought the dry odors of the range with him.

"Wal, howdy, Miss Hallie. Did you reckon I was daid?" he said.

"No, hardly that," she replied, laughing. "Sit down, Nelson. You look tired."

"Shore am. Rode in from Castle Haid this mawnin'."

"Castle Head? I remember Arlidge speaking of that place. Far off our range, isn't it?"

"Yes. It's on what Arlidge an' Allen call their range. Right about heah," replied Nelson, and reached over to put a finger on the crudely drawn up map about Harriet's desk.

"What were you doing way over there?"

"Wal, Ted lost his favorite hawse an' was trackin' him."

"That fiery little pinto. Did you find him?"

"Shore, we found him all right."

"Strayed?"

"Wal, we didn't notice much strayin'," drawled Nelson, which reply seemed to be one of his evasive ones.

"I suppose Ted is pleased," went on Harriet. "He lets Florence ride that pony. She has been complaining. It appears there are not many horses she can ride."

"Sorry to say Ted ain't pleased atall," corrected Nelson. "Yu see we found the hawse in a corral belongin' to a man named Snook. Found it with yore field-glass from the top of Castle Haid."

"Nelson, what are you driving at?" queried Harriet, suddenly.

"Miss Hallie, the hawse had been stolen," said Nelson, mildly. "An' I wouldn't let Tracks go down after him, 'cause he'd have shore shot Snook."

Here it came again – that relentless and insistent feature of the dual nature of the range. She could not escape it, nor the heat suddenly engendered in her veins.

"What will you do about it?" she demanded.

"What would you?"

"I'd go get the horse, without violence."

"How'd yu go about thet?"

"I'd ask Snook for it, assuming that he had kindly put the lost horse in his corral."

"Wal, thet might work if it was backed up by a gun. But I reckon we'd better not let Tracks go after his hawse."

"Will you go?"

"Yes, but not very soon. Yu see, I'd rather wait until Snook gets rid of some of the brand-burnt cattle we seen over there."

"Brand burnt? You explained that to me once, Nelson. What brand has been burnt?"

"Looked to me like the Peak Dot has been burned to a Triangle Cross.... Lend me yore pencil, Miss Hallie.... Like thet."

"Ah, I see. Very simple. So that is another way a rustler works?"

"Yes. We know it, but we cain't prove it, an' even if we could prove it we couldn't do nothin' about it."

"What a damnable outrage!" ejaculated Harriet. "We're to be robbed of our cattle without any redress whatever?"

"Law will be some time comin' to this range. I reckon yu'd better give up cattle-raisin', except what few yu could run in the valley. Yu could let most of us riders go, an' farm it for some years. Course thet would be losin' money. But as losin' stock is losin' money just the same, I reckon it'd be better."

"Let most of you riders go?" echoed Harriet, and by that she meant him.

"Shore. What else can yu do? I reckon it'd be foolish to waste money on riders when there's no ridin' for them to do. I'm shore I wouldn't want to stay myself."

"Laramie!"

The consternation in that word told Harriet vastly more than it told him. Nelson sat somber and downcast of eye.

"You would not leave me – us?" she floundered.

"Wal, no, if yu put any store on my stayin', Miss Hallie. But I'm plumb discouraged."

"*You!* . . . I didn't think that possible."

"Wal, I'm only human, an' it is so. I cain't make my brag good cause yu won't let me run the ranch the way I want to."

"I – I will reconsider," replied Harriet, hurriedly. "What else have you to report?"

"Nothin' much. Lonesome picked up a couple of suspicious riders with the glass. Thet was yesterday mawnin'. He rode out an' caught them meetin' two of our own riders. But they seen him an' all got off down the draw before he could recognize them."

"Our own riders! – That has a bad look, on the face of it. Could it be possible some of our own men are in league with these rustlers?"

"Wal, Miss Hallie, it's so possible thet it's a fact. I've had a hunch for some time. Don't let it fret you. Common thing on the range."

"Oh, those fine gay boys! How could anyone suspect them of being thieves?"

"Wal, I reckon stealin' in the East is different from what it is out heah. Most Westerners have done it, from a beef to a herd. It's keepin' on an' bein' found out that's bad."

"Laramie Nelson! – Did *you* ever steal cattle?" cried Harriet shocked.

"Shore. A beef heah an' there, when I was hungry, but I'm glad to say never no more."

"Oh, what am I going to *do?*" burst out Harriet. "Father is getting better. He's so happy. He trusts you and me. He believes we are doing well.... It makes me sick. What will he say – how will it affect him – when he finds out we're ruined?"

"I've a hunch the old man will never bat an eye," returned Nelson, and Harriet realized no greater compliment could be paid her father.

"But what shall I *do?*" repeated Harriet, at her wit's end. "What will become of us?"

"Wal, thet ain't so hard to see, if yu go on like yu've begun," replied Nelson, not without bitterness. "Neale will go the way of common clay on the range. Florence will coax Ted to make up with his rich folks an' they'll leave yu heah. Lenta will go on drivin' the cow-punchers mad until one of them throws her on a hawse, an' thet'll be the end of her. Yore dad an' maw will settle down to disillusion an' sorrow.... An' as for you, Miss Hallie, wal, I reckon, considerin' the queer nature of women, thet yu'll marry the boldest an' handsomest of the range-riders, Luke Arlidge."

"Don't insult me," flared Harriet furiously. "All the rest you predicted is horrid enough – without making me out such a – a shallow creature.... I wouldn't marry Arlidge if he was the only man on earth. I – I wouldn't give your little finger for the whole of him."

Harriet had not calculated upon the betraying power of temper. She had not meant to say so much; she had not really known she had felt that. But she could not be sorry when she saw his transfigured face.

"I'm glad I riled yu, Miss Hallie," he said, rising. "Shore I didn't mean all thet – though I reckon I was scared yu might do the last. Please overlook it. I've been plumb down-hearted lately. Lonesome an' Tracks have been ridin' me about everythin'. An' – wal,

230

never mind. Thanks for bracin' me up. I'll go back to my job an' make it the best one in this heah country."

Nelson went out. Harriet heard his soft jangling step cross the court entrance, toward the room he shared with his two rider comrades. She stared after him, all her feelings held in abeyance. "Good heavens!" she whispered, with his radiant face, his suddenly intense and vibrant change, confronting her. "Is he in love with me?" Then she was shot through and through with a wholly new and tumultuous emotion that assumed instant domination over her consternation, regret, and revulsion.

Harriet was in the throes of this onslaught when Lonesome shuffled up the steps to rap. When she bade him enter he laid his chaps, gloves, and sombrero on the doorstep.

"Howdy, boss," he said, with a gallant bow. "Did you hear the turrible racket as I come in?"

"No, Lonesome. I didn't hear a thing."

"Dog-gone! That's queer. For she sure was noisy. But honest I don't know whether it was hystericks or temper or just plain laughin'."

"She? Who?"

"No one but your sweet little sister. I laid for her, Miss Hallie. You know you forbid

231

her ridin' with Chess Gaines. I know, 'cause Lenta told me. An' I also know he's not the kind for her to trifle with. I hate to talk against a rival. But Chess is no good. Laramie is goin' to fire him soon as he finds somethin' out. But Lenta! Do you think she cares – what Laramie thinks, or you, or *me*? Not much. That gurl don't care a d – darn.... Chess bragged about goin' to meet her out an' I watched her an' laid for them. I caught them, too. If you never seen a mad gurl you want to see Lenta. Gaines was ugly. But he didn't have guts enough to throw his gun an' that left the fight between me an' her. I had to chase her a mile before I could grab her out of her saddle. Ride? Say, if she ever was a tenderfoot she's got over it plumb. She screamed, scratched, bit, screeched, kicked, bawled, an' finally tried bein' sweet. But no good. A burnt child dreads the fire! I packed her back, round-about, so none of the punchers would see us, an' I never let her down till we got here. Then I wouldn't let her have her hoss.... I've done my duty, boss, an' that's my report."

"I don't know what to say," admitted Harriet, blankly, when Lonesome's rushing story ended.

"Course I ruined any chance I ever had

of winnin' Lenta, if I ever had one," went on Lonesome.

"My poor boy! Certainly you never had one," ejaculated Harriet, sorrowfully. This was almost too much.

"I found that out, Miss Hallie, when I up an' asked her to marry me, like a man, an' not one of them huggin', kissin', dancin', an' so forth cow-punchers. Would you like to know what she said?"

"Lonesome, I believe I would," risked Harriet.

"She was mad at somethin' I did before. She called me a bow-legged little Lothario, whoever he is. 'Marry *you?*' she says, proud-like as a princess. 'My Gawd! but you flatter yourself!' ... Then I says, 'Lenta, I may be bow-legged from honest ridin', an' that name you called me, an' a lot more, but I do love you true, an' only you can save me from death on the lone prairee.' An' then she shrieked –"

"Lonesome, my deluded boy, that is about all I can hear this time," interrupted Harriet, yearning to burst into both tears and mirth.

"It sure is hard, lady, but don't give up," rejoined Lonesome, soothingly. "I'll stick to you an' so will Tracks – an' Laramie, why, that cool, crazy, fire-eatin' gun-slinger, who's gone out to meet the worst of men an' come back – why, he trembles at your step an' he sees your face in the clouds an' hears your voice in the wind. Don't ever miss that, lady."

He left her and went whistling across the court.

"Bless him!" murmured Harriet. Could that be true he dared to say of Laramie? Verily this Lonesome was Great-heart, Valiant, and Ananias all in one.

Harriet reached for her little gold-mounted pencil which she had laid on the face of the ledger just before Lonesome had come in. It was gone. She looked every-where, when she knew she had neither dropped nor mislaid the favorite little gift, of which she had always been duly careful. It had neither flown away nor grown legs. It had been moved. Suddenly she uttered an exclamation of dismay, self-reproach, and certainty, and a light dawned upon her. "Lonesome! – That nice lovable boy! – Oh!"

Shocks were multiplying for Harriet, so she concluded that she might as well annex another. Wherefore she went out to search for Lenta, and came upon her lolling in her homemade hammock. The youngest of the Lindsays looked a tanned, freckled tomboy, with a vividly feminine color and outline. Harriet made the cool mental reservation that Laramie was not far from being right when he had claimed range-riders would not be any good until she was settled. Evidently this much-to-be-desired consummation was still far off.

"Hello, Hal. I had a ripping ride," said Lenta, lazily, with her wide-open baby eyes innocently penetrating.

"So I heard. Lonesome told me," replied Harriet.

"Oh – that's where he went, then. What did he say, Hallie?"

"He talked a blue streak. I can't recall the half of it. But – he rather intimated you preferred the society of other cow-punchers when it would be far better for you to confine yourself to him."

"Squealer! Darn him, anyhow. I'll bet he made it worse without giving himself away." Whereupon Lenta frankly launched into a story that held fairly close to Lonesome's up to the time that he snatched her off her horse.

"It was the chance he wanted, Hal, don't you overlook that," declared Lenta, resentfully. "He got me in his arms over the front of his saddle. I fought like the dickens, but he's a giant. Finally he slid his left arm round my neck and under my left arm, which he held. As I was pressed tight against him I couldn't do anything but kick. That scared his horse, and me too, so I quit. Then he began to kiss me, square on the mouth. I screamed, I raved, I swore. I called him every name I could think of – that is, when he didn't have my lips shut with his. After a while I wilted. He took darn good care to ride me away around out of sight of the draws. He said some day he'd pack me off that way and make love to me scandalously. Finally I bluffed him by pretending hysterics. At that he didn't stop kissing me right off – too good a chance, whether I went mad or not! But after a while he quit and let me off. That was just below the house."

"What became of your horse?" asked Harriet.

"He tagged after us. He's out there now with Lonesome's. I was just working up spunk enough to ride back to the stables, so that darned thing wouldn't look so bad."

"It does look bad," replied Harriet, seriously.

"I know it, dearest, just as well as you. But what's a poor girl going to do? Let these rough-necked conceited jackass Westerners get the best of me, just because I'm a tenderfoot? Not by a darn sight!"

"It looks to me that Lonesome, at least, did get the best of you."

"He did not! I certainly didn't let him kiss

me.... But, Hallie, I'd hate to give myself away to Lonesome – I *do* like him. Heaps. There's something so droll about him. You never can tell whether he's lying or not. He swears he loves me horribly. Asks me to marry him every day. That's something in his favor, anyway. I notice not one of the others have done that. But Lonesome Mulhall thinks he's a lady-killer. And I'll fool him or die in the attempt."

"Lent, I believe he's madly in love with you. That's what worries me."

"Well *that* wouldn't worry me, if it were true. I'd be tickled to death, I'd drive him crazy."

"But, my dear, it seems to me that these young Westerners are not to be trifled with. Laramie Nelson hinted as much. And I feel it. I don't want to scold you, Lenta, or find fault, but I *do* think you are making too free with them – you are going too far. What would mother say?"

"She'd say enough. Worse, she'd tell dad, so for Heaven's sake don't give me away. I'm having the time of my life. I *know* it's not going to last, and that's what drives me. I'm so jealous of Flo! Not that I'm in love with Ted or want *him*, goodness knows. But he's such a handsome, fine, devoted boy. It makes me envious to see them together.

237

Mark my words, Hallie, there's a sure-fire case."

"I'm afraid so."

"We ought to be darned glad. Laramie is. He told me so."

"What does Laramie think of Lonesome's case on you?"

"Not much. He says Lonesome is no good and that if I don't let him alone, I'll be sorry."

"Oh, I wouldn't say Lonesome is no good. There are some lovable and splendid traits in him. He respects women, I think. He's really gallant."

"You're right, Hallie. I feel safe with Lonesome, despite his love-making and threats. I wouldn't be scared if he did pack me off on a horse."

"Mercy! Don't let him. Think of your mother and me.... All this distresses me, Lent. You see I just can't imagine Lonesome as a husband for you."

"Lord, who can?" retorted Lenta, savagely. "I see red when I think of a husband among these swearing, drinking, fighting riders. There never will be another like Ted Williams. The ranchers I've seen are old, dusty, tobacco-chewing codgers. It's good I don't want to be married, but if I *did* – if I ever *do* – what then?"

238

"You might send for Lane Griffith or Eddie Howe," suggested Harriet, demurely.

"My old schoolmate beaus!" And Lenta let out a peal of laughter. "No, I wouldn't wish this awful West on Lane or Eddie, even if I hadn't changed."

"Awful West? . . . I guess you are right. It does have some awful aspects."

"But Hallie, just think! I wouldn't go back for worlds. Would you?"

That was a query Harriet did not desire to confront. Surely something insidious and profound was imperceptibly coming between her and the old humdrum Upper Sandusky. She could only detect it by looking back.

"Lenta, there's no chance of our ever going back now," went on Harriet, soberly. "We have to earn a living here. And now that father is out of danger we must go to work earnestly, with hope and enthusiasm."

"I'd like to know what the deuce we've been doing. Look at my hands, Hal Lindsay. Look at them! – Baby hands you used to pat and kiss. They look like a washerwoman's. But I'm darned if I'm ashamed of them."

"No indeed. Did you notice the hands of those Liley girls, who called on us last Sunday? Their father is a big rancher halfway between here and La Junta. They must do real work. . . . But to come back to

239

our own troubles. We started out with the idea of making this ranch pay, at least a reasonable income on investments. But we haven't made any start. We are poorer by some thousand cattle than when we arrived."

"Hal, I know more about the ranch than you and dad put together," spoke up Lenta, spiritedly. "I'm glad you cared enough to broach the subject to me. I've learned a lot this last month. You seldom go down to the corrals and then only with Nelson. That shuts up the riders like mouse-traps. But I've hung around with Neale and alone, sitting on the high corral fences, watching and listening. And I've ridden ten thousand miles, it seems, with Lonesome, Chess Gaines, Slim Red, and others. I may be a madcap, as dad calls me, but I'm no fool. And I've seen a lot and heard a good deal more and made deductions of my own."

"Suppose you give me the benefit of all this, Lenta Lindsay," suggested Harriet, not without humor.

"Well, you can gamble on this. The Peak Dot outfit is a house divided against itself. Laramie, Lonesome and Ted line up here with us. That has caused no end of jealousy. But Laramie is liked by most of the riders and feared by all. Such tales they tell of Laramie's fights! Why, Hallie, I hate to shock you, but Laramie Nelson has shot no end of men. Killed them! ... To be sure maybe most of it is talk. Anyway Laramie's respected. I'd like to hint to him that it's struck me Luke Arlidge still runs this Peak Dot outfit. Only I wouldn't dare. ... Chess Gaines is riding for us, but he hates Laramie and he's thick with Arlidge. Rides over there at night! Oh, I put two and two together. One reason I've flirted with Chess was to find out. But he's deep and he's cute. That made me want all the more to lead him along. Slim Red was a pard of Gaines', but he was switched. Laramie did that. And Gaines is sore. This Slim Red – the one that was such a devil our first night here – he's not a bad fellow at all. He's the most bashful person I ever saw. He'll run, hide, ride over a precipice to escape me. But I'll have him coming around soon. Then Fork Mayhew, Clay Lee, and Dakota have also come over to Laramie. But the others, in my opinion, are taking wages from you, Hallie, and all the time in cahoots with Arlidge. This Luke Arlidge is a villain, Hallie. Lonesome told me, but I felt it that first Sunday he called here. The way he watched you! That man has terrible eyes, like those of some cruel bird of prey. Laramie's eyes you just can't look into, but not for the same reason. You feel when Laramie looks at you that he's uncovering your soul. Look out for Mr. Arlidge, my handsome sister!... I like Wind River Charlie. He's a big wonderful looking fellow, simple as a, b, c, but governed by Gaines. Same with Juan Mendez, the Mexican, and Nig Johnson, the Negro. That leaves Archie Hill, and I don't know what to say about him. He's got me buffaloed, as Lonesome says. You can't keep your eyes off him. How that fellow can ride! Lonesome can't hold a candle to him."

"Lenta, I'm downright surprised," declared Harriet, humbly. "You've made use of your eyes other than *making* eyes, anyway. If what you claim is true, Nelson is not so badly off for riders who'll stand by him. Counting Lonesome and Ted, he'd have six, and of course Neale, who swears by Laramie."

"Yes, Laramie has enough men, according to Lonesome, to beat the rustlers and run the ranch, if only you'd let him."

"I! What do you mean?" exclaimed Harriet, weakly. It was common gossip then – her hampering Laramie in his hard task.

"Hallie, to me and to all of us you are the best ever," declared Lenta, warmly. "But to these Westerners you are a joke. You can't ride worth a cent. You're afraid of a horse or

242

a steer or even a cow. You wouldn't watch the boys rope and hog-tie that mean old outlaw stallion. You wouldn't watch the branding of calves. Smell made you sick, you said. Sight of blood makes you faint. The idea of a fist fight to you is horrible. You should have seen your face that night Lonesome hit Slim Red. You have the funniest frozen look when Laramie happens to bump into you with his gun. You won't let him go after the rustlers, because you fear he might shoot or hang some of these nice, sweet, gentle, Christian robbers who are ruining us."

"Oh... I *am* a tenderfoot, a poor soft-hearted female tenderfoot!" exclaimed Harriet, flayed by Lenta's candor.

"Hal, old girl! Why don't you get your dander up?" went on Lenta, with affectionate persuasion. "Don't you remember when the Curtis and Gibbons kids used to maltreat me – how you'd chase them and smack the stuffings out of them? ... Why don't you get mad now? We're out West now and we're stuck here for good. Dad will be raring to fight soon. I see signs of that. You're the only Lindsay who'll turn the other cheek when you get one slapped. That won't do out here."

"I –I see it won't" replied Harriet, faintly.

"What'd we do if Laramie happened to leave us?" queried Lenta.

"Oh!" cried Harriet aghast at the mere idea.

"Or if he got shot!"

Harriet stared mutely at her executioner.

"There! That digs you," flashed Lenta, passing from eloquent appeal to devilish glee. "Darned if I don't believe you're in love with Laramie!"

"Lenta, you can – go – too far."

"Never mind, honey," laughed Lenta. "But it'd shore be great for this heah outfit if you were."

Chapter 9

It was a night in late June, and Laramie, with his now inseparable comrades, sought an interview with their employer.

All the members of the Lindsay family were assembled in Mrs. Lindsay's sitting-room, the most spacious and pleasant in the house.

"Laramie, I'm beset by wife, son, daughter to take them to La Junta for the Fourth of July races, cow-puncher contests, dance, and what not," declared Lindsay.

"John, we have not been out of this house since we moved in," complained Mrs. Lindsay. "I want to see some people, if there are any in this blooming West."

"Tell you, dad, it'd be a sort of a family jubilee to celebrate your recovery," said Neale, sagely.

That statement was accepted by his sisters in marked contrast to the way most of his sallies were regarded.

"I'd love to go, papa," pleaded Florence, who never used that endearing finial term except in extreme situations.

"And I tell you, dad, that I *am* going," added Lenta, decisively. Then as an afterthought: "If I have to elope!"

"Father, we are not getting acquainted very fast with our neighbors," said Harriet. "And this will be an opportunity. All the countryside will be there, so I hear."

"Laramie, what do you think about it?" queried Lindsay, as he faced about to the three riders, standing, sombreros in hand, just inside the open door.

"July Fourth cain't be no wuss than any other day an' it might be better," drawled Laramie, his eyes twinkling at the girls. "First-rate day for peanuts, pink lemonade, elopin', an' such. We shore don't risk nothin' leavin' the ranch to the Mexicans. There ain't much stock left to steal. Rustlers waitin' for us to buy a few thousand more haid. All the cattlemen, riders, rustlers, gamblers, outlaws will be there. I reckon we-all better go."

"Whoopee!" yelled Neale, and tried to stand on his head.

"Laramie, you dear!" screamed Lenta, and she hugged him.

"Miss Lenta, I got him to say that," declared Lonesome, boldly.

"Dad, can Ted and I have one of the buckboards?" begged Florence.

246

"Yes, to everything," replied Lindsay, affected with the general rejoicing. "Laramie, you can drive Hallie and Lent, and Lonesome can drive me and mom."

"Aw!" groaned Lonesome, sagging. "Boss, I'm the poorest driver in the outfit. Remember when I broke a wheel on the wagon comin' out. The other boys will all go in – or throw up their jobs. An' any one of them can beat me drivin'."

"Very well, Lonesome. I will relieve you of all responsibility.... It's settled. We're going. So, mom, plan what you'll need to ride in and dress in after we get there."

"It's a day an' a half drive," said Laramie. "So yu better figger to leave early on the mawning' of July second, an' drive till dark, stoppin' at some ranch."

"Now there, I hope you're satisfied," declared Lindsay, to his beaming womenfolk. "I have a presentiment this trip will bring dire results. But go we will.... No, Laramie, I'm ready for any serious confabs. Let's get out where we can smoke."

Laramie conducted him, with the two boys following, to their quarters at the end of the court, but did not go inside.

"Wal, boss, it's serious, but it'll be short," announced Laramie. "I'm askin' yu, whether yu consent or not to give me a free hand, to keep this confab under yore hat."

"Certainly, Laramie. I shall respect all you say as confidence," replied Lindsay.

"Wal, we've been heah nigh two months, an' all the range knows we're an easy outfit. Arlidge, who knows me, an' Price, who knows Lonesome, were leary at first. But for thet we'd been cleaned oot long ago. As it stands we've got aboot five hundred haid of cows an' calves left."

To Laramie's satisfaction this statement fetched some good round profanity.

"An', wuss, from a rider's standpoint, about all our hawses air gone. I've got Wingfoot yet, an' reckon I can keep him, 'cause nobody is damn fool enough to steal him. But Tracks' two hawses air gone an' Lonesome's bay. An' all told there ain't a dozen hawses grazin' about, outside of the bunch in the pastures. They air yore hawses, of course, but thet outfit Arlidge left heah looks on them as theirs. We had more'n two hundred haid of range hawses."

"Allen claimed there were five hundred, and that he threw these in with the bargain," declared Lindsay.

"Wal, Allen said a lot we're findin' out ain't so. . . . Now, Lindsay, so far as me an' my pards heah air concerned, rustlin' is one

248

thing an' hawse-stealin' is another. We cain't abide a hawse-thief."

"I don't blame you. I'm seeing red myself."

"Thet's good. Now what I want is a free hand to go about this business as I should have done in the first place. But right off I seen Miss Hallie was daid set against any violence. An' to be honest, up to now I just couldn't hurt her feelin's."

Lindsay swallowed hard, and in the dusk his face could be seen to shade gray.

"We needn't waste words, Laramie. I think the more of you for your forbearance. And so would she. But we don't know how to run a ranch. I'll agree to any course you want to take and back you up. I feel a new man now. Perhaps I've shirked my duty too long, but it's been so good just to loaf around getting well."

"Wal, boss, thet's more'n enough from yu. It's straight talk, plumb from the shoulder. An' I'm shore obliged for yore trust in me."

"Then we start over right here?"

"Thet's it. Right heah."

"What's the exact case, Laramie?"

"Wal, we had it figgered for some time. But out heah in the West yu got to ketch a man red-handed. It ain't enough to suspect. Yu've got to know, an' then yu have to act

249

quick.... Yu remember what Buff Jones told yu about the range, how rustlin' had come in strong, an' these bands of slick men rode from one range to another. Some of them ranch it, some of them buy cattle an' sell, an' the rest ride for somebody. But they air all in cahoots, thet is, a particular outfit. Arlidge is the crookedest, slickest kind of a cattleman. I ran into him over on the K Bar in Nebraskie. I should have shot him long ago. Allen is no doubt one of these shady cattlemen who never stay long in one place. He got this ranch from the Seward Company, an' he never did a lick of improvin'. He's now ranchin' over heah forty miles on Sandstone Creek. We rode over to see what his place looked like. Fine range, but no ranch. A log cabin an' some log corrals. Arlidge is purportin' to be ranchin' it at Castle Haid, with a man named Snook as foreman. All a lot of slick lyin' work. Between them all they've sold half of yore cattle, after sellin' it to *yu,* an' presently they'll do away with the rest. Then, if they see yu're not goin' to stock up soon they'll hit the dust for other diggin's some thirty thousand dollars, more or less ahaid."

"Good God! – Laramie, how is it done?"

"Easy. There's always some honest ranchers on every range, an' they make the

250

way easy for the crooked ones. 'Cause nobody can tell a crooked cattleman right off. Some of them work for years withoot bein' trailed. An' some never get found out. But I happened to know Arlidge. Thet put the shady brand on Allen, an' this heah outfit of riders."

"But you're not telling me how all this robbery is done," fumed Lindsay, impatiently.

"Wal, boss, give me time," drawled Laramie. "In the first place before we got heah Arlidge drove half yore herd way across the Sandstone, an' sold it from there. Some of the riders yu're payin' now were in thet drive. An' since then, at picked times, these crooked riders operated to run off more stock when the honest riders were asleep or somewhere else on the range. Yore brand was blotted into another brand on considerable stock. An' a lot of it wasn't branded atall. We couldn't brand calves when we were buildin' this house over. But we did do some little ridin' about. Tracks heah tracked his first stolen hawse to thet Castle Haid corral. An' I rode over with him another time. An' I seen things. Then Lonesome has had his eye peeled on this Chess Gaines, an' thet greaser Juan an' the nigger rider Johnson. All this counted up, but didn't amount to such proofs as yu got to have in this country. An' these, I'm tickled to say, Lindsay, we got from no one else than yore lass, Miss Lenta."

"NO!" cried the rancher, apparently thrilled.

"It's true, Mr. Lindsay," spoke up Ted, quietly. "We've all been making fun of Lenta or worrying ourselves about her escapades. But all the same these escapades of hers have made clear what all the three of us could not see."

"And what's that?" demanded Lindsay, eagerly.

Both Tracks and Lonesome tried to reply in unison, but Laramie checked them.

"Let me talk, Lonesome, so it cain't be held against yu.... Boss, I hate to double-cross yore daughter. It shore seems mean to me. But I've thought it all out. She's takin' too many long chances with these riders. She's only a kid, an' Colorado has gone to her haid. Lenta is flirtin' too outrageous, if no wuss, an' yu've got to stop her if yu have to lock her up."

"My Gawd, pard, if you're lyin' I'll kill you for that," burst out Lonesome, huskily.

"Shet up!" ordered Laramie, tersely. "Yore feelin's run away with yore haid, too."

"Nelson! You astonish me," declared Lindsay, stiffly. "I was aware Lenta had taken rather – er – wildly to horses and riders, but I had no idea. . . . Hallie has been worried, and so has Mrs. Lindsay. . . . Lenta has been well brought up. Are you sure you're not . . ."

"Lindsay, I'm always shore before I shoot," interrupted Laramie. "Lenta has got three riders, Gaines, Slim Red, Wind River Charlie, all of them, even my pard Lonesome heah, standin' on their haids. Soon they'll be hatin' each other's guts, an' out heah thet means gun-play. I'm not so damn shore it's not too late."

"That's strong talk, Nelson," replied Lindsay, certainly affronted. "You understand, of course, if you do my daughter an injustice –"

"Aw, hell!" ejaculated Laramie, shortly, losing his patience. He did not like this job. "I saw the spoonin' with Chess Gaines, an' he's shore the least attractive of the lot. It just knocked me plumb west! An' wuss, from my side of the fence, I heahed some of these boys talkin' damn free an' plain about Lenta."

"I'll fire the whole caboodle," replied Lindsay, angrily.

"Shore yu can, an' me too," went on Laramie, coolly. "But thet won't help yu any. It'll be jumpin' out of the fryin'-pan into the fire. Maybe the next outfit yu hire

253

wouldn't have one single honest man in it. How'd yu know? An' where'd yu be?"

"I apologize, Nelson," returned Lindsay, hurriedly. "It's upset me."

"Wal, thet's natural. Yu've been concerned about gettin' wal. But it's time now yu began showin' yore hand. An' to come back to this outfit of ours, just try to savvy thet yore daughter is more to blame than the riders. What could yu expect? A sweet, pretty, fresh wild-rose of a girl throwin' herself into their arms! The boys on these ranges air as women hungry as the men. Yu'll see thet in La Junta next week."

"All right, Nelson, I swallow it, and come up smiling," rejoined the rancher, and he did smile, though at the cost of effort.

"Now yu're talkin'," flashed Laramie, as swift to change. Lindsay was aggravating, but he had the making of a solid Westerner. "Thet's all about Lenta, except what she told me. It 'pears Gaines was waitin' for her to ride out to their meetin'-place, an' Lenta forgot about it, or said so. I've a hunch she didn't forget atall. Wal, she rode out with Slim Red. Thet's the way these riders have been attendin' to my orders. Shore riles me. Wal, they run plumb into Gaines, an' when he an' Red locked horns over the girl up comes two strange riders. An' heah's where

254

Lenta showed how smart she is. Gaines didn't seem to care a damn about them meetin' him with the girl. It was Slim Red that stuck in his craw. The two strange riders made no bones of the fact thet Gaines had agreed to meet them, an' pay up. Thet led to a hot wrangle, Lenta got the hunch thet these strangers figgered Slim Red was still one of *their* outfit. She heahed Gaines cuss them an' swear they'd have to kill him. Which they tried to do, Lindsay! But Slim smelled a rat an' was on the go when they pulled guns. Slim told me he shore heahed bullets all about his haid.... Wal, Gaines sent the riders off, an' fetched Lenta home. She was cute enough to act stupid an' pretend not to savvy. Gaines hesitated in a moody an' thoughtful way, she said. It scared her, an' so she played up to the idee thet she hadn't heahed much of the argument an' reckoned Gaines took this opportunity to vent his jealousy of Red. She was cute enough to play it off sentimental, an' so fooled him. When she got home she came straight to me."

"So help me Jehoshaphat!" ejaculated Lindsay. "My youngest child mixed up in shooting scrapes!"

"Wal, it's a bad mess. But we can thank our lucky stars yore youngest child has a haid on her shoulders. Now, what to do with Gaines. Any orders, boss?"

"I'm all at sea. How – what to do?"

"Wal, we can let Gaines go. An' Mendez an' Johnson will stick with him. Thet'd help, I reckon. If we wait till we ketch Gaines one of two things will happen. Either we'll shoot him or hang him. Thet depends on how an' where he's ketched. Unless we surprise him, hold him up, he'll shore show fight. Gaines is not so young, either, in range life or years. He's a bad hombre. An' if we're to believe his brag an' thet of his pards he's been in a lot of shootin' frays."

"Nelson, what'd you rather do about this?" queried Lindsay, nervously.

"Wal, I'd like to go down, call Gaines out, an' have it over with," replied Laramie, tersely.

"No – no! – That would scare my wife and distress Hallie. . . . Let's discharge him. I suppose that other thing – that strange ruthless range law – will come, sooner or later. Sufficient to the day, Nelson. Anyway I'll be better prepared."

"All right, boss. But from then on I'll have to act on my own judgment, 'cept in cases where I've time to come to yu. One thing more. I've an idee of havin' Lonesome do some slick work. An' it's got to look like he's drinkin' hard. But he'll only be pretendin'. I want yu to know so yu can clear him with Mrs. Lindsay an' the girls, in case they heahed of it."

"Very well, Nelson," replied Lindsay, as he rose wearily. "Anything you say. I'll do my damndest to bear up under all this."

Whereupon he walked slowly away as if burdened, and it was noticeable that he went out of the gateway, instead of back into the court. Ted Williams stood up.

"Fine and dandy, Laramie. You are a wonder," he cried. "The old boy is sagging, but he's game. I feel sorry for the kid. Only she's got to be hauled up. I have my doubts, pard. Never saw a girl like Lenta."

"Tracks, if *you* say one word – Aw hell!" burst out Lonesome, miserably. "I'll be losin' my pards soon – all for a – a – sassy little tenderfoot of a hussy. Only the hell of it is I can't believe it."

"What's eating you?" demanded Tracks, giving the prostrate Lonesome a kick. "If she is a little hussy – which I don't believe – she has given *you* the inside track. Run the race out, you love-sick rider, if you want the girl. She's going to need her friends."

Williams stalked away across the courtyard. His quick steps were drowned in the soft flow of running water. The night was still, with a smell of burning brush wafting up from the valley.

"Pard, did you hear what Tracks said?" asked Lonesome, presently.

"Shore I heahed. An' I put a lot of store in him. He's got more brains than you an' me put together. I reckon he about sized up the deal for yu."

"Pard, I don't see how. Thet you told Lindsay was the last straw. I wouldn't see myself. An' it'll kill me, Laramie, sure as the Lord made little apples."

Laramie was silent for several minutes. All these things had slowly worked toward a climax. He sensed events. That old cold mood was hovering near again. Just what should he say to this lovable but rudderless boy, who long ago would have gone on the rocks but for him?

"Pard, my – heart is – broke," gasped Lonesome, almost with a sob.

"Wal, if it is, maybe thet'll make a man of yu."

"I just don't care about nothin'. You won't need to have me pretend to drink. I'm gonna swim in red likker an' get drunk an' stay drunk."

"Yu air like hell! Lonesome, some day I'm goin' to beat the livin' daylights out of yu. What've I loved yu for all these years?"

"I never could savvy that, pard, 'cause I'm no good on earth," replied Lonesome, in a terrible despondency.

"Shore yu air," retorted Laramie, grasping that this was the crucial moment. "Yu heahed what Tracks said about Lenta shore needin' her friends?"

"Course I heered him."

"Wal, she's only got three, me an' him an' yu. We're goin' to save her, Lonesome."

"Bah! You cain't save a rotten egg. If she lets Gaines an' Slim – Aw – faugh! Makes me sick."

"She let yu, didn't she?"

"What? Hug an' kiss her? ... No, I'll be damned if she did ... Anyway, not till I wore her out. But that was different, pard."

"How was it? Yu never were no good. Yu were a rotten egg yourself. Yu made a grab for every girl yu ever seen. Yu're no better'n Lenta, if yu're half as good."

"Hell, man!" exclaimed Lonesome, writhing and breathing hard. "Whatever I'd done this time I was different an' that made it different. I asked her to marry me before I ever laid a hand on her."

"Wal, air yu goin' back on thet now?" drawled Laramie, settling to the old task of compelling Lonesome.

"Yes, I am."

259

"No, yu're not. Lonesome, old pard, I've a hunch this heah is the time I've hoped an' prayed for."

"What? To see me down in the dirt?"

"Yes, an' confessin' it.... Boy, did Lenta say no when yu asked her to marry yu?"

"She didn't need to. But she didn't. That always got me, somehow. Lord! how sweet she can be! ... An' to think –"

"So yu love her turrible?"

"Pard, I do – honest. I love her so I'm – Oh! I can't tell you."

"Then this triflin' of hers won't make no change in yu."

"Triflin'. What would you call serious, Laramie?"

"She's a child. She's out of her haid. Shore she'll go to the bad pronto if we don't save her."

"Aw, who'd ever took Laramie Nelson for an old fool?"

"Lonesome, yu're disappointin' me plumb deep. Yu're hurt an' yu're thinking only of yoreself. Come out of thet. It's now or never. Whether yu make a real man of yoreself!"

"Rave on, pard; you're lickin' me. You always do lick me. What you want? How'n'hell can *I* ever make a real man of myself?"

"Just tell me yu'll love Lenta the same –
no! more, if she *does* go to the bad?"

Lonesome's tense frame jerked with the
shock of that. He sat up. His face was gray
in the gathering darkness.

"Pard, why do you torture me this way?"
he asked, hoarsely.

"Pard, yu say? Wal, show me yu're worthy
of such a pard as I've been."

"All right, Laramie. You win.... The wuss
Lenta gets the more I'll love her.... It's
tearin' me inside, but you've dug it out."

"Wal, now I'll tell *yu* somethin',"
whispered Laramie. "Yu're wuth confidin'
in.... I'm in a far more turrible fix than yu.
Lenta's only a child an' I've a hunch she likes
yu best. I feel it, Lonesome.... But my case
is hopeless. If I ever had a lovesickness it was
far back when I was sixteen. I don't
remember clear. There were two or three
girls. But they're ghosts. An' this woman I
love is the sun. It's Lenta's sister, Hallie. I
reckon yu never guessed. But I've just lived
an' breathed thet girl since I found it out.
Thet's one reason why I've been such a
failure runnin' this ranch. Not thet I had any
hope of her ever carin' for me. God – no! But
I couldn't bear to sicken her with a sight of
me. I just went on from day to day, with only
one feelin' – to see her – to be near her. It's

261

shore hell, Lonesome. But I wouldn't have missed thet for anythin' in the world. I never lived before.... I'll go out now an' clean up this ranch an' call myself lucky."

"For Gawd's sake!" gasped Lonesome, overcome. "Why didn't you ever tell me before, pard?...So that's what's been wrong?...This Lindsay outfit of girls hasn't done anythin' to us atall? First Ted, then me, an' now you! – Jumpin' grasshoppers!...It's set me wonderin'."

"Wal, keep yore wonderin' to yoreself, Lonesome. I reckon I'll go to bed," replied Laramie, and he rose to go in, leaving his friend out there whispering to himself.

Lonesome came in, however, before Laramie fell asleep.

"Pard Laramie, I've a powerful good idee," he announced.

"Cain't yu hold it till mawnin'?"

"Nix. I'm makin' a deal with you," rejoined Lonesome, eagerly. "First off, pard, this pretendin' to be on a drunk trick of yours didn't tickle me to death. Lenta hates fellars who smell of the bottle an' she made me swear I'd quit. An' I have. But your plan is all right. We gotta find things out. An' I'll do it proper on one condition."

"Ahuh," growled Laramie.

"You gotta make Lenta believe you told

me what you seen her do, an' that I went to the bad pronto. All for her sake! Broke my heart – ruined my life – goin' plumb to hell! . . . Will you promise to do it, pard?"

"Shore. I reckon thet's not such a pore idee – to come from yore haid, anyhow. If the girl's got a conscience it may fetch her up short."

"Dog-gone, I must be dotty," concluded Lonesome, ruefully.

Laramie awakened next morning with a zest he had not felt for long. Resolutely he set his thoughts on the details he had planned, and smothered the dreaming melancholy under which he had labored for weeks.

"He's not such a rotten actor," remarked Tracks, as Lonesome slouched ahead of him and Laramie, on their way down to the ranch. Lonesome had stuck a black bottle in his hip pocket, some of the contents of which he had spilled on his shirt, and he had otherwise assisted nature in the simulation of a cow-puncher under the influence of rum.

"Shore is a hard-lookin' customer," agreed Laramie. "I'm 'most feared he'll make the best of this job."

"Watch him! Laramie, when you told him

to pick a fight with everybody, I saw an unholy glitter in his eye."

"Wal, we're shore in for a spell of natural range happenin's. An' I'm glad, 'cause I want to be my old self once more."

Laramie hardly believed that could ever be. He lagged behind his friends a little. The yellow road wound down to the green level valley floor, that owed its fertility and color to the never-failing brook. Part of his task had been to add to the natural beauty of the place. Riders with little riding to do had been set to cleaning up, painting, building fences, and other such tasks that they hated. Barns, sheds, corrals, cabins, all, in fact, of the valley adjuncts to the ranch, had been built and used by the cattle company preceding Allen. They were picturesquely located in a grove of cottonwoods, through the middle of which ran the brook. Beyond were the big pastures leading out to the open range. It was indeed a ranch to delight the heart of riders, wholly aside from the house above, with its fascinating Lindsay sisters.

Half a dozen saddle horses stood bridles down under the big cottonwood tree in front of the yellow stable. Mexican boys were cleaning out the stalls. Neale Lindsay appeared, leading the bay horse Lonesome had taken a fancy to, after his own had been stolen. A group of riders lounged around in the shade, waiting. Laramie promised himself that they had not waited in vain this morning.

Lonesome halted some paces in front of Tracks, who apparently remonstrated with him.

"Hey, Lindsay, wot'nhell you doin' with my hawse?" yelled Lonesome.

"Your horse? Say, cow-puncher, this horse is mine. I'll have you know," replied Neale, getting red through his sunburn. Two months of range life had toned him down considerably, but he was still a tenderfoot, still vain and pompous enough to be a thorn in the flesh of the riders. Innumerable tricks perpetrated upon him, and sundry hard falls and knocks, and a couple of minor scuffles, had not cured Neale to the extent desired by Laramie.

"Ump-umm! Fade away, tenderfoot, before I blow on you."

Lonesome slouched over to snatch the bridle from Neale, whose face turned as red as a beet.

"Mulhall, you're drunk!" he burst out, angrily.

"Who's drunk?" roared Lonesome.

"You are. If you weren't I – I'd crack your ugly mug.... Laramie –"

265

He was interrupted by Lonesome slapping his face.

"We can't all be handsome – like you Lindsays," snarled Lonesome. "Look out, young fellar. I'm easy riled. An' I'm about through with this outfit."

"You bet you are! I'll have you fired," raged Neale, and he ran at Lonesome. That worthy stepped aside, to stick out his foot, over which the Easterner tripped and fell. But he leaped up, thoroughly aroused now, and plunged at the little rider, swinging his fists wildly. Lonesome had dropped the bridle of the horse, which moved away.

"You won't be so bootiful after I get a couple whacks at you," said Lonesome, and forthwith met the boy's onslaught with a blow on his nose. Neale staggered back as blood spouted from the rather prominent member.

"Damn bow-leg rooster! I'll kill you!" yelled Neale, and he rushed at Lonesome, raining blows upon the doughty little rider. Lonesome took a good many before he returned one, and that was a fairly rough tap in the region of Neale's abdomen. It sent young Lindsay to his knees, gasping for breath, his face convulsed with pain and rage.

"How you like 'em on your biscuit-basket,

Neale?" shouted Lonesome, gleefully. He had forgotten the ugly contrariness of the part he was supposed to play. "Come on. I'll give you the sneezel jab next on your kisser. Then I'll give you the raspitas –"

"Nelson," interrupted a sharp voice, "stop that puncher's pickin' on Neale, or I will."

Whereupon Chess Gaines strode down out of the stable, his light eyes full of fiery, ugly gleam, his full handsome lips curling. His heated face suggested a late intimacy with strong drink.

"Wal, Gaines, suppose yu stop it," drawled Laramie, tossing gloves and chaps aside.

"You bet I will," declared the rider, forcefully, as he stepped in front of the heaving Neale. "Stay out of this, kid, an' you'll see who your real friends are."

Like a flash Lonesome was transformed from his grinning self to the half-drunken leering rider.

"Hell you shay, Gaines?"

"You leave Neale alone or I'll batter your face into a mud pie," replied Gaines.

"Say, Gaines, you're terrible keen on Neale all suddenlike," sneered Lonesome. "When you've been meaner'n any of us to him. Aw, I'm onto you. Makin' a bid to stand in with his sisters, huh?"

Gaines let out a furious imprecation and swung a violent side blow at Lonesome, as if to slap his leering face. But Lonesome ducked with a surprising quickness.

"You're a little late all around, Chess," snapped Lonesome, viciously. Then as Gaines made at him, Lonesome danced from side to side and backwards, suddenly to charge at his antagonist like a bull. Lonesome's stature had always led to deception. Laramie expected to see here a repetition of many former encounters. For Lonesome was a master at this game. His body blows sounded solidly. Under their impact Gaines staggered, lost his balance, when Lonesome came up with a tremendous swing to thump him on the jaw. The rider went toppling back to collide with the barn where he sank to his knees. But he had been only upset, not stunned. His eyes flamed livid murder as he snatched at his gun.

"*Heah!*" thundered Laramie, leaping in front of Lonesome, with his gun out. If Gaines' hand had vibrated so much as the breadth of a hair it would have been his last move.

"No go – Nelson," he rasped, as if half strangled. His face had turned a dirty white. "I savvy.... You put up a job –"

"Drop yore hand! ... Now get up.... *Stiff,*
268

damn yu! . . . Turn about. Now get yore pack an' fork yore hawse. Yu're shore through with the Peak Dot."

"Don't be too – sure, Nelson," hoarsely replied Gaines as he brushed the dust and dirt off his clothes.

"Wal, I am shore. An' I advise yu to shet up, unless you have somethin' to say to yore pards."

"Nig, you an' Juan fetch your hawses an' mine over to the cabin. We're packin' to leave this —— —— —— flathead tenderfoot outfit," ordered Gaines. "Do we get robbed out of our wages?"

"Wal, yu were paid Saturday," drawled Laramie. "An' considerin' everythin' I reckon yu'll still be ahaid."

Gaines gave Laramie a piercing glance, as if recognizing in him now a character he had mistaken or had repudiated.

"You bet your sweet life I will," he hissed, with a passionate gesture.

"Ride off the range, then, before yu dangle at the end of a rope," said Laramie, in his soft cool voice, as if he were advising a thoughtless young man.

Here the rider's face blanched to the very lips. The tone as much as the content of Laramie's drawling speech rang the iron creed of the range. Although his brazen

269

effrontery upheld him that shot went home. He stalked away with his two comrades, and the horses.

Lonesome bawled after them. "Three of a kind! I'll bet I see you-all stretch hemp!"

"Like you damn near did, you measly two-bit rustler," yelled Gaines, with a harsh haw-haw.

Lonesome whipped out his gun, but before he could level it Laramie seized his arm.

"Leggo!" bawled Lonesome. "You're breakin' my arm." He relinquished the weapon to his friend, and cupping both hands around his mouth he yelled in stentorian voice.

"Sure, Chess, I was a two-bit rustler once. But you're the real sneakin' breed – the two-faced breed! An' —— —— ——, if you don't get off this range you'll swing."

"Thet'll do, Lonesome," said Laramie, dragging him around. "Yu're shore drunk. Where'd yu get your likker?"

Here Neale Lindsay made himself manifest again.

"We didn't fight it out," he cried, resentfully. "You hit me below the belt."

"Whoop! Lemme at him, Laramie!" shouted Lonesome.

"See heah. If you two don't shake hands

pronto I'll fire the both of yu," declared Laramie. "Think it over."

Whereupon Laramie turned to a tall light-haired young man, Wind River Charlie, who stood staring after the discharged riders.

"Charlie, where yu standin'?"

"On one foot, boss," replied Charlie with a grin. He had clear yellow eyes, the direct gaze of which did not waver, and under the fine fuzzy beard his tanned face appeared to struggle with a smile.

"Wal, hadn't yu better get down both feet – on this heah side of the fence?"

"I'd reckon I'd better, if it ain't too late, Nelson," slowly replied Charlie.

"It's never too late – when a man's honest. Declare yoreself right heah before what's left of the outfit."

Wind River Charlie spent an undecided moment with his yellow eyes sweeping over the silent riders. Then they came back to Laramie.

"Nelson, I ain't double-crossin' nobody when I say thet I never had any idee what the deal was here. I was ridin' a grub-line an' pretty low-down."

"Wal, yu found out pronto what Arlidge was, didn't yu?"

"I had a hunch, but never knowed for

sure. He kept me doin' odd jobs. I never made no long drives."

"Ahuh. Thet ain't declarin' yoreself as free as I'd like, Charlie."

"Sorry. Best I can do, 'cept I'd be sure glad to stay on if you'll keep me."

"Wal, we'll talk about it again. Where's Archie Hill an' Slim?"

"Archie's doin' cook chores this week. An' Slim has been keepin' mighty scarce."

"Fork yore hawses, boys," concluded Laramie. "Tracks, saddle Wingfoot for me. I'll want a word with Archie. Then we'll ride out an' count what calves air left."

"Boss, look!" suddenly ejaculated Lonesome, pointing. "Chess an' his pards slopin'.... There, he's lookin' back. Shakin' his fist! I reckon you let him off too easy."

"I reckon so, Lonesome, but it shore was a close shave," replied Laramie, watching the three dark, sinister riders vanish down under the trees. "He's in company thet fits him – Juan and Johnson air both bad 'uns."

Three hours later Laramie wended a thoughtful way alone up to the ranch-house. His interview with Archie Hill had been favorable, but failure of Lonesome and Tracks to return with Slim Red occasioned his uneasiness. It was not impossible that

Gaines had paid his parting respects to Slim, and that that was what had detained the boys.

One thing, however, cheered Laramie on his slow ride up the winding road. He espied Lindsay working in the garden below. The movements of the Easterner betrayed both energy and satisfaction. Laramie rejoiced. In something like three months Lindsay had become a new man. Laramie soliloquized that Colorado might be infested with rustlers, horse-thieves, skunks, coyotes, and other vermin, but it was good for something.

When about to dismount before the wide gateway Laramie was halted by hearing his name called in low, trilling accents. Then he espied halfway down the stone wall a little hand waving from one of the small iron-barred windows. Laramie rode down even with this window from which the hand had protruded, and peered in.

Lenta's pretty, tearful, woebegone face greeted him.

"Laramie, I'm locked in," cried Lenta, resentfully.

"Wal, wal!" ejaculated the rider. "Dog-gone! This is too bad. How come?"

"Dad! He's shut me in like I was a kid! And I had a date with Slim.... Oh, I am wild."

"So I see. But to be honest, lass, I'm shore relieved."

"Laramie dear, sneak around into the court and let me out," pleaded Lenta.

"But, child, we put locks on all the doors. An' shore yore dad kept the key."

"Oh yes.... Then get a pole or pick-handle and bend this iron-bar. I've busted two chairs on it. I can almost squeeze out now."

"Ump-umm. I wouldn't dare do it, Lenta."

"Laramie, don't you love me any more?" she asked, reproachfully.

"Wal, I reckon I do. An' thet's why I'm shore glad yu're locked in."

"Laramie, I'll be awfully nice to you, if you'll let me out," returned the girl, seductively, with both little brown hands held out between the bars.

"I cain't do it, Lenta," replied Laramie.

"Please. Dear old Laramie! I – I'll kiss you as often as you want."

"Wal, thet's shore a temptin' prospect, lass. But I don't care to lose my job an' yore sister's trust."

"Laramie, it won't take *much* to make Hallie fall into your arms," whispered this provocative and bewildering little lady. "She's leaning to you now. Only she doesn't

274

know it. She'd be lost without you. And *I* can make her see it!"

Laramie was mute for a moment. Never had he encountered such a minx as Lenta Lindsay. The alluring thing she hinted rendered him weak. No wonder she had the riders out of their heads! How bewitching the pleading face!

"Come, Laramie. Be a good fellow. I'll do something terrible if I don't get out."

"No. I reckon yu will if yu do get out."

"Then send Lonesome. He'll help me."

"Lenta, I'm sorry to inform you thet Lonesome is drunk."

"Drunk!" cried Lenta, aghast.

"Shore. An' fightin', too."

"The bow-legged little liar! He swore he'd never drink again. For my sake!"

"Wal, it's all on yore account thet he's drunk. An' rarin' to kill some one. I had to tell him how I saw yu carryin' on. An' thet was the last straw for Lonesome. Yu see, lass, he believed in yu."

"Laramie! you gave me away?" flashed Lenta, in passionate amaze.

"I reckon I did. Lonesome's like a brother to me. An' I –"

"You squealed! About how you sneaked up on me – and – Slim?..." Lenta choked with emotion.

275

Laramie began to be sorry he had made promises to Lonesome.

"Yes, I squealed, Lenta. I reckon I'd never have done it if I'd any idee how crazy Lonesome is about you. For now he's goin' plumb to hell."

"Oh!"

"An' I fear he's not the only one."

"I don't care a – a – damn," returned Lenta, in a voice that denied the content of her words. "But for you to be a squealer! *You* – Laramie Nelson – whom Hallie and I thought the most wonderful man! . . . Oh, you – you four-flusher – you two-bit range-rider – you big calf-brander – you bluff of a Southern gentleman. . . . I hate you! . . . I'll make Hallie hate you. . . . Run – you coward – run from a girl and the truth –"

Laramie did not run exactly, but he surely spurred his horse out of earshot of that choked, furious face. He dismounted before the gate and wiped his hot face. His ears tingled, his cheeks burned. There was a riot within his breast.

"My Gawd! what a little wildcat!" he ejaculated. "Whew! . . . who'd a thought it of thet little baby-eyed lass?"

Then through his chaotic mind whirled the thunderbolts of her words. Truth! He was all that she had called him. But until this

276

very moment he had never realized that he had been idiot enough to believe he might win Hallie Lindsay. What jackasses men were! The moment they met a woman, regardless of her class or position, they immediately surrendered to a monstrous egoism and believed they could get her. It must have been some kind of instinct. He was glad Lenta had flayed him back to his senses. Perhaps he had better ride away from Spanish Peaks Ranch before –

"Laramie, what's the matter?" called a voice that made him jump. Hallie Lindsay stood in the door of her office, watching him. The day was hot and she was dressed in some flimsy white stuff that revealed her beautiful form. A rich color ringed with gold had displaced the former pearly paleness of her face. Her wonderful gray eyes, intent and grave, regarded him thoughtfully, almost with a sweet doubtfulness.

"Aw – nothin', Miss Hallie," replied Laramie, suddenly beset by a totally different army of emotions. He dropped Wingfoot's bridle and slowly plodded through the gate.

"Don't call me Miss Hallie," she said, with a surprising petulance.

"Wal, what shall I call yu?" demanded Laramie, helplessly. She used his first name for the first time. Laramie! Verily he was on a downhill grade.

"My name is Harriet."

"But I cain't pronounce thet."

"It certainly is a very difficult name," she rejoined, dryly. "I hate it, myself.... Everybody calls me Hallie."

Laramie stared up at her. "Do yu reckon yu're givin' me permission to call yu thet?"

"I reckon I am," she laughed, and averted her eyes momentarily while a spot of red appeared in her cheeks.

"Thanks, I'm shore proud," replied Laramie, somewhat recovering his dignity. There was less aloofness about her.

"I heard Lenta call you," went on Harriet.

"Wal!... An' yu heahed how she ended up?"

"Yes. Isn't she a perfect little devil?"

"Yu heahed it *all?* "

"I think so. My window is open. It's a still day. And she certainly spoke clearly."

"Aw!" expelled Laramie, heavily. He could no longer look up at her.

"I am glad you are loyal, Laramie. Lenta would turn the heads of most men. She is a distracting, terrible child."

"Wal, she's no child.... An' I reckon my haid was already turned."

"Oh, I see," she returned, hastily.

"Laramie, come in and make your report. I know something has happened."

Laramie felt that he dared not enter that office – to be alone with Hallie until he had gotten hold of himself.

"Nothin' much come off about the ranch," he mumbled.

"Don't lie to me," she retorted, impatiently. "Of late I have suspected you of deliberately deceiving me. To spare my feelings, father acknowledged. Because I'm a tenderfoot! You and your riders treat me with less – less respect and confidence than you show Lenta."

This was the truth. Laramie could not deny it. He stood there like a fool, bareheaded, running a hand round his sombrero.

"Yu cain't always tell the truth to a – a lady."

"Laramie, until father gets fully well and capable, *I* am boss of this ranch."

"Shore I know thet.... An' I wish you'd discharge me."

"Nonsense! I wouldn't do that," she replied, disconcerted and startled. Laramie conceived an idea that he had a certain hold on her. "You are – wholly satisfactory. What would I – we do without you? ... But I insist that I won't be treated as if I were a little girl."

"Wal, yu are a little girl so far as innocence an' softness are concerned," drawled Laramie, finding himself once more.

"But I – I mean business," she insisted, blushing in confusion or anger. "What has happened to upset you?"

"Wal, if I'm upset yu can gamble it's not the ranch business thet's to blame," he said, coolly.

"Very well."

"Lonesome is drunk."

"Drunk!"

"But thet didn't upset me.... An' he picked a fight with Neale. Then Chess Gaines busted into it. Lonesome lammed him one an' Gaines pulled a gun. I had to interfere.... Wal, I discharged Gaines. An' his pards Nigger Johnson an' Juan Mendez went with him. I reckon I can swear by the rest of the outfit."

"Well! – And you declared you had nothing to report."

"Reckon it's not much compared to what's goin' to happen about this heah ranch," he returned pessimistically.

They fell silent for a moment. Laramie felt her eyes upon him and he shifted uneasily on his feet.

"There's a rider coming," suddenly broke out Harriet, descending the steps.

Laramie jerked out of his trance to espy Lonesome astride a sweaty horse, riding up the last stretch of the road. A mere look at Lonesome told Laramie some untoward event had made him forget the rôle he was playing. Even at a distance he appeared stern and grim.

"Oh' it's Lonesome," ejaculated Harriet.

"Shore is, an' I'll bet a double-eagle Lenta will waylay him."

As the rider reached a level and turned toward the ranch-house a sweet, high-pitched, excited voice pierced the warm air.

"Lonesome! Oh, Lonesome – here – here!"

Harriet whispered hurriedly to Laramie: "If he's drunk he'll let her out."

"Not much," replied Laramie.

Lonesome halted, and appeared to be collecting his wits. Laramie saw him grow wary.

"Here I am, Lonesome," cried Lenta.

At last Lonesome located the imprisoned girl, but it was a long moment before he replied.

"Whash masser?"

"I'm locked up. Dad locked me up," wailed Lenta.

"Aw! Show you're in callaboos?"

"Ride over here to the window."

"Me. Ump-umm."

"Lonesome dear."

"Not much. Not atall. No, b'gosh!"

"Won't you let me out?"

"I should smile not."

"*Lonesome!* . . . Do you want me locked up?" begged Lenta, appealingly.

"Shore do. Great idee. You auch be behind bars forever. Dangerous female."

"Lonesome, I *do* think heaps of you. I'll promise –"

"You won't promise me nothin'," interrupted Lonesome.

"You bet I won't, you drunken cowpuncher!" flashed Lenta, surrendering to rage. "What are your promises worth? You swore you'd quit drinking for me."

"Shore. An' you swored you'd never kiss nobody but me. . . . Haw! Haw!"

"I *would* have kept it. *Now* I'll kiss every damn rider on the ranch."

"Nope. Not me or Slim Red."

"Yes, Slim Red! I'm going to meet him right now if I have to tear this wall down," shrieked Lenta.

"Tear away, Mish Lindsay," taunted Lonesome, riding on.

"You faithless hombre!"

"You flirtin' jade!"

Lonesome came riding on, reeling in his saddle. Lenta's final cry pealed out on deaf ears. Then the rider espied Laramie, and a moment later, when he reached the gateway, Harriet came into his view. Lonesome rode in and tumbled out of the saddle. An observer of experience would have noted that he was far from being drunk. Still he deceived Miss Lindsay, who fixed him with grave, disapproving eyes.

"Miss Hallie, gotta report Slim Red – bad hurt," said Lonesome.

"Hurt! – How? When? What has happened?" exclaimed Harriet, startled.

"Hawse piled him up."

"Oh! – Is it – serious?"

"Reckon. He's gotta have doctor pronto."

"I'm sorry.... Laramie, will you take charge of this," replied Miss Lindsay, soberly, and hurried back into her office.

Lonesome dropped his bridle, and with a significant jerk of head for Laramie to follow he trampled into the court. A moment later Laramie entered their room behind him and closed the door. Lonesome tore off his chaps and then began to divest himself of a wet and grimy shirt.

"So they got the kid locked in?" he queried, coolly.

"Shore have. She nailed me same as she

283

did you," replied Laramie, eyeing his friend thoughtfully.

"Sort of tickles me. She's locoed the outfit."

"Me too. But thet youngster will do somethin' bad yet."

"Yet! Say, pard, she's done it already."

"Aw, Lonesome – not bad."

"Wal, bad fer me, anyhow. Laramie, this bluff I'm throwin' ain't so good. I may hang on till we get back from La Junta."

"Ahuh. What's on yore mind boy?" drawled Laramie.

"We found Slim out on the trail. He's all shot up. Said he run plumb into Gaines with his pards. They throwed on him. Killed his hawse under him, or he'd got away. Gaines shot him three times while he lay on the ground. Left him fer dead. He was damn near croaked when Tracks found him. But he come to an' I reckon he's got a chance for his life. The boys air hitchin' up the old buckboard. I'll take Charlie with me an' we'll drive Slim straight to La Junta. Suits me better'n drivin' over with you-all, tryin' to keep up this drunken bluff."

"Ahuh. Yore idee is to keep the Lindsays from knowin' Slim was shot?"

"If we can. But Neale seen him. That boy

has stuff. You should have heard him cuss Gaines."

"I'll speak to him about it."

"Laramie, we oughtn't go to this La Junta circus."

"I reckon not. But to get out of it we'd have to lie wuss than we're lyin' now."

"Wouldn't surprise me if some of thet outfit showed up in La Junta. An' if they do, pard, what's the deal?"

"Wal, so far as Gaines is concerned yu needn't ask me," replied Laramie, darkly. "We're about at the end of our rope."

"Now, you're talkin'.... Gaines would look good at the end of a rope, not to say Price. Huh?"

Laramie sat down on the bunk and eyed the stone floor. He could not understand why he had hoped and believed he could spare the Lindsays the ruthless reactions of range life. It would have been better not to allow troubles to accumulate.

"Shore. An' Arlidge, too," returned Laramie, slowly.

"No such luck. You'll have to beat him to a gun, Laramie.... I'm glad Lindsay an' the girls are goin' to meet up with a lot of Western folks. They'll get an earful. Then when we come back –"

Lonesome ground his teeth over an

unfinished statement. Laramie nodded his head gloomily.

"Pard, don't take it so hard," spoke up Lonesome, brightening as he watched his friend. "Shore the brunt of this will fall on you, as it always does. But don't fool yourself about Hallie Lindsay. In the end she'll be game."

Chapter 10

"Can it be only nine days?" murmured Harriet, as she dropped her bags and packages on the floor of her room and flung herself upon the bed, where Lenta already sprawled in an abandoned posture of exhaustion.

"Nine wonderful days!" exclaimed Lenta, dreamily. "They'd been perfect but for that Lonesome Mulhall."

"Don't be so hard on the poor boy," replied Harriet, wearily.

Lenta growled something which sounded like profanity.

"You treated Lonesome outrageously," went on Harriet. "And but for him we.... Oh, well, what is the use?"

"No use, my locoed sister. Lonesome may have been the whole show, but for me he was a beastly jealous, drunken little bow-legged duffer."

"All your fault. Lonesome was growing to be a nice dependable boy. Now, look at him!"

"Don't worry, Hallie, I won't look at him," retorted Lenta.

"Nonsense! You like him."

"Me? Ump-umm! I did, but nix no more."

"How can you change so suddenly?"

"A woman's privilege, my dear."

"Woman! You are a spoiled baby.... Lenta, I'll tell you this. As soon as I've recovered from this trip you're in for a lecture from me," declared Harriet.

"Oh, you make me sick, Hallie, you used to be a good fellow. But since we came out West and you got moonstruck over that handsome dumb Laramie Nelson you've become a pill."

Harriet wanted to sit up and roundly slap this impudent sister, but she did not have the energy.

"I hate to tell you what you've become – a shallow conscienceless flirt," she substituted instead.

"I am not," snapped Lenta. "Self-preservation is the first law of life. Catch me letting these range-riders get the best of me."

"If you keep on, one of them *will* get the best of you," rejoined Harriet, bitterly.

"Hal Lindsay!" exclaimed Lenta. But she did not deceive Harriet. She might be petulant and peevish, but there was no genuine ring of sincerity in her voice. Harriet had to face the apparent fact that her sister had become incorrigibly wild.

"I suppose you are sore because I coaxed that rider Stuart to come back with us?"

"No, not sore. Laramie said he would give Stuart a job. But I'm sorry for him."

"You waste your pity, Hal. You don't savvy these cow-punchers."

"Yes I do. That's just it. I do. And I know you can't play fast and loose with them."

"You're worse than mother."

"Lenta, somebody must beat sense into your head before it's too late."

"Reckon it is too late," said Lenta with a giggle. "But, gosh! I've had a good time."

"You carried on outrageously in La Junta. Especially at the dance."

"All the same I didn't elope with one of them, as our darling, proud sister did," declared Lenta, scornfully.

"Ted Williams is different. He comes –"

"Oh, pumpkin-seed sunfish! Ted is like all the rest of the riders. He's got you all fooled, especially Flo. I've had six of them ask me to elope. And that's not counting Mulhall."

"Ted and Flo didn't elope," replied Harriet weakly. "They were just afraid to ask father. But they did ask me."

"Oh-ho! So that's why you've championed them? Does dad know?"

"Yes. I told him."

"Gee! so everybody but me knows everything? How'd dad take it?"

"He was hurt and furious. Said he had a couple of fine dutiful daughters."

"Couple! He's liable to have three – if I don't miss my guess. God help us, as ma prays, when *you* break out, Hal."

"There is not much danger of me disgracing the family, sister dear," rejoined Harriet.

"As *I* have disgraced it. And Flo, too. . . . Oh, fiddlesticks! – *No!* I don't mean that. I mean – oh, well. . . . Laramie says I've saved the Lindsays from poverty, murder, and what not."

"Laramie was humoring you. Even he is not impervious to your blandishments."

"Jealous cat!" ejaculated Lenta, sweetly. "I shall certainly throw myself at Laramie."

This dire threat was unanswerable, because Harriet knew that Lenta was capable of doing it."

"I'm sorry, Lent. I guess I'm – just all broken up," faltered Harriet.

"Shore, we're all broken up. I heard dad tell me what the West had done for the Lindsay outfit. I had gone to the bad. *You*
290

had turned out a mollycoddle. Neale had taken to the bottle. Flo had run off. And ma had become a fussy old fool."

"Lenta, you are making that up," replied Harriet, with all the vehemence she had left.

"Nope. I wasn't. Dad had had a few drinks himself."

"Mercy! What will become of us?"

"We'd turn out all right yet if only you would get acclimated," drawled Lenta.

"*I!*" That was the most unkindest cut of all. Harriet succumbed under it. She got up, and dragging herself into the sitting-room she went to bed on the couch, only half undressed.

Still, tired as she was, her mind kept active and she lay thinking. Presently her resentment and consternation were swallowed up in memory of the past nine days that seemed packed full of nine weeks of experience. She could only dwell on the outstanding events: the myriad of lesser ones were kaleidoscopic. Although their effect had been tremendous. And out of the whole she deduced astounding facts. She liked Western people. She loved the West and surrendered to the bewildering assurance that it had claimed her. She would have fought against going back to Ohio, even if her family were in favor of that. She had met other pioneer families and found them kindred spirits. The Colorado range was endless, the distances frightful obstacles, but there were neighbors, nice folk, kindly people, wholesome and attractive girls, splendid men, scattered all over the purple land. To realize this was a vast comfort. They were all in one category, most of them comparatively new to the range, dependent upon the boundless acres of grass, the streams, and the cattle. And likewise at the mercy of the rustlers as every cattleman realized! Harriet had gained more understanding of the complex situation. The striking thing about it was the fact that only few rustlers were known. Any cattleman, even her father, according to the mystery of the range, might be one of them. Harriet had been forced to accept the need of drastic treatment of these parasites of the country. She had tried, and failed, to make Laramie see a change in her. But that was his fault – the droll, aloof, incomprehensible and fascinating man! She felt that she was about to succumb to something. And every time the conviction forced itself upon her she drove it away. Mollycoddle! So that was what they all thought her, and probably Laramie, too? She would show them presently.

But these weightier matters had to be

given time. When they flooded back in memory Harriet laboriously put them aside for other things – the sudden passion she had conceived for horses and her resolve to learn to ride and manage them; her thrilling interest in the races and the tricks of the riders; the disturbing presence again of the bold Arlidge, who had hounded her at the dance; the shyness of Laramie in such strange contrast; the perplexing problem of the cattle and her failure to solve it; the undoubted confusion and let-down of all the Lindsays in this new invironment; and lastly the perilous conquests of Lenta and the elopement of Florence.

They were sufficient to keep Harriet awake for a long time, without listening to the insistent call of her heart. At length she heard Lenta moving around in their bedroom, yawning and mumbling to herself. Then the light went out. Harriet was left in total darkness. It made a difference. Besides, she discovered that she was cold. Presently she slipped back into the other room and stealthily got into bed. Lenta was already locked in slumber. But half disturbed, she unconsciously reverted to her old childish habit of snuggling close to Harriet. Harriet, deeply grieved with Lenta, had the instinct of repulsion, but there came an intervention of an old, stronger feeling. It was not long thereafter that her pillow was wet with her tears.

When Harriet awoke the sun had long climbed above the wall of the opposite wing of the ranch-house and she wanted to leap out of bed in the excitement of a dawn that was new and strange. But she restrained herself. Lenta's tanned and rosy face showed on the far pillow. How arresting in its sweetness! Harriet marveled that the girl could possess such a guileless sweet face and be such a devil. But Harriet did not gaze long at her sister. She had troubles of her own. She owned to a rebellious heart and she knew she had awaked another Harriet Lindsay. It thrilled her. The old self ventured feeble protests that were cried down. No longer would she be an obstacle to the success of Spanish Peaks Ranch. And that last triumphant decision landed her on her feet in the middle of the room.

Harriet donned riding garb that she had tried on only once, to her intense embarrassment. Her cheeks burned as she vowed she did not care. The summer days were growing hot and thin clothes were desirable. What would Laramie Nelson think of a young woman, twenty-five years old, in such a rig? It gave her a panicky feeling, which incensed her only the more. Then, snatching gloves and sombrero, she sallied forth in full possession of the realization that she was going out to meet disaster of one kind or another. Nevertheless, she would meet it and hide her feelings or die in the attempt.

At breakfast, Jud, who was devoted to Harriet and liked to talk, divulged much information. Mrs. Lindsay had had her breakfast in bed. Lindsay, glad to get back to the ranch, had whistled himself off early. Neale's drinking and failure to return from La Junta, Florence's elopement, and Lenta's incorrigibleness, Laramie's dark face that boded trouble. Lonesome's bottle, and the news of another cattle raid during their absence – all these had rested lightly on the head of John Lindsay.

"So dad's done with worry!" ejaculated Harriet. "Thank goodness! But, Jud, how do you account for it?"

"Wal, Laramie said the old boy was feelin' his oats," replied Jud, with a grin. "An' I say thet trip to La Junta done him good. He found out half a dozen stiff drinks of red likker couldn't phase him. He's goin' to be a well man. Thet's my hunch."

"I believe you are right, Jud," said Harriet, earnestly. "In the light of the blessed truth of returned health and growing strength all these troubles are nothing."

"Wal, I reckon myself they ain't much."

Harriet deferred seeing her mother for the present, and hurried out into the court to tarry a moment under the great green cottonwoods. How cool and shady under their spreading canopy! The brook went sparkling and singing down the stone steps. Blackbirds and mockingbirds, catbirds and swallows, were melodiously in evidence. This was a restful, beautiful, strength-giving spot, so old and thought-provoking. She would never tire of it, nor of the strip of purple range-land through the wide portal between the walls.

On her walk down to the valley below she espied Lenta's latest acquisition, the young rider, Stuart, approaching up the cottonwood-lined road. He was leading two saddle horses. Harriet stepped aside into the cover of the brush so as to avoid meeting him. If she had encountered him she would either have had to greet him civilly or have advised him to return to La Junta; and she felt that she did not know which she ought to do. So she let him pass. He certainly was a handsome young stripling. Besides Stuart, poor Lonesome would have resembled a little banty rooster. It was too bad that Lonesome appeared to be the only ugly, insignificant boy in Laramie's outfit. They were all absurdly attractive, young, red-cheeked, fire-eyed, lithe, and graceful chaps. Harriet thought she would like to have liked this newcomer Stuart. He was whistling gaily. He had not a care in the world. Probably he had not a dollar, nor anything but a horse. It pleased Harriet to observe that Stuart did not pack a gun. And this reminded her of Laramie. She both desired and feared to see him. Stuart passed on up the road, no doubt to keep an engagement with Lenta made the day before. And Lenta was in bed sound asleep.

Harriet resumed her walk toward the stables and likewise her thoughts of Laramie. She had not laid eyes on him since the dance at La Junta. That, however, had been the last event of the several days' entertainment, and they had all driven away next morning early. But the hours seemed long. Laramie had reason to avoid her. Had he not transgressed? Once could have been forgiven. But a second and unpardonable offense! Harriet felt her veins swell with heat that ran along them tinglingly to culminate in a hot wave on neck and face. She was ashamed and furious that she had unwittingly yielded to memory, yet once admitted, the incident augmented in her mind. Indeed there was no use to deny her pleasure at that dance. She had actually held her own with Lenta. Florence, probably, would have eclipsed them both, but Florence had eloped with Ted. Most of the riders had been atrociously poor dancers; not so Laramie Nelson. Early in the evening he had asked for a dance with her and had waited for it. So had she, with a pleasurable expectancy. She might be his boss, but all such distinctions were leveled this night. Laramie had not talked while he danced. And after Harriet had made a few attempts at conversation she had desisted. This was no ordinary dance. Laramie was no ordinary partner. Not until the dance began had she thought of being held in a man's embrace. And then after two turns around the thronged hall she had discovered why. Laramie was holding her close. She had hoped it might be merely accident. But presently she realized it was not. Then she protested: "Laramie, you're holding me – too tight!" His reply had been a cool drawling: "Aw, excuse me, lady, I shore haven't danced for years." And he had loosened the coil of his powerful arm. Again Harriet had fallen under the spell of the dreamy waltz. She did not remember how soon, but presently she felt that almost imperceptible drawing of the muscle-corded arm around her. The incomprehensible thing was that she had wanted to surrender to it. And she had done so for a moment, long enough to feel her throbbing breast flatten against his. Then: "Laramie – you – you're – hugging me!" she panted, and halting she drew away. "Aw, no! I wasn't atall, Hallie," he expostulated. "Don't yu reckon I'd know?" Harriet gazed up at him, feeling that a woman's eyes, intuition, intelligence must go far with this man. "Well, if you didn't know it –" Then the music stopped, saving her from she knew not what. Laramie had begged for another dance and she had promised it. But that second dance had never transpired. Harriet, in her excitement and pleasure at being so importuned by Westerners of all ages, had lost her head a little. This, with an intense added embarrassment when Luke Arlidge had accosted her, had resulted in a dance she did not actually desire or accept. In truth, Arlidge had simply swept her away from another partner. The enormity of her offense had not dawned upon Harriet until the dance was over, when she met Laramie's glance. Never had he looked that way to her. Recollection of the enmity between these two Westerners flooded over her then and she anathematized her stupidity. It chilled her, too. She had waited for Laramie to come to claim her, but she had not seen him again.

"Laramie was surprised – disgusted with me – and cold.... Uggh!" mused Harriet, as she walked on. "But what could the darned Southerner expect? I couldn't make a scene." She felt contrition, but she was not greatly concerned that Laramie might not come around. Still she did not really know him. She caught her breath and then she laughed. Always she could resort to what Lenta called a woman's prerogative. If she said to him, "Laramie, I'll go with you to the next dance and dance a lot with you – *no matter how you hold me,*" he would fall all over himself accepting, as these young riders did for Lenta. Here Harriet caught her unbridled imagination and concluded her reverie with, "I'm getting what they call loco."

She espied several of the riders in the distance, but caught no glimpse of either her father or Laramie. That afforded her relief. At the stables a Mexican lad, Pedro, saddled a gentle horse she had ridden before. Harriet took the bridle and led the animal away across the green valley to a secluded sandy spot shaded by cottonwoods and surrounded by brush, where she felt safe from prying eyes. Here she took the initial step in a procedure she had resolved upon – to overcome her fear of a horse to learn to mount and to ride. First she led the horse to a high rock from which she could easily get into the saddle, and rode around the enclosure a number of times. She trotted Moze, cantered him, galloped him, and finally rode him running. It was a goodly space, so she had ample room. There were thrills and fun, and also fright in this speed. But she stuck on, and finally established a permanent relation between her and the saddle. It was not impossible, where no critical eyes were seeing her. Once warmed up, she got the swing of it. So far as Moze was concerned, all she needed now was practice.

Then she reined him in and slid off in one step as she had seen the riders do. That was easy. She felt elated. Presently she meant to boss this ranch from the back of a horse instead of an office chair.

Harriet's next attempt was to mount. There were two ways to get upon a horse – any old way and the right way. She scorned any but the latter. Moze was about medium height and so was she. By stretching she could just get her left foot in the stirrup, while she gripped the pommel. First she

301

tried with both hands. It was a failure. She fell flat and hard enough to hurt. Reasoning that she had not sprung quick or hard enough from her right foot, she essayed again, and this time got astride. Whereupon she performed that action until out of breath. After resting, she attempted what she desired to emulate in Laramie and Lonesome. If she ever learned that, how she would astound the rest of the Lindsays!

The idea was to grasp the reins in the left hand, pull the horse around a little so he could see what she was doing, slip her left toe in the stirrup, and then seize the pommel with her right hand and spring up. On her first attempt her toe slipped all right, but out of the stirrup, with the result that she bumped her nose on the saddle and then fell ignominiously. This roused Harriet to battle. She tried again. She kept on trying. She succeeded. Then patiently for hours she stuck at the job until she had mastered it.

"Dog-gone-them!" she panted. "I'll show – them.... *Him!* The girls rave – about my shape.... But if anyone asks me – I'm too darned fat.... I ought to be skinny – and I'll get skinny."

Nevertheless, her earnestness did not extend to the limits of meeting Lenta and Stuart face to face, when on the return to the stables she espied them lolling in their saddles, horses close together, in the shade of the cottonwoods. Very lover-like for such short acquaintance, thought Harriet! She rode back and around the other way to avoid them. This time she ran right into Wind River Charlie and Dakota, who appeared as if by magic directly in her path. They doffed their sombreros. Dakota was bold and Charlie shy.

"You-all been workin' Moze out," declared Dakota, much pleased. "An' I reckon he piled you, miss?"

"No. I was learning to leap astride, as you boys do, and I fell in the dirt about nine hundred times," replied Harriet, with a laugh. "Please don't give me away."

Their astonishment and delight with the formerly dignified Miss Lindsay shone in their honest faces.

"Wal, I'll shore keep mum, lady. An' if Windy Charlie heah blows on you I'll half kill him," sang out Dakota.

"Never fear, Miss Lindsay," spoke up Charlie for himself. "I'll keep yore secret till h – h – er – always."

"Thanks, boys," she rejoined, and dismounted brazenly, she imagined. But it was not so bad. "Turn Moze over to Pedro."

"Shore you ain't a-gonna walk all the way up?" queried Dakota, aghast.

"I need the exercise."

"Wal, if you knowed what we know I'll bet you'll ride and run," grinned the rider, with a side glance at Charlie for corroboration.

"Yes? What do *you* know?" inquired Harriet, coolly. She had restrained a start. And she was proud of this dearly bought new demeanor. In time she would rival Laramie himself.

"Wal, Tracks Williams is back," announced Dakota, importantly. "He an' your sister drove right by us an' never seen us atall. They looked plumb scrumptious, but shore scared."

"Is that all you know?" accomplished Harriet, easily as she brushed the sand off her suit.

"Nope. Lonesome rode in, too, drunker'n a lord."

"What else? I thought you had some news."

Dakota tore at his tawny hair. "You win, lady. There ain't nothin' else, 'cept something about Laramie. It shore was funny to us. But I reckon you'd not be interested."

"Now, Dakota, yes, I would," flashed Harriet, forgetting her rôle.

"Ump-umm," rejoined the rider, his keen hazel eyes intent on her.

"Very well, then. As your boss I demand," she continued, with a smile. She saw that the smile, not the threat, gained her point.

"Aw, course I was foolin'...You see Larry must have had orders, didn't he?"

"Not from me."

"Wal, from yore dad, then, fer he chased Lin Stuart an' yore other sister all over the valley. They dodged Larry, we reckon, till he run bang into them heah. He was red in the face. Shore thet was new work fer him. 'Stuart,' he says, 'yu get off the ranch.' – An' Stuart laughed. 'All right, Laramie, but I ain't hurryin' none.' Then Laramie yelled: 'Lenta, yu go home an' I'll deal with this gazebo.' Thet little gurl came back at Laramie: 'Don't you insult my friend'...Haw! Haw! It was shore good as a circus."

"Well, what more?" queried Harriet, keeping her face straight.

"'Lenta, you go home!' busted out Laramie.

"'Larry, you go to hell!' re-lied Lenta, cool as a cucumber.

"'By thunder! thet's jest what I'll do!' roared Laramie, an' he rode off like mad up toward the ranch-house."

"Indeed! Had Laramie been drinking, too?" inquired Harriet, innocently.

"No. He ain't took to drink yet, but we reckon it won't be long now."

Harriet had to turn away to keep from betraying herself to these boys. She could not blame Lenta for liking to be with them, for a fiendish glee in tormenting them, in giving them back as good as they sent. Harriet suddenly felt a weakness to do that herself. Thoughtfully she walked up the road, but once out of sight she sat down on a rock to rest and ponder. So Florence had returned. Harriet was glad and sorry at once. Flo and Ted would not exactly meet with a parental blessing. Father Lindsay would rage. He was capable of turning them out. Harriet thought that she would let the guilty couple receive a sound scare before she intervened in their behalf. And Lonesome Mulhall, too, had returned, drunk again, or still drunk. That was serious. Harriet found that she had a tender spot in her heart for this wild, harum-scarum, thieving, lovable range-rider. But what could be done? Lenta had goaded the sentimental boy to madness. Worse would surely come of this. Laramie's ridiculous attempt to compel Lenta to anything and his equally ridiculous threat to go to hell proved how impotent and enraged he was. Harriet wondered if this last affair of Lenta's, or any order given by her father regarding the willful youngster, could so completely warp that cool, strong, quiet man out of his orbit. Harriet just wondered and pondered. Laramie, however, might well be upset on behalf of his beloved Lonesome.

Harriet slowly resumed her homeward walk. She lingered in likely spots. There would be pandemonium up at the house when she arrived, and she was in no hurry to run into it. Nevertheless, in the course of another hour or more she reached the ranch-house and the gate. There she halted to fortify herself against the inevitable.

Before Harriet had steeled herself in the least, however, she heard angry voices, not loud, yet certainly trenchant. She recognized Laramie's. To her amaze she espied that the door of her office, which was on the side of the entrance nearest her, stood open. She recalled having given her father the key last night. Had he forgotten to lock it or was he in there with Laramie? She took a step, another, and presently stood on the stone porch behind the door. The thick door swung outward and hit Harriet. She had no conscious intent to play eavesdropper. But there she was and Laramie's next speech froze her in her tracks:

"Sneaked in heah reckonin' Hallie would save your hide, didn't yu – yu gol-durned exasperatin' liar!"

"Aw cheese it, can't yu, Laramie?" That growl and appeal in one were certainly couched in Lonesome's plaintive voice.

"Cheese nothin'. Yu run in heah, hopin' Hallie would save yu."

"Wal, wot if I did?"

"It shore wouldn't save yu if she was right here."

"Bah!"

"Lonesome, I found this red scarf in yore chaps pocket," went on Laramie, relentlessly. "Yu stole it from Lenta thet first day of the races. The kid was ravin' about it. She swore some bull-haided puncher stole it. An' she was right."

"Naw. I didn't stole it," rasped Lonesome.

"Yu're a durned liar, boy."

"All right, then, I am. What you gonna do about it?"

"Wal, the last time I ketched yu, which wasn't so long ago, I swore I'd beat the stuffin's out of yu."

"Aw, you ain't man enough," blustered Lonesome shuffling his feet.

"Lonesome, I could rope one hand behind

my back an' lick yu all hollow," declared Laramie, in a slow voice.

"You jest try it, Laramie Nelson, an' see what happens. I'll give you away to Hallie."

"How give me away?"

"Thet you're loco about her. Thet you're wuss off than I am about the kid. Thet you cain't eat or sleep – or fight, either, by Gawd, 'cause of her!"

"Lonesome, if yu double-cross me thet far, I'm through with yu forever," drawled Laramie, solemnly.

"Wall, mebbe I won't do *that*. But I ain't agonna play off this drunk gag of yours any more. It makes me madder'n hell. I've queered myself with Lent an' the old lady, an' I'm afraid with Hallie, too. All for nothin'."

"I don't agree, an' neither does Ted or Jud. It shore worked an' I could square yu with Hallie an' her ma in a jiffy. But whether yu keep on pretendin' to drink or not, yu're shore goin' to get licked aplenty."

"Hold on, Laramie! or I'll start in real drinkin' an' you know what a hell's rattler I am," threatened Lonesome, fearfully. His steps gave evidence that he was backing to the wall.

"Yu won't do nothin'. An' shore yu won't steal no more. Why, yu've disgraced Ted an' me. Scared us sick! Yu'll ruin us yet. Shore as God made little apples yu'll ruin us heah with this nice old couple an' their lovely daughters!"

"Hell! Ain't we ruined already?" A dull thump answered this violent exclamation. A gasp of pain followed, then sundry thuds, rasping of boots, a wrestling of bodies in violent strain, and at length a sodden crash on the floor.

"La – re! Quit or I'll – draw on you," choked Lonesome, in a fury.

"Shet up, yu bow-legged bluffer.... I'm gonna straddle yu an' beat the damn thievin' stuffin's out of yu!" There followed sliddery sounds, and then a bam that attested to Laramie's sincerity.

"Aw! – Larry, don't – don't.... that's my weak spot.... *Aw!* ... for Gawd's sake! ... *Aw!* ... kill me – an' be done! Somebody'll ketch us heah. Dear old Larry, let me up. I'll be good. I'll promise.... *Aw!* You —— —— —— ——!"

"Shet yore profane mouth, son!" rejoined Laramie, grimly. Bang! ... "Take thet on your kisser!" Wham! Bam! "There's a couple on yore nose!" Biff! "How yu like thet, Lonesome? I see yu've got some real red blood, after all." *Smash!* "There's another for yore gizzard. Aha! Thet's

the place. Thet's where yu live!"
Bummm!... "Now, ketch yore breath, an'
tell me if yu'll stop this low-down stealin'?"

All sounds except a gasping intake and
expulsion of heavy breaths ceased to fill
Harriet's distraught ears.

"Who'd athunk – you'd treat me – this
way!" panted Lonesome.

"Say I'm only warmin' up. But I'll give
yu a chance. Will yu stop this heah stealin'
forever?" returned Laramie.

"Hell no!" burst out Lonesome, still
consumed by rage, but significantly weak of
voice, "I'll steal every —— —— —— I see!
I'll steal the cussed kid's clothes – so she'll
have to go naked. I'll steal jewlry –
money...an' cattle an' hawses! – Thet'll
make you sick. I'll be a hawse-thief an' get
strung up by the neck."

"Very wal. Now I am good an' mad. Shore
I was only foolin' before," declared Laramie,
sternly. "Heah's for yore breadbasket."
Wham!... "Heah's for yore yellow gizzard."
Bam!... "Heah's for yore white liver." *Bam!*
"Now I'll treat yu to the raspatas with both
fists." A succession of rapid terrific blows
ensued. Then a pause. "Dog-gone," panted
Laramie. "I just wonder where this disease
of yores is located. It cain't be in yore haid.

311

So it must be in yore belly." Bum dum – *bum* BUM BUM!

Harriet could not endure this situation any longer. She had to fight to keep from screaming in mingled mirth and fear. What manner of human beings were these range-riders? Or were they human at all? She checked her impulse long enough to decide upon a course of procedure.

"What's this? Who's in my office?" she cried, in pretended amaze. Then she mounted the steps and rushed into the room.

Laramie straddled Lonesome's hips, and on the moment he had a red fist aloft. It remained aloft while his head jerked up and his piercing eyes appeared to pop. Laramie's visage expressed a righteous anger. It slowly changed. His fist fell.

Harriet's gaze traveled to the prostrate Lonesome. He lay limp as a sack and almost as flat. His face was a bloody mess.

"Laramie! – For heaven's sake! What are you doing?" screamed Harriet, dropping quirt, gloves and sombrero. "Are *you* drunk, too?"

"No – I'm not – drunk," mumbled Laramie.

"You've murdered this poor boy!" went on Harriet, wildly, thrilling to her part. "Get up, you monster!"

312

"I was only – lickin' him," replied Laramie, rising to his feet and backing away from Harriet's flaming eyes.

"You great big stiff!" went on Harriet, trying to recall some choice rider's slang. She might go to the extent of a little profanity. "To pick on this boy!"

"Pick on Lonesome? It couldn't be did. Look heah. See thet?"

Harriet had noted the swelling on Laramie's chin and another over his eye, but she gave no heed to Laramie's appeal. She had her cue.

"You brute!" she replied.

"He hit me terrible hard – in a place I cain't show you. He may be little, but he's a bull."

Harriet dropped upon her knees beside Lonesome. "Oh, you poor dear!" she cried, tenderly wiping his bloody face with her handkerchief. "Lonesome, are you dead? Has he killed you?"

"I was most dead, Hallie, till you come," murmured Lonesome. Verily he would have had to be almost wholly in that state not to take advantage of this golden opportunity.

"What'd he beat you for?" she queried, trying to keep her voice steady.

"It's his vicious nature. You'd never think

313

Laramie could be so onhuman," said Lonesome, earnestly.

"Did you quarrel?" asked Harriet.

"Not eggzackly."

"How did you come to be here?"

"Wal, I run in heah for protection. I seen the door open an' I thought you'd save me from him."

"Poor boy! I surely will," replied Harriet, with all the tender solicitude she could muster.

Suddenly Laramie started as if he had been struck with a whip.

"Lonesome, how can yu lie to *her?*" he rang out.

Lonesome lay still a moment with one eye open and the other half closed gazing from Harriet to Laramie. Then he moved to take the stained handkerchief from her and struggled to a sitting posture.

"Help me up. I'm licked, all right," he said, and appeared to be a different Lonesome."

Harriet rose to assist him and it was her conviction that he needed more than her arm. Laramie stood like a statue. Lonesome flopped into a chair, where he pulled out his scarf and with trembling grimy hand wiped the blood out of his eyes. With his other hand he put Harriet's handkerchief in his pocket.

"Keep yore mouth shet," ordered Laramie. "Yu're out of yore haid. I'll tell Miss Lindsay about it."

"Too late, pard. You beat all the deceit out of me," returned Lonesome.

"What *are* you saying – both of you?" asked Harriet.

"Hallie, I'm a thief," replied Lonesome, looking up at her. There was a light in his eyes that rendered even that homely battered face beautiful.

"Why – why, Lonesome! How you talk! You must be flighty," cried Harriet, in great concern.

"Listen, Hallie," went on Lonesome, while Laramie threw up his hands and strode to the window. "I'm a low-down thief. Not to make myself any richer, but jest because I couldn't help appropriatin' things I liked. I've stole for years. An' since I come heah it's got wuss. I've stole from you. Thet little gold pencil on your desk! Don't you remember? Wal, I stole thet. An' all the things Lenta lost I stole. . . . An' I stole Miss Florence's nightgown!"

"Lonesome Mulhall!" ejaculated Harriet.

"Laramie stood fer my stealin' fer years," continued Lonesome, frankly. "An' so has Ted. But lately they both got sore on me. I let on it was a disease. But it was jest plain

315

low-down cussed stealin'. I had a hankerin' fer pretty things – 'specially what wimmen wore or owned. Laramie kept swearin' he'd beat me half to death if I didn't quit. An' today when he found Lenta's red scarf in my chaps he went after me. He chased me in heah – an' I reckon he did a good job of it."

"Lonesome! Of all things! . . . I am simply stunned," murmured Harriet. "You – whom we all thought so fine a boy!"

"Don't rub it in," he begged, hoarsely, a little bitter. "I've come clean. An' I'm cured. Course you'll fire me now. But thet's not what matters. I won't have you layin' this on to my pard, Laramie. He done jest right. I deserved all I got."

"You say you're cured?" queried Harriet.

"I wouldn't steal even a hunk of beef off'n a lost steer if I was starvin' to death," declared Lonesome.

"Then if you'll promise not to drink so – so terribly, I will not discharge you," replied Harriet, sweetly.

"Lord, Miss Hallie, you're good," said Lonesome, feelingly. "But even if I could promise you an' keep it, I'd not want to hang around heah with everybody knowin'."

"I will keep your secret, Lonesome, the same as Laramie and Ted have done."

"But I – I can't promise –"

"Shore yu can," spoke up Laramie, turning from the window. "Miss Lindsay, all this heah drinkin' of Lonesome's lately has been a trick."

"Trick! It's no trick to fool us," retorted Harriet, feigning heat.

"Wal, I wanted Lonesome to let on he was drunk so's to find out more about Gaines an' his hombres. An' Lonesome agreed, providin' I'd let on he was goin' to hell for Lenta."

Harriet did not know what to say. The tall rider was quite pale and his wonderful eyes pierced her. Up to this moment she had been mistress of the situation, but her composure was breaking and she could not trust herself longer. Laramie's presence seemed to pull her like a magnet.

"Miss Hallie, I don't want Lenta never to know the truth," added Lonesome, earnestly. "'Cause if it hadn't been for Laramie I'd done plumb wuss than I pretended."

"I will keep that secret, too," returned Harriet. "You have lied to me. I'm not such a tenderfoot as you imagine. I mean about things pertaining to the ranch. May I be assured that you will tell me the truth from now on?"

"I swear I will," replied Lonesome.

"Wal, so far as personal matters air concerned, I promise," drawled Laramie, somehow retreating to his old cool self.

"Thank you," returned Harriet, hastily. "I advise you to take Lonesome to your quarters and look to him before anyone else sees. He surely is a sight."

Laramie laid powerful hold on his disfigured friend. "Come on, pard."

"Dog-gone, I'm knocked out," replied Lonesome, ruefully, as Laramie dragged him up and half carried him out. Then right before them appeared Lenta in the courtyard. She had just come in hurriedly on foot and she halted stockstill to gaze at Lonesome.

"Say!" she cried.

Harriet, who peered out over Lonesome's shoulders, detected an inflection of Lenta's voice that gave food for reflection. Nor did the girl wholly conceal a flash and start.

"Pass on, Lenta," drawled Laramie, "or yu may feel bad."

"Lonesome! – somebody throw you in a threshing-machine?" queried Lenta.

"It's nothin' to you, girl."

"Lenta, my pard heah suffered this cripplin' in yore behalf," added Laramie, coldly.

"*Mine!*" Lenta's face flamed scarlet, and

318

then slowly paled till her tan appeared obliterated. Instinctively she moved as if to step toward them, but something inhibited a natural impulse, and turning she fled up the court.

"Laramie, old pard, thet wasn't so bad!" exclaimed Lonesome, thrillingly.

Harriet watched them out of sight. Then ponderingly she picked up her gauntlets, which suddenly she slammed against the wall. "Damn it!" she whispered. "I love that boy Lonesome, and it's beautiful. . . . I'm going to love that cold, blood-curdling Laramie – and – it's – terrible!"

Presently Harriet remembered Florence and Ted, which thought instantly switched the direction of pondering and emotion. She found herself in a Homeric mood that augured well for her erring sisters. Fearing she might lose this exalting excitement and sense of power, she ran out to find them.

Chapter 11

The porch in front of Florence's open door was littered with parcels and bundles and grips, evidently left where they had been thrown from the buckboard. This was an indication of the eloping bride's mental state, for Florence was usually the neatest and most fastidious person with her possessions. Harriet burst in upon the young couple.

"Congratulations, you prodigals!" she cried, gaily. She saw Ted first. He looked exceedingly well in a new dark suit. His handsome weathered face showed no sign of worry, concern, or remorse. It broke into a warm smile at sight of Harriet.

"Oh – Hallie!" cried Florence, poignantly. On the moment she did not look a happy bride. Her lovely face was pale and tear-stained. She was most becomingly gowned. Harriet's surmise proved correct, for Florence rushed into her arms to laugh and cry and kiss her with a warmth seldom expressed by the beauty of the Lindsays.

"Well, Flo, you've been and gone and

320

done it," murmured Harriet, holding the girl close.

"Hallie, don't I come in for a kiss, too?" queried Ted, brazenly, as he rose from the bed. "I was there when it happened."

"Two, if you want them," laughed Harriet, as she extended a hand. Ted was not slow to kiss her. "Boy, you don't look sorry over your deportment."

"Me? I'm the happiest man in the world," he declared.

"So you should be."

"Oh, Hallie, I was happy too, till we got home," wailed Florence. "Dad wouldn't even see us. He wouldn't let us go in to mother. And when we tried, he yelled, 'Get the hell out of here!'"

"Did he!" ejaculated Harriet. "That's a lot for father. I'm afraid he is angry. You should have asked him. I *told* you. What'd you run off that way for?"

"Oh, it was Ted's fault. He coaxed – so – he made me. . . . And I – I guess I wanted to. . . . But, Hal, darling, what on earth will we *do?* We spent every dollar we both had. Where could we go? But I won't be separated from you all. It'd be dreadful. I didn't elope for that. I just didn't think."

"Don't cry, honey," replied Harriet. "Maybe it wasn't such a fool thing, after all.

We're out West now. What was the sense of waiting? Still, it'd been better if you'd asked father."

"I wanted to, Hal. Honest I did. But Ted wouldn't let me.... Won't you persuade dad to forgive us?"

"I'll try, dear. I guess I'm not much scared," returned Harriet as she released her sister. "He's not in a good humor. You see, Lenta broke out again."

"Again! She has stayed broken out. I hope she didn't fetch that Stuart fellow home with her."

"That's just what she did," said Harriet.

"Oh, Lordy!" cried Flo, aghast, and looked to see how Ted took the news.

"Did Laramie know it?" queried Ted.

"Not until we got here, I'm sure."

"Hallie, young Stuart is a bad hombre," rejoined Ted, seriously. "We heard all about him. Reckon he's not a rustler like Gaines, but he's just plain no good. Married, for one thing. Ran off with Alice Webster. She worked in a restaurant at La Junta. And she had to go back. Lenta has barked up the wrong tree this time."

"Whew! So he's married? That's one thing we mustn't tell father."

"I'll tell Lent at once. Where is she?" interposed Florence.

322

"Laramie is the one to tell," added Ted.

"One thing at a time. Wait till I see if I can persuade father not to cast you off forever," said Harriet, gravely.

"Oh, Hallie, I – I couldn't bear it," cried Florence.

Harriet hurried over to her father's quarters and knocked without any misgivings. His bark was worse than his bite. And even if he was furious, Harriet knew she could coax him around.

"Go away," called a rough voice.

"But it's Hallie."

"Oh ... ma, it's Hallie. Let her in."

Harriet was admitted by her sleepy mother, who did not appear otherwise upset by the misfortunes of the family. Lindsay sat at the window, with his back to Harriet. She was careful to stay behind him, but finally leaned over his chair.

"How are you, daddy?"

"Humph! You must want a lot – callin' me that. Out with it!"

Harriet gathered all her forces of eloquence and launched forth: "Flo is scared and heart-broken. Poor kid! She's so deeply in love that she didn't know what she was doing. And Ted is penitent. They both realize now that they should have asked you. They *did* tell me and made me swear not to betray them. Ted's a fine young fellow. We need him here. Besides, if you sent him away Laramie and Lonesome would go too. Then where would we be? Flo could not be separated from us all. Daddy, darling, we've got this infernal cattle business to conquer, and from what I've gathered it'll be no fun. For goodness' sake, let's *keep* the riders we know are honest, no matter how queer they are!"

"Fine talk. Can you keep that hombre Laramie here?" returned Lindsay.

"Why – why, father!" exclaimed Harriet, utterly routed.

"Don't why me. *Can* you do it?"

"Can I! . . . How on earth – What –"

"Daughter, you understand me. *Will* you keep Laramie here? We're ruined if you won't."

"I – I will," faltered Harriet, in a tumult.

"Very good. That relieves me," declared Lindsay, heartily. "Now you can call Flo and Ted over. I was only bluffing about them, anyhow. But you needn't tell that."

Harriet shakily opened the door and called, hurriedly. "Oh, Flo . . . Ted. Come!" She waited to receive them. Florence came running, but her husband was slower. Meanwhile Lindsay told Mrs. Lindsay to present herself in the sitting-room.

Florence stared with appealing question at Harriet. The proud dark eyes were not proud now. She went in. "Dad – p-please forgive me." Ted strode up on the porch, and tossing away his cigarette he winked at Harriet and went in. Harriet followed. She would have been frightened if she had not been aware of her father's duplicity. He had arisen. He apparently did not see the trembling bride, but fixed stern gaze upon the groom.

"Well, young man, what have you got to say for yourself?" he bellowed. Before Ted could reply, Laramie strode jinglingly in at the door.

"Aw, 'scuse me," he drawled.

"Stay, Laramie, I may require your assistance," said Lindsay.

"Mr. Lindsay, I haven't got so much to say," replied Ted, frankly. "Fact is, I've deceived you all."

"Deceived us?" demanded Lindsay.

"Oh *Ted!*" moaned Flo.

"See heah, Tracks," interposed Laramie. "I've had a couple of shocks today. Go easy now."

"Yes I've deceived you," resumed Ted, coolly. "It looked all right at first thought. But now I'm afraid it's pretty low down, especially to my wife. . . . But anyway, here goes. About six weeks ago I wrote to my parents – first time for years. And I told them what a wild life I'd led – and how falling in with a fine family and the sweetest girl in the world had changed me. That she'd promised to marry me. . . . Well, the answer didn't reach me until two days before we went to La Junta. It came with the mail that Manuel brought on the freight-wagon. . . . The governor, mother and my sister Edna – she was a kid when I left home – are coming out to set up in the cattle business. It sort of knocked me. I was sure locoed. It means a big ranch for me or I could throw in with you here and we could run a hundred thousand head of stock. But the funny thing is I didn't want to tell you. I guess I was crazy to see if Flo would marry me just as I was – a wild range-rider without any future. That, sir, is my excuse."

Ted's listeners were all stricken. Flo most of all. Rapt, fascinated, she gazed at him. Lindsay scratched his grizzled beard in bewilderment. The tables had been turned on him. Laramie appeared to be the only one at a loss, and astounded.

"Yu double-crossin' son-of-a-gun," he drawled. "Don't you ever reckon yu could boss me."

"Laramie, we've shared blankets and

crusts – good and bad all these years. And we're not going to change now. When the governor comes out to set me up this fall you and Lonesome will be my pards as always," declared Ted, warmly.

"Oh Ted! you wonderful wretch! Not to tell *me!*" cried Flo, and flung her arms around his neck.

"I reckon I cain't wait to tell Lonesome about thet," beamed Laramie, and plunged out of the door to clink rapidly down the courtyard.

"Looks like I've gained a partner as well as a son-in-law," declared Lindsay. "Hallie – ma, it sure takes a tickle out of my surprise. They'll never believe me now."

"Indeed they will," cried Harriet, joyfully.

"Flo – Ted, the 'tarnal truth is that I wasn't mad at you. I was tickled to death. I just wanted to throw a bluff."

Florence screamed and ran from her husband to her father, to envelop him ecstatically. Ted followed her and gripped the hand that clasped round Flo's shoulder.

"See here, pop, you've played a low-down trick on me. You've not only got well but you've got Western. You've made a tenderfoot out of me. I was scared stiff."

But it soon developed that joy in the Lindsay

household was not unmitigated. Presently Lenta appeared upon the scene, distractingly pretty and as baby-eyed as ever.

"So you've come back pronto?" she asked coolly, without any preliminary greeting to Florence. "I'll stay away awhile and have some fun when I elope."

"Lent, aren't you going to congratulate us?" rejoinèd Florence, reproachfully.

"Well, I congratulate you all right, but I'm not so sure about Ted."

Then Mr. Lindsay fixed his youngest daughter with an icy stare and was evidently about to address her when Laramie came in, carrying a saddle-bag. His eyes were twinkling. Harriet felt a sudden rush of liking for him. How seldom did he show humor!

"Folks, reckon heah's Christmas come middle of July," he drawled, and emptied a bright mass of articles upon the table. "There! Lonesome's respects an' he said he'd got a lot of fun out of his joke."

"Joke!" echoed Ted, fiercely.

Lenta let out a scream, and leaping at the table she snatched a red scarf out of the tangle. "My darling scarf! I knew I never lost it.... Lonesome, the darned little thief!... Look! here's more I thought I'd lost. My locket with my picture! My glove!

328

My bracelet! Well, I'll be jiggered! . . . I'll bet two-bits I'll find my garter here –"

"Oh, Lent, there's my gold pencil," cried Harriet. "The rascal! But I'd forgive him anything – I'm so glad to get it back."

"For the land's sake – my nightie!" ejaculated Flo.

Ted made a lunge. *"What?* Your nightgown? How'n'h – the deuce did he get this?"

"Not off me, darling," laughed Flo, recovering the lacy garment.

"Lonesome snooped thet off the clothes-line," drawled Laramie. "Fact is, he took about everythin' thet wasn't tied down. Heah's a double-eagle I've packed with me for years. I wouldn't have spent it for worlds. An' many's the time we was near starvin'. It saved my life once."

"How?" queried Lenta, eyeing the gold piece in Laramie's extended palm.

"Wal, it was in my vest pocket an' it stopped a bullet thet would shore have done for me. There's the mark where the lead hit."

"Let me see," spoke up Harriet, answering to irresistible impulse. Laramie handed the coin to her. It was a twenty-dollar piece, worn smooth, and it had a very perceptible dent in the middle. What a little thing to save a man's life! Harriet shuddered. There

329

seemed to be a raw, sinister violence in that very dent. Suppose Laramie had not been carrying this coin in his vest pocket! An accountable speculation as to what difference that might have made to Harriet whirled through her mind.

"No wonder you cherish it," she murmured, her hand trembling visibly as she returned the coin. "If it stopped a bullet – some one must have shot at you."

"Wal, if I recollect, some one did," drawled Laramie.

"May I ask what happened to him?" queried Harriet, curiously. She was to see the twinkle die out of Laramie's eyes and an almost imperceptible shade pass over his face. He made no reply, but flipped the coin and turned aside.

"Hallie, why don't you ask me?" queried Ted, with a laugh.

Lenta and Florence were recovering more lost articles, and were squealing in glee.

"Dad, here's your cigarette-holder," chirped Lenta, suddenly, and she tossed it to him.

"So 'tis," replied Lindsay, pleased as a child.

"Mother, if I don't miss my guess here are your little scissors, the pair you raved about disappearing from your work-basket," added Flo.

"It is.... Well, if this doesn't beat the Dutch!" returned Mrs. Lindsay, receiving the coveted instrument.

"Folks, don't be mad at Lonesome," spoke up Laramie. "He's just a boy at heart. An' thet was his way of havin' fun. I took him to task about it an' I reckon he won't steal no more."

"Mad? Why, we couldn't be mad at Lonesome," said Harriet, and as there was no disputing this, evidently she spoke for all. Laramie went his way then, and presently Flo and Ted, sensing trouble brewing for Lenta, beat a hasty retreat. Mrs. Lindsay retired to her bedroom, and that left the refractory Lenta alone with her father and Harriet.

"Lenta, I forbade you to leave your room today," began Lindsay, severely.

"I'm young, dad, and full of go. I can't stay indoors," replied the girl, petulantly.

"Where'd you go?"

"Out."

"Riding?"

"Yes, sir."

"Alone?"

"It's not safe to ride alone, Laramie says. So I always ride with some one."

"In this case no doubt your companion was the rider you annexed at La Junta. What's his name?"

"Stuart."

"Did you persuade him to come here?"

"Well, dad, I can't say I discouraged him. I told him we needed riders. And he's wonderful on a horse."

"That's not the point, my daughter. I don't approve of you meeting one of these strange Westerners today and fetching him dangling after you tomorrow."

"I can't help it if they dangle after me," said Lenta, resentfully.

"Lenta, I don't blame these boys for liking you. And I don't blame you. But you are nearly seventeen. You must use more sense – or trouble will come of it."

"I can take care of myself."

"You could back East. But not out here," protested her father. "This is the unsettled West, you headstrong child. Any one of these riders may be a rustler, a horse-thief, or worse. Laramie Nelson is authority for that. My objection is you are too free – too reckless. You will not wait till we know this or that young fellow is all right. And I propose to stop you one way or another."

Lenta tossed a rebellious head.

"How do you know this Stuart is a fit companion for you?" went on Lindsay.

"Anyone could see he's a perfectly wonderful fellow," retorted Lenta.

"He might be that and all the same be a desperado," returned her father, dryly.

"Lenta, dear, you are quite mistaken in young Stuart," interposed Harriet.

"Hallie! Do you know anything about him?" asked Lindsay.

"Yes, I regret to say."

"Keep it to yourself, sister, for I sure won't believe it," snapped Lenta, suspiciously. She had been rubbed the wrong way.

"Hallie, tell me," ordered her father, peremptorily.

"Stuart is a bad hombre, according to Ted. He is married to a girl named Webster in La Junta. She left him or he deserted her, for she went back to work in a restaurant there. Laramie must know, for he ordered Stuart off the ranch this morning. You heard him, Lenta."

"It's a – lie!" gasped Lenta, passionately. "You're all picking on me."

"Nonsense! We are trying to keep you from making a fool of yourself," replied Lindsay, impatiently.

333

"Lenta, what has gotten into you?" asked Harriet, in amaze.

"Laramie said he reckoned it was the devil, Hallie. Eastern girls run wild out here sometimes," said Lindsay.

"Aw, that for Laramie!" burst out Lenta furiously snapping her fingers. "He's only sore at me because of Lonesome."

"Lenta, are you going to stop riding around alone with these fellows?" demanded Lindsay, gravely. "Are you going to stop carrying on with anyone? Are you going to stay at home and help your mother?"

"No I'm not," flamed out Lenta.

"Very well. I'll lock you in your room until you change your mind," replied her father, and taking Lenta's arm he dragged her out. Lenta looked back at Harriet with eyes vastly different from a baby's.

"I'll get even with you, Hal Lindsay," she cried.

Most certainly this was not the hour for Harriet to have the long heart-to-heart talk with Lenta that she had determined upon. She sighed heavily. Lenta might be going to turn out the black sheep of the family. For that matter Neale was not so white a sheep. At La Junta he had caroused with the cowpunchers, so it had been reported until they laid him away under a table. He had not yet returned from La Junta. One grain of comfort Harriet extracted from all this trouble was the way her father took it. He had evinced a most surprising imperviousness. She remembered when even little things used to infuriate him. But now he was out West. Out in the open! It was magical. She had changed herself, and as she strolled through the courtyard toward her office she drew a full deep breath of that sweet, dry, hot sage-laden air. It expanded her breast.

As she passed the lodgings of her three range-riders she heard sounds of merriment. Lonesome laughing after he had been beaten to a pulp! Then Ted's low, less coarse laugh rang out. Harriet distinctly heard from the half-open door: "Who's gonna tell her?" And the answer in Laramie's drawl: "Reckon Tracks better do thet. I shore don't stand ace high no more." To this Lonesome replied: "Hell, you got four aces up with her sister." And again Ted laughed and spoke: "Girls hate jealous, glum blokes. Listen to me. Larry, if instead of being afraid to look at Hallie you grab her and kiss her dumb, and Lonesome if you brace up and do the same with Lent we'll all be happy. My governor will stake us –"

Harriet drew out of earshot. Her ears certainly tingled and her cheeks glowed. She ran up into her office and shut the door. "Oh, the brazen wretches! To parcel us girls out that way!" she whispered, hot and cold by turns. "Ted is the cunning one. So that's how he won Flo? . . . To advise Laramie to – to grab me – oh-h! . . . if he *did* –" Harriet hid her burning face in her arms as she leaned over her desk, and shook from head to foot. What had outraged pride and reserve to do with the tremendous tumult in her breast? She had been waylaid and surprised by an unknown self. One self seemed shamed and horrified; another thrilled and throbbed, and cried out in demanding voice for the very thing that had stricken her.

Harriet kept to herself the remainder of that day, and when night came, owing to the fact of Lenta's confinement in another room, she was alone. She felt relieved. She bore a secret in her bosom and she could not everlastingly hide it. Her mirror told her many tales, as well as forced her to gaze at this flush-faced, wild-eyed stranger. Nevertheless she slept deeply and long.

Next morning she again dressed to ride, and discovered that she had awakened in a sublime and heroic mood. She had no fear of a horse. She would ride the little beast of a mustang that had thrown her or break her neck trying.

She had breakfast with Ted and Flo. They were a delightful couple, when Harriet could forget Ted's duplicity.

"I want to ride, too, darling," said Flo, coaxingly. "You promised to teach me. I've got such a gorgeous riding-habit."

"Listen, sweetheart. You'll ride in overalls," quoth Ted, masterfully. "Pants – my stylish wife!"

"Well, anyway, just so you take me. I never thought Hallie would come to it. Look at her. Getting Western."

"Sure. She looks great. I'll take you this afternoon, honey. Laramie has a job for me this morning."

"Job? Do you have to work?"

"I should smile I do. I've got you to support now – you wonderful girl. . . . It's a job finding horse tracks. Lonesome is in bed – done up – and I've –"

They went out with their arms around each other. Somehow Harriet suffered a queer pang. How happy she was for Flo! That boy might be a gun-throwing cowboy, but he worshipped her and she was safe. If only Lenta had –! Her father came in, dusty and warm, a cheerful presence.

"Hello, Hal. I've been up with the boys,"

337

he announced, gaily. "Hungry as a bear!... Hey, Jud. Ham and eggs. Coffee – and a couple of your sour-doughs.... Neale rode in late last night, Hallie, I'm glad to say."

"That's good. How – was he?"

"Didn't see him till this morning. He was all right. Looked rocky. Laramie routed him out early and put him to work."

"At what?"

"Digging fence-post holes. Gosh! how the riders hate that sort of work. I used to like it. They sure rode Neale. That Wind River Charlie – he's a dandy chap – I heard him say for Neale's benefit, 'Laramie, dog-gone if the boss's son ain't the plumb best hole-digger I ever seen.' And Laramie said: 'Shore. I seen thet right off. I'll put him on thet mile stretch we want fenced down the valley.'"

"And what did Neale say?" queried Harriet, keenly interested.

"I couldn't tell it to a lady," laughed her father. "But at that, it tickled me. He's game, Hallie. And that counts out here. Laramie said: 'Don't worry no more about Neale, boss.'"

"Well, let's stop worrying – then," replied Harriet, her voice breaking a little.

"I shall. But Lent's a different proposition," returned Lindsay, gravely

338

shaking his head. "As I came up the road just now she saw me. She's so little she can sit up in that window. What do you think she called me?"

"Lord only knows."

"Guess I'd better not tell you.... Aggh! Thanks, Jud. That ham sure smells good."

Harriet wondered if Lenta would espy her as she passed on the road, which turned somewhat along that side of the ranch-house before going down. Before she had reached the head of the descent Lenta hailed her.

"Mawnin', dear sister," called the girl in her sweetest most dangerous voice.

"Why, good-morning, Lenta dear. I should think you'd decide to obey father," replied Harriet, feeling like a hypocrite.

"If you don't get me out of this I'll queer you with Laramie," threatened Lenta, viciously.

"Nonsense. You couldn't queer me – even if –"

"Oh, couldn't I? Laramie believes you're a saint. But you're not, old girl! I'll squeal about your affair with Emery and you bet your life I'll make it something to drive even Laramie to drink."

Affronted and stung, Harriet retorted: "Child, how you talk! There's nothing between Laramie and me."

339

"Sure. You're too cold-blooded to love anybody, even your own sister. But that big stiff of a rider would adore you if you'd –"

"Hush!" commanded Harriet. "How dare you speak so – so insultingly – to me?" With that Harriet wheeled to hurry down the road. Presently a shrill voice pealed after her, and suddenly its content forced Harriet to clasp her hands over her ears and run. This encounter and the violence of action were not conducive to composure, or a reasonable judgment for the issue at hand.

Harriet had a little bay mustang saddled instead of the gentle Moze, and such was her state of mind that she mounted him right in front of the Mexicans, and also Dakota, who gaped at her. True, Pedro was holding him.

"Miss, he ain't been worked out lately, an' he might pitch. Better let me go with you," advised the rider, anxiously.

"Thanks, Dakota. I could ride an outlaw this morning," she replied. Nevertheless, after she was out of sight, she concluded discretion would be the better part of valor, and she would be wise to put the mustang through his paces over in the secluded sandy plot she had utilized the day before.

Presently she became aware of sundry sore spots on her anatomy. She had not felt at all spry, still she had not known she had sore muscles and aching bones. The mustang wanted to run, yet he appeared tractable, and Harriet believed she could manage him. Suddenly he bolted and tore off at breakneck speed. Harriet had all she could do to stick on. But instead of getting panic-stricken she grew angry. She did not care whether she fell off or not, only it would never be from any lack of her trying to stay on. The wind tore at her hair; branches of trees stung her face. When he leaped a log she shot sky-high to come down in the saddle with such a jolt that she thought her head would fly off her shoulders. If he had needed any guiding, it would have been a desperate predicament. But the mustang was not running away; he was just racing for fun. He tore out of the cottonwoods, down the pasture road, all around that pasture, across the valley and up on the other side of the woods again. Harriet stayed on him until he slowed down.

"Son-of-a-gun!" she panted, in true Western expression. Hot, wet, her sombrero gone, her quirt lost, her hair flying, she made the astounding discovery that this strenuous action of her extreme agitation had done away with her pains, at least for the moment. Suddenly her anger gave way to elation. She was still in the saddle. "You darned little wild nag! I'm on you yet!" she cried.

Before she realized it she was back in the neighborhood of the sequestered natural corral which she had started out to find. She headed the mustang there, and soon felt safe from curious eyes, at least. The mustang grew cranky. He certainly was a self-willed animal. Still he did not appear to want to leave the oval, so she let him have his own way. He pranced around, side-stepped, champed his bit, half-reared, and all of a sudden bolted again. But just as he got going faster he made a terrific leap, and landing stiff-legged he threw Harriet in a parabolic curve far over his head. She fell in the sand and scooted along on her face, her hands out, until she dug in so deep that she stopped. Breathless, stunned, she lay still. Am I dead – she thought? Her consciousness seemed real, though all outside was dark. The smell of sand roused her to the fact that she had her face buried. She was smothering. To her amaze she sat up easily. She was not hurt, apparently, but she surely presented an undignified spectacle for Harriet Lindsay. The mustang stood there meekly, as if waiting. A mere sight of him inflamed Harriet to a degree she had hitherto never dreamed of.

"You ornery little Western mule!" she ejaculated. "You're like all the rest of this darned West. You're laughing at me. You've got the soul of these tricky cow-punchers in you. But I'll get the best of you. I'll ride you if it's the last thing I ever do."

Whereupon she got up and essayed to mount him, forgetting that Pedro had held him for her at the stable, and that he was one of the horses trained for a flying mount. As she leaped up he leaped forward and spilled her. Harriet spun around on her head and went down to roll over. Strangely she was not hurt, only enraged. When she shook the sand out of her hair she strode over to the mustang and kicked him in the belly as she had seen Lonesome do to a mean horse. Still it was not a brutal kick, but just something to show him her spirit. Then all set, careful, nerved, she slipped her toe in the stirrup and sprang off her right. She appeared to be swung up into the saddle with marvelous ease. If Harriet had not been so furious she would have whooped at this feat. But the mustang was in action, headed around the enclosure. From gallop he changed to run, and after a couple of times around the corral he turned toward the center. Harriet was ready for him, so that when he executed the tricky stop she stuck like a burr.

"Fooled you, didn't I?" she taunted.

He might have understood her, for he did

something new. He bounced up and came down on stiff legs. Harriet thought every bone in her body was broken and her teeth jarred loose. She could not keep her head up. He bent double and pitched her high. He was bucking with her. While high off the saddle Harriet realized that, and instead of frightening her it only made her furious. She lit in the saddle and desperately clutched the pummel. He pitched again – up – down – up – down – up – down. Next time Harriet missed the saddle and slid off his back like oil. She sat right down in the sand. It was ignominious but no more. It did not hurt. If that was all she had to stand from pitching she could do it all day. The mustang led her a long walk around the corral before she could catch and mount him again. Whereupon he promptly began to pitch again. On the third buck he threw her ten feet aside, to alight on her shoulder and head. The soft sand saved her from injury. She got up and went at him again.

In the succeeding hour or two, or whatever period it took, Harriet was thrown often after sticking on longer each successive time. She knew she was going to ride him eventually and the mustang knew it too. That made him worse.

"Tomorrow I'll wear – spurs," panted

Harriet. "Then I'll rake you over.... You won't throw me – either – you – ornery – white-eyed little Western horse!"

No doubt the truth of this was assimilated by the mustang, for in the last and valiant effort of pitching he gave her the worst of her falls.

Harriet lay on her back where she had struck just outside the wall of brush. She was stunned, helpless, but conscious. She realized she was conscious, for she saw the blue sky, the white clouds, the green cottonwoods, and she heard a jingling musical step. Then the rush rustled and parted right close to her. A tall form loomed over her.

"Wal, this last spill wasn't so funny," drawled Laramie's familiar voice.

His face blurred in her sight. She tried to speak, but no sound came. A tight bound sensation encompassed her chest. But she was aware of his kneeling beside her, straightening her legs and arms.

"Aw, nothin' cain't be broke," he muttered. "She lit square – an' this heah soft sand –" Then he lifted her head. "Hallie, air yu hurt?"

As she gazed up her sight cleared. The dark piercing apprehension in his eyes seemed the sweetest thing she had ever realized.

"Laramie – I'm – killed," she got out, in a husky whisper.

"Killed yore eye! Air yu hurt – an' where?"

"My spine! – I feel – paralysis – stealing over me!" This was not such an arrant falsehood, because some paralyzing affection was attacking her modesty and dignity.

"For Gawd's sake, girl, don't tell me yu broke yore back?" entreated Laramie.

Whatever she had yearned for had its fulfillment in his tone, his look, in the big hands she felt tremble.

"Perhaps not so – so bad as that," she whispered, weakening. "Help me sit up."

He did so, very gently, though with strong clasp. Harriet got all the way to her feet. "I'm all right – I guess. . . . Dizzy. I –" she swayed, and instinctively clutched him.

"Yu're hurt. Yu cain't stand up," he declared, as he held her.

"Oh no. I don't feel any pain – yet. I can stand."

But Laramie did not give her a chance to prove it, for promptly taking her up in his arms, as if she were a child, he strode off up the valley.

"I can pack yu home. Yu're more of a load

than Lenta, but yu don't weigh much at thet," he said, coolly.

"I do – so," replied Harriet, confused and startled. "I weighed one hundred and twenty-six at La Junta."

"Is thet all? Gosh! I reckoned yu was a big girl."

Harriet closed her eyes and tried to think. There was something terribly wrong. If it was not an internal injury it was most assuredly an internal commotion. But what could she do? For the sheer, feminine, inexplicable glee of it she had practiced an innocent deceit just to see what he would betray. She would have to keep it up. What if Lenta was still at the window? Nothing would escape her eagle eyes. The thought of Lenta seeing her in Laramie's arms was unendurable.

"Laramie, let me down now," she said.

He did not pay the slightest attention to her. How silly of her to ask that when she had her eyes closed and looked as if she had fainted! Harriet opened them, to her sudden discomfiture. Laramie was carrying her through the willows. Her head was quite high upon his shoulder, with her face turned partly inward. He had one arm under her shoulders and the other under her knees. How powerful he was! She might have been as light as a feather for all the sign he gave. She turned her face farther inward so that he could not see it. Then she made the disturbing discovery that her right side and breast were pressed tight against him. Her left hand had instinctively grasped his vest above his pocket. She saw it. All of a sudden an absurd and incredible impulse assailed her – to slip that hand and arm up around his neck. She even let go her hold on his vest before the enormity of such an act swept over her. That shattered what nerve she had left.

"Let me d-down, Laramie. I can walk now," she entreated.

"Say, Lady, I'd do this for any girl," was his astounding reply. "I'm not crazy about packin' yu – if that's what ails yu."

"But you are holding me too – too tight," objected Harriet, in a smothered voice.

"Shore. I heahed yu say thet when we danced together. An' there was no cause for it atall."

"You are a liar, Laramie Nelson," retorted Harriet, anger coming to her rescue. "I know when I'm hugged."

"Wal, Lonesome said he'd bet yu'd been hugged a lot. But I kinda reckoned –"

"Put me down this instant," commanded Harriet, who realized that if he did not she would give up abjectly.

"Aw now, Lady."

"I'll yell," she threatened.

"Wal, so yu take me for the Luke Arlidge brand?" drawled Laramie, coolly setting her upon her feet. "I'm tellin' yu flat thet yu can crawl home for all I care."

By this time they had reached the foot of the zigzag trail at the head of the valley. Harriet found that she would not have to crawl. She was unsteady on her feet and had to stop to catch her breath, but she climbed to the fringe of sage and oak-brush just under the rim without any assistance. At the last step or so, however, Laramie's iron hand detained her.

"Wal, look there, Lady," he whispered, and his icy tone like his clutch on her arm sent a cold stiffness all through her.

Harriet gazed out between two sections of brush in the direction indicated by Laramie's leveled hand. She saw a horse close under a window of the ranch-house, then a rider leaning away from the saddle, his sleek dark head halfway inside the bars. She gazed spellbound. That was Lenta's window. Stuart! Then she espied two little brown hands clasped around the rider's neck. Lenta was kissing Stuart through the bars.

"What shall I do, Lady?" whispered Laramie.

"Send him – away," choked Harriet.

"Wal, yu step down the road a little, for this hombre may throw a gun on me," advised Laramie.

A hot bursting gush of blood raced over Harriet, liberating she did not know what.

"If he does –" she flashed, and then broke off. But it was not fright. Strangely she realized that it was not fear that gripped her. Stepping out she hurried down the road – hesitated – stopped. Lenta and her latest admirer were oblivious to their surroundings. Suddenly a voice with a cold ringing drawl broke the silence.

"Hey, Stuart."

The rider jerked as if he had been lashed, and breaking the clasp of the girl's arms he whirled and straightened up with face flashing pale.

"Don't draw, boy," called Laramie, sharp and quick. "If yu're half decent yu won't force me to kill yu before her eyes."

"Aw, I – ain't drawin', Nelson," cried the rider, hoarsely.

"Wal then, rustle pronto. An' if I meet yu again around heah yu'll have to draw."

Stuart let out a mirthless laugh, and spurring his horse rode around the ranchhouse out of sight.

"Lent, I reckon yu're no good," declared Laramie, in profound regret.

"Howdy, Romeo and Juliet," replied the girl, flippantly. But her face was distinctly red, with either anger or shame. "I'll bet you've been spooning yourselves.... Hallie, you shore look mauled."

Harriet ran to get into the courtyard. If she had been furious at sight of Lenta's action, what was she after such an insinuation? Never in her life had she been so possessed with wrath. She feared to trust herself on the moment. Repairing to her room, she removed her garments and washed the dust and dirt from her person. Then she discovered some bruises, a skinned elbow and sprained wrist. All the while what mental force she was capable of had been directed to the restoration of calm. She could not attain it. Nevertheless, she refused to wait longer. As soon as she had dressed she hurried across to obtain the key of Lenta's room from her father. But he was out and her mother said she thought he had the key in his pocket. Harriet went to Lenta's door, anyway, and pounded upon it with no gentle hand.

"Who's there?"

"It's Harriet. I've a word to say to you, young lady," replied Harriet.

351

"You don't say? Well, I can't let you in and I wouldn't if I could," drawled the girl, insolently.

"Lenta, I really don't care to see you," returned Harriet, striving for steady deliberate scorn. "You can hear me.... I think your conduct disgraceful. I think you are a shameless little hussy.... Laramie had it right. You *are* no good. You have turned out bad.... My hopes for you, my prayers are ended. I don't want anything more to do with you."

Harriet stopped. She expected a tirade of abuse. But all was significantly silent. She hurried away to the seclusion of her room. And she did not present herself at the supper table this day.

Her sleep was restless and troubled. She dreamed or imagined she heard noises in the night. As gray dawn approached she sank to deeper slumber. And she awoke late. Somebody was knocking upon her door.

"Yes. Who is it?" cried Harriet, sitting up. The sun shone bright in her window.

"It's me, Hallie," replied her father, and his voice heralded calamity. "You needn't let me in. But – listen...." His speech broke, gathered strength. "Lent ran off last night. Some rider – Stuart we think –

broke the bars of her window – got her out. . . . Laramie says it happened before dawn. He took Ted – Lonesome, and I don't know who else. . . . He said to tell you and ma that the girl was only playing a joke. But he didn't look like it was a joke. . . . They'll trail them . . . and I've an idea we're in for – some real West at last."

Chapter 12

Toward dawn Laramie awoke with a start. A gray space marked the open door. Some noise had aroused him, or it might have been a dream. Laramie lay on his side, breathing quietly and regularly. Tracks, of course, no longer shared their quarters. Then a clip-clop of shod hoofs sounded from the far side of the ranch-house.

The sound died away. It had not been unusual for Laramie to hear hoof beats outside the walls, especially on his side of the old fort. There were always loose horses and strayed horses. These, however, were never shod, and they were always grazing around. But this horse had been shod and he was not grazing. A rider had gone by.

Laramie rolled over to go to sleep. But sleep did not come. He realized after a little while that there had been a regurgitation of one of his old trail habits. Men of his calling slept lightly. Always they heard steps on their trails. Any slight noise around camp brought him instantly wide awake and listening. He had an intuition, an

354

inward ear for unusual steps, as well as untoward events.

Wherefore Laramie sat up in his bunk. The darkest hour had passed some time ago, and the gray light that he had noticed upon awakening had perceptibly increased. Laramie felt for his clothes on the floor, thinking the while that there was no sense in his not responding to this feeling. Since living with the Lindsays he had scarcely been his real self. Old instincts had been gladly lulled. And Hallie Lindsay had made him forget who he was.

Slowly he dressed and pulled on his boots, very quietly, for Lonesome likewise slept with one eye open. Laramie buckled on his gun-belt and slipped out of the room into the courtyard. The brook murmured softly; off on the range a solitary coyote yelped. He walked to the gateway and out on the road.

Daylight was spreading from the eastern horizon, a wonderful soft brightness coming up from the undulating prairie. A faint tinge of rose lighted the sky. He listened. The range still slept. The valley was steeped in gray. Laramie stood a moment, inhaling the fresh cool sage-breath of the morning, running his appreciative gaze far out and down, along the battlements of the distant ranges, and the obscure patches and streaks that meant leagues and leagues of open country. Cattle out there, herds and mavericks, horses and squatters, riders and hustlers, life of the West! But it was to the north that his gaze swept and held. The ruggeder gray north, swelling to the foothills, with the dim Rockies beyond! Months ago Laramie had located menace to the Lindsays there.

He searched the road for fresh hoof tracks and that slow action seemed to still a restlessness. By that Laramie judged how dissatisfied he was with himself. Finding none, he stood a moment ponderingly, then made his way toward the gate. As he reached a point even with the wall that ran north he thought he saw something dark projecting from one of the windows. He did see something. That was Lenta's window. Laramie leaped along the wall.

Before he reached the window he espied one of the iron bars projecting out. It had been bent and broken. On the ground lay pieces of stone and mortar, and a pick. Laramie recognized the tool. Only yesterday he had seen it leaning somewhere down by the stables. Fresh tracks of a shod horse cut up the ground directly under the window.

"Wal, heah we air," soliloquized Laramie. "Thet awful kid has eloped. All the time I reckoned somethin' was goin' to happen. Now what'll I do?"

Laramie made sure that Lenta could have squeezed out of the window and then of the direction the horse had taken. After which he strode back to awaken Lonesome. He hated to tell his friend of this last proof of Lenta's waywardness. But it had to be done. Lindsay would send them out on the trail to fetch her back. For that matter, coming to think of it, Lonesome would go of his own accord, and Laramie would not let him go alone. Stuart, besides having a bad repute, was married. Somehow the handsome rider had intrigued the susceptible madcap Lenta and had made off with her. Lonesome would kill him.

Laramie went in and put a reluctant hand upon Lonesome.

"Wake up, pard," he called grimly.

"Ahuh," Lonesome stirred and groaned. His face was swollen and blackened in spots, but he could open his eyes. "What's the idee, wakin' me early? I'm gonna stay in bed. My Gawd! ain't you been mean enough –"

"Hell to pay, Lonesome," interrupted Laramie.

His words, his tone fetched Lonesome up in a trice.

"Excoose me, pard. What's up?"

"Lenta is gone. Run off...eloped, I reckon."

"Aw!" Lonesome let out a great breath. His disfigured face underwent a nameless change.

"I heahed a hawse some time before daylight. I sat up an' listened. Struck me queer. Yu know what I mean. Wal, after a while I went out. It'd come daylight. I fooled around an' found Lent's window bars busted out, a pick on the ground an' fresh hoof tracks. Reckon I didn't need to call to see if she was gone."

"Who with?" queried Lonesome, coolly.

"Stuart, I reckon. He was foolin' around heah yesterday. Hallie an' I were comin' up the trail.... An' we seen him, Lonesome."

"What doin'?"

"Wal, he was straddlin' his hawse under the kid's window. In fact he had his haid in between the bars."

Lonesome got out of his bunk. "Go tell Lindsay thet Lent broke out last night," he said, cold and hard. "Say she's jest playin' a joke on them an' thet we'll fetch her back. Then call Tracks. Rustle now."

Laramie lost no time striding to the rancher's door where he rapped softly.

"Who's there?" called a voice.

358

"Lindsay, come to the door. Yu needn't dress. It's Nelson."

To do him credit Lindsay complied without undue noise.

"Why, Laramie!" he ejaculated, when he saw the rider.

"Lenta has broken out of her room," announced Laramie, bluntly. "Somebody helped her. Used a pick on the window. Reckon it was Stuart. The crazy kid was just playin' a joke on yu. Gettin' even 'cause yu locked her in. . . . Tell Miss Hallie – an' don't worry boss. We'll fetch her back."

Without waiting for a reply or to look Laramie made haste across the patio to arouse Williams. His knock brought instant response.

"Tracks, get up an' dress for ridin'," he called. "Yore honeymoon is over."

"Nix pard, but I'll be with you pronto," replied Ted, with his footfalls thudding on the floor.

"Tell Florence thet Lent has eloped an' we're to fetch her back," concluded Laramie, as he passed on.

"Ho! Ho! Flo, wake up. What you think?"

Laramie heard no more, except a startled sleepy cry from Florence. He found Lonesome putting on his chaps. That worthy appeared unusually quiet.

359

"Tracks will be heah pronto," said Laramie, and sat down on his bunk to wait. In a few moments Ted came in, ready to ride, with black fire in his eyes. "Come out, boys, an' have a look."

On the way around the wall Ted was the only one to vouchsafe any remark and this was that he had always expected Lenta to do something crazy. Soon they stood under the broken-barred window, where Laramie left them to make their own deductions. He back-trailed the hoof tracks to where Stuart, or whoever had ridden the horse, had come up out of the valley. When Laramie turned to retrace his steps Ted was far out on the level, evidently seeing where the hoof tracks went, and Lonesome had climbed up the wall to look in the window.

Presently they met again.

"He hit straight north," declared Ted, snorting his disgust. "He aims to get a horse from some of those lousy outfits and then travel west. Denver, likely."

"Wal, I reckon it makes no bones with us," added Laramie. "Our job is to ketch him an' save Lent before he has the damn little fool all night. Thet'll be easy unless he finds a hawse pronto."

"Laramie, if it wasn't for her family I'd say let her go," replied Ted bitterly. "We may save her this time. But what good will thet do?"

"Shore I savvy. All the same if we taught a lesson to one of these gay gazabos thet Lent's drove wild mebbe it'd stop the rest of them."

"Stop that kid? Hell no," replied Ted, snorting again.

"Wal, I been givin' up about Lent for some time now," said Laramie, resignedly. "An' if yu want to know I lost my hopes when Miss Hallie lost hers. Thet was only yesterday."

Lonesome did not even sag under these combined scornful estimates of his inamorata. "Lent didn't elope," he ground out. "She's jest showin' her folks they can't keep her locked up. An' I don't blame her. Mebbe after they get a good scare they'll treat her decent."

"Pard, yu die hard," rejoined Laramie, admiringly, ashamed of his opinions.

"Heavens, Mull, do you need any more proof than *this?*" ejaculated Ted.

"Than what?"

"That she's gone – run off – eloped with a strange rider."

"Reckon I do. I wouldn't go back on Lent any more'n I would on you fellows."

"Oh, hell! – Would you risk laying off their trail?"

Lonesome pondered that a moment. "I would, yes, if we had only the kid to figger on. She'd come back an' laugh in our faces. But this fellar Stuart has a bad rep. Lent must trust him, but we can't."

"All right. Let's get going," replied Ted, impatiently.

"You an' Laramie light out on their trail. I'll go down an' fetch the hawses."

Lonesome strode off at a rapid pace and quickly disappeared down the road. Ted and Laramie turned away from watching him.

"This will ruin him," declared Ted. "— — that pretty little imp!"

"Nope. It'll make a man of Lonesome – if thet's in him.... Come on, Ted. Trackin' is an old game of ours. We used to bet on it. What'll we gamble on now?"

"Not on Lent Lindsay, that's a cinch. It would be throwing money to the winds.... Trail is plain enough.... He walked his horse."

At the end of a few hundred yards the tracks turned east to follow the rim of the valley, zigzagging among the patches of brush. This was a surprise to both of the riders. In two distinct spots, not far apart, the horse had been halted long enough to

362

leave a number of extra tracks; and these places appeared significant in that they were screened by trees from the ranch-house. But there were no signs of any one dismounting.

"What yu make of thet, Tracks?" inquired Laramie, in perplexity.

"Damn funny! Looks like they were undecided.... Maybe they stopped to hug and kiss."

"Wal, if they was set on thet they could do it ridin'."

Presently the tracks left the rim and took out on the hard gravel floor of the ridge where they could not be followed rapidly. The riders worked across, however, to the head of another intersecting draw, out of which led one of the range trails. Meanwhile the sun had come up hot. Here they waited for Lonesome, pretty sure that he would count on heading them off. They did not have long to wait. Before Ted and Laramie had arrived at a satisfactory opinion as to why the trail did not abruptly leave the valley, Lonesome appeared mounted and leading two saddle horses. He did not evince any surprise at finding them there.

"Huh. Thought you said their trail headed north," he growled, sarcastically.

"It did. Now it's haidin' east," returned Laramie.

"Heah's some biscuits an' meat. An' I slung on a waterbag."

Ted led off along the trail, eating as he rode, and bending a little to the left, following the tracks. Progress was slow because the dusty trail showed other horse tracks, and sometimes it was difficult to distinguish the fresher ones. Soon, however, the hunt swerved from the well-trodden path to the grassy upland where it proved no longer easy to follow. Ted had to walk his horse. High ground rose some miles off to the northeast, and cedared ridge-tops showed dark against the sky. This certainly was no direction for a couple to elope. It headed directly away from La Junta or any other settlement. Laramie confessed he was puzzled. He surely remembered that Lenta invariably rode out this way, and had often spoken of the wonderful view to be had from the high ridge-tops.

The morning was far advanced and waxing hot when the three riders ascended the lower slope of a ridge that ended in a wooded escarpment, looking down on the gray gulf of the prairie-land. Laramie, whose gaze kept to the fore, sighted a flock of buzzards soaring low over the end of the escarpment.

"Look. Somethin' daid up there."

364

"Buzzards. . . . Well, what of it? We always see them. Dead cow or calf, likely."

Lonesome did not express an opinion, but it was noticeable that he paid less attention to the tracks they were following, and also he took the lead up the ridge. Ted, however, stuck to his task of trailing, though neither he nor Laramie fell far behind.

On top they met a pleasant breeze. Cedar trees straggled along the ridge, thickening to a grove toward where the escarpment ended. The height afforded a magnificent view of the vast prairie, the leagues of range east of Spanish Peaks, the old fort like a black dot on the gray, and the rich green valley. Small wonder that Lenta had loved to ride there! Laramie had a premonition that she had ridden this way once too often.

At this juncture Lonesome reined his mount to wait for his friends. They joined him. And he pointed off into the cedars.

"Dead hawse," he said, coolly. "What color was Stuart's?"

"Black. Coal black, with some white. Shore was pretty. . . . Where?"

"Heah . . . to the right of thet spreadin' cedar. . . . Black hawse with white spots – all right."

"Yes, thet's Stuart's hawse," declared Laramie, grimly. "Saddle's on yet."

The riders galloped an intervening fifty rods. Buzzards took wing from the cedars to join the soaring ones aloft. Laramie's comrades were out of their saddles in a twinkling, but he swept wary glances all around. Over under a cedar he espied the blue-shirted form of a man lying prone, in a terrible laxity that he well understood. All at once Lenta's so-called elopement assumed tragic proportions. He leaped to the ground and joined his companions.

The black horse was dead, though not yet stiff. It had been shot in several places, according to the visible wounds. Blood had clotted and dried around them. The bridle was gone, and the saddle had been stripped.

"Shot in his tracks. He wasn't runnin'," asserted Laramie, his eyes scrutinizing the ground.

"Mouth full of grass," said Ted.

"Wal, come over heah, an' yu'll see Stuart, I reckon," called Laramie, sharply turning away.

In another moment they were gazing down upon a dead rider, a young man whose handsome features wore a tortured ghastly fixity. He lay in a pool of blood. Evidently he had been riddled with bullets. One hole showed in his brown wrist; another in his neck near the shoulder. All his pockets had been turned inside out. Sombrero, belt, spurs were gone.

"Pard, is it Stuart?" queried Lonesome, thickly.

"Yes. No doubt of thet," replied Laramie, cold and sharp. "Spread out an' let's figger this heah deal."

They separated. Laramie stalked to the clump of cedars on the rim. This was one of the famous lookout points on the range. Indians had once spied upon the fort from here. Laramie found unmistakable evidence that this shady vantage had been occupied for some time by a man or men who had reason to watch the ranch, even as Indians had watched soldiers and settlers, and the caravans before them. But there was no signs of a camp. Some one had rested there, lounged on mats of cedar, smoked innumerable cigarettes, read tatters of an old newspaper, and whittled sticks.

"No more'n I expected," muttered Laramie. "Who now? Rustlers watchin' cattle, shore, but what else?"

Laramie hunted to and fro along the rim, then circled back to where Stuart lay, a sickening sight with the flies buzzing around him. Ted was coming from down the slope of cedars, and before he reached the corpse, Lonesome hove in sight from along the ridge.

He waved something white, and appeared propelled by a singular force.

"Ted, what's thet Lonesome's wavin'?" queried Laramie, as the rider arrived, breathing hard.

"Looks like a girl's handkerchief – Lent's I'll bet," replied Ted, after a moment. "And it's not any whiter than Lonesome's face."

"Pard, the fire's out! I never saw him look like thet – even when Price had a rope round his neck."

They waited. Lonesome stamped into their presence and exhibited a small linen handkerchief.

"Smell it," he said, huskily, and waved it in front of Ted's face, then Laramie's. The faint perfume was indeed memorable of the girl. "Reckon it's Lenta's."

"What else yu find?" queried Laramie.

"Hoss tracks. Five or six hawses sloped out of heah this mornin'. An' Lent Lindsay was on the back of one of them."

"Wal! – Ted, what'd yu find?"

"There's a camp down the slope," replied Ted, quickly. "Hid in a thick clump of cedars. Place has been used on and off for months. Dry camp, but there's water down below somewhere. Three riders have been staying there for days. They had a couple of pack animals, one of them a mule. These men rustled in a hurry a couple of hours ago – maybe longer.... And, pards, the lead rider's horse belonged to Chess Gaines."

Neither Lonesome nor Laramie showed any surprise.

"Wal, I saw where scouts have been layin' on the rim, watchin' for days," added the latter.

Lonesome folded the precious handkerchief and carefully stowed it in his breast pocket, after which his hard and glinting eyes searched the faces of his friends.

"Plain as print now, Lonesome," spoke up Laramie. "I reckon Tracks an' I were sore an' judged Lenta pretty bad. When mebbe she's not bad atall. I'm beggin' yore pardon."

"Me, too," chimed in Ted. "But hurry."

"Ahuh. S'pose you bright fellers read all this for me," retorted Lonesome, in no wise softened.

"Wal, Lenta must have persuaded Stuart to get her out," went on Laramie. "Thet must have been before Hallie an' I saw them. Anyway he got her out. Lent's idee, as I see it now, was to stay away all day, so's to scare hell out of her folks. She had Stuart ride her up heah. An' they run plumb into Gaines an' his cronies, waitin' heah for thet very thing. Thet's all."

"It's as plain as the nose on your face, Lonesome," corroborated Ted.

"An' thet elopin' idee?" queried Lonesome, in passionate sarcasm.

"Our mistake. We're sorry. But what's it matter now?" rejoined Ted, impatiently.

"You always had it in for Lent. Both of you," declared Lonesome, "An' now I'm makin' you eat small. You're gonna clear her with Hallie an' the rest of them."

"She shore wasn't elopin', pard," agreed Laramie.

"Yes, an' she shore wasn't doin' anythin' bad," went on Lonesome, fiercely. "I know, because I was jealous an' suspicious of her.... An' I tried it, by Gawd! Thet's what queered me with Lent. An' all the time I knowed she was good – I *knowed* it! But jealousy is hell.... She was only turnin' the tables on her dad. Stuart must have been square, after all. There he lays dead. You fellars didn't see the five shells on the ground. I found them after you left. Stuart fought for the girl. But Gaines an' his outfit killed him, robbed him, shot his hawse, an' then made off with her. Gaines has been layin' up heah for thet – reason – to get Lent."

"Wal, he's got her," agreed Laramie.

"Pards, you both know what thet means,"

370

went on Lonesome, hoarsely. "Chess Gaines won't hold her for ranson. An' he won't risk takin' her to some town where he could marry her. Reckon he is as turrible in love with her as any of us. But he's black-hearted. He'll maul her – violate her – first chance he gets. It ain't reasonable for us to reckon we can save Lent thet. But we can save her life an' kill him. Thet's what we've got to figger on. . . . It'll be awful for the poor kid. But it won't make no change in my love for her. I tormented Lent. . . . Mebbe if I hadn't she'd give me more chance to protect her. . . . Now, Laramie, pard, thet's all."

Laramie did not need to ponder. "Yu an' Tracks hit their trail," he flashed. "Make it easy for me to follow at a trot from heah. I'll ride the hell for leather back to the ranch. Have Dakota an' Charlie pack grub, grain, water, rifles, while I make up some story to tell Hallie an' her folks. It cain't be the truth. Some day mebbe – if we save Lent. I'll send two of the boys up here to bury Stuart an' hide his saddle. Charlie, Dakota and I'll light out on yore trail. If it comes dark before we catch up with yu we'll camp right there till daybreak."

Lonesome swung into his saddle. "Pard, you've got the head. I'm thinkin' –"

"Yes, but it's not working," ripped out

371

Ted, as he mounted. "He's thinking about Hallie – the big stiff.... Laramie, don't waste time telling anybody anything. Let 'em stand it. Think of that poor kid. You hear me!"

"Shore, I heah yu," replied Laramie, as he made for his horse. "Reckon I am loose in my haid.... I'll ketch up with yu before sundown. Look out for Gaines. Mebbe he saw us. He might lay for yu."

"Hope to Gawd he does," sang out Lonesome. "Ride now, pard!"

Chapter 13

Laramie rode the short cut down to the ranch in fast time, less than an hour, but he bade fair to lose some in locating Wind River Charlie and Dakota. These boys, as well as the others, were not to be found at the respective jobs Laramie had assigned them. That morning the droll and angelic humor for which the Lindsay girls had given him credit had gone into eclipse. Laramie had reverted to the cool hard ranger of Panhandle days. At length finding four of his riders playing cards on the cool runway of the big barn he laid into them:

"Heah yu air. Yu —— —— —— —— ——! Whaddyu mean loafin' on me?" Laramie broke out.

To Laramie's amaze they were not in the least concerned. Dakota mildly asked Laramie what was eating him? Clay Lee smiled in a mysterious way. Archie Hill never looked up at all: "I'll see you, Windy, an' go you one better," he said, while the rider he addressed nonchalantly fingered his cards and gave Laramie a tranquil fleeting glance.

"Say, come out of yore trance," added Laramie, with biting scorn. "Do yu call yoreselves a bunch of range-riders?"

"Laramie, old scout, our boss took us off them jobs you gave us," explained Wind River Charlie.

"Yore boss!"

"Sure, Miss Hallie. She said she wouldn't have us gettin' sunstroke." The tremendous sustained glee of these riders might have at any other time been entertaining to Laramie.

"Wal, I resign. I'm no foreman for this heah outfit," declared Laramie, coldly.

This was different and serious. The four boys responded as one, each expostulating in his way.

"Save yore breath," interrupted Laramie. "Yu reckon I rode in on a picnic or to play poker? Look at my hawse out there!... Listen, an' keep yore traps shut.... We've been trackin' Stuart an' Lent Lindsay. This mawnin' he broke open her window an' got her away. Tracks an' I reckoned it they was elopin'. Lonesome had it figgered Lent was just havin' fun. But it didn't turn out funny. Up on Cedar Haid they ran plumb into Chess Gaines an' his pards. We found Stuart daid. All shot up. An' Gaines kidnapped the kid!"

"My Gawd!" ejaculated Wind River Charlie, his face going gray. He rose as if on springs, and the others leaped up.

"Thet – Gaines!" rasped Dakota. "Stuart wasn't nothin' to us. But Slim Red was, an' Slim's lyin' over there at La Junta all shot up.... Laramie, I reckoned you looked different. Excuse us."

"We've got to rustle," returned Laramie. "Archie, yu fetch fresh hawses. Charlie, yu an' Dakota air goin' with me. Pack saddlebags. Meat, biscuits, dried apples, salt, sugar, coffee. Stick in a little pot. Don't forget some grain an' water-bags. Clay, yu fetch me two or three forty-four Winchesters with shells an' saddle-sheaths. Pronto now while I snatch a bite to eat."

Like startled turkeys the riders scurried away. Charlie, exiting toward the front, was intercepted by Harriet Lindsay.

"What's all the loud talk?" she inquired, curiously.

"Aw – it's only Laramie. He's loco or somethin'," stammered Charlie confusedly. This was not a situation where he could readily lie. He rushed away.

"Laramie!" she cried, in surprise, and

wheeling she espied him, and came in almost running.

There was no help for Laramie. She wore that same riding-garb which lent her such irresistible charm, and robbed her of years and dignity. She was just a girl, sweet as a rose.

"Laramie, why are you here?" she asked, swiftly, as she reached him.

"Mawnin', Lady. I had to have a fresh hawse.... Yu've seen yore father?"

"Yes, before mother or Flo. And he didn't tell them what he told me."

"What was thet?"

"You said Lent's breaking out was only a joke. But you didn't *look* as if it were," returned Hallie, excitedly.

"Aw, wal, I reckon, it was thet – this mawnin'."

"You found her?"

"Not yet. Ted an' Lonesome air on her trail. I'll ketch up pronto."

"Lenta was not close by? She has gone far?"

Laramie felt that he might have parried her queries, but he could not be cool and collected when she drew close to him like this, to drop her gauntlets and quirt, and catch at his vest, and look up at him with wonderful darkening eyes.

"Wal, she might be hidin' out on one of the ridge-tops, laughin' at us."

"Laramie, you are a clever liar, but you can't lie to *me*," she cried.

"Who says I'm lyin'?"

"I do."

"All right, I cain't help what yu say. Reckon if I told yu how awful sweet yu look this mawnin' –"

"No compliments, Laramie Nelson. You are hiding something," she retorted, and actually shook him.

"Wal, I'm not hidin' how powerful dangerous yu air to look at," he drawled, with a cool and easy boldness not characteristic of him at all.

Hallie scarcely appeared to hear this significant speech. She was becoming visibly affected by some strong compelling emotion.

"I tell you Lent did not play a joke. She did not elope. She has run off! . . . I know because I drove her to it."

"Aw now – Hallie! Yu're jest upset," replied Laramie, failing to be convincing. Indeed he was astounded at this new angle, at her agitated face.

"Upset? I'm nearly crazy. I tell you I drove her to it. You remember yesterday – when we saw her at her window – both hands tight around this Stuart's neck? . . . After that

377

I went to her door. Oh, I was furious. I don't know what I called her, but it was so terrible she never answered.... Not a word from Lent Lindsay! By that you can estimate what I must have heaped upon her head.... I'm scared. I'm sick. And meeting you makes it worse.... You know something. You lie to me.... Oh, Laramie, don't think me a coward. I love Lenta. It'd kill me if she – threw herself away."

Her beauty at that moment, her abandonment to remorse and fear, her unconscious clinging to him, was about all Laramie could stand. He did not want to tell her – to horrify her – to give her days and nights of anguish over some possibility that might not come to pass. On the other hand he was not an adept at falsehoods with anyone, much less Hallie Lindsay. If he did not do something very quickly he would be blurting out all about the murder of Stuart and the abduction of Lenta by desperate and ruthless range-riders.

Hallie was leaning upon him, on the verge of weeping, if not hysteria. Her look, if not her intent, was one of exceeding appeal. As if he could help her! Suddenly he divined a way out of his predicament. Born of her nearness and sweetness, it struck him as a remedy for two evils.

"Come heah," he said, and with powerful arm half lifted, half dragged her out of the wide aisle of the barn into one of the stalls partly full of baled hay.

"Why – Laramie!" she faltered, completely surprised.

He did not release her. If anything he held her closer.

"Yu laid off my boys today?" he queried.

"What if I did? Sunday is the same to a – a heathen like you as any other day.... But it's not to me. Is it necessary to hold me –"

"This heah job is too much for me. Those boys made game of my orders. An' I quit. They crawfished then. But all the same, I'm through."

"But, Laramie," she cried, wildly, "I promised father – I – you – Oh!... What of Lenta?"

"I'll fetch her back."

She strove to get out of his half-encircling arm, then suddenly desisted, either from lack of strength or resignation. Nevertheless her spirit revived.

"I insist you are deceiving me. I *feel* it.... And this grip you have on me... Why, it's outrageous. Let go!"

Anger perceptibly acquired dominance over her other feelings, but she could not control the trembling of her lips. Laramie

379

gazed down at them instead of into her eyes. What he intended to do was madness, still it seemed a release for him, and it would infuriate her so that she could not divine the truth about Lenta. How sweet the curved lips, drooping a little at the corners, tremulous! As he bent swiftly to them he just closed his eyes and kissed her. He seemed to whirl and float away. He felt her string tight as a stretched cord under his embrace. And he drew back frightened. What had he done?

"Lar-amie Nel-son!" she gasped.

"What'd yu think of thet?" he drawled, brazenly.

Her eyes glazed like those of a female panther. "You insult me!"

"Wal, I didn't mean it thet way, but if yu reckon –"

"*This* is what I think," she flashed, and swinging her free arm she struck him across the mouth with stinging force.

That broke Laramie's hold. It also awakened in him the truth of his folly and the bitterness of the lover who was relinquishing hope. His hand came away from his lips stained with blood. She saw it. His eyes dilated.

"After all – you – another Luke Arlidge!" she panted. "You range-riders are all alike."

That capped the climax for Laramie's

380

riotous feelings. The comparison to Arlidge roused all the savageness in him. Snatching her fiercely to him he slid his left arm clear around her to clutch her left wrist. Thus he had her powerless. Then he bent her back.

"Laramie! You are mad. I – I take that back about Arlidge. I'll forgive the once if – if –"

He closed her lips with a terrible kiss that made her sink limp and unleashed all the primitive hunger in him.

"Shore we're all alike," he said, passionately, as he drew back to look at her. But where was the fury, the hate, the battle in her eyes? Even in his chaotic mind that query lodged. Yet he was too far gone. It was like falling over a precipice. "There!" he whispered, kissing her again. "Reckon Arlidge – did thet."

"Mercy! – Oh – Laramie do I de-serve this – at your hands? Arlidge did *not!* I swear to you."

"Aw yu women! Yu proud white trash, as the niggers say! Yu Eastern tenderfeet – queenin' it over us pore devils!"

And he kissed her with a slowly lessening passion, with a sense of returning manhood. The moment came when, spent and shaking, he relinquished her lips. In the struggle she had sunk down upon the bales and he was on one knee, lifting his head. Her heavy eyelids were shut tight. The pearl-whiteness of her face a moment before had undergone a transformation. Even as he gazed a scarlet wave spread upward from her pulsing neck. He found that in his passion he had let go of her arms, and if he was not demented one was round his neck. He saw her right hand feeling a shaky way up his shoulder.

"My – Gawd!... Hallie – forgive me! I didn't know – what I was doin'." The savage intent to insult and hurt her had wrought havoc – an incredible, insupportable transformation. He could not meet it. He could not realize. All he knew was that he must flee from something like an avalanche. As he released her it became plain that she did have hold of him. The action of rising lifted her with him. Then her hold broke, her arm came sliding down from his neck. That ended uncertainty for Laramie. She sank back upon the bales and her opening eyes, soft, strange, like midnight pools, fixed upon him accusingly. He leaped up and ran out of the barn.

Half an hour later he rode up the draw ahead of Dakota and Charlie. Armed to the teeth, grim and cold and silent, he deceived these riders. But he knew himself to be distraught, to be haunted. He knew the tumult under his wet and panting breast. He knew that only tremendous exertion and bloody fight could restore his equilibrium, and he rode hard to meet them.

Once out on the range, Laramie led at a brisk trot, keeping to the low country and making for a point east of Cedar Head. By this he hoped to avoid any upgrade until he rounded the promontory. This short cut took him out on the grassy range where cattle wearing the Peak Dot brand should have been abundant. But in the eight-mile ride he saw only a few lone steers, a small bunch of yearlings, some cows and calves. The rustlers had made a clean sweep of Lindsay's stock. What easy picking, no doubt, for cattle-thieves like Gaines and Price! Arlidge and his rancher associate would never have been so unwise as to steal all a cattleman's stock. They were big operators, and engaged in many legitimate deals to one that might look shady. No continued association could have existed between them and common rustlers, and cow-punchers gone crooked, such as Gaines and Price. Just so long as Lindsay ran any stock, this kind of rustling would continue until some drastic check had been administered. "About time we was rarin'," muttered Laramie.

Under White Bluff, Laramie and his two

followers, working up a deep brushy draw, came across a waterhole, the existence of which they had not known. It was fed by a spring which showed signs of having been visited often of late. This water, of course, was what made it possible for Gaines and his outfit to camp indefinitely up on the promontory.

Laramie did not climb the ridge, but kept on up the slowly ascending draw to emerge several miles east and north of the cedars where he had left Lonesome and Ted. At this point he began to scrutinize the ground in search of their trail. Three – four miles or so he covered, with Dakota and Charlie spread out one on each side, without a sign of the trail he was hunting. They had turned north beyond the head of the draw toward the ridged and heaved-up range-land in that direction. Finally, Laramie halted to confer with his comrades.

"We cain't have crossed it," he said. "But I'm plumb worried. Right heah we're almost turnin' toward the ranch."

"Boss, I'd say from the lay of the land an' what's ahead, any riders wantin' to get away an' hide would work north," said Wind River Charlie.

"Shore I figger the same," replied

Laramie, quick to appreciate that this Wyoming rider was one to listen to.

"Lemme have your glass. I believe I see somethin' red," added Charlie, pointing. Upon receiving the field-glass he leveled it and adjusted it to his eyes. "Yep, there's a bit of red scarf wavin' from a bush."

"Ahuh. I see thet now. Wal, let's rustle."

In a few moments they were passing from hand to hand a piece of handkerchief, taken from a high sage-bush, which Laramie identified as belonging to Lonesome.

"An' heah's their trail, plain as print."

It was about mid-afternoon, and Laramie began to have misgivings about catching up with Lonesome and Tracks that day. Still, the trail was now easy to follow at a canter for long distances, and always at a trot. They covered ten miles in less than two hours. After that the roughening of the country into which the trail entered slowed travel to a walk.

By sunset they entered a long oval swale through which a deep cut meandered. The slopes on each side were heavily brushed. Antelope were plentiful, and jack-rabbits scurried through the sage. At the upper reach of this long swale they found water running over the shallow sandy bed.

"Wal, I reckon we'd better camp heah," said Laramie, thoughtfully. "It's about dark. An' we might not find grass an' water ahaid."

"We'll do all the better tomorrow. I'd say we was around three hours behind Mulhall an' Williams," rejoined Wind River Charlie.

"In thet case we'll shore ketch up with them before tomorrow night. The thing is – will *they* ketch up with Gaines?"

"I'd gamble on it."

"So'll I.... Gawd! though, I wish it was tonight! To think of thet kid ..."

"It's tough, boss. But she's a game an' smart kid. Mebbe she'll soft-soap Gaines, playin' for time."

"Smart? Wal, I reckon. But Gaines mightn't be easy to fool. Funny I didn't savvy him sooner. Aw, I was loco myself. I ought to have shot him thet day."

"No use cryin' over spilled milk, Laramie," replied Charlie. "I've a hunch how you feel. But *I* think, with Mulhall out ahead of us, fightin' mad, an' with Williams trackin' thet bunch, we're goin' to save the girl."

"Alive – yes. But.... Dakota, water an' grain the hawses. Then hobble them. Charlie, you fix a snack of grub. I'll pack in some firewood."

Darkness fell upon the riders eating their

meager meal around a ruddy fire of red coals. The heat of the day was gone. A cool night breeze rustled the cedars. Coyotes had begun their yelping quest. A lonesome owl hooted, and frogs were trilling from the watercourse.

Soon Laramie left his smoking comrades, and repairing to a near-by cedar he spread his saddle blankets wet side down, and with his saddle for a pillow stretched himself for rest, if not slumber.

He should have fallen asleep at once. But Laramie Nelson had departed from the way of peace and serenity. Even with Indians on his trail or a brush with rustlers at hand he had never been so disturbed. He strained to find the old cool, easy, all-solving mind. The conditions of the hour were familiar, and it felt so good to realize that. The stars blinked white overhead; the cedars whispered to him; his old friends the coyotes were wailing their wild music; the dry sweet night breath of the lonely range blew over him; the thump of hobbled horses came reassuringly to his ears. Once more he was out on the trail. He had not even removed his spurs. Tomorrow, surely, he would gain freedom from this oppressed heart, from whirling thoughts, from sweet and agonizing memories.

But just now he was helpless, at the mercy of the solitude and loneliness he loved so well and knew he needed so much. The action of the day was past. And ruthless memory, with remorse and exultation, with misery and ecstasy, worked its will.

If he had to die right here, or at longest in the morrow's fight, he could not have been sorry that he had kissed Hallie Lindsay. At the worst those kisses would not cost her more than a moment's disgust, an hour's fury. But for him there had been something all-satisfying, a fulfillment of he knew not what. He had yielded to longing, surely, but still he had done the thing with eyes open and with a purpose other than selfish. He had felt it a duty to swerve that clear-eyed, keen-minded young woman away from the appalling facts of her sister's peril. That had not given rise to his regret. It had come from a dismaying, unbelievable, unforgettable fact that Hallie had struck him across his violating lips, and then presently, precisely for the same offense multiplied, she had put her arm around his neck. The thing was incredible. Had she? Was that not his bewildered fancy? It did not seem logical, reasonable, possible that any girl, much less Hallie, could hit a man with all her might for kissing her and then embrace him for doing it again. But there it was. Her left arm had been clear up around his neck, and her right hand had been creeping up. He had seen it. He had felt her cool quivering fingers on his hot neck. Well, what then?

There was absolutely no doubt as to his mental aberration. But had she been crazy, too? If such an act were possible it could mean only one thing – that his violence had overcome her on the moment, and not only had she surrendered to him, but had been about to respond with a woman's love.

Laramie had his bitter battle here. He could not believe the evidence of his own senses. He had been mistaken. If she had caught hold of him it must have been in the frenzy of repulse. "But I'll never – never know!" he whispered, poignantly, to himself. "My Gawd! why didn't I wait to see? ... Then, if it'd been true ..."

Thus he tortured himself. But in the long run, when the night was far advanced, he persuaded himself that his perceptions had been as faulty as his reasoning. There was left then only the certainty that the sweetness of her lips had been his – that he had spent his honest passionate only love upon them – that in his heart he knew he had offered her no insult, and as time passed she might come to realize it. Here ensued the break between his wretchedness and the still small voice of renunciation. With that over, Laramie

Nelson began to come to himself. In the future he might dream over his only love-affair and pity himself and wallow in sentiment. But now he had to call on all that the ranges had made him, to take Lenta home at least alive, and to weave a bloody trail around Spanish Peaks Ranch, so that these fine good Lindsays could settle down to the happiness they deserved. Then he would ride away as he had often ridden before. When all that had worked itself out inevitably in Laramie's mind, he found himself again. And he went to sleep.

Wind River Charlie awakened him in the gray dawn. A fire was crackling. Dakota appeared riding bareback, driving in the horses. Jays were squalling in the cedars. Laramie arose as if many nights had elapsed since he had laid down. There was very little talk, and that was only commonplace. They ate, saddled, mounted, and rode out in a silence that boded ill to the objects of their pursuit.

An hour later, at sunrise, they climbed high to see the foothills of the Rockies scarce two days' ride to the west. Laramie calculated they were forty-odd miles from Spanish Peaks Ranch, and therefore east of the range used by Allen and Arlidge. It was new country to Laramie. Dakota claimed to have been in there once, and knew they were not far, as a crow flies, from the squatter's cabin where Williams and Laramie had trailed the stolen horses, and had stumbled upon, as well, some of Lindsay's stock.

The plain trail led on to the north, and kept to the levels. High ridges and narrow valleys alternated here, and gradually augmented their characteristics. Cattle began to show in impressive numbers, but they were so wild that Laramie, without departing from the trail, could not read their brands. They passed an old log cabin. The hill tops here showed a sparse growth of pines. The white flags of deer moved up every slope. Grass and water grew abundant. At length the riders crossed a wide cattle road running east and west. The fresh tracks pointed west, proving that the last herd had been driven toward the uplands.

"What yu make of thet?" asked Laramie of Wind River Charlie, remembering the rider's questionable standing with Arlidge.

"It's a big country, boss," replied Charlie, evasively. "There's a hundred thousand odd head of stock range in here, not countin' what's movin'."

"Ahuh. But rustlers wouldn't be drivin' big herds to Denver. I'd reckon all stock in any quantity would be sent east, down on the Kansas an' Nebraskie ranges."

"Boss, it's my hunch you'll clear up some of them knotty questions this hunt," was all the rider would vouchsafe. But it was enough for Laramie.

Noonday brought the pursuers to a puzzling halt. The trail split at the juncture of two valleys, where a low pass between high hills afforded a magnificent view of wild country, marked by cattle dotting the gray-green levels, and patches of black timber, and threads of shining water. Laramie was quick to discover that additional horse tracks had been added to the trail. Gaines had met some more of his outfit here or certainly had encountered three, possibly more riders. At any rate, the trail split. The pursuers were puzzled until Laramie's roving eye caught sight of another strip of Lonesome's red scarf. It waved high from a cedar branch, where it had been tied by a rider standing on his saddle. That appeared to be the reason they had not espied it at once. Again Wind River Charlie proved his worth, as well as his experience in trailing fugitive riders.

"Look, boss. Two sticks fresh cut, one pointin' down thet draw an' the other down this one."

"Shore do. Thet's old cowman making'

Injun sign. Wal, one outfit went this way an' the other thet way. Reckon Lonesome an' Tracks split heah. So will we. I'll take the left trail. Yu boys take thet to the right. It's a stumper to see which outfit had the girl. We just cain't. But same as Lonesome an' Ted – we'll take no chances."

"It weakens us, boss, same as it does them. But we can't do nothin' else."

"Wal, we're losin' time an' this trail is gettin' hot. Mebbe yu will meet Ted or Lonesome back-trailin'. Mebbe I will. We're trackin' them an' they're trackin' Gaines. This other outfit has throwed them off. But they'll nose it out. Rustle now, an' for Gawd's sake use yore haids an' yore guns if yu come on Gaines' outfit with the girl."

Laramie had not proceeded far when Charlie hailed him.

"Boss, here's a juniper bush broke off fresh at the top."

Waving an encouraging hand, Laramie turned to his task. Soon his way led into a narrow aisle of grassy descent between wooded slopes. He could follow the trail by the different shading and shape of the grass that had been parted and trod upon. Presently he espied the top of an oak shrub leaning over distorted and striking. It had been rudely wrenched, and not so long ago.

Either Lonesome or Ted had passed that point.

Laramie searched the long gray valley below for dust clouds made by riders. Cattle appeared numerous, but there were no moving knots of riders or tell-tale streaks of dust riding. To his amaze he found he had over-ridden any signs. He wheeled to return and sighted another mutilated bush before he reached an abrupt sheering of the trail up the slope. He followed, pondering this change. It looked queer. But he was not surprised. The tracks of rustlers and outlaws left crooked, wandering trails.

This slope was easy of ascent, open in places, thicketed in others, with scrub oak and jack pines growing at intervals. The trail doubled back in a long slant over the ridge toward the other valley. Laramie made a deduction. The outfit that had turned back here surely had done so to spy upon the other which had taken the valley to the right. Laramie grew certain of this, and once on top he absolutely knew it. Mounted horses had been halted time and again under trees on the verge of the slope. Laramie could read the minds of men of the open in the signs they left on the ground. Gaines and his men with the girl had not been accountable for this trail. It belonged to an outfit that had reason to spy upon Gaines, to follow him, or more likely to head him off for purposes of ambush.

This valley below was a whole range in itself. It must have been thirty miles to where the hills converged again. The floor was narrow just beneath and covered with a scattered growth of cedar, but miles farther on it opened to wide gray space. Cattle were far less numerous than in the valley behind Laramie.

A well-defined, hard-packed trail led on the crest of the ridge to the north. Riders who had reason to watch must frequent it. And the tracks Laramie was hot on worked below along the edge where the slope began. Presently they ploughed off the rim in great fresh furrows and went straight down.

"Wal, I'm a son-of-a-gun!" ejaculated Laramie. "I wonder how long it took Ted or Lonesome to figger this. Not much longer, I'm gamblin'. He'd make pronto for thet other trail.... But if this heah outfit is aimin' to haid off Gaines, why shouldn't I beat them to it?"

Laramie tried to shake the idea. It would not shake. Weight strengthened it with the evidences of former inspirations. He gazed up at the sun. Already westering! Could he afford to trust to any old instinct? This deal was not his, but Lonesome's. And the abducted girl was Hallie's sister. Nevertheless, a strong impulse, cold and inscrutable, took possession of him. It quickened and directed his calculations. Four hours at the most would see Gaines come to a halt for the night. The outfit that had turned to trail him knew this and where he would make camp.

Suddenly Laramie bethought himself of the field-glass tied to the horn of his saddle. Securing this, he leaped off to steady himself against a tree and search the valley. He began at the right. The distance was far for a naked eye, but with the glass he could command all of it. Cattle, deer, antelope passed under his range of magnified vision. And the last band of antelope was on the move. But Laramie could not make out any other moving objects directly under him.

Whereupon he took a comprehensive sweep of the valley where it widened to the north. Grassy barrens merged into alkali flats. Out there no live object showed. The far side of the valley yielded nothing. Then beginning far to the left, and along the line where the timber met the sage, Laramie studied the land minutely. Eight or ten miles down he sighted a log cabin close to the wall of green, or a square rock that closely resembled a cabin. From there toward him for several miles the green and gray level appeared lonely.

Suddenly a string of horses slipped as if by magic into the magnified circle. Laramie sustained a shock. He nearly dropped the glass. What havoc Hallie Lindsay and her sister had worked on his nerves! Steeling himself to recognize the certainty he expected, he found the group again. Six horses, four riders, two packs! That would fit Gaines' outfit, according to Ted's calculation. They were traveling slowly. The horses were tired. Laramie's eyes fixed upon the second rider, small, a mere bright dot in the saddle. That would be Lenta.

Laramie wasted not another second. "My hunch!" he soliloquized. "Funny about thet. . . . I can get ahaid of Gaines." With swift decision he led his horse back to the trail, and tying on the glass he leaped astride. The big rangy sorrel answered to spur and in a moment Laramie was speeding along the ridge. The trail appeared open and hard. No dust would puff aloft to betray him, and he could not be seen from either valley. The ridge top widened to a big country and the trail kept to the middle of it. Laramie ran the sorrel over the long level reaches and otherwise governed his gait according to the ground. He calculated that a quarter of an hour's rapid travel had brought him to a point where he should cut across to the slope again. This he did, finding it long but good going.

He came out upon a beautiful prospect. A timbered bench below reached out to the sage, and as luck would have it, there stood the cabin that he thought he might have mistaken for a rock. He did not look for the string of horses. They would be five miles at least down the valley. And at the pace they were moving it would take an hour and a half for them to reach the cabin. That was Gaines' objective. Laramie meant to be there to meet him.

Without more ado he dismounted and gave his attention to the task of descending from the ridge. He found a place and started down, leading the sorrel. It was steep but passable, and did not concern him. Below, however, he might find difficulties, though he had to take that chance. Zig-zagging down through brush and over benches, he came to a slant which bothered him for the reason that, though the sliding down would be easy, he could not retrace his steps. His range of vision here was restricted. He tried to see below. Finally he undertook the descent and made it without mishap. Soon after that he got into rough ground and had to puzzle and

398

toil a way out, up and down, along the shelves and back again. He lost valuable time. Fortunately he had marked his direction by a crag across the valley. The sinking sun had long gone down behind the ridge he had descended. Shadows were thick. He had not miscalculated, but he had encountered bad luck – that factor always impending. Finally he crashed down over the last wooded barrier to a level.

A stream flowed out from under the bluff. Laramie let the sorrel drink. And as there was fresh grass for the taking, he decided to let the horse graze, and push out to the open on foot.

The main timber was spruce, thin and spear-pointed, interspersed with oak and brush. He could see the gold and purple of the valley beyond. The cabin stood out a little from the timber, marked by low-branching oak trees. Laramie was about to leave the woods when he espied the string of horses half a mile below. Turning back, he strode under cover until he had the cabin between him and the approaching riders. Then he ran across the open. When he reached the cabin door he drew his gun in case there were any inmates. He stood panting and peering. Then he rapped. No answer! Like many cabins, it contained one large room and a loft of poles halfway across under the roof. A leaning ladder with steps missing led up to it.

Laramie entered. He would shoot Gaines on sight, then hold up the Negro and the Mexican, unless they showed fight. It was Laramie's idea that he would make the Negro talk. With this plan made, he awaited their arrival.

Chapter 14

Through a chink between the logs Laramie discerned a flash of white and the next instant heard a thud of hoofs. Gaines' outfit had no white horse!

The situation demanded quick thinking. If a fight with these other trailers was unavoidable, Laramie felt ready for it, but as he was after Gaines he preferred to meet Gaines first. It might facilitate developments for him to hide up in the loft. He had to be quick, for the horses were close. Gruff voices sounded plainly. Laramie's hand tightened on his gun. Almost he waited, but the sixth sense of his operated at last.

He ran to the ladder, ascended it, and stealthily lay down, facing the opening. The loft was not dark. Light came through a square hole at the back. This afforded Laramie satisfaction, despite the fact that it rendered detection easier than if the loft had been shrouded. On the other hand, he could not be cornered. If he were discovered he could shoot, then leap through the window and meet anyone on the outside. Plainly the advantage was all his.

Horses thudded up to the cabin. Instead, however, of stopping at the door they went behind, and halted with leathery creaks. Rattling spurs attested to the dismounting of riders. Laramie perceived then that the roof of the cabin extended out on this side, probably over some stalls for horses. He observed also a closed door near the corner of that side, and crude shelves extending from the corner to the rough stone chimney.

Low voices, their content indistinguishable, preceded the flop of saddles on the ground. The door opened to disclose a man in the act of entering. He half turned, looking back.

"Water the hawses, Jude, but don't turn them loose," he said, then he stepped high, with spur jangling on the door sill, to come in. His voice was familiar and Laramie knew the coarse dark thin-bearded face. Price! But he had changed markedly in visage, and his once portly form appeared lank. His garb did not lend him a look of prosperity. Close at his heels followed a short man, no longer young, with round, dull, blotched face and leaden eyes.

"I ain't hankerin' for this deal," declared

this worthy, in gruff impatience. "What's your idee, anyway?"

"You never was bright, Beady," returned Price. "I'll agree the deal wasn't so good or safe when we fust doubled back on Gaines' trail. But we seen thet fellar on a black hawse trackin' Gaines. An' *thet* makes our deal. I'll tell Gaines we seen he was bein' trailed an' thet we rustled over to put him on."

"Ahuh. Thet'll go, mebbe. An' then what?"

"We'll see what comes off."

"Price, you want thet girl."

"I ain't denyin' it, Beady."

"Wal, what fer?"

"Lindsay will pay handsome for thet little lady," declared Price, rubbing his hands with satisfaction. "Arlidge had left us only some two-bit cattle-rustlin'. Let's make a stake an' leave the country."

"So far your reasonin' is good," replied Beady. "But you underrate Gaines an' ain't takin' any stock atall of Nelson an' his outfit. I'll bet, by Gawd! thet it's one of his riders trackin' Gaines right now."

"I am wonderin' myself," said Price, seriously. "I'd as lief meet Nelson himself as thet little cuss Mulhall. Bad blood between us, Beady."

"Wal, thet won't help. But if the rider we

seen is one of Nelson's outfit he won't tackle Gaines alone. He'll have to go back to the ranch. Thet'll make a delay, sure, an' you might pull a trick with Gaines an' git the girl. But it won't change the end. Thet gun-throwin' Texan will trail you till hell freezes over. So if you don't want the girl jest fer herself, I advise you to pass the deal up."

"Beady, I swear I don't want thet kid for herself. It'd be robbin' the cradle," protested Price. "But you're givin' me a better idee. You sure are. Let's get the girl if we have to kill Gaines, an' take her home to her father. He'd sure reward us."

"Thet's a better idee. But it ain't so good, either. Suppose we run plumb into Nelson an' Mulhall, an' thet hawk-eyed Williams who tracked us when we stole his hawse?"

"Thet wouldn't make no difference, if we was on the way home with her."

"Haw! Haw! Mebbe it wouldn't," snorted Beady.

"Wal, enough of this. Ar you on –"

Their colloquy was interrupted by a lanky individual with a sallow face and long drooping moustache. A wide-brimmed sombrero hid his eyes.

"They're comin'," he announced.

"Where?" queried Price, swiftly, moving toward the door.

404

"Around thet point of timber. About a quarter, I reckon."

Price took off his sombrero and guardedly peered out. When he withdrew his head he had the eyes of a ghoul.

"He hasn't seen us an' doesn't know he's bein' trailed.... Now, men, let me do the talkin' an' if I start anythin' come in pronto.

Laramie, listening to this man, contemptuously relegated him to the fifth class of border outlaws. The little man called Beady would bear watching, and the other, Jude, did not look cool and unconcerned enough to be dangerous. He sat down on the side bench beside the table and bounced up to take a seat again; Beady leaned against the chimney, while Price, pulling himself together, went to stand with one spurred boot on the high door sill.

"Like as not this is what'll happen," spoke up Beady. "Gaines an' his outfit will roll in heah. An' then Nelson's. It'll be lovely."

"How soon?" queried Price, sharply.

"Couldn't say. Tomorrow at the latest."

"Thet gives us time."

"Fer what?"

"There's only three of them. I'll shoot Gaines when he's asleep an' hold up the greaser an' nigger. It'll be easy."

"In his sleep, huh?...Price, how'n hell have you lived this long out heah?"

"Shut up. They're comin'."

Soon then Laramie's strained ears caught a soft pound of hoofs. The sound increased until it reached the cabin where it slowed and ended. Then followed a creak of leather, a metallic clink, and quick thud of boots hitting the ground.

"Price, I reckoned it was you comin' off the ridge. What you mean, bracin' me again this way?"

That ringing, dry voice, with its note of disgust, belonged to Chess Gaines. For Laramie suspense ended. The chance he had taken had been justified. And the worry and doubt it had engendered passed away.

"Chess, I was aimin' to do you a favor," replied Price, coolly.

"You call it a favor aggravatin' me to bore you?"

"Somethin' aggravated you, sure. Mebbe them bloody scratches on your face....I done you a good turn an' see what I get for it."

"Say, you can't trick me. You never did any man a good turn in your life. An' damn me if I wouldn't bore you for two bits.... What'd you head me off here for?"

406

"I seen a rider on a black hawse trailin' you," declared Price.

"You're a damn liar!"

"No, I'm not. Ask Jude an' Beady in there," protested Price, sullenly.

"Jude would swear to anythin' you said. But I don't know your Beady. Call 'em out."

Price stepped across the threshold and called his men to follow. Laramie appreciated that these two would be subjected to the gaze of a Westerner who realized he had crossed the pale. After the three men went out there ensued a moment's silence.

"So you're Beady, huh?" queried Gaines. "Beady what?"

"Jest Beady," came the laconic reply.

"Did you see a rider trailin' me?"

"Nope. sorry I can't say so. But I was behind. I'll say, though, thet I took Price's word."

Suddenly a shrill high voice pealed out: Chess Gaines, you can bet your life that rider was Lonesome Mulhall!"

Laramie thrilled back into his intensity. That was Lenta. It surely did not sound as if her spirit was broken. All Laramie needed more was a peep at her.

"Come off thet hawse, you little spit-fire," growled Gaines.

"Keep your dirty claws to yourself," cried the girl. "I *told* you. . . . I'll get off myself."

"An' I *tell* you, for the benefit of these grinnin' apes, thet not so long ago you didn't mind my dirty claws," retorted Gaines.

"Let go!" shrieked Lenta. A moment later Laramie saw her clutched in Gaines' arms, kicking like a little mule. He threw her into the cabin, where she alighted sitting up, to slide until her back came against the corner of the chimney. She had no hat. Her hair was a bright dishevelled mass, her face sunburnt and dust-begrimed, with tear-streaks down her cheeks. No humiliated and shamed maiden could ever have possessed such blazing eyes. Laramie actually jerked in the release of his fear. All Lenta's shortcomings were as if they had never been, and he reveled in the courage that had sustained her. Tenderfoot? She had all of the West in her heart.

"Nig, throw the packs," went on Gaines, wearily. "Juan, you look after the hawses. We're gonna stay here tonight, no matter what comes off."

Lenta sat still, watching the men through the doorway. She wore overalls, top boots, and a short red coat over a blouse. The coat was soiled, and rent in many places. She looked like a boy, except for her slender

408

shapeliness. Eyes and lips began to lose their fury. Then her face showed the havoc of fright and fatigue. Laramie thought he could estimate what she had endured.

Meanwhile, Laramie ascertained, twilight was falling. This caused him concern for a moment, until he calculated that it was almost a certainty Lonesome and Tracks had either sighted both of these outfits or had been close enough on their trails to be out there now, waiting for night. Moreover, they had, no doubt, been reinforced by Wind River Charlie and Dakota.

"Price, have you fellows got any decent grub?" Gaines was asking.

"Sure, an' I'm some punkins of a cook myself," came the reply.

"Throw in with us tonight. We're out of grub thet dainty tenderfoot will eat."

"Haw! Haw! I'll make her pretty mouth water."

"Rustle some firewood."

"Plenty stacked inside, Gaines," spoke up Beady. "Dry pine knots and split oak."

"Jude, help me with the packs," added Price.

Dark forms entered the cabin, and presently a sputter of fire followed. Soon a blaze lightened the interior of the cabin, showing Lenta sitting with her back to the wide fireplace, Price and Jude kneeling on the other side, busily preparing supper, and Beady and Gaines on the bench by the stationary table of boughs. Beady's back was turned to the lynx-eyed Laramie, but Gaines sat full-face to the light. He appeared to be a disgruntled, defeated cowpuncher whose ambitions had mounted beyond his years and discretion. He stood out to Laramie then as a thoroughly evil man, capable of anything desperate, but not great enough to carry this issue to success. If he had been older he would not have been risking so much. But he had a touch of egotism and for some reason he was angry. Looking for that reason, Laramie imagined he detected it in the distinct scratches on his face, and in the smoldering gaze that now and then reverted to the girl. She had fought him like a wildcat. It did not seem impossible to Laramie that Gaines had waylaid Lenta with an old idea of elopement dominating him. Perhaps even with the murder of Stuart on his hands he had still attempted love-making with Lenta. At this hour he entertained dark and sinister motives.

"Gaines, if you'll excuse me, I'd like to ask somethin'," spoke up Beady.

"Fire away," rejoined Gaines, wearily. His

fiery eyes studied the older man, to that individual's favor.

"Ain't it reasonable to expect riders on your trail?"

"Why, yes, but I'm not worryin' none yet."

"Wal, you'll please excuse us fer not bunkin' with you tonight."

"Sure I'll excuse you, an' my outfit, too. I'm bunkin' here tonight with my lady friend."

"Only by force, you yellow cur!" spoke up Lenta, witheringly. "Any big stiff of a hombre like you could manhandle a slip of a girl. I'm worn out now."

"What's the idee, Gaines?" queried Beady, coldly. "Price said your deal was ransom. But her talk don't argue thet.

"None of your damn business. An' Price better keep his trap shut," snapped Gaines.

Lenta stood up, back to the wall. She made a brave little figure. Only the most hardened of men could have resisted it.

"Say, you they call Beady," she burst out. "This cow-puncher rode for my dad. I lost my head over him, same as the other riders. And I flirted with him. I let him kiss me. Then when I suspected he was a cattle-thief, one of Arlidge's outfit, stealing from the man who hired him, I led him on till I found out

411

sure. Nelson discharged him. Then he hid on the range, laying for me. Yesterday I rode to my old place with a boy named Stuart. They shot him – Gaines and his pards. Murdered him! – Oh, it was ter – rible. . . . Then the idiot tried to talk marriage to me – to run away with him. He's crazy. He kept wrestling me till I tried to scratch his eyes out. . . . Now, you – any man could see – what he means, the dog! . . . I'm only a tenderfoot, but I'm not afraid of him – or any of you. Lend me your gun – and I'll show you. . . . You all must be a lot of white-livered brutes – to let – him –"

"Shet up, or I'll smack your face," interrupted Gaines. "You're sure layin' hell for yourself, young lady."

"Gaines, your deal is none of my business, but I'm surprised if you're ridin' for Arlidge," said Beady.

"I'm ridin' for nobody," declared Gaines, darkly.

"But you were Arlidge's right-hand man," flashed Lenta, pointing an accusing finger at him. "I coaxed that out of Slim Red and Wind River Charlie. You were trying to make them crooked, too. You're a low-down rustler, Chess Gaines. And if it hadn't been for my sister, Laramie Nelson would have shot you. And you can bet your sweet life *now* that Lonesome Mulhall WILL shoot you!"

"My Gawd! how a woman can rave!" he got up, and reaching out a long arm he clutched her coat and blouse at the throat. With one pull he swung her clear off her feet against him. Bending his tawny head, he stuck it close to her face. "You brag a lot about this puncher Mulhall. You must like him."

"I wish to Heaven I'd liked him more, instead of wasting my feelings on a lousy dog like you," replied Lenta, in deliberate passion. He could neither intimidate nor frighten her. Fiercely he gave her a fling, sending her back to the wall, where she slowly slid down to sit as before.

"Wal, you're game an' you got a sharp tongue," he rasped. "I've wasted words on you. There's only one way to tame you, Lent, an' by Gawd! I'm goin' to do it."

He ended with a malignant passion that rang through the cabin. Laramie quivered in his tension. Why did not the boys come to hold up this careless bunch? Pretty soon he would lose his patience to kill Gaines, and that might start an uncertain fight. Laramie got himself in hand. It was only the girl's presence that disturbed him. Reason argued him to wait the limit.

"So Nelson fired you an' then Arlidge did the same?" queried Price. "You're gettin' in my class, Chess."

Gaines straddled the bench and almost tore his tawny hair out by the roots. He wrenched force from his desperation. It struck Laramie that Gaines could have coped with this situation if he kept cool. Truly the girl's presence was like a red flag to a bull.

"Price, you can't deal me in your class," he returned, icily. "The fact thet you double-cross Arlidge an' me before this rancher's daughter proves your class."

"Have it your own way. But I'll gamble I couldn't tell thet kid much she doesn't know," said Price, with a mildness which did not deceive Laramie. He turned to address Lenta. "Say, kid, sure you know Arlidge rustled your dad's cattle?"

"I sure do," retorted Lenta.

"An' thet he burns your Peak Dot brand into the Triangle Bar brand?"

Lenta regarded the speaker with quickening eyes.

"An' thet the rancher Lester Allen sells this brand in Denver an' Nebraskie?"

"There! That's what I've wanted to find out," shrilled the girl, clapping her hands. "Thanks, Rustler Price, I'll bet Laramie Nelson will be tickled to hear that."

Gaines whipped out his gun and held it low on Price.

"I reckon I'll bore you for thet."

The offender's face turned as white as his flour-covered hands. He had overstepped himself. Laramie could not gauge what the fool was driving at, unless for some incredible reason he wished to betray Arlidge and Allen to the daughter of Lindsay. The news was welcome to Laramie and verified his suspicions. As for the issue at hand, let Gaines make it one less for him to contend with – or two – or three.

"Wal, all I'll say more, Chess – is you're sure achin' to bore – somebody," gulped Price.

"Hold on, Gaines," interrupted Beady, markedly the only cool one present. "Is thet a matter for throwin' your gun? Price is windy, sure, an' plumb irritatin'. But you've no call to kill him for tellin' what we all knowed."

"Thet jack-rabbit-eared kid didn't know," rang out Gaines.

"No, I see she didn't. But what difference does thet make when she'll never get a chance to tell it?" returned the imperturbable Beady.

Laramie, watching and listening like a ferret, divined that he had gauged this

415

stranger well. Neither Price nor Gaines knew what Laramie saw – that if Gaines pulled the trigger it would mean death for himself as well.

"Huh?" croaked the rider.

"Gaines, you know you'll never let thet girl go now," concluded Beady. "So what's the sense of shootin' him? We'll all be in the same box an' have to ride out of the country."

Gaines' face turned a flaming red and he flipped the gun up to catch it by the handle, and sheath it.

"You're —— right I'll never let her go!" he flared, passionately.

At that Lenta got to her feet in an action which appeared to be a drawing taut of every muscle. "Chess Gaines, to – to think I – I once liked you! . . . You dirty monster!" she screamed at him, the very embodiment of horror and scorn. "Were you born of a woman? Hadn't you a sister?"

"So help me Gawd, I'm goin' to have you, Lent Lindsay!" he shouted, stridently.

"Never alive!" she cried, and leaped for the door. As quick as a cat she would have made it, too, but for something that checked her with a smothered scream.

Then Gaines in a leap was on her like a tiger. He tossed her up and caught her

416

kicking in the air. "Alive you bet!" he ground out in fierce exultance. She beat at him with flying fists, and supple and strong, she twisted out of his arms to thud against the wall. Here he pinned her and was crushing her right in a mingled anger and passion when suddenly he stretched high as if galvanized by a burning current.

"Aggh!" he bawled out, and with a spasmodic wrench he tore loose to wheel in the firelight. Blood squeezed out between the fingers with which he clutched his breast. She had bitten him.

Laramie had his gun almost leveled. Another move of Gaines toward the girl would be his last. With visage distorted by pain and frenzy Gaines lifted high a quivering open hand.

"You she-cat! Bite me – will you?" he hissed.

"Howdy, Chess!" sang out a voice through the door. Its mirth had a deadly note.

The hand Gaines held aloft froze in the air. Only his eyes moved – to stare – to pop wildly.

"Hell's fire, but I hate to kill you quick!" pealed that outside voice, terrible now in its certainty.

Laramie's blood leaped. A fraction more of pressure on his trigger was diverted.

Lonesome! A red flame shot through the door – a puff of smoke. Then the cabin filled to bellowing thunder. Chess Gaines' brains spattered the chimney and he went hurtling down as if propelled by a catapult.

Chapter 15

Laramie raised himself silently on his left arm, his gaze switching to Beady. Hardly had that booming report died away when Beady drew his gun and leaped off the bench in a single action. Another leap carried him to the cabin wall where in the shadow near the door he shoved out the gun to kill Lonesome when he entered. That was a signal for Laramie to shoot.

Beady fell forward in a heap as the cabin reverberated to the heavy shot.

"Hands up – yu men. *Quick!*" ordered Laramie, getting to his knees.

"Reckon thet'll be Laramie," sang out a grim voice, and Lonesome entered over the dark huddled form inside the door. Then the opposite door crashed inward to admit Williams with rifle forward, and Wind River Charlie, who jumped to a position beside him.

Three gun-barrels glinted darkly in the dimming firelight. Jude and Price knelt among the packs and utensils, hands rigidly aloft, their pallid faces gleaming. Lenta had collapsed apparently in the chimney corner.

"Laramie!" called Lonesome.

"Heah I am," replied Laramie.

"Where?"

"Up in the loft."

"You been there all the time," asserted Lonesome, "I might have knowed thet.... Come down an' make a light."

Laramie descended the ladder, face to the fore, but after a glance at the stupefied prisoners he sheathed his gun, and threw pine needles and pine cones on the fire. It blazed up brightly.

"Where's Dakota?" demanded Laramie, sharply. "Johnson an' Mendez air out there."

"I hear Dakota comin'," replied Wind River Charlie.

"Git in there with you, nigger," ordered Dakota, from outside.

"I'se a-gittin', boss. Yu needn't jab me n-n-no mo' wid dat gun," came the reply.

"Stand aside, Ted. Let them in," called Laramie.

A yellow-faced rolling-eyed Nigger shambled in, trying to bend away from a rifle barrel shoved against his back by Dakota.

"Heah's Johnson," announced the rider. "The greaser must have heard us an' sneaked away."

"Where is he, nigger?" demanded Lonesome.

"I dunno, sah. I was jus' talkin' to him out dere wid de hawses. He never sed nuffin', an' when I looked fer him sho he was gone."

"Saves us the trouble of hangin' him," went on Lonesome, who seemed to assume leadership here. "Charlie, get ropes somewhere."

"Saddles jest outside, Charlie," added Laramie.

The rider disappeared out in the darkness and presently could be heard tearing at saddles in the stalls. Soon he reappeared, carrying coiled lassos.

"Charlie, you an' Dakota cut one of them in three pieces an' tie these hombres' hands behind their backs," went on Lonesome.

This order was soon complied with, whereupon Lonesome sheathed his gun and sat down upon the bench to throw his sombrero on the table. His face resembled an ashen mask.

"Now drag these dead hombres back in the corner, so sight of them won't spoil our supper."

Meanwhile Laramie knelt beside Lenta. She lay half propped between some firewood and the chimney. Her small face shone white and it wore an expression of torture. Her eyes

421

were now vastly far from resembling those of a baby.

"Wal, I shore reckoned yu was daid to the world, Lenta," said Laramie, and it seemed that with sight of the pathetic torn little figure and her eyes all his affection for the wayward girl rushed back. She had what Laramie respected most – courage. He lifted her to a more comfortable posture and tried to smooth out her disheveled hair.

"I – I didn't faint," she whispered, clinging to Laramie. "When I ran – I saw Lonesome out there. I knew then – I was saved.... But I've seen – heard it all. I'm sick, but glad.... Oh, Laramie, *he* hasn't looked once – at me. What does he – think? ... Tell him – I – I'm all right – that –"

"Shore yu're all right," interrupted Laramie, softly. "I heahed yu, Lent, an' was plumb happy. Yu're the gamest kid I ever met, an' some day I shore got to get yore forgiveness. Brace up now. Yore troubles air past."

"Maybe they are ... But tell him, Laramie – please," whispered the girl.

"Pard," called Laramie, addressing Lonesome, who sat dark and grim at the table. "Lent's all right. Weak an' sick, shore, but unhurt.... An' not harmed atall!"

"Yeah? ... Thank Gawd then fer her an'

422

Hallie," responded Lonesome, without emotion, and without a glance in that direction.

Lenta pulled Laramie down to whisper: "See! He doesn't believe – or care. . . . And I – Oh – Laramie –"

"Hush, child. Yu're upset. Don't try to figger out anythin' now. Keep on fightin' off hysterics. Think of the facts. Yu're neither hurt nor harmed. In the mawnin' we'll take yu back home – to Hallie an' yore mother. That's enough to think of now."

It was not easy to unclasp Lenta's twining little hands or to turn from her big beseeching eyes.

"Come heah, Laramie. You ain't no nurse, an' if the girl's all right, why, let's tend to the deal," said Lonesome.

"Reckon the rest can wait will mawnin'," rejoined Laramie, crossing to Lonesome and speaking in a low tone of voice.

"No. An' I reckon you'd better let me boss the party."

"Shore, if yu want. But why?"

"On account of Hallie," returned Lonesome, speaking low. "In case the story of what happens ever leaks out. Savvy, pard?"

"Wal, I don't know as I do," drawled

423

Laramie. "This heah's a funny time for yu to be dreamin'."

"Aw, hell!...Heah, I'll take the responsibility an' I'll lie to Hallie. Only you must coax Lent to keep quiet about this bloody mess."

"Shore. I reckon I can guarantee thet."

"Good. Now have you any suggestion?"

"Only one. Daid men's evidence isn't so shore as thet of livin' ones. I've heahed the truth about Arlidge an' Allen. It's what we reckoned, Lonesome, but couldn't prove. I say scare the nigger half to death. Then agree to set him free if he squeals."

"Ahuh. Anythin' you say, Laramie, though it galls me not to see him stretch hemp with the rest of them."

"Shore I reckon I feel thet way, too," rejoined Laramie, ponderingly, not so certain of himself.

Price watching the dialogue between Lonesome and Laramie, but unable to hear them, burst into shaky speech: "Mulhall, we had – nothin' to do – with Gaines' kidnappin' thet kid."

Lonesome gave no sign that he had heard the appeal of his old enemy. He rolled a cigarette with steady fingers. His impassiveness struck even Laramie, and his stony visage might have been the mask of

424

doom itself. Certain it was that Price realized this, for a second attempt at speech failed in his throat.

"Aw, keep it out of your neck!" interrupted Jude, in harsh bitterness. "You got us into this. Now take your medicine."

"Dakota, we'll want a blazin' fire outside, so we can see," spoke up Lonesome.

"No, we won't," interposed Laramie. "Throw some more wood on heah.... I'll pack the girl out." Wherewith he stepped to Lenta's side and bent to lift her.

"What you want, Laramie?" she asked.

"Wal, the fact is, lass, yu'll be – it's nicer outside – more air, an' later I'll fix yu a bed," replied Laramie.

"I can walk," she said, and rose to prove her contention. Laramie led her out.

"Set heah, Lent, where I can see yu," concluded Laramie, and gently forced her to a sitting posture against the wall. Then he turned back and sat down in the door, facing those inside.

"Laramie, what is Lonesome going to do – with them?" whispered the girl, fearfully.

"Wal, yu never mind. It won't be much, I reckon."

"But he won't let that Price go scot-free, will he?" protested Lenta, with decided force. Laramie began to feel ashamed to

425

deceive her, so did not have a ready answer. Whereupon the girl got up and peered into the cabin, her hands on Laramie's shoulders. The renewed fire brightly lighted the forward end of the cabin.

"Lonesome!" cried Lenta, shrilly. Every face inside turned toward her, gleaming darkly. The pine cones cracked. "That man Price is worse than Gaines. Today when he met us – he kept eyeing me.... Oh, I read his mind. And he waylaid us here to kill Gaines. He meant to get me."

"Yeah?" responded Lonesome, with a composure that sat so strangely upon him. "Much obliged, Miss Lindsay. We're right glad to have our suspicions confirmed."

Lenta stared at him and then slowly turned away, muttering. Laramie told her to move along the wall, away from the door, out of hearing.

Lonesome's sharp order rang out:

"Charlie, throw a noose over thet high rafter."

The lanky rider strode to the center of the cabin, rope in hand. This left the open door on that side unguarded. Quick as a flash Jude leaped toward it. "By Gawd! you'll never hang me!" His leap carried him through but the crash of Dakota's gun ended his flight.

The rider went out, to return and close the door.

"Reckon we'll never have to," he said, grimly.

Wind River Charlie swung the coil of lasso dexterously through the small triangle between the rafter and the roof. The noose streaked down and dangled with a sinister action like the head of a snake.

"Ted, keep yore gun on Price, an' if he as much as winks, shoot him in the belly," said Lonesome, in a low voice. "Charlie, gimme the rope an' you an' Dakota drag the nigger heah."

They did so and threw the noose over the Negro's head. Lonesome hauled on the lasso, stretching Johnson to his toes and held him there a moment.

"How you like thet, nigger?" he whispered, slacking on the lasso.

Johnson came down flat-footed, choking and writhing. Charlie loosened the noose. The Negro gasped, his yellow face worked hideously, his eyes rolled with the whites startlingly prominent.

"Yuse oughtto – kills me – decent," he said, in a strangled whisper.

"Thet all you gotta say, Johnson?" queried the imperturbable Mulhall.

"Fer de Lud's sake – don' hang me. . . . I'se done nuthin'."

"You're a hawse-thief."

"No, sah, I ain't. Nebber."

"But you're a cattle-thief."

"Yas, I is. But I nebber – wuz – till dat Arlidge man – made me," protested the Negro.

"Wal, thet's too bad, 'cause we gotta string you up."

The Negro presented a pathetic figure. But he was not without courage.

"Nelson, yuse boss heah. . . . Cain't yuse make him shoot me? . . . I sho hates – to have my neck – wrung."

"Sam, I reckon I might if –"

Lonesome slowly threw his weight on the lasso and pulled. "Heah, give me a hand, Charlie. . . . Easy now. Don't break nothin'." Together they slowly drew the Negro up until his head and neck appeared to be those of a turtle. One foot left the ground, then the other. He swung free. His knees drew up spasmodically while a horrid sucking sound issued from his mouth. Suddenly he was dropped back to solid earth. This time he swayed and would have fallen but for the rope.

Laramie took a glance at the livid face of Price. The rustler's eyes were shut tight.

Again Charlie loosened the noose. Johnson appeared almost strangled. He coughed, and the intake of breath was a wheeze.

"How you like thet, nigger?" asked Lonesome.

"I done – reckon – I's gone – den."

"Sam, then you love life, huh?"

"Lud, I nebber – knowed – how much."

"Wal, what'd you do to save yore life? Would you talk?"

"Yas, sah. I'd tell – all – I knows," replied the Negro, in hoarse accents of hope.

Here Laramie intervened: "Sam, tomorrow we'll ride down to see Allen. Will yu talk in front of him?"

"Yas, sah, I shore will."

"Is Allen a cattle-thief?"

"I nebber seen him – rustle no stock, sah. But he sells burned brands – sah – he shore does."

"How about Arlidge?"

"He's a ridin' rustler, sah. He led de outfit dat fust drive – before you-all come wid Lindsay. I heered him tell Gaines dat Lindsay had bought Allen out."

"Wal, jest who rode in thet drive, Sam?" went on Laramie.

"Dar wuz Gaines an' Juan an' me, an' Arlidge – an' dat's all I remembers, sah."

429

"Don't lie, Sam. Heah's the time to save yore neck. Try to remember."

"Wal, sah, dere was Fork Mayhew, an' – an' –"

"Me!" chimed in Wind River Charlie, with passion. "But, Laramie, I swear I didn't know thet drive was rustlin'. Not till after. Me an' Fork an' Red wasn't in the secret. We didn't like the deal, but we didn't pry into it. Afterward Gaines told us Lindsay had bought Allen out an' we was really rustlin'."

"Ahuh. Thet was Arlidge's hold on yu, Charlie?"

"Yes, boss, an' no more."

Laramie lifted a hand to signify he was through with the proceedings. Lonesome whipped the rope so that the noose jumped from round Johnson's neck.

"Make way, Sam. . . . Ted, will you prod thet gent over heah?"

But no amount of prodding with a rifle could move Price. His dead weight clung to the wall. Whereupon Lonesome grasped the noose, and pulling the lasso over the rafter to sufficient length he took three long strides and cracked the loop over Price's head.

"Price, you remember when you did thet same trick to me once," he said, cold as steel. More than border justice rang in that terse statement. Price appeared far gone, at the
430

mercy of primal instincts, but even so he saw the uselessness of supplication.

Lonesome strode back to leap high and drag down the end of the lasso. "Ted, Dakota, come lend me an' Charlie a hand."

The four hauled in unison, dragging Price away from the wall, over the bench, and upsetting the table, and then with a concerted heave swung the rustler into the air.

"Hold – there," panted Lonesome, and while the three sustained Price at that height Lonesome tied the end of the rope to one of the loft supports. "Leggo. Reckon thet'll do." As they complied the lasso strung and stretched, letting Price down a foot, but it held. Then Lonesome, hands on his hips, his short stature and sturdy bow-legs singularly expressive, stood at gaze, watching the strangling man.

Laramie sat in the doorway, likewise watching. He had been present at numerous lynching bees, first of that most hated of border outlaws – the horse-thief, and then of late years the rustler. It was common practice, inaugurated, he remembered, in order to intimidate cow-punchers going wrong. Not greatly had it succeeded.

This crude justice brought home to Laramie now its hideousness as well as its futility. He seemed to be sitting in judgment upon Price and his kind, and his executioners, of whom surely he was one. Had he not hauled on many a rope? But he seemed also to be sitting there and seeing this appalling spectacle with Hallie Lindsay's eyes. She had changed him. The law of the West was what it was, and he could not alter it. But he divined here that the advent of women on the frontier would alter it. Price in his contortions kicked so violently that he got to swinging to and fro across the center of the cabin space. Once a jumping-jack kick nearly reached the statue-like Mulhall. That indeed jerked the avenging rider out of his rigidity. He wheeled away, his face gray and dripping with sweat.

"Pack this grub outside, boys," he said, huskily. "I'll fetch some fire."

That broke the suspense. They all leaped into action. Laramie, diverted as well, was about to rise and step forward when he heard a gasp behind him. Swiftly he wheeled in time to see Lenta sink to the ground beside the door. The incorrigible girl had watched from behind his back, had been a witness to this gruesome spectacle, and at last had succumbed to what indeed would have been sickening and devastating to the hardiest of pioneer girls.

Laramie turned to pick her up in his arms. She was a dead weight. This time she had fainted. "Dog-gone," he muttered, as he carried her out under the spreading tree. "But I never thought. She shore beats hell, this kid."

He laid her down on the grass, deciding that it would be well not to help her return to consciousness. Then he lent a hand to his comrades. They carried out the packs and the camp utensils with the food. They built a new fire for light, as well as shoveling out the red coals to cook upon. Johnson was brought out to be sat by the wall. Then Laramie went to find his horse. It was dark under the trees, but in the open places the starlight enabled him to find his way, and eventually the horse. He removed saddle and bridle. These he carried back to the cabin, plainly visible in the camp-fire glow. The riders moved to and fro, dark suggestive forms, fitting the scene. Lenta lay as he had left her. Laramie dropped his burdens and went back into the woods to cut some pine or cedar brush for her bed. Securing a bundle, he retraced his steps, to find Lenta sitting up.

"Wal, heah yu air all right again," said Laramie, cheerfully, as he dumped the fragrant mass. "We're shore goin' to have a soft bed for yu so yu can sleep some."

"Sleep. Will I ever again?" she asked, huskily.

"Nature is wonderful, lass. . . . Now see heah. I spread the pine nice an' thick. An' a saddle blanket on top with another to go over yu. An' a chunk of wood for a pillow. There!"

"Laramie, will you stay right close – by me – all night?" she queried, falteringly. "Now that it – it's over I'm losing my nerve."

"Shore. I'll set right heah an' hold yore hand all night. Reckon I ain't sleepy. But I can sleep settin' up jest the same."

"Some one doused me with water. Do you think it was – Lonesome?"

"Like as not. He's most unconsiderin' when he's riled."

"Riled? Uggh! If he only was mad!"

"Wal, don't pay no more attention to him, Lent."

But she evinced an inability to keep her dark haunted eyes from following the little rider everywhere. He kept busy around the camp fire, lending a hand to Charlie, who was cooking supper. Finally Ted came over.

"How are you, Lent? This has been the

toughest deal I ever saw a girl stack up against. Flo would have croaked."

"Ted, I'm sorta sunk. Feel like a poisoned pup."

"Some nice hot potato soup will be good for you."

"Come an' get it," sang out Charlie.

"I'll fetch yu some," said Laramie, suiting action to his words.

"Laramie, you flatter me. I haven't had a mouthful since yesterday. But I can't eat," replied the girl.

Lonesome pricked up his ears in a manner that suggested they were keenly sensitive in a certain quarter. He was kneeling with a heaping pan in his hands.

"Say, young woman, do you want to give us pore devils more trouble?" he asked. "We got two hard days ridin' an' one fight sure before we can get you home. An' if you won't eat you'll give out an' delay us."

"I – I'll eat," hurriedly whispered Lenta, receiving the pan from Laramie. And she did eat, though she forced every swallow. Laramie felt sorry for her and angry with Lonesome. Certainly it was no time for sentiment, yet Laramie saw no reason for Lonesome to be as hard as flint. The only break in the silence after that was when

435

Lonesome told Dakota to untie the Negro and let him eat.

"I'm so stiff and sore," said Lenta, presently, and got up. "I'll walk a little."

"Thet's a good kid," rejoined Laramie. "Dog-gone yu, lass, I'm beginnin' to like yu again."

"Thanks, Laramie. I'm suffering a change of heart, too."

Laramie arranged his saddle and a blanket on the other side of Lenta's bed, so that she would be between him and the tree.

"Pard, do yu reckon there's any chance of thet greaser prowlin' round to take a pot shot at us from the dark?" queried Laramie.

"Not if I know greasers," replied Lonesome.

"One saddle-horse missin'," added Dakota. "I reckon Juan got it. He's pushin' leather now."

"All the same, we'll keep guard," said Lonesome. "An' I'll be first on."

"There won't be a hell of a lot of sleepin', I reckon," added Laramie.

Lenta came stealing back to plump down on her bed and stretch out. Her eyes appeared unnaturally large and bright in her pale face.

"It'll be cold towards mawnin'," said

Laramie as he covered her partly. "Then I'll pull this up over yu."

"You'll stay close all night?"

"Shore, lass."

"I never was afraid of the dark and I never had nightmares. But...let me hold your hand, Laramie."

She held his hand in both hers, and then her heavy eyelids fell. Laramie expected her to go to sleep, and she did, almost immediately, when she unconsciously released her hold on him. Laramie sat gazing down upon the disheveled head, the pale face, the gently heaving breast, with mingled feelings. If this experience would be a lesson to her, all would yet end well. He decided it would be – even for such a madcap as Lenta Lindsay. And he rejoiced. After a while he softly arose to approach the squatting riders.

"Wal, you old wiz, how'd you come to be in thet cabin, waitin' fer us?" queried Lonesome.

"Wal, after I left yu pretty soon the trail forked back an' up over the hill. I got leary an' reckoned there was more'n yu hard after Gaines. When thet trail took off the ridge I searched the valley with my glass. Soon saw Gaines an' his outfit with the kid. I figgered I might haid him off by ridin' fast an' gettin' down. I did. I found this cabin an' I seen hawses comin'. But one was white an' then I was shore some one else had haided off Gaines, too. Thet was Price. So I took to the loft."

"You old wolf!" ejaculated Ted, warmly. "It was Lonesome who split off after Price. I rode slow, and soon Charlie and Dakota caught up with me. We saw Price's outfit pile down the hill and sneak after Gaines. So we waited for Lonesome. When he came we expected you soon afterward. But you didn't come pronto, so we knew you were up to your old tricks."

"Wal, we shore had luck," drawled Laramie. "If I hadn't been in the loft some of us would have got plugged. Thet stranger, Beady somebody, who was with Price – he sized up dangerous to me. He was playin' Price against Gaines. An' when Lonesome opened the ball I had an eye on Beady."

"Wonder who he was. What'd he do, pard?" returned Lonesome, in gruff curiosity.

"Wal, Gaines hadn't stopped fallin' when thet Beady leaped behind the door, his gun throwed.... I hope yu wasn't about to step in, then."

"I was, you bet. I had my foot up when your gun bellared. You see our plan was like this. Dakota was to take care of the two hawse wranglers, Charlie an' Ted was to be ready at thet back door, while I'd plant myself by the front door. Course it was on the cairds thet I'd pay my compliments to Gaines. Then the idee was for us to bust in quick, not givin' them a chance to hide, an' hold 'em all up."

"Well, it'd sure been all day with you, an' me, too, and maybe Charlie if Laramie hadn't been here," broke in Ted, gravely.

A sober little silence ensued. Lonesome poked the red embers with a stick. "Another time – huh?" he queried, with an odd break in his voice. "Wal, I own up to recklessness – 'cause of the girl.... But you was there, pard."

Chapter 16

Hallie sank back upon the soft hay, blinded by tears, so shaken and overcome with emotion that her mind seemed a whirling chaos. But the burn of Laramie's rude kisses upon her cheeks and neck, the sting of them on her lips, suddenly realized, cleared her consciousness at least of uncertainty.

She struggled up wildly, wiping her wet eyes. Gone! She heard trampling, jingling steps wearing away. She peered out of the stall. No other rider in sight! That catastrophe had had no witness. "Oh-h!" she whispered, thickly, as she gazed at her disheveled blouse and felt of her hair. One sleeve was up above her elbow. A fine dust of hayseed covered her habit. "The – savage! ... He nearly – tore me to pieces.... And I – I – Oh-h –"

This poignant expression, dying in her throat, had not to do with the furious blow she had dealt Laramie. That sprang from a panic-stricken shame – at a fearful realization. Laramie's volley of kisses had reacted terrible upon her – to her undoing.

She could not comprehend, but she knew. They had seemed to burn some cold strange barrier from around her heart and set it free to leap up against his. First she had been shocked, inflamed, then carried away on a rising flood of strong, sweet, irresistible madness.

There it was! Tragically she whispered the inevitableness of it. What a wreck she felt – what a wreck she must look! She brushed off her clothes and buttoned her sleeve. There was a red stain on the waistband. Blood! Whose? Then she remembered his bleeding lips. And he had kissed her with them! Frantically she found her handkerchief and wiped her face. Yes – more red – more –! She tried to stop her stream of consciousness – as if to dam a torrent. She picked up sombrero, gauntlets, quirt, and fled out at the back of the barn like a guilty thing. No rider in sight! She ran under the cottonwoods into the trail and far from the corrals; in a shady green covert she fell spent and breathless, to lie there staring up at the blue sky.

At last she agonized it out. Laramie had sickened of the Lindsays – of their milk-sop idea of ranching. And like other riders, in a reckless and perhaps poignant moment, he had responded to such an opportunity as they all answered. He had kissed her. Then, at her blow, enraged, he had – what had he not done – the brute? But the fierce, hard, brazen primitiveness of him had transformed her into his mate. One more moment of his strangling embrace – nay, one more rough kiss – would have seen her arms close around his neck. That was the terror of her realization. Oh, she knew! She could not delude herself. One hand had gone around his neck and the other was on the way to meet it when he had torn free. He did not know – he had not dreamed of her wild response. What had this West done to her? It had made a wife of Florence before she was out of her teens, it had ruined Lenta, it had torn her asunder, her – Harriet, who had been through with love – it had found in her depths another woman like a savage, a tigress, free, defiant, who loved with blood, flesh, mind, in a passion that relegated her old attachment to the strength of a candle-flame.

A grind of wheels rolling down the gravel road brought Hallie's long vigil to a close. Peeping out through the foliage, she espied two buckboards going by down to the barns. Horses, vehicles, drivers were all strange to her. Company! She was startled. What a time to be visited by some of the friendly ranchers whom the Lindsays had met at La Junta!

This event changed the current of Hallie's thought. She hurried up the valley trail and reached her room without meeting anyone. Here she proceeded to remove the stained and wrinkled riding-garb, which she vowed with a queer passion she would never put on again. Then she dressed hurriedly and endeavoured to look as if the world had not come to an end. She essayed a smile, and her mirror told her that that would do much to eliminate the havoc from her face.

Jud scowled at her as she passed her open quarters. "I don't want any lunch, Jud," and he replied that she did not eat enough to keep a jack-rabbit alive. Laughter and voices from the living-room confirmed Hallie's suspicion about company. Presenting herself at the open door, she looked in.

Flo, looking unusually excited and therefore lovely, sat holding the hand of a striking brunette girl of about nineteen, who was certainly a sister of Ted Williams. Then Hallie, suddenly breathless, espied her mother, radiant as always when she had company. A handsome gray-haired woman of distinction sat with Mrs. Lindsay, and beyond were two men talking to Hallie's father.

"Here she is," said Flo, leaping up.

Lindsay called, gaily. "Come in, daughter. Mrs. Williams, this is my eldest girl, Harriet.... Mr. Williams, you and Strickland meet the boss of Spanish Peaks Ranch... Hallie, of all the good luck! Ted's mother, father, and sister have come west to find Ted.... And this gentleman is Mr. Strickland, whom you met at La Junta. He is the largest cattle-dealer in eastern Colorado."

"I'm happy to meet you, Harriet," responded Mrs. Williams, graciously, as she extended her hand. "I'm glad there's one of the Lindsays who hasn't eloped yet."

Ted's sister, Kitty, had a shy greeting for Harriet. Mr. Williams was gay and flattering in his acknowledgement of the introduction, and Mr. Strickland, a tall, eagle-eyed tanned Westerner past middle age held Hallie's hand gallantly. "Miss Lindsay, I shore am glad to meet you again. An' if you're the boss of the Peak Dot Ranch I'm confident of the success of my call."

"Mr. Strickland, are you like all the rest of the young Westerners?" queried Hallie.

"Wal, if I was twenty years younger, yu'd see about that," declared the rancher, with a hearty laugh.

"It is too bad you-all did not come a day

444

sooner," said Hallie, to the visitors generally. "We are upset. Lenta has – run off, and Ted, with the other riders, has gone to fetch her back."

"Married or no?" asked Mrs. Williams, with a smile.

"In any case."

"Do you approve of the young man?" queried Mr. Williams, jocularly.

"Hardly. He is handsome, and wild enough, surely, even for my wild little sister. But he has – scarcely any more to recommend him."

"And how do you feel about our son running off with your other sister?" added the smiling mother.

"I'm very happy about that."

"Oh, so am I," murmured Kitty. "And just crazy to see Ted."

"I knew you at once to be his sister.... Ted is very handsome."

"Thank you. Handsome riders must be plentiful out here. Can't you find me one? I've heard enough about this Laramie Nelson to make me eager to see him."

"Oh, Laramie –" replied Harriet, constrainedly, conscious of a queer sinking sensation within her breast. "Yes, he is quite good-looking, too.... Perhaps with all their talk they have not told you, he's a gun-fighter. It was he who led the riders after Lenta. I dare say Laramie has killed some one already."

"Gun-fighter? – Killed some one!... Oh, how dreadful!" exclaimed the Eastern girl.

"And Ted has been a – what do you call a rider – a range-rider, all these years?" queried Mrs. Williams, aghast.

"Ten years, I think he said. And the last four he has been closely associated with Laramie Nelson, and another of our riders, Lonesome, they call him. They are like brothers."

"Lonesome? How cute!" cried Kitty.

Mrs. Williams gazed in apprehension at her husband. "Father, I fear Ted is going to give us a shock."

"I'm prepared for anything," replied Williams, happily. "But I'm not worried any more. I'll take the West as I find it. And right here I find it most satisfactory. For years I've feared Ted had become a disgrace to us – an idle, drunken cow-puncher. But I'm sure I'll have to apologize."

Florence gave him a proud little smile.

"Indeed you will. Ted is the farthest removed from that. He is just the finest boy in all the world."

"All's well that ends well," returned Mr. Williams, feelingly.

446

"Mrs. Williams, of course, you will stay?" asked Harriet. "We can make you comfortable and will be most happy to have you."

"Thank you, we will stay – unless one of your wild riders makes up to Kitty."

"One of them! They'll all make up to her. . . . And I warn you, Kitty, they make love like – like cyclones."

"It'll be just great," replied that demure young lady, her eyes shining.

Here Strickland interposed: "Lindsay, now that your range boss is here suppose we get our little confab over. I'll have to leave at daybreak tomorrow. An' as my business with you is important, I'd like to get it off my chest."

"Range boss?" echoed Hallie, wonderingly. "Am I he?"

"So your father gives me to understand," replied Strickland.

"Oh, I – I've made a mess of it. All I'll ever do after this is handle the money."

"Wal, that includes about everythin'."

"Ma, you folks please excuse us a while," said Lindsay rising. "Come, Hallie, we'll go to the office. Mr. Williams, didn't you say you might back Ted in some cattle deal or other?"

"Yes, I said I might, if he was half decent

and it would help him," replied Williams, genially. "Now after hearing what you say about Ted, and meeting his lovely wife, I'm inclined to buy them a corner of Colorado for a wedding present."

"Fine. Then you sit in with us on this little game. Come."

He led the way with Hallie, while Strickland and Williams followed.

"Mr. Williams, are you really serious about settin' your boy up in the cattle business?" Strickland was saying.

"I am indeed – if the boy will only forgive me. I guess I wasn't –

"Shucks! That'll be all right. Dads will be dads. I had a boy who disappointed me turrible. He went to the bad an' – never come back."

"Ah! That's sad. I'm sorry."

"But I have two other sons, both doin' wal, one out here, an' the other in Kansas City, at the receivin' end of our cattle business. . . . It's not a bad idee your backin' the boy now. This particular range is due for a boom, an' it'll run half a million haid of stock."

"Half a million!" echoed Mr. Williams.

Harriet led them into her cool and tidy office with a conscious pride.

448

"Wal, this looks like business to me," declared Williams.

"She was my right-hand man back in Ohio," replied Lindsay.

"What'll you do when one of these buckaroos rides off with her?" queried the Easterner bluntly.

"That isn't likely," stammered Harriet, with a furious blush.

"Isn't it?" dryly added Strickland. "Wal, sufficient unto the day.... Now, Lindsay, to get down to talk, I want you an' Miss Harriet to glance over these papers."

"What are they?" asked Harriet, as the rancher slapped a bundle of long envelopes upon the desk.

"Wal, I calculate they prove my status. Letters from bankers, stockmen, an' so forth. One from a Denver judge, an' executive of the Santa Fé, an' others, all well-known men."

"I see," replied Lindsay, fingering the letters, which Strickland had opened. "What's the idea? Your status?"

"These are references, I take it?" inquired Harriet.

"Exactly, an' to your evident kindly objection to see any reason for them I have this to say," returned Strickland. "I am an old cattleman an' you are a newcomer. This

449

cattle business has grown so complicated, as it has prospered, that no rancher knows whether his neighbor is stealin' his cattle or not. That's the gist of the matter."

"Ridiculous, in your case, Mr. Strickland," replied Harriet, warmly.

"Thanks, miss. That's nice from you. But do me the favor, you an' your father an' Mr. Williams, too, to run over them."

The request was acceded to, at the conclusion of which Mr. Williams said to Lindsay: "These are unquestionably and legally a guarantee of Mr. Strickland's position. I should say leading position."

"Agree with you, Williams," replied Lindsay.

"An' you, Miss Hallie?" queried the cattleman.

"I read them to please you, Mr. Strickland, but I did not need to."

"You can see through men?"

"Hardly that, Mr. Strickland. But I have a woman's instinct. I think I know whom I can trust."

"Did you trust Lester Allen?" queried Strickland, bluntly.

"I did not," retorted Harriet. "I told father Allen had cheated him."

"How about Arlidge? I remember you were – evidently interested in him at La

Junta. Pardon me. This is business. Would you trust him?"

"Mr. Strickland, you must make allowances for an Eastern tenderfoot," replied Harriet, blushing as usual, to her annoyance. "I was interested in Arlidge, perhaps somewhat fascinated – but as surely repelled. I would not trust him in any way."

"Thank you. That is straight talk. I like it an' I like your eyes, aside from their beauty," rejoined Strickland, and then he turned to Lindsay. "You are fortunate in your right-hand man. May I ask if you have relied wholly upon this – this woman's instinct she called it?"

"No, I haven't, and I've lived to regret it," rejoined Lindsay, frankly.

"Wal, I've taken the trouble to find out all the range knows about you an' your family an' your riders. It'd surprise you. Westerners take stock of any newcomers, but they're slow aboot it. Sometimes it's unhealthy."

"You're very kind to be so – so interested, Strickland."

"Not at all. But I've become sort of a leader in eastern Colorado. Now, for the reason. You'll see in this list of names – here – all the reputable cattlemen in this section, an' that runs over into Kansas an' Nebraskie. I'll be frank with you. There *may* be

451

cattlemen listed there who are crooked, and we may have left out some honest ones. But we've done our best. Bain, Stockwell, Halscomb, an' myself are responsible for this organization I'm representin'. We call it The Spanish Peaks Cattlemen's Protective Association. Our object is to band together for protection against rustlers. There always has been rustlin' in the West, an' so long as cattle are raised there will continue to be rustlin'.... You have lost considerable yourself, I understand?"

Lindsay nodded and spread wide his hands. "I came West to recover my health. I did. And I'm glad about it that I'm not kicking over my losses."

"How much stock have you lost?"

Hallie replied for him: "We are cleaned out. Father bought ten thousand head from Allen. The actual number here upon our arrival was much less than that. Now they are all gone."

Mr. Williams leaned forward in genuine amaze. "Is it possible? Ten thousand head of cattle! I am shocked. Why, this rustling must be a business."

"Bane of the cattlemen, Mr. Williams," replied Strickland, tersely. "Wal, naturally you have suffered most, Lindsay. But some of the rest of us are losin' stock, more an'

452

more all the time. There's a wave of rustlers swellin' on us, about to swamp us. It's a big range, with thousands of cattle spread all over, easy pickin' for thieves. There must be a number of gangs, perhaps none of them large. An' when mixed brands can be driven an' sold to one of half a dozen markets – wal, it's somethin' for us to stack up against.... Lindsay, we want you in our organization. We want your son also, an' young Williams, too, if he is becomin' a rancher."

"I accept, and thanks to you, Mr. Strickland," replied Lindsay.

"Gentlemen, I can't swear for my son yet, but I'm strong to see him go in with you and fight these robbers," spoke up Williams, forcibly.

"So far so good," declared Strickland, with satisfaction. "But the rub has been, an' still *is,* how to operate against these rustlers. Every growin' range sees somethin' of the same trouble. But ours is particularly lax, mainly because we have only one or two men capable of controlin' riders an' wipin' out the rustlers. My foreman, Stevens, was one. Unfortunately, Stevens was shot a week ago. Not fatally, I'm glad to say, but he'll be out of harness for a while. We must get the other men to lead our forces, or else import some one. That I don't approve of, because it'd be

453

hard to get the right one. We might hire a man who would fall in with the rustlers. That has been done often."

"Who, is this – other man you speak of?" asked Hallie, with a sudden sense of catastrophe.

"Your foreman, Laramie Nelson," answered Strickland. "I don't know Nelson, but I have heard of him. I dare say, Miss Lindsay, that neither you nor your father have any idea who this Nelson is."

"Buffalo Jones got Nelson for me – told us a lot about him," replied Lindsay.

"Yes. I met Jones in Denver recently an' I told him about our troubles. An' he growled about what'd come over Laramie Nelson. That acquainted me with the fact of Jones' interest in you. Wal, he told me though he recommended Nelson highly to you, he did not tell you altogether who an' what Nelson was."

"I see. All right, it's not pertinent right now to waste time on who and what Nelson was or is, jest so long as he's the man you need."

"He is. An' now I must get – wal, sort of personal, Miss Lindsay. I hope you'll forgive me. We're all deeply concerned.... The talk of the range is that Nelson has laid down on his job."

454

"What?" demanded Lindsay.

"Mr. Strickland, you mean La – Nelson has – has not lived up to his reputation – that he had not done anything to – to end this rustling?" queried Harriet, hurriedly.

"Exactly. He has not."

"I – I am to blame. I have kept him from – from violence. It made me sick to think of this – spilling blood.... Oh, indeed, I have been – I am the most chicken hearted of tenderfoots."

"No one would suspect that," returned Strickland. "But I think I understand you. We all wondered about Nelson.... May I presume to ask – are you engaged to him?"

"Oh!... No, indeed," murmured Hallie, and this time her skin blanched cold and tight instead of burning.

"Wal, that's too bad, for us an' Laramie, too," went on Strickland, wholly unconscious of flaying Hallie. "The range gossip has it that Nelson is so sweet on you he can't run the riders, much less go out an' hang a rustler."

"Such gossip is a – a great injustice to him," replied Hallie, lifting her head.

"Wal," drawled Strickland, his eagle-eyes piercing and warm upon her, "such things always right themselves. That gossip won't hurt Nelson so long as he corrects it, particularly the report that he intends to quit your father."

"Quit me!" ejaculated Lindsay, astounded. "No, Strickland, he'll stick to me."

"Father, I must confess to you," said Hallie, fighting for composure, "that Laramie quit this morning. He assured me he would fetch Lenta back to us – then he was through."

The significant glances of the three men were not lost upon Harriet. At the moment she was more concerned with concealing her secret than with anything else.

"Lindsay, I'll gamble Nelson quit so he'd have a free hand. I know Westerners of his stripe. With all due respect to Miss Hallie's feelin's, I'm glad he quit. There'll be hell out there on the range. Don't worry, he'll fetch the little girl back safe an' unharmed....*But,* his quittin' is serious now. He might take a shot at some one, then ride away. The thing is – he must be got back – he must be the man to lead our protective organization."

"Maybe a good big offer of money would help," suggested Williams.

"No," replied Strickland, decidedly, and he shifted his gaze back to Hallie.

"Strickland, I had a hunch Nelson was going to leave us. And I asked Hallie to persuade him to stay.... Hallie, you must have failed."

"Father, I – I did not try," responded Harriet, and she walked to the window to look out. Then ensued a silence that enabled Harriet to find herself. She turned. "Dad," she began, and the fact that she called him that was revealing, "and Mr. Strickland, if Laramie Nelson is so – so vital to our interests I promise you I will do my utmost to keep him here – and no longer influence or hinder his actions."

Hallie shirked facing what she actually meant and how she should proceed in such a crucial situation. She had an inkling that if she shunted aside her too sensitive delicacy and reacted in a wholesome and unrestrained way she might be better off. Moreover she was resisting a suspicion that she was being false to this new character. Sufficient unto the day! She did not dare think of meeting Laramie again, while she knew that she must. Would that meeting give her the shock she needed?

With congenial company to entertain, Hallie seemed to put off the inevitable for the time being. When it came to dinner, Jud did the ranch proud. Then the evening passed swiftly until the tired visitors reluctantly retired. Hallie said good-night to Strickland with a feeling that he would indeed be the friend and adviser her father needed.

Strong as was her longing to see Lenta home safely, and to get her forgiveness, Harriet felt relief when the hour of eleven arrived without the return of Laramie and his riders. They had been detained. Had they succeeded in trailing and catching Lenta and her companion? Hallie felt no divination of that in her heart, but she knew Laramie would fetch her back. And when she reflected that here she relied upon his Western force – the bold and relentless violence which had repelled her, then she realized she was nearing an eclipse of old standards.

She shared Flo's room and bed that night, to her benefit, for the excited girl, so full of delight with Ted's people, did not give her a chance to think of herself. And at last sleep brought oblivion.

The next day, given over to walking and riding with the Williamses, passed swiftly, though punctuated by recurrent and increasing concern about Lenta. Neale, too, had been absent for two days. By dinner time, which arrived with no riders in sight, Hallie gave way to dread. Something had happened. It could not be that Stuart had been able to elude Laramie. Absurd! Nevertheless, the unexpected could always happen. Hallie passed a miserable night.

If another, a third day, passed without sign or word of her sister, Hallie felt that she would be frantic. The hours wore on. There was now no attempt to entertain the guests. Indeed, they shared the suspense. Hallie had to get away from everybody, to pace her room alone, in an agony of accusation. Had she not driven Lenta to such a rash act?

A clatter of hoofs out on the hard court brought Hallie up short. She rushed to open the door. Clay Lee was in the act of reining a wet and panting horse.

"Lee," she called, hurriedly. "Are the riders coming? – Have they got Lenta?"

"No, I'm sorry to say," he shouted.

Lindsay strode out upon the porch.

"What's that?"

Hallie, in her hurry across the court, did not catch Lee's reply. But it was bad news, judging by her father's paling face when she reached the porch.

"Father!"

"Neale has been shot," said Lindsay, with stunned blank look.

"Oh, my God! ... Don't – don't say he's –"

"He's not dead or even hurt fatal, Miss Lindsay," interrupted Lee. "A rider jest went through. Didn't know him. He said there was a cattle drive over here at Meadow Wash. Thet's half way to Allen's ranch. Neale was there. It seems he took offense at a remark an' went for his gun an' got shot."

"A – remark?" faltered Hallie.

"Yes, ma'am. It was about your sister – about her runnin' off."

"Oh!. . . . Is he – badly hurt?"

"This rider said not. Bad gun-shot through his arm, but no bones broke. Arlidge jest shot to cripple the boy."

"Arlidge!"

"Yes, Miss Lindsay. Arlidge made the remark an' did the shootin'. I reckon thet was a bad job for him. Hadn't I better ride over?"

"Please go – hurry," whispered Hallie. Then as Lee wheeled his horse to gallop away Hallie did battle with the hottest gust of fury that had ever taken possession of her. Arlidge had maligned Lenta and then crippled her brother. But Hallie suppressed this strange new heat for the moment, and thought of her mother. "Father, let me break it."

"Sure, Hallie," he replied, hoarsely. "But I'm going to break something myself and that pronto."

Chapter 17

The day with its sustained suspense and final tragedy had worked its deadly havoc among the riders. Laramie felt the steely, ruthless clutch, though he showed it least. The creed of the range kept such men justified in their own minds; nevertheless, the dealing of death visited upon each its icy touch.

During the night Laramie dozed at intervals. He tried to woo sleep. The morrow would bring even a sterner encounter for him – one he had to seek deliberately. His comrades expected it of him. Though he had contempt for Arlidge, still he wanted steady nerves and clear eyes, and brain swift as lightning. For years he had trained himself to have these. And even during these lax months, when he had smothered old instincts, the habit of self-preservation, exceedingly tenacious in him, had forced him to continue his old secret practice of throwing his gun. Not even subjugation to the charm and command of Harriet Lindsay had been able to eradicate that. And in the

461

wakeful lonely hours of night he felt that it was well.

The Negro, Johnson, and the girl were the only ones who slept the night through. Ted, Dakota, Wind River Charlie, and Lonesome, beside doing guard duty, were awake and up at intervals. Alone, and sometimes in couples, they patrolled a beat before the cabin. Lonesome was the most restless. Laramie, in the shadow of the tree, watched his friend understandingly. Often Lonesome gazed at the spot where Lenta lay asleep. Often he halted at the door of the cabin to peer in. Once he entered. What had that been for? The interior of the cabin could have received only faint starlight. It was ghastly, still, reeking.

As the long night wore on Laramie sensed a gradual fixing of his own mood. Lenta's slight prone form, her sad wan face, her clasped hands, held this mood off less and less, and at length failed. But so powerful was his will that presently he forced himself to a sleep that lasted until gray dawn.

Lonesome was raking the ashes of the fire over fresh dry cones and chips. "Howdy, pard," he said, deep in his throat. "It's different the mornin' after. . . . Kick 'em in the slats. . . . We gotta rustle."

Laramie did not exercise such roughness

462

as that. It was noticeable that each of the remaining riders sat up quickly, instantly awake, silent as the gray dawn.

"Help me wrangle the hawses."

By the time the riders had found and caught their own mounts, and the other horses necessary, day had broken clear and beautiful. Laramie saw it without feeling. The rosy east, the long ragged ridge-top, the alternate patches of black timber and grassy slope, the sage-gray valley, soft and misty, awakening from sleep, the antelope grazing with the cattle and the coyotes slipping away with last yelps – these were merely details of a morning which Laramie wished had never dawned.

Lonesome and Charlie had breakfast ready. The girl slept on. Laramie roused her, brought her food and drink, but was not responsive to her overtures this morning.

"Laramie, I'm buckin' you from heah on," said Lonesome, tossing away his empty cup.

"Ahuh. . . . Boys, pack a little grub an' water for tonight," replied Laramie. "Leave everythin' else – jest as it is. An' saddle pronto."

Presently he addressed Johnson.

"Nig, how far to Allen's?"

"I don't know zactly, sah. But I sho knows de way."

"Half a day's ride?"

"More, sah, onless we rustles."

"Climb yore hawse an' lead. . . . Ted, look after the girl an' stop us if she weakens."

Early in the afternoon Johnson led out of a winding wooded gulch down upon the open range. The scene was grand. Laramie recognized it, though he had never sat his horse to see it from that point.

A mile or so down the gray-green slope of sage stood a picturesque squat cabin, half ringed by trees. This was the ranch where Allen and Arlidge held forth. It had belonged to the settler Snook and no doubt was now being exploited and offered for sale as had been the old fort Lindsay had bought. Strings and herds of cattle afforded marked contrast to the vacant range around Spanish Peaks Ranch. Ten miles to the east, down the line of green willows, nestled the gray cabin and corral to which Ted had tracked his horse.

Westward rolled the range, swelling, billowy, dotted by cattle, bright in the afternoon sun. It rose to the low foothills, which in turn mounted step by step to the purple-sloped, white-peaked Rockies.

Laramie studied the Allen ranch cabin with his glass. Evidences of occupation were

464

manifest, but he did not make out a single rider. He remembered that the wide porch of this cabin fronted toward the west and he could not see it from this angle.

Laramie led the riders at a brisk canter down the slope, keeping the line of willows and cottonwoods between them and the cabin. Behind the last clump of trees he halted.

"Wal, who wants to ride up an' tip me off about what to expect?" he queried.

They all volunteered, and Ted, particularly, wanted to go.

"I told yu to look after Lent," rejoined Laramie. "Anyway, it wouldn't do for yu to brace this outfit. Yu've been heah before with fire in yore eyes. . . . Charlie, yu go."

"Fine, boss. What'll I do?" replied Charlie.

"Ride up to the porch," went on Laramie, swiftly. "Halt jest outside thet hitchin'-rail. Make some excuse for callin'. If you don't see Arlidge, ask for him. An' if he's there take off yore sombrero careless like. Savvy?"

"Shore. An' how'll I signal if there's some of Arlidge's riders?"

"Nig, how many in Arlidge's outfit?"

"Four on steady jobs, sah, not countin' me an' Juan an' Gaines."

"Only four. Who drove those big herds?"

"Allen had riders come from other ranges."

"Ahuh. Wal, Charlie, never mind about the outfit. Jest –"

"Pard, what's your idee?" interposed Lonesome.

"I won't make up my mind until Charlie tips me off," responded Laramie, tensely, and waved Charlie away. Both Ted and Lonesome questioned him then, but he gave no heed. It was hard to sit there watching, waiting. Charlie rode the hundred paces at a trot, and halted before the cabin, just as any lonesome and travel-worn rider would. Through the web of foliage Laramie would make out patches of figures on the porch, but he did not care to risk clearer view. Plain it was, though, that Wind River Charlie engaged somebody in conversation. Tight and cold, with the faculty of action in abeyance, Laramie bestrode his horse. Charlie did not remove his sombrero. Laramie waited a moment longer. He knew then that if the rider used the signal he would wheel his horse and gallop swiftly around to the back of the cabin. But Charlie's head remained covered. Laramie expelled an oppressive breath. The time seemed not yet.

"Wal, come on, boys. Ted, ya hang heah a little with Lent."

Ted consented, but not until he had vigorously protested. Laramie heard the girl cry out as he led the riders away. "Let's go anyhow, Ted," she said. And Ted replied: "Whoa, Calamity Jane! Laramie's mad enough now."

"Now, boys, ride, but not too fast," ordered Laramie. In a moment they were cantering toward the cabin. Laramie's hawk-eyes swept the scene. Charlie sat sidewise in his saddle, rolling a cigarette. Two bareheaded riders dangled chaps down over the edge of the porch. Two men in shirt sleeves lolled at a table next the cabin wall. Quickly the horses covered the intervening distance. Looking back, Laramie saw the girl riding out of the grove and Ted trying to catch her bridle.

Next moment Laramie faced frontward and dismounted. Dakota, Lonesome, and the Negro joined Charlie, opposite the two seated riders. Laramie's long stride took him around the hitching-rail.

"Howdy, gentlemen," he drawled, as he stepped upon the porch. Both men appeared aware that this encounter was unusual. The one standing, a tall Westerner with an eagle eye, Laramie had seen before somewhere. The man sitting at the table did not strike Laramie favorably. A pallor showed under

467

his coarse tan. He had hard, bright blue eyes and rugged features that fitted them.

"Howdy," replied the man standing.

"Didn't I see you at La Junta?" queried Laramie, slowly. He stood so that he could see the slightest movement of both men at once.

"You may have."

"What's your name?"

"Strickland."

"Ahuh. Yu're John Strickland?"

"At your service, mister –"

"Wal, I'm sorry to meet ya heah. What yu doin'?"

"I have been tryin' to persuade Mr. Allen here to join a cattlemen's protective association I'm organizin'," returned the rancher, impressively. Laramie was swift to catch an inflection of a voice, a glint of eye that he did not read to Allen's favor.

"Humph. I'll bet two-bits Mr. Allen ain't keen about it," drawled Laramie, with cool sarcasm.

"Strange to say he –"

Allen interrupted by bursting out of his amaze to pound the table and bark:

"You impudent cow-puncher! What d'ye mean, bracin' in here this way?"

"I've a little business with ya," replied Laramie, softly.

468

"Then you can get out. I want none of it. . . . The nerve of these punchers, Strickland! He must be one of that insolent Peak Dot outfit."

"Shore. I happen to be Laramie Nelson."

Allen leaned back, his face livid, and he eyed Nelson with dark speculation. "I don't care who in hell you are. Get off my land!"

"Say, for a Westerner yu air sort of testy. Had yore own way a lot, I reckon. Wal, yu're at the end of yore rope, Allen."

"Is this deal a hold-up?" demanded the other, hoarsely.

"It shore is, an' about time. . . . Strickland, step to one side."

"What you want – Nelson?" yelped Allen.

"Wal, I reckon I want a lot. . . . First I'll acquaint yu with the fact thet Beady is daid – Jude is daid. . . . An' we hanged Price."

"What's that to me? I don't know these rustlers."

"No. How about Gaines? He's daid, too. Arlidge's greaser got away. But we have the nigger heah."

"No – matter," shouted Allen, stridently, beginning to fail of nerve.

"Nig, come up heah," ordered Laramie. In another moment Johnson stood on the porch, rolling his eyes at Allen, and evidently not perturbed.

469

"Nig, yu know this man?"

"Yas, sah, I knows him."

"Who is he?"

"Calls hisself Lester Allen."

"Have yu rode for him?"

"No, sah. But I don ride for his pardner, Arlidge."

"Do you know what became of the cattle Allen sold Lindsay?"

"I sho do, sah. They was rustled. Tree big drives an' some little ones. I was in them all."

"Did Arlidge lead one of these drives?"

"Yas, sah. The first one."

"What'd yu do with the cattle?"

"Druv it over heah. Allen sent thet herd out an' nebber burned a brand. But all the rest ob de stock we put de iron on, sah."

"Can you prove Allen took these cattle an' sold them?"

"No sah. But we all knows dam' wal that he did."

Allen leaped up with blanched face and staring eyes. He jerked at his hip for the gun that was not there, and which Laramie had noted was not there.

"You lyin' nigger!" he yelled. "Arlidge will kill you for this."

"No, Arlidge won't," retorted Laramie, deliberately. "Allen, yore bluff is no good.

470

Anyone could see through yu.... How about thet, Strickland?"

"Nelson, this substantiates what I suspected before I came here to interview Allen," replied the rancher, gravely.

"Ahuh. Thet's interestin'. I wondered about yu. Jest happened along right. Wal, it works out thet way sometimes."

Allen made as if to go into the cabin, but was deterred by a sharp call from Lonesome.

"Riders comin', pard.... Arlidge!"

Allen dropped heavily upon the bench, his face pallid and clammy, his eyes suddenly gleaming. "Hah! - you tell all that to Arlidge. He's been achin' to meet you, Nelson. Old grudge, he said. But I kept him back. Now, by Heaven, you'll get your bluff called!... An' you, Strickland - you'll have to answer to him for your - suspicions!"

Laramie's three riders peered beyond the cabin, their necks craned, then quietly slipped out of their saddles to stand behind their horses. Laramie could not see what had actuated them, but he heard a rhythmic beat of hoofs, coming fast. Strickland answered to the suspense by striding across the porch to stand back to the wall. Allen sat staring with distended eyes.

Laramie recognized the moment that would be his, as if fatefully ordered long ago.

471

He did not need to gamble on the element of surprise which decided so many encounters, but he welcomed it. He too backed against the cabin wall. Then all the iron of muscle and steel of mind gathered as if to leap.

Ringing hoofbeats pounded closer. Gravel and dust flew ahead of a furious horse, pulled on its haunches. Arlidge leaped to land with a thudding clink of spurs. As he strode for that end of the long porch two other riders dashed into sight.

Lithe and erect, intense in action, his face darkly passionate, his eyes like daggers. Arlidge stepped upon the porch.

"Bad news, Lester, cuss my luck!" he pealed out. "Had to shoot young Lindsay –"

Then his piercing gaze took in the strange horses, the riders stepping out, Allen plumped on the bench with extended shaking hand, and Strickland flattened against the wall.

"What the –" he hissed.

At that Laramie stepped out.

Arlidge saw him. With one foot forward he turned to stone. Then his visage underwent a marvelous transformation. Perception, surprise, hate, motive, and realization swept with kaleidoscopic swiftness across his countenance. And the last gripped him horribly. As clearly as if he had spoken he expressed wild fear and certainty of death.

With audible intake of breath he crouched slightly, desperate as a wolf at bay, his eyes like points of fire. As he lurched for his gun, Laramie's boomed in its outward leap. Arlidge died in the act of his draw, falling backward off the porch almost under the plunging horses.

One of the riders fired off a rearing horse. Laramie heard the bullet spring off the gravel beyond him. Lonesome shot – then Charlie. The rearing horse plunged away with rider sliding off to be dragged by a heel.

"Up with 'em. Hennesy," called Charlie.

"Up they air," returned the other rider, sweeping his hands aloft. His horse pivoted to a trembling stand.

"Whoa, Sandy – whoa, boy," called Dakota. The other horses stood restlessly. Still there came a pounding of hoofs, Laramie wheeled. Ted and Lenta sat prancing horses, out beyond the others.

"Lonesome, grab yore rope," ordered Laramie, turning to the stricken Allen.

Mulhall sheathed his gun and leaped in a single action. Tearing the lasso off his saddle he thumped around his horse, ducked

473

under the hitching-rail, and came up with a sinister snarl of lips.

"Toss a loop about Allen's neck," went on Laramie.

Like a snake the noose glided out to circle Allen's neck. Lonesome gave the rope a whip. Then Allen leaped up, fumbling at the noose. "God Almighty! Would you – hang me?"

"I should smile we would," replied Lonesome.

"Hold – hold! Nelson," ejaculated Strickland, in agitation. "I don't want to interfere . . . but will you give me a word?"

"Go ahaid," replied Laramie.

"Nelson – you riders – I question the wisdom an' justice of such a proceedin'. You are hot now – blood-set on this. But wait a moment. Think! Let me –"

"Wal, do you need any more'n to look at him?" queried Lonesome.

"Any man about to hang would look like that."

"Ump-umm!" declared Lonesome. "I didn't. This heah gazabo is a big thief. The wust kind, 'cause he hires pore riders to steal for him."

"Strickland, we know Allen's crooked," put in Laramie.

"But can you prove it?"

"Wal, I reckon we cain't," replied Laramie. "All the same.... See heah, Allen. Take your choice. Hang or leave Colorado."

"I'll – leave," panted Allen, tearing off the noose.

"All right. Jest as yu air. Fork Arlidge's hawse an' rustle. If we ever see yu again on this range neither Strickland nor anyone else can save your neck."

In another moment Allen was on his way, heading west.

Laramie voiced a query that had hammered at him. "Heah, rider, what about Arlidge shootin' young Lindsay?"

"Thet's right. He did."

"Kill him?"

"No. Only winged him."

"Where'd this happen?"

"Over at the Meadows. Snook was roundin' up stock with two of his punchers. I seen Lindsay throw a gun on Arlidge. Don't know what for. An' I seen Arlidge shoot him in the arm. Lindsay is layin' over there bleedin' like a stuck pig. Snook sed, 'Let him bleed.'"

"Lonesome, yu an' Charlie an' Dakota pile over there," ordered Laramie. "Strickland, where yu headin' now?"

"I've a buckboard behind the cabin," replied the rancher. "I'll drive with you an'
475

take young Lindsay over. . . . Hello, who's the girl?"

"That's Lindsay's lass – the one we went after. Take her with yu, Strickland. . . . Ted, beat the dust after Lonesome."

Scarcely had Laramie given this order when Ted, with a word to Lenta, spurred away.

"Get yore hawse from Snook," yelled Laramie, after him. Then Laramie spoke to the two riders who had slid off the porch to the ground. "Get up an' move. Thet goes for yu, too, Hennesy. Remember yu're marked riders on this range from now on. Better go honest."

"Nelson, we ain't liable to fergit," returned Hennesy, turning his horse down the lane, with the two riders hurrying after him. Strickland appeared in the buckboard he had mentioned, driving a spirited team.

"Get off an' climb in, Miss Lindsay," called Strickland. The girl complied, showing in her actions that her strength was almost spent. Strickland drove away, calling for Laramie to follow.

"Be right along," replied Laramie. Then he turned to Johnson, who sat on the bench.

Nig, yu squared yoreself with me. What yu want to do?"

"I doan know, boss. Dere's no sense in

rustlin'. I'se long hed cold feet, sah. Ebberybody's daid. . . . I doan know where to go."

"Get on an' lead the girl's hawse. We'll follow the buckboard."

Laramie sheathed his gun, and plodded over to his horse, to kick the stirrup straight and step into the saddle. Then he surveyed the scene. Arlidge lay flat on his back, one arm flung wide. His right arm lay across his body and his hand clutched the half-drawn gun. The years rolled back. Always Laramie had known this thing would come. What had held it back these last incomprehensible months? Once again thought impinged upon that gloomy mood.

It was ten miles and more to Snook's ranch. Laramie and Nig did not catch up with Strickland, though they kept him in sight. The sun was setting when Laramie halted before the Snook cabin. He espied the buckboard, unhitched, and a number of horses in the corral. Ted and Strickland emerged from the cabin, and the latter advanced to meet Laramie. Wind River Charlie appeared with an armload of firewood. Again Laramie felt the easing of that cold, sick oppression.

"Nelson, we'll spend the night here, if you

don't object," said the rancher. "The girl has about collapsed an' it won't hurt young Neale to be kept on his back."

"Wal, mebbe it's as well all around," pondered Laramie. "It's a good thirty miles for the buckboard. An' our hawses are all in."

"Boss, one of Snook's riders said Jerky sloped off," called Dakota. "He'll stop at Lindsay's."

"Wal, I reckon a little sooner or later won't matter," muttered Laramie as he slid off. He could be glad to lie down in the darkness and quiet and spend the endless hours of a long night wearing out of this vise-clutched grip upon his senses. "Nig, look after these hawses."

It struck him that Ted had no more desire to be approached than had Laramie to approach him. But Lonesome came whistling out. The vicissitude lay behind this rider.

"Hullo, pard. You look seedy," he said. "Ted got both his hawses back."

"Thet's good. What'd Snook say about it?"

"Aw, not much."

"Wal. What yu mean?"

"Snook got plumb ugly, so Ted just eased a forty-five slug through him."

Chapter 18

Wind River Charlie's call to supper had no allurement for Laramie. Finally Lonesome brought him a cup of coffee and a biscuit.

"Pard, reckonin' from your looks, you an' me will be ridin' away after this," he said, sagely.

"Wal, thet hadn't struck me yet. But I reckon so," returned Laramie, gloomily.

"Ted is on. He jest taxed me about you. It'll go tough with him, Larry."

"Shore. But he's married now an' he'll have to stick. An' we haven't got anybody to care." Lonesome sighed. "Out on the lone prairie for us, pard."

"Dodge an' Abilene for us, Lonesome, an' the flowin' bowl," rejoined Laramie.

"Aw, hell!...Dreams don't amount to nothin'....Say, Larry, this rancher Strickland has been pumpin' me about you. Like him alright, but I couldn't be civil jest now. I reckon he's afraid to brace you. I see him lookin' hard."

"Wal, I don't want to talk."

479

"Let's say hello to Neale. He's been askin' for you."

"Go ahaid in. I'll come."

The cabin was comfortably furnished, and well lighted by lamp and open fire. Strickland stood with his back to the grate. Lenta lay locked in a deep slumber of exhaustion. Ted sat beside Neale who lay on the floor, his head upon a folded blanket. His face deathly white and his eyes burned black.

"Wal, son, how yu makin' out?" inquired Laramie, kneeling beside the lad.

"Laramie! – I'm all right now. My arm hurts like hell, but I can stand it. Ted fixed it up."

"Any bones broke?"

"No. I can move it, anyway. But there's a big hole and I bled terrible."

"Son, how'd yu happen way over heah? This ain't our territory."

"I tracked a rider. Thought it was Stuart."

"Ahuh. An' yu was plumb sore?"

"Yes, but I kept my head. I sure didn't get any welcome from this outfit. When I saw Ted's horse and a lot of Peak Dot yearlings I just up and asked Arlidge how they got here. He told me to run along home. Then I cussed him and told him about Stuart eloping with Lent. He haw-hawed and made a dirty remark about her and said he'd be eloping with Hallie next."

"What'd yu do then, son?" queried Laramie.

"I kicked him good and hard. He knocked me flat. I tried to throw my gun while I was on the ground. Then he crippled me. It wasn't an even break when I was down.... Oh, it was decent of him not to kill me, I know. All the same, I'll lay for him and get even."

Laramie was silent, pondering what seemed best to say to this lad too suddenly thrust among hard characters of the West.

"Neale, old man," spoke up Lonesome, "you won't never need to get even with Arlidge."

"What! ... Why not?"

"Arlidge finally run into the wrong man."

"*Laramie!*"

Lonesome nodded, and giving Neale a kindly pat he rose to his feet and went out.

"Son, I feel sort of responsible for this," went on Laramie. "I shore didn't spend time enough with yu to get yu started right out heah. But there's been so many things.... An' I let yu run amuck. I'm shore sorry."

"Laramie, it was all my fault. I've been bull-headed. But I'll do better after this."

481

"Thet's straight talk. Don't get into any more jams, an' don't throw yore gun unless in self-defense. This little gunshot hurt ain't nothin'. But let it be a lesson to yu. Lay off the bottle an' cairds, an' keep yore haid with the riders."

"Laramie, I promise," replied Neale, eagerly.

Long hours Laramie paced and sat under the cold white stars. Somewhere in that vigil peace came back to him. Then he slept, and when morning broke there seemed to be far distance and time between this rosy dawn and that fading dark yesterday. He had done well, even if almost too late. And no matter where and how the future trail led, he had memory to sustain him.

Soon the riders were up and doing. Clay Lee had gotten in late the preceding night, having been advised of the fight by Jerky. By sunrise Strickland drove off with Lenta and Neale in the buckboard. If a night had calmed Laramie, what had it done for Lenta Lindsay? Her pretty face bore the pallor and strain of fatigue and fright, yet appeared all the more bewitching for that. Laramie observed that Lonesome had avoided her, though he could not escape her haunting eyes. Laramie made the startling observation

482

that no doubt he would be riding away from Spanish Peaks Ranch alone.

The riders wanted to take the trail across country, as it was shorter, but Laramie held them to the road and Strickland's buckboard. Of all the rides Laramie had ever made, this one was the strangest, the most endless. He imagined he grew old upon it. There were hours like years. But they passed, and the miles fell behind. Finally from the last rise of rangeland they viewed the magnificent scene dominated by the old fort. The westering sun sent gold rays across the peaks to glorify the rolling sea of grass and sage, the green spreading valley, and the ribbon of shining stream.

When Strickland reined his team inside the court Laramie dismounted to approach the occupants and say: "Strickland, let Lonesome or me do the talkin'. We reckon it'd be kinder to sort of hold back the truth, yu know.... Neale, can I depend on yu?"

"Mum's the word, Laramie."

"An' yu, lass?"

But either Lenta did not hear or care. She was staring at a dark-eyed girl who had come out of the living-room, followed by a man and a woman, also strangers. Lindsay next appeared, his face working. Then the riders arrived.

"*Ted,*" screamed the strange girl.

"Holy Mackeli!" yelped Ted, falling off his horse.

"Laramie, help me – or I'll keel over," cried Lenta, and as Laramie wheeled she half leaped and fell into his arms. Then Hallie appeared running across the court. Laramie met her.

"Oh, Laramie – you brought her home!... Bless you! I can never – never repay you for.... My Heaven! Is she..."

"Fainted, I reckon. She was all right when we got heah."

"Thank God! – I – I was terrified. Bring her to my room, Laramie.... Hurry!"

Laramie strode across the court with his light burden, and entering Hallie's room behind her, laid Lenta upon the white bed. Her eyes were open.

"Sister! – Lenta dear, you're home," cried Hallie, softly, leaning over. "My prayer has been answered.... Are you – all right?"

"Sure I'm all right. When I stood up – I went dizzy.... Hallie, old honey, I've had a hell of a time – but I'm home, safe – a sadder and wiser girl."

"Do you forgive me?" whispered Hallie, poignantly.

"Yes. You and everybody – even that damn Lonesome," replied Lenta, and

484

wrapping her arms around Hallie's neck she hugged and kissed her.

"Honey, I too am – sadder and wiser," said Hallie, brokenly. "I never knew how dear – you were to me."

"Same here, Hal. Maybe it was a good thing. But we can talk about that some other time. . . . Hal, I'll bet the girl who yelled to Ted is his sister."

"Yes indeed. Ted's family is here, and they're the nicest people you ever met."

"Dog-gone. I'm sure glad. Do they like Flo?"

"Love her."

"Gee! the luck of some girls!"

"Lenta, I'll call mother – dad – all of them."

"Wait a minute," cried Lenta, sitting up. "I'd rather see Lonesome first. . . . Laramie, call him – *make* him come."

Laramie stepped to the door and yelled. "Mulhall, where air yu?"

An answering shout came out of the babble of voices across the courtyard.

"Come heah pronto!" added Laramie, in a voice no rider would have failed to obey.

Lonesome came, but he did not run. He had removed his chaps, coat, and sombrero. A hint of some apprehension gleamed in his eyes.

"What you want?" he growled.

Laramie met him at the edge of the porch and laid a firm hand on his shoulder.

"Come in heah."

In another moment Lonesome stood before Lenta, in mingled consternation and resentment.

"What's the – idee?" he queried. At that moment Lenta Lindsay was not a girl to retreat from.

"Lonesome Mulhall, you've been perfectly rotten to me," she said, accusingly. Tears in her eyes did not hide their soft, eager, mysterious light.

"Aw! ... When?"

"Ever since you saved me from that devil Gaines.... What'd you shoot him for – if you hated me afterwards? I'd just – as lief – he'd ..."

"I didn't hate you, Lent," interrupted Lonesome, evidently stung into self-defense. "But you can't expect men engaged in a bloody business to go cuttin' didos around to – to please a cantankerous kid of a girl."

"Oh! So you don't hate me?"

"No, I don't," retorted Lonesome, as flippantly as she. But Laramie saw that he was lost.

"You know I – I'm right, don't you? ...

486

That Gaines – that I suffered no harm? . . . You believed it? . . . Lonesome!"

"I wouldn't have to be told – after I seen you," returned Lonesome, loftily.

"Well, then, why have you been so – so indifferent? Ever since you blew the brains out of that dog; I couldn't help it if he had evil designs on me. . . . You've never spoken to me. You've never done one single little thing for me."

"Lent, I reckon I didn't savvy I was thet mean. But what's it matter now? You're home safe with yore family. I'm ridin' away tomorrow with Laramie. We've done our best, an' lookin' at it from range-riders' point of view, thet hasn't been so bad. You'll realize it some day."

"I realize it now," she cried, reproachfully. "Do you think I've no good in me at all?"

"Wal, I haven't jest been overwhelmed with thet," drawled Lonesome, essaying a hint of his old self.

"Lonesome, you shan't go away. . . . Laramie, would you let him leave us *now?* Would you leave Hallie in the lurch? When we know now you're the wonderfulest man?"

"Lass, I reckon the kind of work – Lonesome an' me air good fer is about – done," rejoined Laramie, haltingly. He did not dare to face Hallie with that. Out of the tail of his eye he had seen her start and pale.

"Well, I won't let you go," declared Lenta, passionately.

"Aw now – who won't?" asked Lonesome.

"*I* won't."

"Miss Lindsay, with all doo respect to you – jest why won't I go on my lonesome way once more, ridin' the lone prairee?"

"*Because!* . . . I didn't like you much before –" whispered Lenta, radiantly, and held out her arms. "But I – I love you now."

Lonesome uttered a gasp and fell on his knees beside the bed, to be clasped by those eager arms. As Laramie turned to the door he felt Hallie join him, slipping her arm through his.

"Wasn't that – sweet? Oh, I'm so – happy," she murmured.

Her touch effectually obviated what little reply Laramie might have been capable of.

"Look! Everybody's coming," cried Hallie. "This will never do. Let's go out – hold them up."

She stepped out and Laramie closed the door behind him.

"Dad – mother – Flo – and friends," began Hallie, eloquently, "please wait a few moments."

"Hallie, I want to see my dear child," cried Mrs. Lindsay.

"What's happened? Ted said she was all right," added Lindsay, anxiously.

"What's she doing in there – alone?" queried Flo, giggling.

"She's not alone. It's a very serious occasion," returned Hallie, gravely. "If I am not deluded our dear child is about to make it impossible for her to play any more wild pranks.... Laramie, is not that your opinion?"

"Wal, if I was Lonesome I'd shore be ridin' the clouds," drawled Laramie.

Some hours later, after supper, when they all assembled in the living-room, the story could no longer be withheld.

"Folks, I'm shore no good at tellin' stories," drawled Laramie, in answer to their insistent demands. "If yu must heah all about it I reckon Lonesome is yore man."

"Me? Aw, I'm turrible shy in company, an' I hate to talk, anyhow," replied Lonesome, in voice and manner calculated to insure more importunity. He received it in full measure. "All right. You-all set down now like we was round the camp fire. When was it Lenta got kidnapped? Seems a long time. But fact is it was only three

489

days. . . . . Laramie got me up thet mornin' early. He had heard a hawse. We found tracks under her window an' the bars broke an' Lenta gone. By the way thet hawse went we figgered Lent an' her – her friend were jest playin' a joke on her dad because he'd locked her up. Wal, we got our hawses an' trailed them tracks up to Cedar Point. There we found a camp. An' soon spied Stuart – that was Lent's friend, ridin' for dear life across the range. Gaines an' his pards had been hidin' there to kidnap Lent. They chased Stuart off an' throwed Lent on a hawse. Tied her hand an' foot, an' gagged her too 'cause Lent shore can holler."

Lonesome coolly surveyed his audience, nonchalantly unaware of Lenta's wide eyes and open lips. Laramie prepared himself to hear the greatest liar he had ever known, now at the supreme hour of his rider's career. Strickland edged back, a slight smile on his fine face. Hallie wore an expression of extreme bewilderment. The rest of the listeners, especially the Williamses, were enthralled.

"We hung to thet trail all day an' made camp late," went on Lonesome. "Thet was Ted, an' me, 'cause Laramie had gone home to get grub an' fetch Wind River Charlie an' Dakota. Next day about noon we came to a

490

place where Gaines had run into another outfit. They split an' so Ted an' me had to do the same, one on each trail. Now the trail I took soon doubled back an' I figgered thet outfit had evil designs on the other. So it proved. I found where they went down off the mountain to head off the other bunch. Presently Ted came along an' between us we figgered it. The other outfit was after Gaines, so we trailed e'm to a lonely cabin an' as we hung around waitin' for dark who should slip up but Dakota an' Wind River Charlie. They had come on with Laramie, an' had split same as we. They didn't know where Laramie was. But I'd been with thet Suthern gennelman so long I could figger him. An' I bet the boys a month's pay thet Laramie was in the cabin with them two outfits. When it come on dark we sneaked up to the cabin. Would you believe it, folks, there sat Lent on the floor gamblin' with them desperadoes. They had a bright fire. No sign of Laramie! I seen thet the second outfit was bossed by a rustler named Price. I met him onct under pecooliar circumstances, an' never forgot him. Wal, you could see easy thet he was mad in love with Lent already. They was playin' poker. Lent won all their money. I've got thet roll in my saddle-bag, Laramie. You could choke an elephant with it. I didn't

491

know Lent was such a good caird sharp, but then I hadn't figgered a lot about her. After she won the money, Price proposed to Gaines that they gamble for the girl or fight. Gaines didn't like the idee. But Price had a gun-slinger in his outfit, a bad hombre named Beady. So he wilted an' they played one hand of draw-poker. Gaines won. He was so dog-gone tickled thet he imagined winnin' the game was winnin' Lenta's heart. So he got obstruperous with her. Lent slapped him an' cursed him, an' finally scratched his face. Thet made Gaines ugly."

Lonesome, warming to his narrative and wiping his sweaty face, paused for breath and to see if he was holding his audience. Satisfied, he resumed.

"I hate to tell you-all this. So I'll hurry it along.... Gaines began to wrestle Lent an' was tearin' her clothes off right there. I stuck my gun in the door about to bore him when Price blew his brains out. I seen Lent crawl under a shelf, as hell busted loose in there. Wal, when it was over we found three or four dead men, one gone, an' the nigger, Johnson, sittin' there turned clean white. We got Lent outside. She'd never turned a feather. An' she laced it into me like this. 'Fine slow outfit you are! You dam' near got heah too late.' I didn't say nuthin'. We was havin' supper outside when Laramie rode in an' asked what all the shootin' was about. We went to bed then, an' next mornin' the nigger led us down to Lester Allen's ranch. Mr. Strickland was there, an' we seen he was tolerable suspicious of Allen. Laramie had Nig face Allen an' expose his guilt as a pardner of Arlidge an' a buyer an' seller of stolen stock. Allen roared like a bull an' raved about what Arlidge would do to Laramie when he got back. Just then I seen Arlidge ridin' up, hell-bent for election. Two riders behind him! We-all slipped off an' got our hardware. But Laramie stood there rollin' a cigarette, sort of careless like. Seein' him thet way, I went cold to my gizzard an' I wouldn't of been in Arlidge's boots for a million. Arlidge rared off his hawse, so mad he couldn't see quick, an' he yelled to Allen: 'Hell to pay – hadda shoot young Lindsay!' . . . Then all of a sudden he seen Laramie. They was old enemies. Years ago Arlidge had killed a pard of Laramie's. . . . We all froze an' nobody breathed. All the same I wasn't worried none. Arlidge showed he knowed he was a goner. But for a low-down rider-bullyin' range thief he was game. . . . Folks, there's no law on the range but this kind of law. An' Laramie gave this rustler his chance. As I seen it Arlidge moved first . . . but . . . wal, these things have to happen on the range or no nice people like you-all are would *ever* be safe.... After thet Laramie offered Allen his choice – to hang or leave Colorado forever. Allen left right then, without his coat or hat.... We rode over to the Meadows, where we learned Neale had been in a little scrap. He can tell you about thet better'n I can. We made camp, started early this mornin', an' heah we are, with the little lady who upset us as lively as a cricket."

Not long after this amazing recital, when Laramie stood at his open door, gazing out into the moon-blanched patio, he heard quick steps on the flagstones. Hallie appeared, the moonlight shining on her hair.

"Laramie, come walk with me or sit under the cottonwoods. I want to talk to you."

He joined her hesitatingly and thrilled anew as she slid a soft hand inside his arm.

"What did you think of Lonesome's story?" she inquired.

"Wal, I reckoned it'd do."

"Such an atrocious falsehood! ... Laramie, my sister told me every detail of that terrible experience."

"Dog-gone the kid!"

"Why did you sanction Lonesome's lie?"

"Wal, we reckoned the truth would horrify yu."

"It did. But the truth is always best. I *know* now. And I can adjust myself to the – the violence and bloodshed Mr. Strickland explained to me must prevail on the frontier for a while. I have been mawkish, chicken-hearted. But I will overcome it, because I love the West."

"I'm shore glad to heah yu say thet last, Hallie," Laramie said, feelingly.

She had led him down the courtyard, across the entrance, up the other side, and now they were mounting the stone steps under the cottonwoods. Laramie experienced a sinking of his heart. How impossible to understand this composed young woman!

"You know what Mr. Strickland proposes organizing, do you not?" she went on.

"Yes, an' it's a splendid idee. Yore father can retrieve his losses now. There won't be any more wholesale rustlin' on this range."

"Still, he claims there will be need of such protective measures.... Are you aware that you have been chosen to lead this cattlemen's association?"

"Me! No. Strickland never hinted thet to me," ejaculated Laramie, in vague alarm.

"Well, I'm glad to be the one to tell you."

"Wal, of all things! I reckon I'm shore proud, Hallie.... But it's out of the question. I cain't accept."

"Why not? It seems to me to be an exceptionally fine opportunity. You have been a rolling stone, so to speak. Surely some day you will settle down to – to one place. I asked Mr. Strickland if your life had been such that you could not ever be happy to accept something tame and colorless. He laughed and said it'd never be tame here for many years."

"Wal, yu told me the truth was best – an' the truth is I reckon I can't stand it heah no longer."

"I divined that. But why?"

He did not have an answer ready. Meanwhile they had reached the oval surrounded by the boulders. Gleams of silver played in the murmuring pool below the spring. A soft rustle of leaves mingled with music of running water. She came quite close to him and looked up, her face clear in the moonlight, her eyes dark, inscrutable, strange. He saw her throat swell. He seemed forced to gaze at her, to impress her lovely face upon his memory forever.

She threw her scarf on the stone seat and stepped a little nearer to him. It was then Laramie caught his breath with a realization that he knew little of a woman, and that there was catastrophe in the presence of this one.

"You are going away from Spanish Peaks Ranch?" she asked.

"I told yu."

"From me?"

"Wal, as yu're heah – of course from yu."

"Laramie, you have not apologized for your conduct the other day, down at the barn. Will you do so now?"

"No!"

"But, be reasonable. We can't get anywhere – until you do."

"I'm shore sorry, but I cain't."

"Where is all that Southern chivalry with which Lonesome and Ted always credited you? . . . You treated me rudely – brutally. Aren't you sorry?"

"Shore, in a way, but not the way yu mean."

"Not sorry you treated me as Mr. Arlidge once tried to – and failed? Not sorry you dragged me into that stall as if I were an Indian squaw – and crushed me in your arms – and kissed me blind – and deaf – and dumb? . . . Laramie Nelson, not sorry for that outrage?"

"So – help me Heaven – I'm not," he choked out, driven mad by the sweet, strange, soft voice, the challenging, accusing eyes, the hand that went to his shoulder. "But I swear to yu it was no outrage."

497

"Then explain why?"

"God help me, I was out of my haid.... I meant to kiss yu good-by.... But yu struck me.... An' then I had to – satisfy somethin' queer an' savage in me. But, Hallie, it was no insult – not in my heart. No matter what I said."

"Still, Laramie, you have not explained your motive."

"Wal, it was jest such love as no man ever before had for a woman," he replied, simply, strength coming with his betrayal.

"Oh, so that was it?... Love? For me!" How wonderful she appeared then! He backed away from her until the stone seat stopped him. That pressing hand stole higher on his shoulder. Were his senses leaving him? Her face shone white as marble – her lips were parted – her eyelids fell heavily to lift again over gulfs of wondrous depths. "Larry – do you – did you ever know what I did?"

"When?" he whispered, his voice low.

"Why, that time.... You must indeed – have been blind, at least.... Suppose you – do the same – all over again ... right here – now.... Then I will show you!"

The publishers hope that this book has given you enjoyable reading. Large Print Books are specially designed to be as easy for see and to hold as possible. If you wish a complete list of our books, please ask at your local library or write directly to: John Curley & Associates, Inc., P.O. Box 37, South Yarmouth, Massachusetts 02664